PRAISE FO

"Unrelenting thriller . . . constant action, sympathetic heroes, believable evildoers, and absolute authenticity on every page."
—*Publishers Weekly*, STARRED review

"The authenticity of the story makes the tale particularly terrifying, especially at a time when real-life international relations appear unstable. A fine apocalyptic thriller right up the alley of Clancy and Thor fans."
—*Booklist*

"A superb book . . . one of the best thrillers I have read since Stephen Coonts' *Liberty's Last Stand*. I did not want to put the book down. Colonel David Hunt and R.J. Pineiro worked together well to produce an exciting, well-written book."
—*Fresh Fiction*

"A masterful thriller written by men of deep experience. First-rate and very highly recommended!"
—Ralph Peters, *New York Times* bestselling author of *The Damned of Petersburg*

"*Without Mercy* is the ultimate terrorist scenario. Readers who enjoy Tom Clancy and Brad Taylor will find a new favorite."
—Ward Larsen, *USA Today* bestselling author of *Assassin's Silence*

PRAISE FOR *WITHOUT FEAR*

"Outstanding follow-up to their debut, 2017's *Without Mercy*. This military adventure thriller deserves to become a genre classic."
—*Publishers Weekly,* STARRED review

"Not only explosive, thrilling combat, but also realistic characters to root for. Think Brad Taylor, Brad Thor, Ben Coes . . . Smart, skillful, seriously committed action with emotional weight."
—*Shawangunk Journal*

"The story drips with battlefield authenticity, written by someone who has been on the front lines and knows what war looks like."
—*The Real Book Spy*

ADVANCE PRAISE FOR *WITHOUT REGRET*

"In Hunt and Pineiro's rip-roaring third thriller featuring Col. Hunter Stark (after 2018's *Without Fear*), technical problems cause the plane carrying Kim Jong-un, North Korea's president, and his entourage to Washington, D.C., to land at Dallas–Fort Worth International Airport, where they run into ex-president George W. Bush, who loans the North Koreans his plane. That plane is shot down seconds after takeoff, killing everyone aboard. The shooters, Sinaloa cartel member Mireya Moreno Carreon, who has a grudge against Bush, and her henchmen, weren't aware of the switch. Not on the plane was formidable Naree Kyong-Lee, the North Korean in charge of Kim's security, who vows revenge. Several subplots, one featuring Stark's former partner, FBI agent Monica Cruz, entertain, but it's Stark's efforts to prevent WWIII that will keep readers turning the pages. Hunt and Pineiro reinforce their place in the military thriller genre."
—*Publisher's Weekly*

BOOKS BY R.J. PINEIRO

Siege of Lightning
Ultimatum
Retribution
Exposure
Breakthrough
01-01-00
Y2K
Shutdown
Conspiracy.com
Firewall
Cyberterror
Havoc
SpyWare
The Eagle and the Cross
The Fall
Ashes of Victory **
Avenue of Regrets
Chilling Effect
Highest Law
First, Fire the Consultants! ***
The Scars We Cannot See ****

BOOKS BY DAVID HUNT AND R.J. PINEIRO

Without Mercy
Without Fear
Without Regret

BOOKS BY DAVID HUNT

They Just Don't Get It
On the Hunt
Terror Red *

* *with Christine Hunsinger*

** *with Joe Weber*
*** *with Robert H. Wilson*
**** *forthcoming*

WITHOUT
REGRET

A Novel

**COL. DAVID HUNT
AND R.J. PINEIRO**

Copyright © 2020 by David Hunt and Rogelio J. Pineiro

All rights reserved. Produced in the United States of America. No part of this book may be reproduced, scanned, or transmitted in any form or by any means, electronic or mechanical (including photocopying, recording, or information storage and retrieval) or otherwise, without express written permission of the authors.

Identifiers:
ISBN 9798662985124 (paperback)
ASIN B088BBTZ66 (Kindle)

Cover design by Kevin Summers
Cover images: Under license from Shutterstock

This is a work of fiction. Names, characters, places, and events either are the products of the authors' imaginations or are used fictitiously. Any resemblance to actual persons, living or dead, corporations, or other entities, is coincidental and not intended by the authors.

To Angela, Ryan, Jason, Byron, and Travis, the brightest lights I have ever known.
—Col. David Hunt

To the amazing women in my family: Lory, Linda, Dora, Irene, Dorita, Islay, Sarah and Donna.
—R.J. Pineiro

"We give everything we have on every mission for each other, without regret. We do this because they are the right things to do, and we are exactly the right people to do them."
—Colonel Hunter Stark

PROLOGUE
O Romeo, Romeo

JUNE 2004.
CULIACÁN CITY, NORTHWESTERN MEXICO.

"What a shit sandwich, Colonel," Master Chief Evan Larson whispered, keeping his tripod-mounted, custom M2 Browning .50-caliber machine gun pointed at their target.

Larson's right hand rested on the dual handgrips of the heavy weapon's rear buffer assembly—that included built-in squeeze triggers—while his left held a pair of night-vision binoculars. "Definitely a Charlie Foxtrot," he added.

Kneeling next to him, Colonel Hunter Stark frowned. He used a similar set of optics to scan the street from the top of their five-story rooftop, adjacent to a crowded and dark parking lot on the outskirts of Culiacán Rosales, the capital city of the state of Sinaloa. His system also recorded everything into a memory card. The dual-tube device amplified the available light, primarily from surrounding buildings and evening traffic. Streetlights, like so much of this town, were broken.

Unfortunately, as Larson had pointed out, the busy scene below, painted in green, had twice as many foot soldiers guarding the movie theater than had been indicated in the brief provided by their employer, the U.S. government.

The steady beat of *Rancheras* streaming from a nearby nightclub added to the cacophony of horn-blowing cars and buses, swarms of motorcycles, and shouting street vendors.

Scantily-dressed ladies worked the dark corner nearest the club, ironically located next to an old Mission-style church. A pair of nuns in dark habits handed out pamphlets to the same pedestrians accosted by the prostitutes.

Stark had to shake his head at the sight, the forces of good and evil hard at work, hunting for lost souls. At the moment, the latter was certainly winning, the women luring quite the number of guys into a rundown hotel advertising rooms by the hour.

One, a young and handsome man dressed in black carrying a guitar case not unlike the ones Stark and Larson used to haul their weapons up here, had gone inside almost two hours earlier accompanied by one of the Mexican beauties.

"And why the hell does Pretty Boy get to have all the fun?" Larson asked.

"I have PID on nineteen. Mix of MAC-10s and UZIs," Stark said, having positive identification on nineteen hostiles armed with either MAC-10 automatic pistols or UZI submachine guns, two popular Cartel weapons. His words were picked up by a RAP4 tactical throat mic connected to an AN/PRC-148 Multiband Inter/Intra Team Radio (MBITR) strapped to his utility vest. Stark took note that the men armed with the MAC-10s were in the open, by the entrance to the movie house. The men with the UZIs were scattered across the large parking lot, staying low, out of sight of the MAC-10 men.

Are those two separate groups?

"Don't forget *la policia*," Larson said, pointing his massive Browning at a state police pickup truck surrounded by four uniformed officers armed with M4 carbines around the corner from the theater.

"*Plus, hostiles on the roof of the movie house, next to the billboard,*" reported Master Sergeant Ryan Hunt, a former sniper with the 1st Special Forces Operational Detachment (Delta).

Armed with a Barrett M82 rifle fitted with an NVWS-4 Gen3 night vision sniper scope and a sound suppressor, Ryan was on the eighth floor of the motel. "*I see UZIs, but no NODs in sight, sir,*" he added.

And it all meant that the bodyguards of Rodolfo Carrillo, the younger brother and go-to guy of Juarez Cartel boss Vincente Carrillo, had no night vision. They were relying on light from neon signs, headlights, and the dim moon to spot any threat to their principal.

"Got them," Stark said.

"Not sure why anyone in this fucked-up town would pay to see *that*," Larson commented about the marquee advertising the movie,

Hotel Rwanda. "I'd be looking for a damn comedy—anything to make me forget I live in this shithole."

"And we're about to make it worse," Stark replied.

Larson, almost a foot taller and nearly seventy pounds heavier than Stark, wore dark civilian clothes bought in Juarez, as did the rest of his contractor team. The chief, however, had refused to part with his good luck charm: a thick carbon fiber bracelet on his right wrist, embossed with *LERNE LEIDEN OHNE ZU KLAGEN.*

It was German for "learn to suffer without complaining," the motto of the *Kampfschwimmers,* the German Navy's version of the U.S. Navy SEALs. Larson had been on a joint operation with them in a prior life.

In addition to Ryan and Larson, two former Navy SEALs, Michael Hagen and Danny Martin, waited in their respective getaway vehicles, one behind the apartment building and the other behind the hotel. No one wore any ID or anything that could be traced back to Uncle Sam should this SAP go sideways. Special Access Programs was the official name of what the general public knew as "Black Ops."

"And to put a cherry on our shit cake," Larson said, "OGA's got us dressed like fucking mariachis." OGA, or Other Government Agency, was a euphemism for the Central Intelligence Agency.

The comment drew laughs from all the operators, especially Danny, their designated pilot. He'd been a naval aviator before earning his trident, operating in Seal Team Two before advancing to the United States Naval Special Warfare Development Group, commonly known as DEVGRU, or SEAL Team Six.

Per his contract, Stark was to kill Rodolfo Carrillo, known locally as el *"Nįño de Oro,"* or the "Golden Boy," an act that Langley hoped would start a nasty little war of attrition between the Juarez and Sinaloa Cartels.

It was a classic Agency move: goad the enemy into thinning each other's herds before the DEA and Mexico's elite Special Forces Corps mopped up the remnants. And the unofficial word was that the op had been personally sanctioned by no other than POTUS himself.

Stark wasn't really enamored of the thought of carrying out an assassination, even for America's War on Drugs, but the contract did meet his three criteria for accepting a job:

One, would the mission make the world a better place?

Two, did the employer have cash in hand, and was the retainer enough to cover initial expenses?

And three, did all the team members agree to go?

The CIA always had plenty of cash. And Rodolfo Carrillo, their high value target, or HVT, as well as his lovely older brother, were the epitome of evil, truly bad *hombres*, responsible for the brutal deaths of thousands. So, Mexico—and the world for that matter—would certainly be a better place without the bastard, as well as all the bastards that would be gunned down in the days, weeks, and even months to come because of today's kill.

Although Stark had been able to put most of his demons if not to bed, then to rest, he would never be totally at peace with what he was and what he had done or was about to do: an assassination. He could, however, justify doing these jobs and fighting with the best damn men and women on the planet.

So, no regret here.

But the veteran warrior had been around the block enough times to know that no matter how many Cartel monsters were eliminated, when the dust settled, a whole new group of monsters—oftentimes more ruthless than their predecessors—would take their place.

The drug business, like show business, had to go on.

"How's the range, Ryan?" Stark asked.

"Comfortable, sir. Nine hundred yards. Wind five to ten, left to right."

"Yeah, I bet you're real comfy after that señorita loved you long time, left to right and up and down," Danny Martin chimed in.

"Hey, Danny," Ryan said. *"How's your wife and my kids?"*

"Fuck you, man," Danny replied.

"Nah," Larson replied. "Pretty Boy only has eyes for that working girl in Juarez. What was her name? Juanita?"

"Anita," Danny corrected.

"Hey, she's no hooker, Chief," Ryan replied. *"Anita's the daughter of—"*

"But wasn't our boy doing some biker chick in Scottsdale? Veronica, right?" Danny asked.

"Monica," Ryan replied, *"and she wasn't a—"*

"Alright, knock it off," Stark ordered.

"Yeah, Danny," Larson added. "Let Pretty Boy focus on Golden Boy."

Stark sighed. His guys were great operators but also great pains in his ass. But if he was completely honest with himself, Stark would admit to being a tad jealous of Ryan, the all-American, handsome sniper who always seemed to get the girl.

Unlike Stark, who had a knack for ending up in the wrong relationships.

His list of mistakes included Kira Tupolev, a striking Russian intelligence officer he met during a joint op to assist in the Moscow theater hostage crisis in 2002, when fifty armed Chechens seized the Dubrovka Theater along with a hundred and seventy people. And there was the beautiful Seung Yong-Kim, a South Korean woman with an affinity for expensive tequila Stark met in Seoul when he ran security for the FIFA World Cup that very same year. Unfortunately, Seung was a North Korean agent impersonating FIFA security, attempting to disrupt electricity and water to the Olympic Village.

I sure know how to pick them.

Stark pushed the past aside and centered his binoculars on the large double doors of the theater and slowly panning to the street, where three dark Cadillac Escalades and ten armed men waited for their boss. The rest of the soldiers were spread through the street and the parking lot, plus the two Ryan had spotted on the roof. And Stark expected at least a half dozen to exit the establishment with their principal, bringing the number up to around twenty-five—almost twice the CIA count.

The chief's right. This is a certifiable Charlie Fox—

The headlights of a passing truck reflected on the windshield of a parked car, flashing in his binoculars in a way that brought him back to a place he typically kept locked away.

Unbidden, the images of his baby brothers, Bobby and Joey Stark, materialized in his mind. The former, a member of the 15th Marine Expeditionary Unit, had died in Somalia in 1993. The latter, a USMC captain, died almost nine years later when a roadside IED hit his convoy outside Bagram, Afghanistan.

Stark always felt guilt—he was the oldest and should have died first, but he would concede that their violent deaths, combined with the deaths of so many other brothers and sisters, had forged his actions and life forever.

The veteran colonel often thought he was cursed, forced to live with the guilt of surviving those he loved. He was normally able to dismiss such thoughts by thinking, *You fucking arrogant prick, all this death isn't being done to you but done to those who died.*

But as with all things, that didn't always work.

And tonight, on this roof, was one of those times.

So, Stark did the only other thing he could do: keep busy, hoping that the work at hand would help him live with his pain.

Unfortunately, it never occurred to him that drowning his entire being in blood and violence would only darken his already broken soul.

The theater doors swung open and three armed men stepped out, scanning the street and getting nods from the guards by the SUVs.

"*Showtime,*" Ryan said.

Stark willed himself to focus on what was happening to his team. *Shake it off, asshole, you can feel bad later.*

He panned the binoculars to the front of the theater in time to see Rodolfo Carrillo emerge, accompanied by his wife and four more armed men.

And that's when all hell broke loose.

Gunfire exploded from the parking lot, the stroboscopic flashes splashing the streets. People started running for cover. Vehicles accelerated. Street vendors ducked behind their carts. Reports reverberated through the streets like Cinco de Mayo fireworks on steroids.

The courtesans vanished into the hotel in a blur of miniskirts, bikini tops, swinging hair, and stilettos. A few of Carrillo's men were down but most were still returning fire and his bodyguards were trying to rush the drug boss to one of the Escalades.

And in the chaos, the police got in their pickup truck and sped away.

"Gotta love this place," Larson opined.

"*Got a shot,*" Ryan reported.

"Send it," Stark ordered, though he had a feeling that Carrillo was not going to survive the attack. But the colonel and his operators were getting paid to kill him and record the kill.

The drug lord's chest exploded. Ryan's .50-caliber round found its mark before the bodyguards shoved him in the lead SUV.

Carrillo's wife vanished in a cloud of blood, but not from Ryan's shot. Three men with UZIs had flanked the group, peppering them with a barrage of 9mm rounds, as were the two on the roof, firing down on them.

"Sundown," Stark said, satisfied that he had enough footage to get paid.

Removing the memory card and stowing it, along with the binoculars, he grabbed his Heckler & Koch MP5A1 suppressed submachine gun and rolled away from the edge of the building. When he reached the stairwell, he pulled out the crowbar he'd jammed the door with and tossed it aside. Larson was folding the custom—and still classified—carbon fiber tripod beneath the barrel of the M2.

Stock M2s weighed in at 84 pounds, but Larson's sported a custom titanium alloy barrel that reduced it to 59 pounds. In addition, the powerful machine gun typically required the heavy-duty M3 tripod, which added another 44 pounds of weight. Larson's carbon fiber version weighed less than eight.

Larson led the way down the stairs, transitioning his gun to the left handle-grip, allowing him to fire the weapon on the move—something very few people could do accurately. Stark let the door slam behind them, muffling the chaos outside.

"I guess those guns in the parking lot were playing for the other team," Larson said.

"You think?" Stark replied, leaping down three steps at a time, muzzle pointed at each landing, his mind transitioning to the critical exfiltration phase.

Probably the Sinaloa Cartel.

So, while the CIA brief had provided a fairly accurate count of the number of bodyguards, Langley had apparently failed to discover the local plot to take out the Juarez Cartel's golden boy.

Or, the cynic in Stark thought, *the OGA, being the OGA, decided to hold that tidbit of intel back in the spirit of believing that two assassination attempts might be better than one.*

And it reinforced two of Stark's core beliefs: Spooks can't ever be trusted and that no plan ever survived the first shot.

They exited the apartment building through the rear service door into an alley bursting with garbage bags, discarded furniture and mattresses, and at least a dozen rats feasting on a dead cat.

"Figures," Larson grumbled. "Fucking place is so backward that the rats eat the cats."

Images of the old Looney Tunes character, Speedy Gonzales and his *compadres* having their way with *Señor Gato* flashed through his mind.

Shaking the thought, Stark checked out the ridiculously small Kia SUV parked just past the rodent banquet. Rusting along the bottoms of the doors, their getaway ride was full of cigarette smoke, a fraction of which curled from a one-inch gap on the driver's side window.

A man wearing the latest in Juarez fashion labels sat behind the wheel. Muscular and stoic, a half smoked Sobranie Classic—a strong Russian brand—hanging from the corner of his mouth, Michael Hagen barely acknowledged Stark as he jumped in the front passenger seat and rolled down his window. Larson managed to fold his large frame along with his equally large weapon, sitting sideways with his head against the ceiling.

Hagen put the Kia in gear and floored it before Larson could close the door. The chief was thrown back, the side of his face banging the rear windshield as the vehicle's forward momentum shut the door.

"Fucking Agency and its fucking rice burners!" he screamed.

"Kia's from South Korea, Chief. Not Japan," Stark said. Hagen grinned, feathering the clutch.

Larson groaned, rubbing his left temple with a gloved hand then punching the roof. "See, Colonel, we're jammed in this flimsy piece of shit courtesy of the OGA while the Cartel rides in bulletproof Escalades! We should be in Humvees!"

"*Sure, genius,*" Danny said over the squadron frequency. "*Let's broadcast to the whole goddamned country that the gringos are here.*"

They accelerated down the alley and onto a side street in time to catch a glimpse of Ryan coming out of the back of the hotel hauling his guitar case toward a white Kia. Ryan being Ryan, he tossed the case in the back and then made Danny slide to the passenger seat so he could drive.

"Pretty Boy has control issues," Larson commented.

Stark pinched the bridge of his nose. The kid, like the rest of the team, could indeed tax his patience, but he'd never met a better shot. Ryan was gifted.

Stark said, "Anytime, Ryan."

The former Delta sniper took off, tires screeching. *"Try to keep up, Mickey."*

Hagen tossed his cigarette out the window and floored the Kia, staying on Ryan's taillights, following the signs to Highway 15, running north-south through Culiacán.

"Who the hell was that, Colonel?" Danny asked.

"Someone who obviously didn't get the memo," replied Larson. "*We* were supposed to do the dirty deed."

"Either way, it's done," said Stark, on the lookout for any pursuit.

"Yeah," Ryan chimed in. *"We couldn't have planned it better."*

The two-car caravan headed south toward their exfil twenty miles away, a walled compound owned by a shell company in Virginia, where their ride waited to haul them to El Paso, Texas.

Traffic pretty much vanished within ten minutes of leaving the city. The highway wound through farmland under pale moonlight.

Stark thought about killing the headlights but decided against it. *Just a couple of local cars cruising on a local road at normal speed.* It was still dark enough to merit using the night-vision binoculars.

They revealed mixed cattle grazing behind fences flanking the narrow highway, sporadically backdropped by sloped-roof sheds typically used to shelter livestock.

It looked peaceful, serene. If you didn't know you were smack in the middle of cartel country after taking out one of its bosses. They had to BBBG, Be Bad and Be Gone.

Every second counts, he thought, checking their six again.

The lead Kia swerved off the road, kicking up a cloud of dust and gravel before steering back onto the asphalt.

"Ryan?" Stark said. "You guys okay up there?"

"Our boy's sexting with the Juarez hooker, sir," Danny reported.

"Hey, Anita's not a—"

"Goddammit, Sergeant Major!" Stark exploded. "Don't tell me you brought a fucking cell phone to an op!"

"A burner, sir, and—"

"I'll deal with you later!" Stark snapped. "Eyes on the road! Clear?"

"*Wilco!*" Ryan replied. *"Putting it away right—"*

It happened fast. In front of them, a greenish blur careened through a fence directly toward the lead Kia.

"Heads up!" Stark screamed over the squadron frequency. Hagen stood on the brakes. Ryan didn't react as fast, trying to swerve out of the way, but it was too late.

What the colonel now recognized as a massive bull crashed into the side of the little white SUV, its horns penetrating the flimsy roof. The beast's momentum carried it over the Kia with its horns caught in the roof, peeling off a wide strip like opening a can of sardines.

Ryan finally slammed on his brakes and the bull's momentum carried him forward. When he crushed the engine compartment, the impact was powerful enough to lift the rear of the SUV off the ground. Twenty-three hundred pounds of meat slapped the asphalt in front of them, blocking the road.

Stark jumped out first, holding his MP5A1, followed by Hagen and Larson, their weapons drawn, converging on the now-still bovine. White sheet metal was twisted around its horns.

And to complete this insane picture, Ryan and Danny stuck theirs heads through the gaping hole in the roof, with the wide-eye stare of deer caught in the headlights.

You gotta be shitting me, Stark thought. Hagen lit up a Sobranie and contemplated the bizarre scene along with Larson. He kept an eye on the road toward town, in case anyone had spotted them. Stark learned long ago the cartels in this country had eyes everywhere, which made it even more pressing to get to the walled compound *pronto*.

Ryan climbed out, still holding a phone, which dinged with a new text message.

"Yeah, dumbass," Danny said, climbing out through the driver's side. "Now you can tell your hooker friend you just killed a big fucking *toro*."

"Seriously, kid?" Larson groaned. "Sexting Juanita and driving?"

"Her name's Anita and—"

"Everyone in my car! Now!" Stark barked. "We need to get the hell out of—"

"Romeo! Romeo! *Donde estas*, Romeo?" *Where are you, Romeo?*

The shouts came from the field the bull had emerged from.

A short man wearing jeans, work boots, and a wrinkled shirt, came through the exit created by Romeo carrying a machete. He looked in his sixties but seemed in terrific shape as he leaped over the downed fence and screamed, *"Chingados! Mataron a Romeo!"* Bastards! They killed Romeo!

"Sir! Hold on!" Stark said, extending a palm at the rancher to tell him to stop. "Your bull—*el toro*—crashed through the fence and hit our car!"

Six men joined the first, all wearing work clothes and holding machetes. They stared at Stark and team with surprise.

"Son gringos," said one of the men. *"Los gringos hijos de puta mataron a Romeo!"* Son-of-a-bitch gringos killed Romeo!

"No, no," Danny tried to explain. *"El toro* ran into *us*!"

"No, señor," insisted the old man, switching to heavily-accented English. "You break, you pay! It's the law!"

Another chimed in, "Romeo fighting bull, *señor*! Very expensive!"

"Si," the older one agreed. "You pay now, gringo! Ten thousand dollars!"

A few more ranch hands emerged from the darkness but remained on the other side of the fence, using their bodies to block the hole torn to hold back a pair of curious steers.

"Look," Stark said, holding his hand up when the men took a few steps toward them, an action that prompted his operators to raise their weapons. "Romeo jumped the fence and hit our car." He pointed at the torn roof still twisted on the bull's horns, trying to avoid a fight. The last thing he wanted was attention, and nothing would draw more than shooting guns at night in this cartel enclave, especially after the Charlie Foxtrot earlier. And, for all he knew, this damn ranch was owned by drug lords. Plus, they were on a tight timetable to get exfilled.

Before anyone argued the point, Romeo groaned and climbed to his feet, evoking images from zombie movies.

The dark bull shook its giant head, sending the scrap of roof clattering across the pavement. For a moment, the beast just stood there, perhaps getting his bearings, before taking a massive crap, dung splatting noisily on the asphalt.

Making up his mind, the bull took off at full gallop toward the field across the road—trailed by a posse of Mexicans screaming, "Romeo! Romeo! *Ven aca! Regresa!* Romeo!"

Stark made a face when the stench of fresh bullshit assaulted his nostrils and noticed one of the hands was still by the broken fence.

He had a cell phone pressed against his right ear.

A knock on the door made Joaquín Guzmán frown.

He didn't like distractions. So, he ignored it. He was currently embroiled in a delicate negotiation with a South Asia associate for four thousand kilos of pure Afghan heroin with an uncut street value of $80 million.

However, the man—known to the world as El Chapo and who had an $8.8 million bounty on his head from U.S. authorities—only planned to pay a small fraction of that to his al Qaeda brother-in-arms. After all, as overlord of the Sinaloa Cartel, Guzmán had to handle the delicate problem of getting the product north of the Rio Grande.

First, he had to cut it right here in his home state of Sinaloa using a proprietary mix of baking soda, powdered milk, cocaine, and laundry detergent designed to double the volume while enhancing the user experience. Then, he had to manage the routes, paying smugglers and providing vehicles, most of which would be dumped after the delivery run, adding to his operating costs. And that was above ground. Below it, he had to deal with the rising cost of digging tunnels—another operating expense hitting his P&L. Then, there were distribution costs in America for the various layers of "management" down to street pushers, paying for security of transports as well as payoffs to local, state, and federal police and judicial officers. There were unforeseen incidentals to deal with: bad weather, vehicles breaking down, and the occasional run in with a rival cartel. And that inevitable ten percent loss of shipments intercepted by the U.S. Border Patrol. It all added to Guzmán's cost of doing business, none of which the man sitting across from him had to deal with.

El Chapo's current offer of $2,000 per kilo, or eight million bucks, had prompted Mani al-Saud, a former prince from Saudi Arabia, to rub the closely-trimmed beard on his chin.

"The *sheikh* was expecting three thousand per kilo . . . like last month," Mani said, referring to the man he represented: Osama bin Laden.

Guzmán's eyes went from the casually-dressed Saudi to his head of security, a woman named Zahra.

The drug lord had to admit that the Kurdish beauty in her tight black jeans, shirt, and boots was a lot easier on the eyes than the barrel-chested and bearded Miguel Orellana, his own head of security standing behind him.

He had to give credit to the Saudi. He smuggled in style, making his deliveries in a shiny Cessna Citation X business jet and accompanied by such an exotic woman—a sharp contrast with the transports Guzmán used—

Another knock on the door.

The ornate wooden door inched open, but Guzmán held his tongue. It was Orellana's only surviving son, Ricco. The Juarez Cartel had assassinated the rest of his family six months ago.

The boy was barely eleven, but as cold as Guzmán's best *Sicarios*. His eyes, one dark brown and one light green, somehow added to his forbidding demeanor.

As hardened by life as he was, Guzmán still felt a chill each time he looked into the boy's unholy gaze.

Ricardo—or "Ricco" as everyone called him—didn't say a word, glancing at Guzmán, then at his guests, with indifference. He passed a note to his father and left without a word. Since the attack on his family, Orellana kept the boy close, and Guzmán couldn't blame him.

Orellana read the message, his right palm resting on the butt of a gold-plated Desert Eagle chambered with the powerful .50 Action Express round. It was a cartel weapon designed to make a cartel statement.

Orellana handed the note to his boss.

Guzmán read it twice, glad that Orellana's security apparatus, nicknamed the Sinaloa KGB, had eyes and ears everywhere. Rodolfo Carrillo's assassination had not been ideal for business, especially when

Guzmán was already at war with the Gulf Cartel. But it had been necessary as part of his strategy to handle the increased shipments from Cali and Medellín by eliminating all competition across the 328 miles of Arizona border—controlled primarily by the Juarez Cartel—where El Chapo continued to dig a series of super tunnels.

And if that wasn't reason enough, Rodolfo Carrillo had personally ordered the raping and beheading of Orellana's wife and daughters after his chief of security had refused to leave him and work for the Juarez Cartel.

Blood must be paid in blood.

Besides, wars were not necessarily bad for business. They had a way of clearing the landscape . . . as long as he won them.

The assassination of *el Niño de Oro* had gone as planned, but Orellana's spy network had just reported a pair of Kia SUVs loaded with heavily armed Americans driving south of Culiacán shortly after the hit on Carrillo.

That was certainly a surprise, given Orellana's Gestapo-like approach to security.

And while he had no idea what American operators could be doing this deep inside Mexico, he could not think of any scenario where that could be good for business.

"Los quiero vivos, Miguel." I want them alive.

While the Saudi prince and Zahra exchanged puzzled looks, Guzmán added. *"Encargate de eso . . . personalmente."*

Take care of it . . . personally.

Stark believed that to win a war, the monsters he brought with him had to be worse than the enemy's, so when the entire team had to cram inside the second Kia, the first thing he did was pull the heavier hardware from the trunks of both vehicles. Then he made sure everyone wore night-vision goggles. Lastly, he killed the headlights.

Sitting in the rear between Danny and Ryan, Stark busted out the back window, covering the road from Culiacán with an M240L machine gun fed by a belt of 7.62x51mm. His operators handled the flanks with Milkor MGLs—multiple grenade launchers—six-shooters loaded with a mix of 40mm high explosive and XM1060 thermobaric shells.

Hagen drove, Larson now sat in front, having kicked out enough of the windshield to level the Browning's muzzle at the road ahead. A belt of API—armor-piercing incendiary—rounds stowed in a canvas bag fed into the left side of the air-cooled weapon.

In all, four muzzles ready for mixed violence were pointed out, plus Hagen had his MP5A1 on his lap. Unlike the Delta sniper, who couldn't seem to handle sexting while driving, the SEAL had a knack for firing while driving, a required skill for all operators in SEAL Team Six.

Two more miles. Stark checked his Casio G-shock watch, which placed them precisely five minutes behind schedule thanks to the unexpected roadkill, though in keeping with the strangeness of this upside-down nation, it was the car that was killed, not the—

"We've got company," said Larson. Their night-vision optics unveiled a pair of pickup trucks and at least a dozen armed men blocking the road.

"Fire!" Stark shouted, shifting his weapon to face the upcoming threat. He hoped to catch them by surprise.

Danny and Ryan popped two 40mm shells each as Larson opened up the Browning in a blinding display of raw power. The noise was deafening, even with special earplugs. The smell of gunpowder and the hot spent shells combined into chaos that would be crippling to the uninitiated.

Stark widened the hole in the windshield when he fired the M240L. And through their mixed caliber wall of destruction, the grenades arced down toward the men.

Two of the shells were high-explosives, wrecking vehicles and tearing the blockade to pieces. But it was the thermobaric munitions that obliterated the cartel resistance.

The pressure waves ruptured eardrums and internal organs while the high-temperature fuel deflagration burned flesh to the bone. It was a cruel weapon, and by the time Hagen pulled up to the destruction, nothing remained but burning debris, which he maneuvered around without slowing.

But beyond the haze and only a mile from their compound, Stark heard distant helicopters.

He started barking orders.

Miguel Orellana blinked at the carnage wrought on the blockade he ordered, witnessed through his Russian night-vision binoculars.

He knelt in the rear of a Bell UH-1 "Huey" helicopter next to the port-side gunner, who clasped the spade grips of an M60D 7.62x51mm machinegun on a flexible mount. A second man stood behind the starboard M60D while Ricco, who never left his side, sat next to three RPG-22 launchers, each fitted with a 72.5mm HEAT projectile. A second Huey followed them, similarly armed.

Who are these guys?

In less than five seconds they had eliminated the two pickup trucks fitted with similar flex-mounted M60Ds plus fourteen armed veterans dispatched from Las Flores, a town twenty miles south of Culiacán. A larger contingent of men and equipment were heading north from the town of Obispo, but they were twenty miles further south and still fifteen minutes away. Orellana had already deployed over fifty men and trucks, plus another twenty-three from the town of Oso Viejo—all with orders to intercept and hold, not kill.

But the level of violence unleashed by those Americans quickly made him realize it was going to be damn hard to stop them from escaping, much less take them alive.

And where are they going? The border is the other way.

He made sure Ricco had strapped on his body armor, which was ridiculously large, almost reaching his knees. The boy sat quietly with his seatbelt on in a seat next to the RPG launchers wearing a David Clark set.

Orellana made his decision.

"All set, *Romeo*?" Larson said, amusement in his voice. They were waiting in a ditch with a view of the incoming helicopters approaching from the west. "Or should I call you *bullshitter*?"

The Delta sniper had his Barrett again, as ordered by Stark, and was tracking the lead Huey in his night-vision scope.

"Fuck off, Chief," he replied.

"Roger that, Romeo," Larson said, sitting on the ground behind his Browning, back on the custom tripod, ammo sack clipped to the left side of his utility vest.

"Kill the chatter," Stark ordered, setting up his DFP—defensive fighting position—with the M240L a couple hundred feet south of Larson and Ryan. Hagen and Danny drove the SUV another thousand feet.

Then the two SEALs did what they did best: dump the vehicle and vanish into the night, leaving it with its high beams pointed at the incoming threat as a distraction.

It had taken all of twenty-one seconds from the time he'd first heard the helicopters. Stark recognized the sound as Model 204 Hueys, the short-body and underpowered version of the venerable Model 205—the workhorse of the Vietnam War.

"Send it when able," Stark said.

"Roger," Ryan replied.

To the untrained eye, a pair of Hueys skimming the desert floor kicking up twin clouds of debris, their side guns clearly visible in the night, might look ominous.

But to the former Special Forces colonel, they represented targets, and Hunter Stark had remained alive this long by always looking for weaknesses—and then exploiting those weaknesses with just the right amount of deception, a handful of violent operators, excessive use of firepower, a side of balls, and a truckload of luck.

In the case of those early Hueys it was the lack of underside rocket launchers or guns that gave Stark the edge. The helos would have to turn and expose their sides to allow the gunners the angle to shoot.

Or, they could attempt to fly right over the road to give those side-mounted M60s a chance at firing into their DFPs.

Good luck with that.

Orellana knelt between the pilot, a former star in the Mexican Air Force, and his rookie co-pilot, a good stick but fresh out of flight school.

They flew a nap-of-the-earth gun run toward the spot where he had seen the Americans jump out of the vehicle, which they had abandoned with its headlights on as a trick.

His plan was simple: get close enough for his gunners to overwhelm the bastards with suppressive fire and keep them pinned down until his teams converged on this remote spot.

But he never got the chance.

A large caliber round pierced the Huey's canopy and nearly tore off the pilot's head, splashing blood everywhere. The co-pilot tried to react, but a second round punched him in the chest.

Orellana reached for the cyclic—the helicopter's center control column—on the pilot's side, keeping his head below the panel. He pulled it back gently, arresting as much forward speed as he could and forcing the Huey down in his best attempt at a controlled crash, given he only could reach the cyclic, not the collective or the rudder pedals. He also shut down the single Lycoming turboshaft.

The airframe shuddered when the landing skids raked the desert floor. The second Huey was burning from a barrage of antiaircraft fire, flames and debris expanding radially.

His Huey skipped across the desert for a few seconds, then the main rotor struck the ground, arresting the helicopter's forward momentum. The last thing Orellana heard before he slammed headfirst into the center panel was Ricco screaming his name through his headset.

Their methods ruled the opposite ends of the spectrum, but they were also complementary—and each deadly in their own right.

Ryan took out the pilots of the lead Huey with back-to-back surgical shots from over a thousand yards. Chief Larson followed him, painting a wall of armor-piercing violence in front of the second helicopter in a raw and blazing display of power.

The helicopter burst into flames.

What Stark had not expected was for the lead Huey to continue flying, given the lack of a pilot and the unstable nature of helicopters.

Instead of plummeting from the sky, it somehow managed a controlled crash. The airframe skipped across the desert floor like a stone on a pond until the main rotor struck an outcropping of rocks a couple hundred feet from his position.

Stark dug in. Few things created more lethal debris than disintegrating helicopter blades made from sandwiched materials: aluminum, composites, some steel, a dash of titanium, and the obligatory leading-edge abrasion shields.

The rotor broke up, centrifugal force vomiting the metallic-composite shit sandwich in a radial pattern at almost the speed of sound.

Shrapnel swept across the road over their heads with the power of a hundred hand grenades, peppering the field like a meteor shower, tearing down fences and scoring the asphalt, but it was over quickly.

Stark got to his feet and scanned what was left of the lead Huey, less than a hundred feet away. "Negative hostile motion," he said, when there was no movement from the wreck.

"*Concur,*" replied Larson.

"Danny, Sitrep," Stark said, asking for a situation report from his SEALs.

"*On our way in five mikes.*"

"Roger," he replied and picked up his M240L.

A great team could handle any op, especially those going sideways, even outnumbered and operating in an unfamiliar, hostile place.

The night was quiet, even peaceful, save for the burning Huey the chief brought down, splashing hues of orange and yellow-gold on a barren land ruled by monsters.

But tonight, Stark had brought far worse creatures and better equipment, each playing a crucial role.

Even the damn Kia, he thought, glancing at the SUV still parked where Hagen and Danny ditched it, high beams colliding with the burning Huey.

Ricco knelt over his father in the flickering light, a scrawny figure swallowed by the violence of the only world he had ever known.

He did not cry.

He had cried enough six months ago, hearing his mother and sisters being brutalized by the monsters who invaded their home in the middle of the night while his father was away.

It had been a cowardly attack—one he was lucky to have survived. He cowered in a closet, eyes closed, his innocent mind trying to block the terrified shrieks, the agonized wails, the incessant noise that squeezed every last ounce of compassion and empathy from his young soul.

The boy had become a man that night, and he had sworn, alongside his father, to avenge them. But now, it appeared vengeance was up to him.

His father was dying in front of his eyes. His right arm had been torn off above the elbow and something had punched a hole bigger than Ricco's fist in his chest.

And yet, he was still breathing, still staring at the boy with eyes growing vacant, empty. His father used his remaining arm to grab the front of Ricco's vest.

He pulled the boy closer, eye to eye, father and son together for one final time before he had to face eternity, alone.

"It was . . . the Americans . . . avenge . . . me, son," his father whispered. "You must avenge us all . . ."

Ricco clung to his father, lying there, his life draining away.

"Avenge . . ." he mumbled, coughing blood. The labored breathing stopped abruptly and his father's face went slack.

For the first time in his life, Ricco Orellana felt completely alone. He curled his small fingers around his father's Desert Eagle.

Avenge . . . me.

And Ricco Orellana pulled the hefty pistol from its holster and crawled out of the wreckage to do precisely that.

A new sound emerged from the south, around the bend in the road where his SEALs had disappeared less than five minutes ago.

To the untrained ear, it was the sound of the wind, softly whistling between canyon walls. The whisper developed a rhythm almost musical in nature, steady but nearly imperceptible, easily missed among the natural voices of the desert.

The world didn't know the warbird existed—just those with the right Top Secret/Sensitive Compartmented Information (TS/SCI) clearance.

But Stark knew, as did his operators, in particular Danny Martin, who brought the MH-X Stealth Black Hawk helicopter into a shallow hover.

The best way to describe this advanced version of the Black Hawk was to imagine an airbrush artist smoothing every external imperfection of the venerable helo, making it look like it belonged in a sci-fi flick. Engine shields and rotor covers were added, along with an extra main rotor blade for increased lift at slower rotor speed. The final touch was a coat of Radar Absorbing Material.

"Curbside pickup for three in thirty, sir," the SEAL operator reported.

"Roger," Stark replied.

Movement from the Huey caught his eye, a figure emerging from the wreckage.

"Got a live one, Colonel," Ryan said

He was about to order the Delta sniper to put a round through the survivor, then he realized.

It was a kid.

"What do we do, sir?" Larson asked.

The boy walked toward them, his face marred with smoke and grime, his skinny silhouette flickering in the light from the fire.

Stark was surprised, especially by the boy's eyes, even from that distance. They were steady, focused, and cold.

But before the colonel could answer, the boy produced an impossibly large and shiny pistol that reflected the glowing fire behind him.

"Gun!" Larson screamed.

The kid fired once, from a distance of forty feet.

The report was thunder in the desert night. Stark felt the air parting over his head from the .50 caliber round.

The good news was that the boy missed. The even better news was that the pistol was way too big for his little hands, so the powerful recoil made him lose his grip and it punched him squarely in the chest, knocking him down.

Stark was on top of him in seconds, followed by Larson and Ryan.

The kid seemed out of it, eyes fluttering, though Stark noticed they were of different colors, one brown and the other green. The boy moaned, probably dazed by the recoil-punch.

Grabbing the Desert Eagle, Stark removed the magazine and cycled the slide, ejecting the .50 AE round. He pocketed the round and the magazine and raised an eyebrow at the pistol, which was quite the gaudy piece of art, with tiger stripes laser-etched on the gold barrel and the initials M.O. on both sides of the grip.

"Time to go, sir!" Larson said as the stealth helo approached kicking up a whirling cloud of debris from its twin low-speed main rotors.

Danny set the MH-X down next to them.

"Right behind you, Chief," Stark replied.

Larson and Ryan climbed in. He took another look at the crazy kid, who couldn't be older than ten or eleven.

"Your lucky night, kid," he said, tossing the pistol on the sand.

The boy's eyes opened and he looked at Stark. The veteran warrior blinked first.

They were the eyes of a monster.

CHAPTER 1
Monica

"You can never run away from your violent past. It will find a way back into your life and harm those you love."
—Monica Cruz

PRESENT DAY.
EAGLE PASS, SOUTH TEXAS

The shot went high, splintering the bark of a red cedar a few feet behind her, the report echoing a second later.

Monica Cruz had simply reacted, jumping off her Quarter Horse and rolling in the knee-high Johnson grass. The cattle she'd been herding for the past two days, a mix of Red Angus and Hereford, stampeded in the direction of the east watering hole.

What the hell? she thought, adrenaline surging. The rocky ground trembled beneath the pounding of hundreds of hoofs thundering past her.

Ignoring it, Monica used her momentum to put some distance between herself and the spot where she landed, using the tall grass for cover. The mare horse bolted, following the cattle, taking the Winchester in the saddle holster with her.

She instinctively slapped her right ankle, relieved that the .32-caliber Colt revolver was secure in the ankle holster—a backup weapon in the unforgiving South Texas wilderness, along with the SOG knife in its leather sheath clipped to her waist. But the little six-shooter was an anemic substitute for the powerful Winchester .308, equipped with a 40mm riflescope.

In the distance, lightning flashed and thunder rumbled from a late-afternoon storm sweeping across the region, bringing much needed rain.

For a moment, she wondered if the shot had originated from the ranch just west of her family's. Hired hands were always hunting coyotes.

But the sound was wrong.

The ranchers in the area, including Monica and her brothers, Michael and Marty, typically used either .30-30s or .308s to clear annoying pests. The latter doubled as a good deer hunting rifle and—

A follow-up shot confirmed it, the round striking the brush she had just vacated.

Monica hardened her jaw. *That's a goddamned 338*, she thought. A McMillan TAC-338 rifle chambered in the powerful .338 Lapua Magnum round. A sniper's weapon—like the one stored in her closet at the main house.

The wind swirled the tall Johnson grass, concealing her, keeping her alive.

Monica cringed at the thought of being hunted. *But by whom?*

It had been a year since she had resigned from the Bureau.

It had been a mutual decision between her and her bosses following that harrowing week chasing terrorists with a nuclear weapon during a covert mission led by Colonel Hunter Stark and his team of contractors.

Although the mission had been a success, it resulted in Congressional blowback for President Laura Vaccaro, who had not sought approval before signing the directive enabling Stark and team to go after the terrorists.

Monica shook her head, still glad she had turned in her gun and badge, leaving the back-stabbing world of Washington, D.C. to head south, to her family's ranch to help her brothers. She'd hoped that the change would be a much-needed break from the intensity of her years as an Army sniper, then a Los Angeles SWAT sniper, and finally an agent for the FB—

A third round, to the right of the second one, told her the sniper was starting a systematic search, trying to flush her out.

A professional. But why? What is he—

A fourth shot punched the dry terrain just a foot away in an explosion of dirt and rocks, screaming at her to analyze later.

Her shoulders tensing, using the swaying grass to her advantage, Monica crawled away from the kill zone for nearly a hundred feet.

A fifth round hammered the ground behind her just as she reached a cluster of cedars surrounding a pair of baby oaks.

Her older brother, Marty, had wanted to clear the trash trees choking the oaks a week ago.

She was really glad they hadn't. But the thought made her think of Marty and their younger brother, Michael. She had been gone for two days rounding up a couple dozen strays on the north end of their 1500-acre ranch, and her phone had unsurprisingly died.

Are they all right?

Bile rose in her throat.

Did I make a mistake coming back here? But how would anyone know? My service file was sealed. Did someone leak it?

A year ago, when the violence had finally caught up to her, Monica had climbed on her Ducati and pointed it south in search of peace . . . perhaps even someone to share her life with, start a family before it was too late.

But the violence, it appeared, had found her.

Maybe I'm a shit magnet.

A light drizzle, getting heavier, was accompanied by sheet lightning and the clap of thunder as the eastern edge of the storm arrived.

A fast-moving front.

Monica licked her dry lips and counted the seconds, wondering if the lack of a sixth shot meant that the sniper had lost her or was reloading since the TAC-338 came standard with a five-round magazi—

The supersonic round whipped the damp air, striking a boulder a dozen feet away, chipping off shards in a brief cloud of sparks. It was followed by a seventh shot, to the left of the boulders, farther from her hideout, which gave Monica hope.

He's lost me.

She didn't move for a long time. Dusk was falling and the wind picked up, which worked to her advantage. The sniper would have to make adjustments, costing him time and accuracy. The gusty wind presented its own difficulties.

Her patience paid off. Back-to-back shots struck the ground a dozen feet to her right.

She saw the muzzle flashes near the top of a rocky hill that overlooked the meadow as well as the next valley, where the main house plus an assortment of other buildings were located. Farther south, the ranch's perimeter fence almost butted against the tall wall erected by Homeland Security along the north bank of the Rio Grande.

She narrowed her eyes. *Hello asshole.*

A crack of lightning followed by a booming thunderclap and the skies opened up, torrents of rain lashing the dry Texas land.

Although whoever was trying to kill her was well trained, rain was a problem for a sniper. Comfort aside, potential equipment malfunctions and diminished sightlines played hell with accuracy. And that meant that the weather was evening the odds in tonight's live fire exercise.

A narrow and twisting trail connected the valley to the top of the hill, which provided an excellent vantage point to locate cattle.

Or to set up a sniper's perch.

Time to move out.

But she had to assume that the assassin was equipped with night surveillance, meaning a night-vision feature in the scope, like the TAC-338 in her closet. And there was even a chance that the sniper had a spotter, an individual armed with a spotting scope that provided a wider view of the terrain.

But night-vision had a weakness: sudden illumination would either blind the user or, in expensive models—like those used in the military—briefly shut down to avoid doing so. Either way, it meant a lightning flash would prevent the enemy from acquiring her.

Priming herself like an Olympic sprinter at the start of a race, Monica waited for her signal, which came when lightning cracked above her.

She charged from the trees, covering a dozen yards in the few seconds of light, and diving for the cover of the Johnson grass, sliding on fresh mud another few feet, like a ball player sliding head first to steal a base.

Ignoring the rain soaking through her clothes, Monica wiped her mud-spattered face, welcoming the familiar sweetness of the rain, the verdant smell of wet vegetation, and the gusty wind—sensory inputs that briefly transported her to her sniper days. She would wait hours—even days—in any weather, to get her shot. And she could do it again to prevent another sniper from doing the same to her.

She considered her options. At the top of her list: turn the tables.

Lightning streaked across an angry sky and she ran, covering another handful of yards before sliding back into the ooze.

Almost immediately, lightning snarled overhead and Monica burst through the grass stealing another dozen yards, starting a wide arc that would take her to the western foot of the hill.

It took her nearly thirty minutes to cover the quarter mile. By then, the sniper had long since gone silent, probably waiting for the storm to abate.

Now came the difficult part: leaving the cover of the Johnson grass and clambering toward the sniper's perch.

But she didn't have a choice.

So she climbed, pushing through the shroud of rain, staying low. When she was at the top, the rain slowed to a drizzle, and she saw lights in the valley to the south.

The ranch.

But there was something else: A strange yellowish glow between the main house and the largest of the barns, and it was surrounded by people scurrying. There were also three white vans she didn't recognize, parked near the yellow glow.

The fuck's going on?

She fretted about her brothers as well as their half-dozen ranch hands, mostly Mexican migrant workers and—

A shot ripped through the night—the sniper resuming his hunt.

This time, Monica saw a long flash, meaning the shooter was still hunting near the spot where she had come off her horse . . . how long ago?

Her heart pounding from exertion as well as elation that her strategy was indeed working, she continued the climb, progressing slowly, still moving only during lightning.

Monica finally got an angle on the location where she had seen the flashes.

This time she didn't move during the next bolt of lightning. It forked across the night sky, revealing a man's upper torso and the unmistakable outline of a McMillan TAC-338 rifle. Its long and slender barrel, mounted on a swiveling tripod, pointed at the north valley below.

Now Monica used the darkness, inching closer. The next lightning flash brought another glimpse of the sniper no more than fifteen yards away.

Monica reached down and retrieved the Colt, curled the fingers of her right hand on the custom rubber grip. She brought it up, cupping it with her left hand while thumbing the hammer and aiming it into the darkness in the general direction of the shooter.

And she waited in the eerie silence between of thunder bursts.

Lightning flashed a moment later long enough to align the shooter's head in its iron sights.

She fired twice

The sniper toppled over, and she was on top ready with a follow-up shot. But the next flash illuminated a corpse with brain matter oozing from two jagged holes in its forehead, and dead eyes staring at the sky.

Shoving the revolver in her jeans, pressed against her stomach for a quicker draw, Monica was about to search him for ID when the sniper rifle caught her attention. It wasn't just *any* TAC-338.

It was hers.

What is happening?

Monica picked it up, touched the familiar scratches on the stock and on its Leupold scope, made a lifetime ago in Iraq and Afghanistan, and on those sweltering rooftops in LA.

Her hands moved automatically, inspecting the bolt action to make sure there was a cartridge chambered. Then she checked the Leupold scope and its night-vision attachment. Finally, she removed the magazine, verifying it had five rounds in it, and reinserting it.

Monica grabbed the rucksack by the man's feet—*her* rucksack, where she kept six spare magazines already loaded. But the assassin had gone through four of them, which Monica found by his feet next to the rucksack, which also contained a dozen 10-round boxes of .338 Lapua Magnum 300-grain hollow points.

Bastards were trying to kill me with my own gun and my own ammo.

Setting the rifle down, she finally checked the dead sniper and found no ID.

But she didn't need to.

His body art was all the ID Monica needed.

The man's arms and chest were plastered with gory scenes of the dead, including a large one on his chest depicting a skeleton clutching an AR-15 firing into a group of women and children. On his face, seven teardrops ran down his left cheek, which symbolized his confirmed kills. But there was no mistaking the word **SINALOA** tattooed on his back, in between a pair of black wings covering his shoulder blades, that gave him away.

This man belonged to a cartel.

And the realization sent chills through her tired body and made her heart sink.

If indeed the Sinaloa Cartel was behind this, then there wouldn't be any survivors. These bastards never left anyone alive, and not only that, they took pleasure in inflicting the cruelest forms of death on their victims to make a statement.

But I can make a goddamned statement too.

The rain finally subsided, and Monica set up the TAC facing the opposite direction, toward the action down by the house. She reloaded the empty magazines and set them up next to her.

She scanned the ranch with the night-vision scope, taking her time, systematically surveying the field between the main house and the barn, where she had spotted that peculiar light coming out of the ground.

And now, when she settled the powerful Leupold on it, she realized exactly what was happening: The cartel dug a tunnel under the wall that surfaced on her property just south of the house. The opening was at least eight feet wide and equally high, and there were a dozen men hauling long cases or crates out of the tunnel.

She continued scanning, searching for her brothers, and—

She spotted Marty by the front porch with his hands tied above his head hanging from one of the posts completely naked.

He had been emasculated.

Goddammit.

And by Marty's feet, she recognized the grotesquely misshapen body of Michael, also naked.

Monica jerked away from the scope, fighting the nausea as very familiar but very unsettling emotions, dormant for the better part of a year, surged.

Bastards.

Fucking bastards.

Quivering with old, familiar rage—smothered these past months by the endless sixteen hour days of ranch work—Monica took a deep breath, mustering control, forcing herself to focus.

She exhaled slowly, swallowing the fury like boiling tar, and settling once again behind the TAC.

Monica scanned the worthless souls moving about, studying each one, taking the time to sort the foot soldiers from the men in charge.

She discovered something else: three of them were her ranch hands.

Motherfuckers.

And they, along with everyone else, were armed, some with UZIs others with Mac-10 pistols—cartel weapons—which were useless at this distance.

Might as well be armed with slingshots.

She identified the two people in charge, a man and a woman. They were giving the orders to people exiting the tunnel hauling those long, rectangular boxes. At least a half dozen of them were stacked inside the lead van, a Ford Aerostar, before working on the other two.

Then, two men who looked Asian and the woman in charge, a tall and very skinny Hispanic—got in the van and took off in a hurry down the unpaved road connecting to the access road a mile away.

She had the sudden urge to shoot it, but her training and discipline held her back.

Not yet. Let that one go.

She reached inside a Velcro-secured pouch on the rucksack and slid out a foot-long black cylinder roughly two inches in diameter.

She screwed the silencer, which doubled as a flash suppressor, onto the muzzle, surprised that the cartel soldier hadn't, perhaps because it degraded the weapon's accuracy. Or maybe he didn't realize it was there. But whatever the reason, it had given Monica a chance to fight back, a favor that she wasn't about to return.

She inspected the silencer, deciding eliminating muzzle flashes and reports was a good tradeoff for the loss of accuracy, which should be acceptable given an estimated range to target of around 800 meters.

The TAC-338 had a manufacturer's range of twice that, and talented operators, such as the legendary Chris Kyle, had hit targets from over 2000 meters.

Monica, who was once among those elite snipers, went through her sequence three times, feeling she could complete the progression in fifteen seconds, including two reloads.

Verifying the spare magazines were within reach, she got down to the business of ridding the world of evil.

CHAPTER 2
Hand Arrow

"Goddamned war. No matter how justified or necessary, it is still the very definition of hell on Earth."
—Colonel Hunter Stark

HELMAND PROVINCE, AFGHANISTAN

It was supposed to be a cakewalk. It turned out to be a certified, take it to the bank, full-blown shit show.

A U.S. Army Green Beret unit on a routine patrol was pinned down under heavy fire from Taliban forces. So, the NATO commander at Kandahar Airfield dispatched a U.S. military Quick Reaction Force, QRF, to relieve the Green Berets, but they too got into trouble and were now immobilized.

Four Apache attack helicopters followed to provide air-to-ground support. But a combination of heavy machine gun fire from a nearby Taliban compound, plus some unexpected surface-to-air missiles, took out one Apache and kept the other three from getting close to the trapped American forces.

A pair of A-10 Warthogs in the vicinity tried to intervene, but one was damaged by a missile and had to turn back to KAF, and his wingman ran low on fuel and also had to return to base.

More A-10s were dispatched from KAF, but their effectiveness was questionable. The enemy was too close to the Americans to risk a traditional ground-support air assault. Not to mention the Stinger-like missiles in the hands of the Taliban.

Faced with the possibility of losing over forty servicemembers that afternoon, the brass at KAF, at the suggestion of the resident

CIA Station Chief, Glenn Harwich, decided to try something a little different.

Colonel Hunter Stark fast-roped from the Black Hawk, ignoring the ground fire pinging off the belly as Danny Martin kept them twenty feet over the rocky terrain just south of the compound that shot down an Apache, damaged an A-10, and was preventing further air support.

The speed was possible in part due to the heat-resistant gloves over his tactical gloves, that allowed him to slide down the 40mm fast rope, which had a weighed core to steady it beneath the rotor blast.

Exactly three seconds later, Stark bent his knees to absorb momentum and landed, stepping away to make room for Michael Hagen.

The former SEAL careened down the rope like no one else could, using just one gloved hand and his legs to control his drop and firing his MP7SD in the direction of the compound.

Both graceful and deadly, Hagen managed to turn quick ingress, when operators were the most vulnerable, into an opportunity to shoot the enemy from above.

Stark, already poised for battle, did a double-take at the plummeting SEAL and unloaded his own MP7SD at the source of the ground fire. It was one of three reported rooftop machinegun nests, each equipped with Russian PKs, basically the machine gun version of the venerable AK-47, firing the powerful 7.62x54mm round.

Landing while going into a roll—and reloading—Hagen discarded his single heat-resistant glove and took up his defensive position behind Stark, covering the colonel's right flank in classic CQB—close quarters battle—while the third member of his team plummeted from the helo.

His fast-roping technique wasn't graceful. In fact, it was damn ugly, but it sure was effective, fast, and menacing.

Master Chief Evan Larson, his monster 50-caliber M2 BMG, plus an ungodly amount of ammunition in a rucksack, careened down the rope, an oversized apocalyptic warrior.

He landed his combined 350-pounds of muscle, titanium plates in his body armor, and his heavy-caliber weaponry with a single and definitive Earth-shaking thud—no roll. He took up his own CQB position behind Hagen in the stack, opening the Browning on the surrounding threat.

Stark was damn glad the big operator played for his team. Larson made fast work of the machine gun nest, temporarily silencing it with a few short bursts of full metal jacket hell.

Last, but not least, this warrior was lean and moved like a big cat. He casually stepped out of the Black Hawk, his movements fluid and precise, almost choreographed.

Command Master Sergeant Ryan Hunt dropped faster than everyone else, hitting the ground running. He tossed his heat-resistant gloves, unslung his sniper rifle, and fell in line behind Chief Larson in the stack.

Fast-roping had taken all of eleven seconds, and Danny flew the helo out of the range of the guns.

"Sierra Echo One, Bravo Niner Six. Sitrep."

Stark frowned. The controller at KAF had impeccable timing.

"Echo One on the ground and a little busy," he replied into his throat mic.

Before the controller could respond, Larson's fifty-caliber beast drowned all other sound as he aimed the Browning on the closest PK machine gun emplacement. Ryan fired single, perfectly-placed shots.

Their combined firepower quickly overwhelmed the enemy. And that was the thing about .50-cal BMGs—which packed nearly five times the punch of the PK. If a BMG hit you anywhere, you were done. At any range, anywhere. Period. And even near-misses killed with direct hits to nearby objects, as was the case with Larson's and Ryan's volleys, which pretty much evaporated the enemy's nest.

Meanwhile, Stark and Hagen focused their fire on the black-clad insurgents coming around a corner of the mud and stone structure.

The second rooftop emplacement swung away from the trapped soldiers in the courtyard beyond the compound and aimed its long barrel toward him.

"Chief! A little help!"

The air above them parted as Larson redirected the Browning's ferocity over their heads

It was deafening. It was violent. It was teeth-rattling.

And it was damn effective.

The second nest vanished in the brutality that Larson unleashed for all of five seconds, in which the belt-fed monstrosity vomited over a hundred 1800-grain BMG rounds, enough to cut a vehicle in half.

That allowed Stark and Hagen to keep their minds on the ground threat. They were firing their MP7SDs in semiautomatic mode, one round per trigger pull. Their fire was accurate, devastating, and violently effective.

Stark and Hagen approached the compound from the west, opposite where the Green Berets and the QRF contingent were pinned down, executing the three principles of close quarters battle: surprise, speed, and violence of action.

They would take no prisoners, offer no quarter, and show no mercy.

Without an ounce of regret.

Through the cacophony of mixed caliber weapons fired, Stark heard a new report in the mix: M4 carbines, the preferred weapon of the Green Berets, meaning his boys had put enough of a dent in the enemy to allow the snake eaters pinned down in that courtyard to get back into the war.

Almost there, he thought, reaching the northwest corner of the compound with his guys on him.

Before the missiles had shot down the Apache from this very rooftop—and forced the others to hover a couple of miles away—the pilot had noticed an entrance to the compound at this corner.

The colonel spotted the green and quite rusted metal door directly ahead of—

"*Sierra Echo One, you have eyes on those SAMs?*" said Glenn Harwich, Stark's current employer.

Goddammit.

He ignored the spook's ill-timed question, making a beeline for the door. Assisting the trapped soldiers had been the cover Harwich needed to convince the KAF leadership to deploy Stark and team. But the Agency was after something else.

Langley needed confirmation of a suspected alliance between the *Yakuza*—Japan's transnational organized crime syndicate—al-Qaeda, and the Sinaloa Cartel to procure, by any means necessary, a new generation of shoulder-launched surface-to-air missiles.

The Type 91, colloquially known as "Hand Arrow," was manufactured by Toshiba Heavy Industries for the sole use of the JSDF, Japan Self-Defense Forces. But a recent joint audit conducted by the CIA and the PSIA—the Public Security Intelligence Agency, Japan's national intelligence agency—highlighted a deficit of 300 units from a Toshiba warehouse outside Tokyo. While additional audits were underway at other Toshiba locations across the island, the CIA had immediately gone into high gear to track down the missing units.

To put things in perspective, the Agency had provided the Mujahedeen with 2300 Stinger shoulder-launched SAMs to fight off the Soviet invasion of the 1980s. But only 1200 were used by the insurgent force during the course of that war. Of the remaining 1100, a third were eventually bought back by the U.S. The rest were unaccounted for, suspected to have found their way into Croatia, Bosnia, and even North Korea. The Agency believed that the missing Type 91s, with Toshiba's more advanced tracking electronics, could wreak havoc if smuggled into America—or if they fell into the hands of the Taliban, the successor of the feared Mujahedeen.

Fucking Toshiba.

Stark, Hagen and Ryan were standing clear of the door while the chief aimed the Browning at the hinges and the lock.

It took less than three seconds for the heavy door to plummet inward and Stark followed it with an MK3A2 concussion grenade, pulling the safety pin, counting to three, and tossing it into the opening. The count was necessary to keep the target from lobbing the grenade right back at him.

"Grenade out!" he warned, and a moment later the compound trembled from the acoustic energy and a plume of smoke shot through the doorway.

The colonel went first, leading the stack through the haze, shifting to the right to make room for Hagen, then Ryan.

"Clear right," Stark announced, scanning his quadrant.

"Clear left," Ryan replied.

"All clear," Hagen finished.

Larson came in last, protecting their six, and the group moved once more as one, cruising through the first floor and up the stairs to the roof, where they surprised three hajis clustered by the PKs firing into the courtyard. Two more knelt by a set of long metal cases, readying what Stark immediately recognized as Type 91 shoulder-launched SAMs.

Hagen took care of the latter while Larson evaporated the former and—

Another warrior stormed through a door to Stark's far right. He was dressed like a Taliban chief and sported a shiny AK-47.

Stark acted on his instructions from Harwich to try to capture someone in charge. So, he shot him through the left knee from a distance of ten yards.

The insurgent boss went down screaming, and Stark was on top of him a moment later, whipping him across the face with the stock of his MP7SD, knocking him out.

"Compound clear," he reported.

Ryan flex-cuffed their prisoner and also slapped a patch of QuickClot on the wound to keep him from bleeding out.

The Apaches were inbound and the trapped soldiers emerged from their hideouts, when Stark noticed a boy on the rooftop.

No older than ten, in baggy pants, a tan shirt, and a dark vest, he ran towards one of the men Hagen had put down. Kneeling next to the body, the youngster began to cry, shaking the dead insurgent, trying to wake him up.

Goddamned war, Stark thought. *No matter how justified or necessary, it's still hell on Earth.*

And it was always the same, everywhere he went. The jungles of Colombia, the mountains of Peru, the war-torn streets of Mogadishu, and the rocky wasteland that was Afghanistan, the graveyard of empires.

His heart broke for the sobbing boy. The inevitable collateral damage was the worst part of this job.

"Echo One, do you have eyes on the package?"

"Yeah," he said, looking at the cases. "I've got eyes on the package, and I got you a live one for—"

He spotted a man on a nearby roof using a cell phone, very likely a lookout.

"Romeo!" Stark pointed.

Ryan rushed to that side of the roof and aimed the Barrett toward him, prompting the local to disappear into the building.

"Keep running, asshole," Stark said.

He returned his attention to the boy. He was staring at Stark with vacant eyes that evoked memories of that night in Mexico—the kid with the different colored eyes taking a shot at him with that gold-plated Desert Eagle.

They were the eyes of a—

The boy raised his right hand, revealing a detonator. His vest was covering an explosive belt.

Oh, shit.

In that instant, staring in disbelief at the boy, features contorted as he squeezed the detonator, something struck Stark then knocked Hagen aside and threw himself on top of the kid.

Before the blast swallowed his world.

CHAPTER 3
The Abyss

"As I looked into the eyes of the monster, they not only gazed back into my broken soul but fragmented my thin veneer of humanity."
—Monica Cruz

EAGLE PASS, SOUTH TEXAS

She didn't approach the kill zone until long after the storm had subsided, a full moon now casting a grayish glow over her handiwork.

It truly felt like the valley of the shadow of death, as Monica somberly inspected the muddy ground at the mouth of the tunnel and collected an UZI from one of the dozen men sprawled nearby. She felt numb in the foggy aftermath that always accompanied the taking of lives—even if they belonged to a despicable enemy.

Taut muscles moved beneath her bronze skin as she surveyed the kill zone. Her burning gaze glinted from a narrow face caked with mud.

Monica could tell herself that she took them without regret—perhaps even with grim satisfaction—but she didn't like lying to herself. With every kill, however brutally deserved, a part of her died as well. But this acceptance of what she herself lost in combat was the very essence of bravery.

These unwelcome feelings collided with the anger swelling in her throat at the sight of her brothers, brutally tortured, and the ranch hands she found piled along the back of the house. Naked. Castrated.

Fucking animals.

She sensed what was left of her humanity evaporating as she regarded the carnage, headshots from a sniper progression confirming that her skills had not atrophied. She did miss one—a man who'd managed to run back inside the tunnel.

There was an old quote from Friedrich Nietzsche, a warning really, to those in Monica's former line of work, about staring too long into the abyss, about avoiding becoming the very monsters she chased.

She walked among those monsters now, quietly inspecting and verifying each kill. Monica had to ask if they had not only gazed into her soul but were fragmenting her veneer of civility.

This question was at the heart of her decision to step away from the abyss and leave the fight to a new generation while she sought some semblance of peace in a world where peace was as scarce as diamonds.

She approached the tunnel with caution and risked a look—the man she had seen running inside could be nearby.

But the shaft was deserted, at least as far as she could see, as it dropped to clear the Rio Grande a half mile away.

She rummaged through a few rucksacks, finding a number of grenades and other tactical explosives. She spent a few minutes setting the charges in a Daisy-chain down the shaft.

Removing the pin from a grenade Monica tossed it into the entrance and moved aside.

The first few blasts were deafening, causing the ground to tremble. Then the cave began to collapse, muffling a dozen more explosions—sealing it well enough to keep any unwanted visitors from venturing through it while she called for reinforcements.

Satisfied that no one would be coming back, at least through that tunnel, Monica spent a few minutes cutting Marty down from the front porch. She covered Michael and Marty with blankets, tears streaming.

She screamed into the night, giving voice to the pain of losing her brothers, her only family, and her own guilt for failing them.

Monica Cruz, the decorated Army sniper, star of the LA SWAT, and hero of the FBI, had come up short. She couldn't protect the people she loved most in the world. And that feeling, combined with the overwhelming guilt of surviving, threatened to push her over the edge, straight down Nietzsche's abyss.

Pulling herself together, Monica walked away from her brothers and took a knee by the stack of long metal containers that had yet to be loaded.

The containers were stenciled in Asian characters; on closer inspection, they looked Japanese.

Kanji?

But there was a word she could read: **TOSHIBA.**

She opened one and stared at a green launcher system that reminded her of the venerable American Stinger missile unit.

Realizing what it was, and also that the first van had left, hauling at least six of them, Monica pushed everything else aside and sprinted to the house, going straight for the charger in the kitchen and plugging in her phone.

She stood there for a few minutes, arms crossed, waiting impatiently while the phone took enough charge to boot up.

And the moment it finally did, Monica called a number she hadn't called in a year—a number she thought she would never have to call again.

CHAPTER 4
Mireya

"Revenge is an act of justice, where injuries are paid back, where crimes are avenged."
—Mireya Moreno Carreón.

BEAR CREEK GOLF CLUB.
DALLAS–FORT WORTH, TEXAS

They called her *La Flaca*. Skinny Girl.

It was an honorable title that was later used by a number of female cartel assassins that followed in her footsteps.

Although Mireya Moreno Carreón was the original *La Flaca*, responsible for the death of many law enforcement officers, the nickname didn't define who she was, and it especially failed to describe the overwhelming adversity she had faced and overcome in her short life.

A native of California, growing up in the barrios of East LA, Mireya joined *La Eme*—the Mexican Mafia—at fifteen. It was there that she cultivated her lack of empathy and knack for violence—necessary qualities to kill people for money.

Her potential was noticed by visiting officers from Los Zetas, the powerful cartel ruling northeastern Mexico who recruited her and brought her down to Monterrey, the capital of the state of Nuevo Leon.

Mireya became the first women to rise through its ranks by eliminating targets—primarily law-enforcement personnel—using just a sound-suppressed 22-caliber Rugger Mark-V semiautomatic firing subsonic .22-caliber rounds.

It was an assassin's gun with assassin's bullets. Quiet and deadly in the right hands.

*Sicario*s were experts at getting close to their targets, shooting them in the head, then dropping the gun and walking away.

And Mireya did it better than most.

But an unfortunate sequence of events, including a member of Los Zetas who became an informant, resulted in her arrest at the age of twenty-one. Mireya was tried, convicted, and sentenced to life in prison.

And that's when the horror began.

In her jail cell, Mireya was brutalized by her captors, night after night, week after week, month after month. It was unrelenting, designed to break her, to kill her spirit. Sinaloa Cartel Boss Ricco Orellana, her current employer, paid his way through the judicial system eight years ago and got her sentence reduced to time served. He then brought her into his employment as part of his deal to forge an alliance with Los Zetas.

Mireya was a young woman but also an old one, aged prematurely by the horrors she had endured. She had once been beautiful, until the prison guards decided to beat her. Repeatedly. Often to within an inch of her life.

But she took the punishment in the silence of a Los Zetas warrior—the most feared assassins among all of the cartel families.

Then Ricco had come along, freeing her from her captors, giving her a new purpose, an avenue to channel her anger. He had also retained the finest plastic surgeons that money could buy.

The doctors did what they could, but they could never erase the damage completely. Her face remained subtly asymmetrical, faintly unequal depressions beneath her cheekbones, one dark eye that sagged unevenly, and a slightly crooked mouth.

Mireya ran a finger over the thin scar traversing her chin, put there by guards on her last week imprisoned.

Her captors had given her another partying gift: Mireya had been impregnated by one of those lowlifes.

Her first reaction had been to get rid of it, dreading the thought of giving birth to the child of a monster.

But Ricco had convinced her to keep the baby, who was not at fault. And he'd promised to help her raise the child.

Feeling the slim Rugger firmly tucked in her jeans, pressed against her spine, Mireya regarded the runway beyond the chain-link fence separating it from the golf course. She contemplated her violent past, as well as the opportunities given to her by this man who treated her as family, including Antonio, her little boy who was turning nine this year.

She shook her head at the passage of time, at the life she had made for herself and Antonio in the empire that Ricco had built in the state of Sinaloa.

But most of all, *La Flaca* remembered the systematic way in which she had dealt with those prison guards, methodically tracking them down.

One by one.

Revenge is an act of passion, of justice, where injuries are paid back, where crimes are avenged.

She remembered their screams, their cries for mercy as she worked them with a torch and a pair of pliers with the same stoic demeanor that had kept her alive in those horrific years before Ricco rescued her.

And tonight, she planned to give something back to this man whose generosity, kindness, and loyalty had enabled her to overcome the kind of extreme abuse very few humans could. But unlike other assignments, Mireya would not be using the sound-suppressed Rugger on this mission—at least, not according to the plan. And for the first time in a long time, she was not operating alone.

Mireya was being assisted by two men this evening, both from Los Angeles—members of the feared *Yakuza*, the Japanese mafia which had procured the weapons required to execute this mission, and also the required training.

She didn't know their full names, and she didn't need to. One went by Eichi and the other by Aito. Both were plastered with Japanese tattoos. They handled Type 91 launchers like the one she carried.

There were three more launchers as backup.

But if the weapon was indeed as accurate and deadly as advertised by Toshiba, they should not need backup. They had left the Aerostar with the launchers out of sight on the access road a half mile away.

Mireya made the final preparations to execute a personal mission for Ricco Orellana.

Very personal.

And she was prepared to die rather than fail him.

CHAPTER 5
Ricco

"I price loyalty above everything else, for without loyalty, there can be no trust, and without trust . . . well."
—Ricco Orellana, Sinaloa Cartel boss.

CULIACÁN CITY, NORTHWESTERN MEXICO

Ricardo "Ricco" Orellana always made it a point to bring every business associate to his Sierra Madre retreat overlooking the Sinaloa Valley and the Pacific Ocean. The air this early evening hour was cool and invigorating, spiced with the fragrance of Mexican Pinyon and the Michoacán Pine.

Ricco had started the tradition shortly after taking over, in the aftermath of his mentor's capture on January 8th, 2016 by the *Fuerza de Infantería de Marina*, also known as the "Mexican Marines," his country's version of the elite U.S. Navy SEALs.

But the boss of the Sinaloa Cartel brought his guests here neither for the view nor for the soothing forest aromas that reminded him of his youth, or even to show off his steel and glass high-tech complex built into the side of the mountain at a cost that would have made Bill Gates blink.

Ricco brought them here to showcase the portraits, the eleven-by-fourteen images on matching dark wood frames occupying almost forty feet of wall space. Above them, written in 24-carat gold, it read:

MAY WE LEARN FROM THE KINGS WHO CAME BEFORE US.

The pictures, thirty of them, not arranged in any particular order, started with a black and white portrait of Al Capone, with the quote: **I'M JUST A BUSINESSMAN GIVING PEOPLE WHAT THEY WANT.**

Next were Miguel and Gilberto Rodriguez, the brothers who ran the Cali Cartel like an international conglomerate, earning the nickname "The Gentlemen of Cali."

Klaas Bruinsma, the notorious Dutch kingpin and biggest drug lord in Europe during the 1980s.

Osien Cardenas Guillen, leader of the Gulf Cartel and later the head of the feared Los Zetas, the brutal Mexican paramilitary gang.

William Leonard Pickard, "The Acid King," the largest producer of LSD in American history, operating out of abandoned nuclear missile sites in Kansas.

Nazario Moreno, *"El Mas Loco,"* leader of the drug gang the Knights Templar from his home state of Michoacán.

And the wall could not be complete without the famous Harlem heroin kingpin, Frank Lucas.

Ricco paused by the portrait of the Medellin Cartel's unforgettable Pablo Emilio Escobar Gaviria. Below it: **EVERYONE HAS A PRICE. THE IMPORTANT THING IS TO FIND OUT WHAT IT IS.**

Next was Panamanian General Manuel Noriega, the perfect example of why the Americans could never be trusted. He'd gone from a prized CIA asset to the top of the FBI's most wanted list.

Then there was Daut Kadriovski, the biggest boss of the brutal Albanian Mafia and king of a drug network spanning two continents.

Christopher Coke, "Dudus," the powerful Jamaican drug lord whose empire once spanned the Caribbean, North America, and the United Kingdom.

Just for good measure, Ricco had included a portrait of Osama bin Laden to stroke the egos of his heroin compadres from South Asia. Though one should never forget that it was the American CIA who trained and armed bin Laden in the 1980s to fight the Soviet occupation of Afghanistan.

And next to the legendary mastermind of the September 11 attacks was a portrait of a smiling Saddam Hussein, another victim of

America's constantly shifting alliances. After all, it was America who armed and supported Hussein's Iraq during his wars against neighboring Iran back in the late 1970s and early 1980s.

Just below the portraits of bin Laden and Hussein, very fine lines on the wall marked a discreet door leading to his safe room, a vault-like apartment where Ricco could hide if his defensive circles were overwhelmed by an attack.

If there was one thing he'd learned from his predecessors, it was that he could never be too careful.

And that brought him to the last photo, to the man who had adopted him after the death of his father at the hands of those Americans: Joaquin Guzmán.

Tío Chapo.

Below it were the words Ricco lived and died by:

IF YOU'RE GOOD, NO ONE WILL REMEMBER YOU. BUT IF YOU'RE BAD, NO ONE WILL EVER FORGET YOU.

The large TV screen above his desk was tuned to a news channel depicting images of bulldozers and hundreds of workers rebuilding lower Manhattan following that nuclear blast a year ago.

If you're bad, no one will ever forget you.

The words of his adoptive father never failed to inspired him, as well as those images, which, like the videos and photos from the attacks on September 11, showed just how the mighty U.S. could be brought down to its knees.

Ricco Orellana had devoted his entire life—his existence—to do just that, to honor his father's dying wish.

Avenge . . . me.

Two words etched into his young mind crouching inside a wrecked helicopter a lifetime ago.

Avenge . . . me.

Ricco returned his attention to his guests, sitting on plush leather chairs sipping Pappy Van Winkle's Family Reserve Bourbon. The Kentucky straight bourbon whiskey, aged 25 years, was the most expensive and sought after in the world.

Ricco had a full case of it.

Dressed in black jeans and a loose blue shirt, his father's gold-plated Desert Eagle hanging from his right hip, Ricco was a compact man with neat features, a faint sneer, and a perennial weariness in his eyes, one brown one green, imposed by violence.

Or perhaps a reflection of his ungodly soul.

He signaled Miguel and Roman, the two *Sicarios* who always accompanied him, to secure the room.

Both bodyguards were in their thirties; bronzed, muscular, with heavily tattooed arms, and dressed in black. Both had inexpressive eyes, like those of a shark.

Roman, armed with a MAC-10 pistol, did the honors, closing and locking the double doors leading to the stairs, where Ricco had parked three additional guards, then sliding the large terrace doors closed.

Meanwhile, Miguel tapped a panel next to the doors and engaged the jamming mechanism to block cell phones and any remote listening devices, GPS signals, and even lasers pointed at the panoramic windows, which were closed and frosted to prevent anyone from reading their lips.

Extreme measures to be sure, but given the lessons learned from his long line of predecessors, Ricco could never be too careful.

And never being too careful required the support of the local authorities.

Ricco shifted his gaze to the overweight man in the corner sipping his expensive bourbon and talking on Ricco's secure landline.

His name was Rodrigo Chavez, the current governor of the State of Sinaloa, put in power with Ricco's heavy campaign contributions and his influence in the region.

Chavez gave Ricco a single nod.

As part of his financial agreement with the state leader a year ago, a half dozen police posts were erected around the mountain and manned 24/7 by a combined one hundred officers. This law enforcement cordon represented Ricco's first line of defense against unwanted guests, ensuring privacy and security for the business he often conducted here.

Higher up the mountain, Ricco had his own emplacements, men and hardware providing second and third lines.

Above the ground fortifications, Ricco installed a missile defense system that rivaled the one protecting the White House.

One of his other guests was Akari Tanaka, short of stature and as slender as Mireya, with fair skin in stark contrast to her short jet-black hair, black eyes, and dark lipstick. But it was her body art that had surprised a man who was very seldom surprised. Scenes of geishas, Japanese courtesans, emasculating samurai warriors. It was gripping—beautiful, highly artistic, and backdropped by traditional Japanese landscapes.

A Japanese "Flaca," he thought.

Akari was the second-highest-ranking member of the *Yakuza* in Tokyo. But more than that, she had orchestrated the procurement of three hundred of the coveted—and highly accurate—Type 91 shoulder launched missiles.

"I have confirmation," said the guest next to Akari, swirling the inch of bourbon in his thick glass. "One Apache helicopter and one A-10 Warthog. The former shot down, the latter damaged."

Prince Hamid bin Nayef-Darzada, a Saudi royal with ties to al-Qaeda and also second cousin through marriage to Malik Darzada, the Saudi-born Pakistani hero that demolished lower Manhattan a year ago.

"So, they work as advertised?"

Hamid gave him a slight nod.

"I told you they would," Akari said.

Ricco was about to spend upwards of $600,000 per unit—almost four times the price advertised by Toshiba. The Japanese missile launchers were apparently living up to the claims made by the *Yakuza* chief—claims Ricco intended to verify once more in Texas.

"Now it's time for you to transfer the funds to Nakamura," Akari added, looking toward a skinny man with a wispy mustache in a tight business suit standing behind her. He held a tablet computer in his bony hands. "Once my accountant confirms payment, we will release the merchandise to you."

"And I will," Ricco said. "As soon as I get word from my team in Dallas."

Akari sat back and crossed her arms in apparent frustration. "Fine, but be aware I have other interested clients. How many are there, Nak?"

The man looked at his tablet and then at Akari. "Nine parties interested."

"Nine," Akari repeated.

"I will make it worth the wait," Ricco said. "I just need to be certain that what happened in Afghanistan wasn't a fluke."

Akari was a business woman and understood Ricco's hesitancy to transfer close to $180 million until he was absolutely certain.

Returning his attention to the Saudi royal, Ricco said, "Confirmation?"

Prince Hamid had arrived aboard a shiny Dassault Falcon 7X—one of the largest and most expensive business jets ever manufactured—just an hour ago. He was in traditional Saudi attire: a white thawb, or tunic, beneath a black mishlah, which was a sort of Arabian loose jacket, plus a black keffiyeh, a headdress folded into a triangle, which Hamid wore with the fold across the forehead.

Checking the solid-gold Patek Phillipe hugging his left wrist, the Saudi said, "My man in Karachi reported that it happened just an hour ago . . . in Helmand Province." Then he spent a minute summarizing the information from his associate in Karachi, who had been contacted by a Taliban observer witnessing the missile strikes from the rooftop of a nearby building.

The Saudi, basically the broker between Akari and Ricco, had moved the Type 91s from a *Yakuza* warehouse in Tokyo to his mega yacht in Tokyo Bay, and transporting them to the Arabian Sea, where arrangements were made to smuggle six launchers to a Taliban commander operating in southern Afghanistan, to test the weapon's effectiveness and ease of use.

In Ricco's opinion, the simplest way to take American focus away from his border operations was to divert it. And he couldn't think of a better way than shifting the balance of power in Afghanistan by arming the Taliban with Type 91s, essentially doing to the Americans what they had done to the Soviets three decades ago.

The remainder of the launchers had been transferred from the prince's yacht to an old oil tanker docked at the port of Karachi, the Pakistani port city which still bore the scars from that American air raid a year ago.

But Ricco had offered a reasonable advance to acquire eighteen of the powerful missiles for a test run in Texas. In addition to arming the Taliban, he wanted to avenge the death of his father at the hands of the Americans.

A double knock on the door made Ricco turn toward the intrusion. Roman looked at the small screen next to the door and said, "It's Antonio."

"Let him in."

Roman pressed a button and the door swung open.

Mireya's young son, whom he looked after personally while she was executing his orders in Texas, stepped inside.

The boy reminded Ricco of himself. His father had been one of the many guards that raped Mireya during those six hellish months she'd endured in federal prison.

Antonio handed a note to Ricco. He opened it to his guests puzzled glances.

"It seems there was an issue in the tunnel," Ricco finally said. "In Eagle Pass."

"Two of my trainers are with your people," Akari said. "You guaranteed their safe passage."

"Will that be a problem?" asked Prince Hamid.

"No," Ricco replied, still staring at the note, weighing the ongoing cost of smuggling. For every ten runs he successfully delivered in Texas, Border Patrol would stop one, maybe two. In this case, with so much at stake, he had tripled the number of vehicles dispatched to receive the hardware from that tunnel.

As it turned out, one of the vans, driven by Mireya with two of Akari's men, made it out before someone opened fire on the rest of his team, and then proceeded to blow the tunnel.

"Your men are in the team that got away, along with my best operative plus six missiles—enough to execute my test run."

Akari nodded in an apparent relief not shared by Ricco, who pursed his lips at the thought of the Americans discovering and confiscating his missile launchers.

But in the end, it wouldn't matter. Nothing would stop what was coming. Absolutely nothing. Ricco had an old score to settle.

Avenge . . . me.

Regarding his audience, he added, "It will not make any difference. Before the night is over, I will have my revenge and you will have your funds."

Ricco then turned to windows, his eyes gazing north. But his mind went further, beyond barren mountains and desolate deserts under a full moon, past a jagged river separating an impoverished nation from the land of milk and honey—where his best agent was on her way to avenge the death of his father while striking fear into the heart of America.

CHAPTER 6
Human Shield

"The hardest part of combat is finding a way to live with the guilt of surviving."
—Colonel Hunter Stark

HELMAND PROVINCE, AFGHANISTAN

He was covered in blood, but it wasn't his.

And the pressure.

It squeezed his head and chest with every breath he took.

But at least he *was* breathing—he was alive.

Somehow.

Then he remembered . . . the figure rushing past him, also shoving Hagen aside just before the blinding flash.

Stark recalled what felt like the Fist of God punching him squarely in the chest, tossing him a dozen feet.

And now this noise—ringing in his ears.

Tunnel vision narrowed his world as if he wore blinders.

His hands trembled. Palms, spattered with blood, with bits and pieces of . . .

Oh, Christ.

He tightened his fists and took a deep breath, trying to hold it together, to—

A hand on his shoulder.

A blurry man in camouflage cream.

A snake eater.

And he was talking to Stark; at least, his mouth was moving.

But Stark only heard the ringing. His head felt like it was being squeezed in a vice.

Ignoring whatever it was the Green Beret was shouting, he forced himself to do a body check, lifting his arms and wiping his bloody hands to make sure none of the gore layering them was his. Next came his legs, his feet—all still attached, albeit sprayed with the same reddish gore.

Finally, the colonel dropped a hand to his groin and squeezed.

Now he felt two sets of hands on him, but under his arms, lifting him to his feet. The tunnel slowly widened and the ringing abated enough to hear the voices.

"Colonel! Colonel Stark! Are you okay, sir?"

Gently but firmly, Stark pushed the soldiers aside and stood on his own, though not without difficulty, feeling a touch of vertigo.

Shit.

He did a quick survey of the bloody rooftop, now packed with Green Berets. Apache attack helicopters circled the area, and above them flew a pair of A-10s.

Two soldiers were assisting Ryan, who, like Stark, rebuffed the help, and used his Barrett as an improvised cane.

Five were kneeling around Hagen, holding the trembling man down. One of the soldiers was applying a tourniquet just below his right knee, where the bottom of his leg used to be. Another slapped a pad of QuickClot on the wound to staunch the bleeding, and a third jabbed the former Navy SEAL in the forearm to start an IV.

This isn't happening. This isn't fucking happe—

Then he saw Larson.

Or what remained of him.

The blast had torn him apart, spreading pieces of the big warrior across the rooftop and over Stark, less than a dozen feet behind him when he used his body as a shield.

Goddammit, Chief.

He stumbled to the remains, little more than his center mass—no head or limbs—the area protected by the titanium plates in his body armor.

And just to the right, a big gloved hand still holding the Browning.

Dropping to his knees, the coppery smell of blood mixing with that of scorched flesh and gunpowder, Colonel Hunter Stark stared at the carbon fiber bracelet still hugging what remained of Larson's wrist.

And he vomited.

CHAPTER 7
The Return of the Warrior

"I had a feeling you'd be back. I just didn't think it'd be this way."
—Gustavo Porter.

EAGLE PASS, TEXAS

"I'd say what we've got here is a big problem, Cruz. A *big* fucking problem."

Monica considered the comment from her former boss, Gustavo Porter, the FBI's Chief of Domestic Terrorism.

The FBI team had arrived in two Black Hawk helicopters belonging to the Texas National Guard. A pair of FBI analysts were recording the serial numbers of the Japanese SAM launchers in and around the Aerostar vans. Twelve in total.

"Hey, what's going on over there?" Porter asked, pointing at three cruisers from the Texas State Troopers and a half dozen deputies who looked like they belonged in high school and had arrived at the scene almost an hour before the FBI contingent. One of them had a bloody nose and was being assisted by two others.

Monica shrugged, then said, "Same thing that happened at the FBI sniper school. Story of my life."

Porter widened his eyes. "Oh."

Monica had been part of the FBI Sniper School seven years ago. It was the second sniper school she attended, the first being the Army Sniper School at Fort Benning, Georgia. The graduation rate at Benning was less than 20%; the FBI school wouldn't be as demanding as the Army. Monica was realistic about guys' response to her physique.

Most looked, but once in a while one would be dumb enough to grab. The first she could ignore; the second required a violent response. At the FBI school, one of her trainers, Special Agent Dick Head, had spent what Monica judged was way too much time watching her ass and pretending to help her with her shooting position. So, during a break, Monica walked up to him and said, "Sir, do you have a minute?" Dick Head had smiled and replied, "It would be *your* pleasure Agent Cruz, so yes, I have a minute." Monica accidentally dropped the bottle of water she was holding. Dick Head bent to pick it up, and her knee rose to meet the descending nose. All everyone saw was Dick Head hitting the ground. The incident was classified as an accident, but everyone in the Bureau knew what had gone down. Dick Head retired a month later.

Porter raised an eyebrow at Monica, regarded the bleeding deputy, and said, "He didn't."

"At least Dick Head pretended to be helping me. That dumbass thought it was okay to pat my behind as an attagirl for taking out all of those cartel motherfuckers. Seriously? Stupid local boy."

"Jesus H. Christ."

"Fucker's name is Maverick County Deputy Dwayne Turner," Monica said, ignoring the eyes glaring at her over a bloody handkerchief. "In case the dickwad decides to file charges."

"I'll take care of it," Porter said.

"I already did. I promise you, that bloody nose is far better than getting slapped with a sex offender label. Hopefully the dumbass learned his lesson."

"Gotta say, Cruz, I really missed you."

"Yeah, well, I didn't miss you, and I certainly didn't miss this shitshow."

"And you still got it," he said, pointing at the row of bodies that had not yet been bagged.

"If I still *had* it Gus, my brothers would be alive, plus those fuckers in the first van wouldn't have gotten away."

"It was twelve of them and one of you, Cruz. Go easy on yourself."

She knew he was right. Still . . .

"So, how many missiles would you estimate made it out?"

"Maybe a half dozen?"

"Goddammit," Porter cursed

"Yeah," she said, for a moment second-guessing her decision not to take out the lead truck when she had the chance. But it would have meant firing unsuppressed, telegraphing her position immediately.

"And they have at least a seven-hour head start," Porter said.

It had taken that long for Monica's emergency call to reach Porter, who immediately sent word to the FBI offices in San Antonio, Texas, who then contacted the state police to set up roadblocks throughout the southern part of Texas.

But Monica wasn't hopeful.

They were obviously dealing with the Sinaloa Cartel, which controlled the territories south of Eagle Pass. Those bastards had money to burn, including many aircraft at their disposal to move the launchers anywhere in the state—or the nation for that matter—in the time it took her government to get off its bureaucratic ass.

"They could be any-fucking-where by now," she commented.

Two pairs of National Guardsmen went by, carrying her brothers in black body bags.

"Sorry for your loss, Cruz."

It felt like someone was pouring searing acid right down into her core, eating away any semblance of humanity she had left.

She half-laughed half-groaned at the sheer insanity of it all. Those bags held the mutilated remains of her only relatives. But in a strange way, the warrior in her welcomed this darkening of her soul, sweeping away any remnants of empathy, leaving her with only her training, her logic—and an overwhelming desire to exact revenge.

The best way for Monica to honor Michael and Marty Cruz was by taking out those responsible—beyond these foot soldiers—and preventing whatever it was the bastards intended to do with those launchers.

First avenge, then mourn.

And in order to do the former—so she could do the latter—Monica first needed to step back into this darkness she had fought so hard to escape.

"Did you bring what I asked for?" she asked.

Porter waved at of his aides, who brought him a brown paper bag, which he passed to Monica.

She opened it and retrieved her FBI badge and the very same .45-caliber Sig Sauer P220 she had used to terminate Salma Bahmani, a terrorist trying to detonate a 5-kiloton nuclear warhead in Washington D.C. a year ago.

"Had it cleaned, plus fresh ammo. More practical than the rat shooter," Porter said about the Colt still pressed against her belly.

"Yeah, well, the little six-shooter just saved my ass," she replied, returning the Colt to its ankle holster, where it would continue to make a fine back-up weapon.

Monica secured the badge to her jeans opposite the holster for the Sig. But before she holstered that handgun, she made sure she had a full seven-round magazine plus one in the chamber.

Monica breathed in the faint scent of gun oil, filling her lungs in an almost ritualistic way that somehow completed the transition to her former life. Satisfied, she holstered it.

"What about the paperwork?"

"What about it?"

"Isn't there something I need to sign to get back under your thumb?"

Porter grinned and shook his head. "I never turned in your resignation, Cruz. I had a feeling you'd be back. I just didn't expect it to be like this."

"Yeah," Monica said as the Guardsmen loaded her brothers into the ambulance that would take them to the local funeral home.

Marty and Michael had been religious, like her parents. Monica had always had doubts. But as she watched the medics drive away, she couldn't help but think that whoever was behind their deaths had to be working for the devil. And if she believed in a devil, then she had to believe in a balancing power.

In God.

But whether this was the work of the devil or just bad luck—or perhaps payback for what she did to the cartel in Monterrey—her brothers had been killed.

And much as she wanted to scream at the way fate pulled her back into the fray, instead, she asked, "Gus, the question now is: where the *fuck* are those launchers?"

CHAPTER 8
LRM

"Flying isn't the dangerous thing. Crashing is."
—Captain Jay Lamar

DALLAS-FORT WORTH INTERNARTIONAL AIRPORT, TEXAS

In all his years flying for American Airlines, Captain Jay Lamar had never felt so damn nervous.

The former carrier-rated naval aviator with over two thousand hours in Hornets and Super Hornets—most of it in support of Operations *Iraqi Freedom* and *Enduring Freedom*—had joined the commercial aviation world almost a decade ago. In that time, he had flown an additional ten thousand hours, working his way from regional jets with American Eagle, primarily Bombardier or Embraer, to the larger American Airlines domestic routes piloting either Boeing 737s or Airbus 320s.

Today, the experienced captain was at the helm of a fully-custom Embraer 175 jet chartered by the U.S. General Services Administration to fly a very special couple and their Secret Service detail to New York City on the one-year anniversary of the largest enemy strike on U.S. soil in history.

It didn't really matter how many hours Lamar had.

It didn't really matter how many different aircraft he had ratings on.

It didn't matter that he had been fired upon by the Iraqi National Guard, the Taliban, ISIS, and even Chinese MiGs over the Taiwan Strait during a conflict few knew of outside the Situation Room.

And it certainly didn't matter that in his years of service he had been shot down twice by enemy missiles, once in Iraq and five years later in southern Afghanistan—the latter earning him the nation's highest medal for valor, The Congressional Medal of Honor.

There was something about being asked to fly a former president of the United States and his wife that had given him pause. And Jay Lamar had never hesitated when it came to occupying the left seat of a plane—any plane, anywhere.

His first officer Diane Percy, was a former Air Force pilot who flew A-10s in Afghanistan, like President Vaccaro, before retiring from the Air Force just last year to fly Embraers for United Express.

She was wiping her hands on the dark blue trousers of her uniform, and Lamar couldn't help but wonder if she was assigned by President Vaccaro because of the similarities in their military careers. In his opinion there were far more qualified United Airlines pilots to fill that first officer's seat.

"Hands sweaty, Percy?" he asked.

"Never happened before, even in country with hajis shooting at me."

"Well, it's not every day you get to fly a head of state and his family."

"Nope," Diane said. "Pretty nerve-rattling if you ask me."

"Just remember, Percy, flying isn't the dangerous thing."

She rolled her eyes.

"Crashing is," he added.

"Gee, thanks. I'll try to remember that."

"You do that." Lamar pointed at the radio stack. "Now, shall we?"

She resumed communications with ground control. Lamar steered the 93 feet of jet away from the East Air Freight ramp and onto Taxiway November toward their designated Runway, 13L.

He tried to relax, calling up the memory of then-President George W. Bush placing the medal around his neck at a White House ceremony. It seemed like a lifetime ago. And it was that very same president who requested none other than Captain Lamar to fly him to a ceremony organized by President Laura Vaccaro, attended by every living American president plus dignitaries from three dozen countries, including the leaders of the other two world superpowers: Russia and China.

But Lamar wasn't flying the Bushes, and he wondered if that was the real reason for his copilot's nerves.

As fate would have it, North Korean President Kim Jong-un and a delegation that included his wife and his sister were also headed to New York at the personal invitation of President Vaccaro. Kim's wife, Ri Sol Yu, who was given the honorary title of First Lady of North Korea in 2018, had the privilege to counsel the Supreme Leader and also travel abroad with him on diplomatic missions such as this one. His sister, Kim Yo Jong, was the vice minister of the Propaganda and Agitation Department tasked with managing her brother's public image as well as his very busy schedule.

Unfortunately, the private jet of the North Korean leader, a 1960's Soviet-made Ilyushin IL-62, developed mechanical problems crossing the Rockies and was diverted to DFW, where ground control directed it to this remote ramp, away from the hustle and bustle one of the busiest airports in the nation. The ramp was also used by Federal Express, where the Ilyushin would be sequestered for repairs, away from the media's prying eyes.

President Vaccaro asked President Bush if he would mind yielding the Embraer to the North Korean leader and his delegation? Another Embraer would be secured for the former president. And, the Bushes had graciously agreed, remaining in the terminal waiting for their new ride to arrive from Houston.

And here I am, he thought, having spent the better part of the last hour working the Embraer's weight-and-balance charts to make sure the added weight of the North Korean delegation—as many as he could take—plus their luggage, didn't exceed the jet's limitations.

He didn't relish the thought of having any kind of problem transporting the first family of the volatile nation. President Vaccaro had worked for over a year to broker a lasting peace between North Korea, South Korea, and Japan.

Talk about causing a goddamned international incident.

Lamar returned to his preflight tasks, though he managed a smile over the Secret Service detail escorting Kim Jong aboard the Embraer and whispering, "LRM on board," into his lapel microphone.

Curious, he had asked another agent what the initials meant. The response: Little Rocket Man.

He had been unable to accommodate everyone in the smaller Embraer, leaving behind nearly two-thirds of Kim Jong's staff with their aging Ilyushin, including a ridiculous number of soldiers.

The United Nations had banned its member countries from exporting aircraft to North Korea. And that meant Air Koryo lacked access to modern aviation innovated by the likes of Boeing and Airbus, or even Bombardier and Embraer—forcing the state-owned national flag carrier airline of North Korea, headquartered in Pyongyang, to rely on Cold War era technology.

A half dozen FedEx mechanics, under strict orders of secrecy from supervising federal agents, were already at work on two of the four engines. The Soloviev turbofans had started to overheat over Los Angeles, and by the time they had crossed Colorado, it was evident they would not make it to New York.

With luck, the mechanics, assisted by the North Korean pilots who also stayed behind with their plane, might be able to isolate the problem and get the rest of the staff over to La Guardia before the New York memorial ceremony the day after tomorrow.

As he taxied away from the ramp, Lamar noticed one of the North Koreans left behind, a petite woman, alone under the massive empennage of the Ilyushin, looking directly at him.

Her eyes glinted with visible disdain on a ghostly and narrow face. She was dressed in a light-brown uniform that included a belt with a holstered sidearm and shoulder bars designating her rank, which apparently wasn't high enough to get her a seat on this flight.

Lamar waved, but the woman did not return the gesture.

"That was rude," Dianne observed.

"It's just differences in ideology, Percy," Lamar replied.

"Might be," Dianne said. "But that's no excuse."

Lamar looked over at his copilot and decided that sweaty hands or not, she had a point.

He gave the North Korean officer a final look and found her still staring at him, motionless, hair fluttering in the breeze like black smoke.

CHAPTER 9
Naree

"I grew up despising how America exported its deranged view of morality, defining what it should mean to be civilized and rational . . . what it means to be human."
—Naree Kyong-Lee

DALLAS-FORT WORTH INTERNATIONAL AIRPORT, TEXAS

Her given name meant "lily" and in some of the eastern provinces, it translated as "soft" or "gentle."

Naree Kyong-Lee was anything but.

A senior operative in North Korea's Reconnaissance General Bureau, or RGB, she was petite, with milky skin and doll-like features suggesting fragility. Most of her life she saw that as a liability. Until her RGB instructors showed her how to turn it into an asset.

Naree cut her teeth as a newly-minted lieutenant in the military intelligence arm of the Korean People's Army, spending most of her early years protecting the northern border of the Demilitarized Zone, the 2.5-mile-wide no-man's land dividing her land and her people. A perpetual and painful wedge.

It was there that Naree ran response scenarios should its neighbor to the south violate the Military Demarcation Line, the location of the war front when the Armistice Agreement was signed on July 27, 1953.

Armistice my ass, she thought, her delicate features hardening. *We were winning, and we were forced into capitulation by Beijing.*

Her missions also took her south of the DMZ, into Seoul, where she spent the summer of 2002 impersonating a FIFA security agent during the World Cup. Unfortunately, she was only partially successful in disrupting food service to the athlete village because a team of American contractors employed by FIFA intervened.

Naree didn't last long in the KPA. Her talent as a military intelligence strategist advanced her to the rank of captain, and then major in just five years before she was noticed by the RGB, which propelled her into the world of smoke and mirrors, to serve a higher purpose.

The years that followed took her back to Pyongyang then to Beijing, where she trained with the Ministry of State Security, The People's Republic of China's intelligence and security apparatus.

It was there that Naree was schooled to combat their biggest threat: The United States of America. She became fluent in English and in the ways of the Americans, from their customs to their obsession for frivolous things, such as social media, celebrity scandals, and the way in which its pop culture corrupted the cultures of millions around the world. Along the way, she grew to despise how America exported its deranged view of morality, defining what it should mean to be civilized and rational.

What it means to be human.

Such arrogance!

She shook her head, but not at the stupid American pilot waving at her from his shiny jet. Naree was enraged. After all of her training, and her multiple assignments here—posing as a transfer student from Seoul, first in California, then New Mexico, and later in Texas—her superiors in the RGB chose not to take her with them to Washington.

Pigs!

It didn't matter that Naree had provided her nation with intelligence on the American military bases in California for the better part of two years—and without a single incident.

It didn't matter that a year ago, she had seduced a young airman from Beale, home of the 9th Reconnaissance Wing, and given Pyongyang priceless intelligence on America's surveillance assets: AWACs and UAVs like the RQ-4 Global Hawk that routinely flew over her nation.

It didn't matter than she had befriended a lesbian Army lieutenant in Los Alamos and obtained stealth technology documents that

Pyongyang—and Beijing—used to developed new radar systems that could detect a new generation of American stealth fighters.

It didn't matter that she had satisfied the sexual fantasies of an Air Force captain from Vandenberg, home of the 30th Space Wing of the U.S. Air Force Space Command, and was able to steal valuable missile technology from his laptop.

And it had not mattered that for the past six months, Naree had used every skill in her arsenal to secure the technology from the decommissioned Atlas-F intercontinental missile once operated by Dyess Air Force Base in Abilene, Texas.

Nevertheless, when the jet experienced the malfunctions that forced it to land here, her superiors had ordered her to look after the B-players of the delegation.

Meanwhile, the A-players—including generals inferior to her when it came to international acumen, especially in America—continued on alongside the Supreme Leader.

I'm fucking babysitting!

She turned toward the staffers now under her care, most of whom had never set foot outside North Korea. She had ordered them gathered in a circle surrounded by the two dozen KPA soldiers also left behind to make sure there were no defections. Although everyone had been hand-picked by the Supreme Leader's inner circle, Naree was aware that American pop culture had a way of poisoning the minds of even the most loyal, especially the younger generation.

So she had given the order to shoot to kill anyone who dared try and run. Doubtless, CIA operatives were at hand ready to grant asylum to traitors.

While she tried to accept being left behind to guard this group, her skills would have been far better utilized in New York guarding her Supreme Leader.

Shaking her head again in resigned silence, she resumed studying the departing aircraft as it taxied away. It was one of the many models that the Americans had prevented her nation from acquiring.

At least the Americans had not been able to keep the Korean People's Army Air Force (KPAAF) from securing Sukhois and MiGs from China. Her twin sister, Colonel Mina Kyong-Lee had volunteered, along with other veteran pilots, to fly the Supreme Leader on this memorable trip.

But just as Naree had been left behind, so had Mina, passed over for a less qualified pilot.

Who happened to have a fucking penis.

And in the process denying her a chance to see her sister after almost five years.

CHAPTER 10
Flash

"This isn't happening . . . not on my goddamned watch!"
—Captain Jay Lamar

**DALLAS-FORT WORTH
INTERNATIONAL AIRPORT, TEXAS**

Lamar forgot the North Korean officer and returned his attention to steering the jet to the end of the taxiway and holding short of the runway, as instructed by ground control.

His first officer switched them over to the tower frequency.

"DFW Tower, Embraer Three Seven Tango ready for takeoff One-Three Left at November," reported Diane Percy.

"Three Seven Tango, you're cleared for takeoff One-Three Left. Upon departure, turn to one five zero. Contact Departure at one three five point niner two.

As Diane read back the instructions, Lamar inched the dual throttles forward and steered the jet onto the runway, working the rudder pedals to align the nose with the centerline.

"All set?" he asked Diane.

"Ready if you are."

"Alright. Here we go," he said, smoothly advancing the throttles, determined to give the North Korean contingent a very smooth flight.

The General Electric turbofans increased in pitch as the 89,000-pound jet accelerated down the runway, achieving takeoff speed in under thirty seconds.

Lamar was impressed. Even close to its maximum takeoff weight, the jet remained nimble, responding to his slight backward pressure on the control wheel—or yoke—slowly leaving the ground with a gentle rate of climb designed for the comfort of his passengers.

While Diane raised the landing gear, he scanned the multiple parameters critical to this phase of the flight.

And that's when Lamar caught two bright flashes in his peripheral vision. They had originated by the perimeter fence separating the field from an adjoining golf course.

What the—?

His muscle memory reacted before his mind could process what he had seen.

Memories of missile attacks in Iraq and Afghanistan flashed in his mind and the former Navy pilot floored the right rudder pedal while turning the yoke in the same direction.

The Embraer entered a sharp right turn, a textbook evasive move.

Unfortunately, the defensive aerial maneuver against surface-to-air missiles was designed to be used along with flares, which the commercial jetliner lacked.

Still, his quick reaction allowed the Embraer to evade one of the missiles, which went high, streaking past him.

But the second missile tracked the heat plume of his port engine and detonated its high-explosive warhead inside the turbines spinning at thousands of revolutions per second, resulting in a blast that tore up part of the left wing.

Still, Lamar was able to maintain control, shutting off the damaged engine and using opposing rudder to offset the sudden asymmetric thrust and prevent the jet from flipping on its back while he continued the turn, heading to the runway from which he had just taken off.

"Mayday, Mayday, Mayday," Dianne announced. "Three Seven Tango is under attack. Repeat, Three Seven Tango is under attack!"

This isn't happening, he thought. Alarms blared in the cockpit and the control panel lit up like a Christmas tree. *Not on my goddamned watch!*

CHAPTER 11
Coup de Grâce

"It's coming . . . coming right at me!"
—Mireya Moreno Carreón

BEAR CREEK GOLF COURSE, DALLAS-FORT WORTH, TEXAS

Mireya held the pistol-grip of the Type 91 with her right hand, resting the launcher unit on her right shoulder, tracking the wounded jet through the sight assembly.

Her *Yakuza* companions had fired the first two missiles at the departing jet, the tail number confirmed by one of Ricco's men working as a baggage handler.

She released the safety and positioned the surviving turbofan in the center of the range ring. The acquisition signal tone confirmed that the missile's UV/IR seeker had locked onto the starboard turbofan's superhot exhaust.

She squeezed the trigger, and the initial rocket booster shot away from the launcher system and accelerated toward its target, which had begun a tight turn back to the airport.

Then the second solid booster kicked in. The weapon's third-generation guidance system kept it tracking the jet's starboard heat signature.

Mireya followed it all the way to the right engine where it struck with a blinding explosion that separated the outer section of the wing from the fuselage.

Then she realized her mistake. The missile had hit the jet after it completed its emergency turn, meaning the crippled aircraft was now headed toward them.

It's coming . . . coming right at me!

Dropping the launcher and startling her Japanese companions, Mireya broke into a run away from the fence.

CHAPTER 12
The Third Option

"A good landing is one from which you can walk away. A great landing is one after which the plane can be used again. And then, there's the third option."
—Captain Jay Lamar.

DALLAS-FORT WORTH INTERNATIONAL AIRPORT, TEXAS

Lamar knew their chances were slim to none as the crippled jet turned toward the airport at an altitude of just three hundred feet.

With both engines gone and missing a third of each wing, the veteran pilot had little control of the Embraer. But at least he had managed to line up the nose with the runway's centerline.

"Three Seven Tango under attack! Repeat! We're under attack! Mayday! Mayday! Mayday!" Dianne repeated as Lamar fought the controls, trying to keep the jet from pitching down while he dropped the landing gear. The ground was coming up fast to meet them.

He would get only one chance at this. The elevators and rudder responded to his commands, and he tried to get the plane into a landing attitude by getting the jet to flare and keeping the nose aligned with the runway's center line.

The partial wings, combined with the jet's functioning elevators and rudder, and its forward motion, gave it just enough lift and control to keep the jet from plunging into the ground headfirst.

There was a common saying in the aviation community, and as he managed the momentum to try to set the plane down on the ground, it filled his mind.

A good landing is one from which you can walk away. A great landing is one after which the plane can be used again. And then there's the third option.

Lamar was praying for the first one while doing everything in his power to avoid the third one.

Unfortunately, in addition to the array of warning lights informing him of what he already knew, that both engines were shot and he had no aileron control, another light started glowing. The landing gear had failed to deploy.

Are you shitting—

The tail struck the fence separating the airport from the golf course, right over the long row of blinking approach lights.

And was torn from the fuselage.

Lamar felt a deep rumble first—felt it in the yoke he clutched with both hands, vibrating with the same intensity as his rudder pedals and his seat.

They were accompanied by the screech of twisting metal as the belly of the plane, instead of the landing gear, struck the ground just short of the runway. Hard.

CHAPTER 13
Tongues of Fire

"Dead. Everyone is dead. And that actually works to my advantage."
—Mireya Moreno Carreón

BEAR CREEK GOLF COURSE. DALLAS-FORT WORTH, TEXAS

She never stopped running.

Mireya pushed herself as hard as she had ever pushed in her life, racing away from the crashing jetliner, whose fuselage slapped the ground like the hammer from hell.

Powerful.

Overarching.

She felt the impact tremors beneath her boots. She also heard the shouts of the *Yakuza* men, who had apparently decided to follow.

Behind her, an explosion lit up the night.

The ensuing shockwave kicked her in the back, shoving her down the fairway, as if she weighed nothing, and, mercifully, plunging her into a pond next to the eighth hole.

The waters swallowed her just as the fireball, expanding radially, scorched everything in its path for the seconds that it took to consume the fuel, retreating just as suddenly.

Mireya realized she was still clutching the launcher, and she let it sink to the bottom of the pond. She stayed under the surface, watching the brief inferno above her.

Then, slowly, cautiously, she broke the surface.

The air was still hot, extremely so in the direction of the airport. She glared at her creation, at the orange and yellow-gold flames licking the night sky.

She crawled out of the pond and spotted her *Yakuza* associates sprawled some fifty feet away, backdropped by a field of sizzling debris from the burning wreckage.

Neither was moving, likely dead from being closer to the explosion.

But she needed to be sure. In her line of work, there were no prisoners. If the *Yakuza* men could not escape with her, she had to make sure they were dead.

After picking her way through the debris she checked for pulses but felt none.

Dead.

Everyone's dead.

And that actually works to my advantage.

Sirens blared in the distance. Soon, the full force and might of the United States of America would descend on this airport. After all, she had just killed a former American president and his wife.

But with luck, the two dead *Yakuza* and their launchers would keep authorities from searching for anyone else—and also from suspecting the Sinaloa Cartel had anything to do with this, which had been the plan all along.

Mireya ran to Bear Creek Cemetery Road, where they parked the van. She started it and drove down the golf course, past the large clubhouse, to Highway 360, where she turned south, merging with the light evening traffic.

Reaching into a pocket, she found her iPhone, but it failed to power up. She ruined it in the pond.

Mierda, she thought. She would need to find another way to communicate, perhaps a burner phone.

But that would have to wait. Her first priority was to put some distance between her and the plane.

As she drove south, a plan began to evolve in her mind.

CHAPTER 14
Survivor's Guilt.

"How much longer can I really do this?"
—Colonel Hunter Stark

KANDAHAR AIRFIELD. KANDAHAR PROVINCE, AFGHANISTAN

Colonel Hunter Stark always suspected that sooner or later, the law of averages would catch up to him. And he suspected that when it did, it would be violent.

Very violent.

In a way, it felt as if his luck—that law of averages—lived inside a windowless room. And every time he avoided death, those walls moved a little closer together, toward his breaking point, altering the odds against him, even more so when someone he loved died instead of him.

Sitting on the edge of a bed at the Role 3 Multinational Medical Unit while a petite Navy lieutenant shone a damn flashlight in his eyes, the veteran operator couldn't shake the reality of what happened on that rooftop.

A kid had taken out his team.

A goddamned child.

He lowered his gaze to the floor, away from the light, which did wonders for his pounding headache.

The doctor, an attractive Asian with **MAE** stenciled over the left breast pocket of her Navy Working Uniform, apparently got the message because she turned off the flashlight. Then she cupped his chin to force him to look into her dark eyes, though Stark didn't need much help to do that.

Lieutenant Mae had the most incredible eyes, which contrasted with her very fair skin. She evoked memories of a mission from what seemed like a lifetime ago.

Stark studied the eerily familiar curve of her face. He pretended to be looking at the Flight Surgeon insignia above her name: a pair of gold wings flanking a small caduceus, the international symbol for medicine. But he could almost taste that Cava de Oro tequila that he and Seung used to drink after—

"I'm up here, Colonel," Mae said, catching Stark staring at her cleavage, quite visible when she leaned down to examine him.

Ryan Hunt, across the room on another gurney using his SOG knife to trim his fingernails, smiled. He still had camouflage cream on his face, which made his grin more pronounced. The doctor had given him an icepack, which the Delta sniper had ignored, leaving on the gurney.

"Sorry, Doc," Stark replied. "I was looking at your insignia."

Her lips twisted, which only added to the damn resemblance to—

"Pretty lame, sir," Ryan commented.

"Lame indeed, Colonel," Mae concurred.

"Look," Stark said, color coming to his cheeks. "Sorry if I offended you, Doc. I *really* was looking at your insignia. You remind me of someone."

"Oh, boy," Ryan mumbled.

This time Mae smiled. A smile that also reminded him of Seung, the North Korean agent in Seoul who had tricked him back in—

"You really need to work on your lines," she told him.

"He sure does," Ryan said.

Stark was used to the friendly teasing and occasional rudeness—and even crudeness—of his team. And most of the time, he just let it go. But today, Ryan's comment pushed one of his buttons.

"And you think you can do better, Sergeant Major?" Stark retorted, wishing to take it back as soon as he'd said it.

Ryan pressed the icepack against the side of his head and moaned loud enough to attract Mae's attention. "Doc, it's very hot in here."

Stark narrowed his eyes at Ryan. Mae hurried over and pressed a hand on his forehead. "Strange," she said. "No fever."

"No, wait," Ryan said, covering her hand on his forehead with his. "It's you, Doc. Smoking hot."

Mae laughed and retrieved her hand. Ryan grinned and winked at Stark, who gave him the bird.

"What's your name, soldier?" Mae asked.

"Ryan, but my friends call me Romeo."

"Romeo, huh? Should I ask why?"

Stark glared at Ryan in a don't-you-fucking-tell-her-about-black-ops way.

"Gee . . . I'm afraid that's classified," he managed.

"Ah, I like a little mystery in a man. It's very nice to meet you, *Romeo*. Call me Annie."

"What time do you get off, Annie?"

Mae laughed again and whispered something to Ryan.

Stark's jaw dropped. *You gotta be shitting me.*

She then turned back to Stark and her smile vanished.

"Now, about you . . . all kidding aside, we need to discuss your condition. You have a nasty concussion, Colonel."

"Yeah . . . thanks," Stark said, feeling an urge to get out of there. "Am I free to go?"

That only earned him an admonishing look under a pair of arched brows.

"Okay, tough guy, try this on for size: unless you take it easy for a few days and drink lots of fluids, plus fruits and vegetables full of oxidants, you really could fuck yourself up."

That made him blink.

"There's a reason for concussion protocols in contact sports," she continued. "And your profession, in case you don't know, is the *motherfucker* of contact sports. It's *very* real and also *very* ugly. You feel me, soldier? Are we clear?"

Goddamn.

"Crystal," Stark replied, and for some reason, maybe his altered state of mind or because of her resemblance to Seung, he checked for a band on her ring finger—not that he even had a chance given the competition across the room.

But he dismissed the thought. He intended to ignore her advice, and even her resemblance to Seung —assuming that was even her name since she was a North Korean agent.

Mae said, "Keep an eye on your friend, Romeo. And let me know if he starts acting strange in the next twenty-four hours."

"But he's always acting strange," Ryan said.

"You're just too damn cute."

And that was as much as Stark could take.

He thanked her and left the good doctor working on Ryan. Or perhaps it was the other way around. In any case, he walked out of the MMU and into a hot, dry, and very dusty afternoon.

He really needed time alone—needed time to process this.

More times than he could remember, Stark had tempted death and had walked away largely in one piece. But he knew that those walls defining his fate had once more edged closer, and he could only wonder how many rolls of the dice he had before he ended up like Chief Larson.

Or like Mickey.

Unfortunately, this was combat, and in combat there was little time to stop and reflect on what happened. There was always another mission. The enemy didn't take breaks, the world didn't stop, and there was no book or instructions on how to deal with the loss of a brother. There was no pill—at least none that actually worked with no side effects—and few people to talk to. Survivors were adrift in their own lives.

And now Larson, one of the handful of people that he could actually let commiserate with him.

The big chief was gone. It had taken the Army medics almost thirty minutes to gather what remained and stow it in a body bag. And worse than that, Stark had spent another thirty minutes in the helicopter ride back to KAF using a roll of paper towels to remove the bits and pieces of the chief that had been sprayed on him.

Ryan was lucky that Stark dispatched him to the edge of the roof to scare off the local with the mobile phone. That placed him not only outside the severe concussion radius, it also caused him to kneel to aim the Barrett.

Stark, on the other hand, had been on his feet and much closer to the blast, getting a nice dose of the shockwave that not only gave him the mother of all headaches but also spattered him with his best friend.

How much longer can I really do this?

Wars were planned by majors, colonels, and generals but fought by privates, sergeants, lieutenants, and even captains. Young men and women were easier to convince to step into the trenches and fight a war.

When you're young, you feel like you can do anything. You are, if not invincible, lacking an understanding of your own mortality. But as you get older, you grow wiser. Most officers retired from the military and went on to other things; a few were promoted and became war planners, operating from the safety of headquarters.

Stark wondered what it said about him that he continued to fight on the ground, in those bloody trenches.

But he had once more managed to beat the odds. Even with the concussion and the mental scars, he had certainly fared better than the chief and Michael Hagen, who was still in surgery.

In addition to losing the bottom of his left leg, the former Navy SEAL had also suffered lacerations to his face and chest. Surgeons were patching him up before shipping him to Landstuhl Regional Medical Center in Germany for more surgeries followed by a long period of rehabilitation.

Landstuhl was where soldiers whose injuries were too severe or who needed specialized care were transferred. Stark thought of it as the place where long and illustrious military careers went to die.

Landstuhl and the KAF Role 3 MMU tallied the ugliness of the War on Terror, the price paid in flesh and blood by America's sons and daughters for our freedom.

Add that to the even higher price paid by the likes of Chief Evan Larson, who made the ultimate sacrifice.

Stark had been around the block enough times to know that there was no protection from the mental scars he would carry with him, images forever seared in his mind.

The scars no one can see.

And almost on cue, the alarm on his G-shock went off, reminding him it was time for his daily PTSD meds.

Stark headed for a Canadian coffee joint next to the DFACs# 1, or Dining Facility# 1, where he hoped to find a quiet corner.

One of the bartenders usually kept some Canadian Club whiskey or something similar under the counter, in direct violation of the U.S. Military's General Order No. 1, which forbids the possession, consuming, introducing, purchasing, selling, transferring, or manufacturing of any alcoholic beverage.

Blah, blah, blah.

Fortunately, the Canadian bartender—the owner of the establishment who was in cahoots with NATO's commander at KAF—another Canadian—shared Stark's sentiment about the dire need for alcohol on two kinds of occasions: celebration and mourning.

And today qualifies, he thought, as he crossed the dusty street to the coffee shop. Though if Stark were to be completely honest with himself, he'd rather infuse the drink with Cava de Oro tequila than whiskey.

You're a goddamned sentimental fool.

But any spiked caffeine drink would have to wait.

His current CIA handler, Glenn Harwich was standing by the door.

Harwich was as tall as Stark, thickly built, and also completely bald. And they shared that deep in-country tan. But while Stark was clean shaven, Harwich sported a short salt-and-pepper beard that from some angles, and in the right attire, let him pass for a local—an asset in his line of work.

Today the veteran CIA officer was dressed in jeans and a Georgetown T-shirt, his alma mater. As far as government handlers went, Harwich was probably at the top, having worked with Stark on multiple contracts over the years. But even though he had as close to a relationship as a former snake eater could have with a member of a community who lied for a living, Stark just wasn't in the mood to talk shop.

Right now, he needed a stiff drink to wash down his daily dose of PTSD meds. And no, those were not supposed to be taken with alcohol, but the extreme situation called for an extreme exception.

Then he planned to go and sleep it off somewhere. Later, he'd track down Ryan and Danny to figure out how to get the Chief's remains flown home.

Since none of Stark's team were current military, special arrangements would have to be made to get his body into one of those flag-draped steel caskets aboard a Stateside-bound Air Force transport.

Danny had likely holed himself up in their hangar, overhauling some component of their CIA-issued Black Hawk helicopter.

Ryan was probably well on his way to shacking up with that pretty doctor, violating another military rule that Stark felt could be broken in times like this: fraternization.

Stark, well . . . he just needed his drink.

Such was the messy business of mourning. Everybody did it differently.

"Colonel, we need to talk."

Stark shook his head. "Not a good time, Glenn."

"Look, Colonel, I'm very sorry for the loss of—"

"That's the last thing I want to hear from you. What do you want?"

"First, thanks for the prisoner. We're currently working him to—"

"Don't wanna hear that either. So, unless you need something else, I'd like to be alone and—"

"There's someone who wishes to speak with you. It'll only take a couple of minutes of your time."

"Goddammit, Glenn, I just lost—"

"I know, Colonel, and that's precisely why I need you to come with me."

Stark regarded Harwich, counting ways drop him. He wanted to hit something or someone, and Glenn Harwich was certainly a target of opportunity.

But the colonel limited himself to cursing under his breath.

Stark had lost enough soldiers—many of them close friends—in three decades to develop a method to deal with death. And that spiked drink, combined with those meds, was a key step.

"Fine, Glenn. I'll talk to whoever the fuck you want me to talk to."

"Thank you, Colonel. I really appreciate—"

"But I'm taking my goddamned coffee to go," he said, deciding to get some alcohol-infused caffeine into him and hold off on the meds. "And trust me, Glenn, you really, *really* want me to have that fucking cup of coffee."

CHAPTER 15
Ibon-nom

"It was them . . . the Japanese bastards . . . and the Americans. They killed him."
—Naree Kyong-Lee

**BEAR CREEK GOLF COURSE.
DALLAS-FORT WORTH, TEXAS**

Her years of training for the inevitable—the attack against her land—prepared her to react.

Naree Kyong-Lee reached the crash site first, before the airport's emergency personnel.

She had seen the first two flashes by the perimeter fence, and she knew immediately.

First, she ordered everyone back inside the Ilyushin and left two soldiers with AK-47s and orders to shoot anyone who attempted to leave the jet.

When the crippled Embraer turned back to the airport, she was already running toward the fence, followed by twenty-two fully-armed soldiers of the Korean's People Army—veterans all.

Forming a defensive cordon around the wreckage to keep everyone out, Naree walked this field of death accompanied by Captain Hajun Kwo, the senior most KPA officer under her command.

She disregarded the arriving emergency vehicles with their flashing lights and deafening sirens. Holding a flashlight in her right hand and curling the fingers of her left hand around the custom, mother-of-pearl grip of her QSZ-92 semiautomatic pistol chambered in 9mm, Naree inspected the wreckage, ignoring the stifling heat and the smell of burned fuel mixed with scorched flesh.

It didn't take her long to confirm her suspicions: there were no survivors.

The main fuselage continued to burn, fire and smoke billowing from its broken windowpanes, consuming everyone inside.

But she was after something else: the perpetrators who had dared fire those missiles at her Supreme Leader.

And it didn't take her long to locate them just west of the wreckage, both dead from the explosion of thousands of pounds of jet fuel.

She continued to ignore the arriving emergency personnel, which her soldiers held back at gunpoint.

Naree crouched next to the assassins. One of the dead men still clutched the spent missile launcher assembly. It didn't take her long to recognize the unit, running a pair of gloved fingers over the *kanji* characters etched on the launcher tube. But anyone could have purchased it. What sent a surge of anger up her spine were the tattoos. These men belonged to the *Yakuza*. And their faces, albeit marred with burns and grime, were definitely Japanese.

Kwo stared at the tattoos and whispered, "*Ibon-nom.*"

Naree nodded at the epithet. "*Ibon-nom,*" she murmured. "It was them . . . the Japanese bastards . . . and the Americans. They killed him."

She rose and snapped, "Get me the satellite phone. I must contact Pyongyang immediately."

CHAPTER 16
Surprises

"No one ever really retires from the Agency."
—Glenn Harwich.

KANDAHAR AIRFIELD. KANDAHAR PROVINCE, AFGHANISTAN

Stark sipped his coffee on the way to the CIA operations building. It was in one of the thousands of shipping containers stacked two and three high and modified as everything from living quarters to working offices.

And in this case, the resident CIA headquarters.

The coffee infused with 80-proof Canadian Club warmed his chest, cleared his head, and tempered his anger.

He wondered what the feisty Dr. Mae would say about his choice of beverages—his version of a concussion-protocol cocktail packing plenty of oxidants plus a good measure of fermented corn and rye grain. He'd asked the bartender to add a shot of a five-hour energy drink for good measure.

Stark shook the thought away, he was probably the farthest thing from her mind thanks to Ryan and that damn charming smile of his.

They arrived at a nondescript container. Harwich tapped a code on the digital pad next to the door. The magnetic locks disengaged and Stark followed him inside.

The dimly-lit interior held a long conference table facing a large TV screen, which at the moment, was dark.

At the head of the table sat Brigadier General Antoine Pelletier, NATO's commander at KAF.

A burly French Canadian, Pelletier resembled a lumberjack, albeit a lumberjack responsible for roughly ten thousand troops from a half dozen nations deployed here. He had short hair, a thick mustache that dropped at the ends, and a pair of blue eyes that were focused on the screen of the laptop in front of him.

Stark had never met the man, and he preferred it that way. On any op, the colonel's objectives were threefold:

First, to execute ops quickly and efficiently for his employer—currently that being the CIA.

Second, to get the hell out of Dodge.

Third, to get paid—hopefully on time.

Meeting the brass, especially NATO brass, was nowhere on the list. NATO especially had a gift for getting in his way and leaking intelligence like a sieve.

Stark gave the general a slight nod. The only other person in the room was a man sitting to Pelletier's right with his back to Stark. He was dressed like a local in a cream-colored khet partug—a combination Afghan tunic and baggy pants—plus a black pakul, or traditional head gear.

Pelletier resumed his laptop activity, apparently to start a conference call. The other man stood and turned around.

Stark was seldom surprised, but this certainly surprised him. Larger than life, was none other than Bill Gorman, the former Islamabad CIA Station Chief.

Slightly taller than Stark and barrel-chested, Gorman carried his weight like a weapon. He had a square face and jaw under a full head of salt-and-pepper hair, and a prizefighter's nose that looked as if it had been broken more than once.

"Hey, Colonel. Long time."

Gorman had this powerful handshake that could induce paralysis on the average soul, but Stark was far from average, matching the vice-like grip, and even briefly pulling Gorman toward him while asking, "Bill? The hell you doing here? I thought you were retired and holed up somewhere in Maine with that Paki girlfriend of yours. Way too pretty for you, by the way. And what's with the outfit?"

Stark had last seen Gorman in Islamabad following the rescue of Maryam Gadai, the girlfriend Stark was referring to, and a former operative of Pakistan's Inter-services Intelligence agency, that nation's version of the CIA. Maryam had been caught collaborating with the Agency and arrested by the ISI. Stark, whose CIA contract in Islamabad had already been fulfilled, agreed to help him out anyway, extracting her from an interrogation cell in the nick of time.

"Colonel, no one really retires from the Agency," Harwich said. "Not even Bill."

"And at the risk of sounding corny," Gorman said, "Duty called."

"And the girl?"

"Back in Bar Harbor looking after our new baby."

Stark was surprised. "Well, that didn't take long."

"What can I say?" Gorman replied. "Hit the lottery with that one."

If Stark was honest with himself, he'd have to admit a touch of jealousy. That feeling was stronger after a day like today.

"Careful, Bill," Stark said. "Someone might confuse you for a family man."

Before Gorman could reply, Harwich said, "Alright, let's get started," and pointed to the chair next to Gorman.

Stark took his assigned seat and set his coffee in front of him. Harwich sat to Pelletier's left. The general had yet to say a word, though his eyes went to the coffee, which had a faint smell of whiskey.

Stark waited, almost daring the Canadian to say something. But he returned his attention to the laptop.

"So," Stark said to Harwich. "Are you gonna to tell me what this is all about?"

"It's about a problem, Colonel Stark," said a female voice from the screen to his left.

The hair on the back of his neck stood up.

On the large TV there were three people in a conference room Stark was all too familiar with, though he had never set foot in it.

U.S. President Laura Vaccaro stood at the head of the table in the White House Situation Room, the palms of her hands on its shiny mahogany surface. She wore one of her classic dark blue skirt suits. Her short auburn hair framed a narrow face that was both feminine and rugged, with an air of ferocity and a scar tracing her left temple and cheekbone. She'd earned both right here in southern Afghanistan flying A-10 Warthogs as a young Air Force captain.

Vaccaro was flanked by her chief of staff, John Wright, and her National Security Advisor, Lisa Jacobson.

The president didn't seem to have aged one bit since he last saw her, shortly after preventing a suitcase nuke from reaching D.C. a year ago.

Upon closer inspection, however, Stark saw something he had never seen in the American President before: Her gaze was still powerful, focused, like a pair of blue lasers slicing through a slab of steel. But there was something else in her eyes, subtle, like a flicker of gray light in the darkest of nights that cut into him like sizzling shrapnel.

It was fear.

The realization that the bravest and most intrepid woman he had ever met was afraid—if only for a second—made Stark feel as if his heart stopped.

"Madam President," he finally managed, forcing air into his lungs. "What problem are you referring to?"

"A *big* problem, Colonel," Vaccaro said. "Over there and also in Texas . . . and soon, everywhere else."

CHAPTER 17
A Sea of Sharks

"Everything is political."
—President Laura Vaccaro.

SITUATION ROOM. THE WHITE HOUSE. WASHINGTON, D.C.

John Wright terminated the call and sat down when Vaccaro did, as did Lisa Jacobson.

"How in the world did we let this happen?" Vaccaro said to no one in particular, clasping her hands. The assassination of the North Korean leader and key members of his inner circle, including his wife and his sister—and on American soil . . . well, wars had started for less than that.

And that's precisely how President Vaccaro read the situation facing her administration: impending war.

A war she had to find a way to prevent—or, at a minimum, contain.

Vaccaro's eyes drifted to the TV screens on the right side of the room, both broadcasting the mess in Dallas with the sound muted.

Her face hardened in an almost brutal way. Although she had just adjourned a meeting with her war cabinet, dispatching them to execute the Constitutionally-approved processes to deal with this—from diplomacy to military action—the A-10 pilot in her still needed to keep the control stick squarely in her hands. She needed a way to bypass the massive bureaucratic battleship that was the U.S. government.

Vaccaro needed a swift and nimble patrol boat alongside the big ship.

And she knew of only one way to do it, just as she had done a year ago. Vaccaro signed Presidential Directive 769, granting herself presidential powers to form a covert ops team—Colonel Hunter Stark was to lead a select group of operators into Mexico—without that country's approval or knowledge—to track those responsible for the attack, and locate the whereabouts of the rest of the Type 91s.

A second team, co-led by Harwich and Gorman, would be deployed to Pakistan—again without approval or notification, even to the American ambassador in Pakistan—to follow up on information extracted from a captured Taliban chief who provided a single name: Khalid Raza. It appeared as though the powerful Karachi industrialist had sourced six missiles to the Taliban as a test.

Harwich also had reason to suspect that Raza might know the location of the rest of the missiles, undoubtedly staged somewhere in the region for the purpose of altering the balance of the War on Terror.

When Vaccaro had asked how Harwich planned to get to Raza, the veteran CIA officer just smiled and said, "By capitalizing on his weakness."

In addition, the CIA strongly suspected that missiles used against American troops in-country, as well as those used to shoot down the Embraer jet were purchased by the *Yakuza* with funds from the Sinaloa Cartel, and that probably meant someone had acted as the broker between the Yakuza, the Mexican cartel, and the Taliban. But that was hearsay via a prostitute in Culiacán City who had overheard a couple of guards talking, after they were through taking turns with her.

"Are we really doing this again, Madam President?" Wright said. He closed the folder containing the signed directive.

If you looked closely at John Wright, you could still see the remarkably handsome face of his youth, marred now by the chisel strikes of the soul-sucking sculptor that was southern Afghanistan, where he served for four tours—his last one with Vaccaro.

Wright's eyes, large, expressive, and the color of butterscotch, stayed on the president, telegraphing not only his undying loyalty but something else that had started and ended in that remote corner of the world.

"We're still dealing with the blowback from the last one," he added at when she didn't respond.

"That's right," Jacobson agreed. "The inquiries headed by Congressman McDonald about rumors of a black ops teams a year ago are still happening. An aide told me last week that he overheard the house minority leader talk about the potential for . . . articles of impeachment."

Vaccaro regarded her National Security Advisor, an African-American woman with a delicate, aquiline nose on a face that was not young but still fresh, and gray eyes that still had a lot of light in them. Jacobson cut her teeth with the CIA across a half-dozen countries in the Middle East, followed by a five-year appointment as ambassador to Pakistan before Vaccaro tapped her for the NSA job a year ago, shortly after her election landslide victory.

"That's bullshit," Wright said. "It will never get through the house, much less the Senate and—"

"Ungrateful assholes," Vaccaro muttered. "And McDonald's whole damn family lives in D.C. They would have gotten hit by that nuke if it wasn't for . . ."

Vaccaro leaned back, thinking.

About six months ago, after the shock of New York abated and the nation returned to business as usual—or as usual as any nation could following a nuclear attack—rumors began to surface about the way in which the terrorists were really stopped; about a secret team of former soldiers—mercenaries—empowered by the president to bypass the Constitution. And three months ago, the source of the leak had finally come forward: Hollis Gallagher, at the time deputy undersecretary of the Department of Homeland Security, had already testified twice about how this 'Team With No Name' constantly undermined his Congressionally-approved multi-agency taskforce.

Fortunately, Vaccaro's overall handling of the crisis, domestically and abroad, had been viewed quite positively by the nation and also Capitol Hill, where she still had enough political capital to keep McDonald from getting those debates beyond congressional backrooms and bathrooms. But that approval could turn on a dime, depending on how she handled this new crisis.

I have no choice, she thought, there had always been a need for such nimble force to complement the established processes in the Department of Homeland Security.

"And your meeting with Congressman McDonald is in two hours," Wright added, looking at his tablet. "Do you want to keep it or postpone?"

"You know he's going to turn this mess into something political," Jacobson said.

"Lisa, *everything* is political," Vaccaro replied, glancing at her chief of staff. "Keep it."

She could handle the good congressman in her sleep. But those images on the TV screens . . . they were another matter.

And Vaccaro needed far more than the word of a Mexican hooker if she was going to attempt to convince China and Russia, and even the surviving leadership of North Korea, to help defuse the situation. But she held little hope for any reasonable discussion with the latter.

The late Kim Jong-un had been surrounded by a sea of sharks, by conflicting factions, which he controlled with an iron fist, like his father, Kim Jong-il, and his father before him. Vaccaro worried that the current situation there might not be unlike Iraq after the late Saddam Hussein or Slobodan Milosevic in the former Yugoslavia. When those dictators were removed from power, their nations imploded into bloody civil wars as the sharks previously under control found themselves uncaged, free to devour one another.

A sea of sharks.

Congressman McDonald and his ilk up on the hill weren't that much different from North Korea's surviving leadership, circling the waters, smelling the blood, biding their time before coming in for the kill.

And if you empowered those North Korean predators with some fifty nuclear bombs, plus the missile technology to deliver them anywhere in the world . . .

I pray to God I'm wrong.

She hoped that the internal apparatus of North Korea had managed to keep such factions from taking root, thus allowing for some semblance of a civilized transition of power.

But regardless, the attack had taken place on American soil and she had to deal with the implications of that.

"Do we have eyes on the ground there yet?" Vaccaro asked, meaning DFW, where the surviving soldiers escorting the North Korean contingent had sealed off the crash site, preventing local authorities from processing the scene.

"The FBI task force is due there any minute," John Wright replied. "Most left the ranch in Eagle Pass an hour ago in helicopters, except for a small team doing forensic work."

Her chief of staff ran the White House and her schedule with the same calm efficiency with which he led platoons in Afghanistan.

Vaccaro closed her eyes and massaged her temples.

This isn't fucking happening.

Yet it was, and to prevent a bad situation from getting worse, she had personally called the governor of Texas, who ordered the local and state police—as well as a platoon from the Texas National Guard—to stand down and wait for the FBI to arrive at the scene.

The last thing she needed right now was a shootout between the KPA and an American posse of mixed law enforcement and National Guard troops.

But at least she was able to coordinate everything from the Situation Room, located on the ground floor of the West Wing, under the Oval Office. Staffed twenty-four hours a day by more than thirty specialists organized around five watch teams who constantly monitored domestic as well as international events.

First conceived of and built by John F. Kennedy after the failed Bay of Pigs invasion of 1961, and modernized by every president after him—George W. Bush brought it to its current state-of-the-art—the Situation Room, or Sit Room, allowed Vaccaro to contact anyone, anywhere, anytime.

At least in theory.

Today, she was having difficulty reaching her counterparts in China and Russia.

Vaccaro contemplated the two documents in front of her. The first was the President's Daily Brief, prepared each morning by the director of national intelligence, to current events requiring her attention. The second document was the Situation Room Daily Summary, which was prepared three times each day, and which was supposed to cover everything else.

Unfortunately, neither document told her what she needed to know: where did China and Russia stand in all of this, and what was happening in Pyongyang?

Turning to Lisa, she asked, "Any word on Xi or Vlad?"

Lisa Jacobson shook her head, frustration deepening the fine lines around her. "Radio silence, ma'am."

Vaccaro felt like a soldier in the trenches, unable to get the information she needed to get in front of this.

Goddammit.

"Our people next door is still trying to get through," Jacobson added, referring to the staff of the Watch Floor of the Situation Room, charged with fusing the thousands of intelligence findings from operations all over the world and summarizing them into the information that made it to one of the three Situation Room Daily Summaries. But the Watch Floor was also charged with connecting Vaccaro to world leaders for encrypted communications, like the ones she was so desperately trying to hold with Presidents Jinping and Putin.

"But we did get ahold of the Chinese ambassador," Jacobson added. "He's on his way here now."

Vaccaro had hoped to have an emergency meeting with Xi Jinping, President of the People's Republic of China, who had been on his way to the event in New York, as was Russian President Vladimir Putin. Unfortunately, both leaders had returned to their respective countries when news of the attack broke.

And who can blame them? she thought.

But it was entirely possible the target was George W. Bush, not the North Korean delegation—she had no way of knowing at the moment. Kim Jong-un had quite the long list of enemies around the world—but so did the former president.

Vaccaro was certain there were protocols in existence to handle the assassination of a former president, investigating and eventually prosecuting the guilty party. But Vaccaro was certain there was *nothing* in place to handle the assassination of a foreign dictator on American soil.

The President of the United States was trying to get in front of this freight train, fully realizing that before the situation got any better, it would certainly get worse—much worse.

Lisa Jacobson believed in the power of connections, of networking, even when it involved unsavory characters. She learned this skill at an early age, growing up in Harlem, where who you knew and how well you knew them made the difference between dying in the endless gang wars and making it out alive. Lisa had made connections with the gang leaders and made herself valuable to them by mediating peace talks, by establishing territories, by making them see the financial value of peaceful and controlled business versus all-out-shooting wars. During her years with the CIA, in the age of cyberterrorism, she had taken a similar approach, developing relationships with criminal hackers and convincing them to apply their skills for America's benefit in the War of Terror.

Now, with the President facing the crap Congressman McDonald and his minions were generating, it was time to take action and ask forgiveness later.

"Madam President, I have to step out and make a call," Jacobson said.

She walked down to the Situation Room and made a call on a secure line to Jason Savage, the best hacker and cyber investigator anyone had ever met.

He was complicated. Jason's complication was that he was a recovering addict. His solitary nature and unique mental skills came at the price of depression. Jacobson had been his sponsor in AA.

"Jason, it's Lisa. I know you're okay, otherwise I would have heard from you. But we need to meet today. I have a job for you that's so necessary, you can name your own price."

"Ah, yes, I'm good, Lisa," he replied. "And yes, I'm expensive and come with certain requirements."

"Then grab your passport and a toothbrush. There will be a car in front of your place in thirty minutes."

"Where am I going?"

"You're going to prevent a world war."

CHAPTER 18
The Azure Dragon

"The days are gone forever when our enemies could blackmail us with nuclear bombs."
—Kim Jong-un

RYONGSONG RESIDENCE. PYONGYANG, NORTH KOREA

His official title was Director of the Organization Guidance Department, but unofficially, Choe Ryong-Ju was second in command in North Korea.

A former chief of the Korean People's Army, he was promoted to OGD director by the Supreme Leader last year. Choe was alone in the office of his slain leader this early morning staring at the gardens and fountains beyond the second-story window.

A rail-thin man in an ill-fitting, dark suit that hung loosely from his coat-hanger shoulders, Choe had an eternal expression of weariness beneath very soft black hair and dark brown eyes encased in deep wrinkles.

And today, his tired gaze grew sadder as he looked upon the grayish facades of apartment towers and government buildings nestled on the banks of the Taedong River, flowing from the Rangrim Mountains and into Korea Bay at Namp'o.

In the distance, he could already hear the echoing loudspeakers at major intersections playing the prerecorded messages from the Supreme Leader as he looked over its citizens from dozens of banners two hundred feet tall bearing his likeness.

The daily messages, which would soon have to change, reverberated across wide boulevards designed for grandiose military parades rather than for the public who used them daily, giving the city a permanent feeling of emptiness.

Choe's eyes ventured east, beyond the buildings and hills.

Korean cosmology assigned a separate mythical creature to each of the four cardinal points of the compass. The east—the direction of Japan—was associated with the divinity known as the *Azure Dragon*, found in the murals of the Goruyeo tombs in the eastern province of Pyongan.

The *Azure Dragon* was also the name of the plan conceived by former Supreme Leader Kim Jong-il and later improved by his son, the slain Kim Jong-un, to unleash North Korea's ferocity on the islands of Japan in retribution for the atrocities committed by the island-state against the Korean people during World War 2.

Choe tightened his jaw so hard that it hurt as he thought of the *Ibon-nom*, the Japanese bastards who, unlike the Nazis, went largely unpunished after the war, allowed to rebuild their nation with massive infusions of capital from the Americans.

Bastards indeed.

Choe had just hung up the phone with the senior most surviving member of the contingent accompanying the Supreme Leader on his historic trip to America—a trip that had ended in the unthinkable: Japanese agents had fired Japanese missiles at the jet carrying the Supreme Leader to Washington, killing him, his wife, his sister, and the rest of his senior advisors.

I told him the Japanese and the Americans couldn't be trusted.
I fucking told him!

Choe made a fist with his right hand and pressed it against his left palm, his jaws taut, recalling his final conversation with Kim Jong-un, when he advised him not to go—or send representatives, a delegation. But the Supreme Leader had been lured by the attractive American President and also by the foolish belief that she was a trustworthy leader trying to rebuild her nation from the ashes of a nuclear attack.

And besides, Xi Jinping and Vladimir Putin would be in attendance. How could he miss such an event? Such a unique opportunity to be seen by the entire world?

Total nonsense!

It didn't escape Choe that the assassination had taken place in the same city where President John F. Kennedy was murdered, and he couldn't help but wonder if there was any significance to that or was it simply a coincidence.

Kennedy's death, after all, was the prelude to the Vietnam War, opening the door for the evil President Lyndon B. Johnson to wage that destructive decade-long campaign against the peace-loving people of Vietnam.

And I'll be damned if that will be repeated here.

Ever-weary, and ever-paranoid—survival traits required in the harsh political environment that was North Korea—Choe didn't believe in coincidences. The realization that America, with its massive security apparatus, had allowed agents from Japan—a strong American ally—to assassinate the leadership of North Korea while on its soil . . .

And using a jet that had just been conveniently vacated by former American President George W. Bush . . .

They have to be behind this.

And if he explored that possibility, in his suspicious mind it could only mean that an American-Japanese conspiracy had cut off the head of North Korea as the overture to a joint invasion that could also include South Korea, another strong American ally.

General Pak Yong-Gil, chief of the Korean People's Army, had already reported the presence of the American Navy in the Sea of Japan. The aircraft carrier USS *Ronald Reagan* and its armada of escorting vessels were conducting drills just two hundred miles from his coast. And south of the DMZ the Americans and the South Koreans were reported to be running an unusually high number of war exercises that could be interpreted as—

A knock on the door pulled him from his reverie.

Choe turned from the windows and pressed a button on the corner of the Supreme Leader's large desk, and a pair of guards swung open the double doors leading to the office's anteroom.

Pak Yong-Gil stepped through, and the guards closed the doors behind him.

The general was a stout man with precise features in a tight-fitting olive uniform, with a chest full of medals and a peaked cap pressed down over stern, coal-black eyes.

He marched toward Choe as if he were in a parade, a strong military man and a devoted loyalist of the Supreme Leader.

At a time Choe considered to be the worst crisis in the history of his country, he was damn glad that the late Supreme Leader had chosen to leave the marshal of the KPA behind. If the current situation was as dire as it appeared, Choe would need strong people to see North Korea through it, and he couldn't think of anyone stronger than the current leader of the armed forces, who ruled his troops with an iron fist.

Pak came to attention in front of the desk, as still as stone, per protocol, and saluted Choe, who gave him a quick salute in return.

"At ease, old friend," he told him, and Pak visibly tried to relax, though it was impossible given the shocking news already starting to trickle into the closed society.

As much as the late Supreme Leader had worked to control the information reaching his country, the age of the internet and satellite phones had triggered an underground information movement that was already disseminating the events that had taken place in America.

"So, it is true then?" Pak asked. "It was the *Ibon-nom?*"

The call from Naree Kyong-Lee, a senior officer of North Korea's Reconnaissance General Bureau, had first alerted her superior, the director of the intelligence apparatus, Rhee Jay-Koo. Per protocol, Naree then personally notified each of the surviving members of the Supreme Leader's inner circle. The list included Choe, Pak, and also Joon Song-Ju, the premier of North Korea—or third in command—and director of the Infrastructure Systems, the Military Industry Department, as well as leader of the development of missiles and nuclear weapons.

Everyone else is gone.

"Where are they?" Choe asked, referring to Rhee and Joon since it would be up to the foursome, plus any help they could get from Beijing, to manage this crisis.

To that end, Choe had already attempted to contact Xi Jinping, President of the People's Republic of China. Unfortunately, Choe had to speak with an aide because Xi was also on the way to New York for the event, as was his other ally, Russian President Vladimir Putin. Last he heard, both planes had turned around when the news of the attack broke, leaving Choe standing right here waiting to hear from both leaders.

"They're on their way," Pak said.

"It falls on us, old friend," Choe said preparing mentally for the upcoming discussion with his colleague. Together they had to figure out how to respond to this abomination, domestically and also abroad.

The response from his nation would have to be, at a minimum, proportionate, but still meaningful enough to send a message to the world that such an atrocity against the peaceful people of North Korea would not be tolerated.

"We will not be bullied," Choe added.

Pak's eyes glinted and resolutely, he said. "In the words of our Supreme Leader, the days are gone forever when our enemies could blackmail us with nuclear bombs."

Choe's weary eyes became hard; his thin mouth, like a knife, twisted into a grimace of congregating wrinkles he turned to face the stark grayish buildings rising beyond the gardens. "We certainly have them now, old friend. . . *and* the means to deliver them."

Five minutes later, RGB Chief Rhee Jay-Koo and Premier Joon Song-Ju joined General Yong-Gil.

Joon, which meant "handsome and talented" was the youngest of the four at age forty-one, and a cousin of Kim Jong-un. The man indeed possessed a youthful face not yet lined with the decades of stress weighing on Choe. Appointed to premier just two years before, when the Supreme Leader had his predecessor dragged out by his feet and shot for incompetence, Joon had a talent for the job but also shared his cousin's taste for expensive wines and beautiful women, including the secretaries he'd hired to replace his predecessor's aging assistants.

Rhee was the oldest at age fifty-eight, completely bald with skin like paper. His sagging cheeks and tired eyes under a forehead crinkled and even brittle, like on the brink of crumpling from the pressure of running the intelligence apparatus for nearly two decades, Rhee had dutifully served not just the Supreme Leader, but also his father, the legendary Kim Jong-il.

Deep lines of strain and age—and likely fear—formed around Rhee's eyes and he looked oddly shrunken and even hunched, displaying far more worry than his colleagues.

As he should.

After all, it was Rhee's job to anticipate such attacks against the Supreme Leader. But Choe would have to resist the urge to handle Rhee like the Supreme Leader handled Joon's predecessor—and in front of the entire inner circle.

That will certainly have to wait, he thought, deciding that, for now, enough senior leadership blood had been spilled. He would deal with Rhee later, after Choe identified a worthy successor to run the RGB.

"I think it is time," Choe said.

Pak's flat-black eyes signaled understanding under his peaked cap.

Choe found reassurance in his old colleague's eyes, unlike the inexperienced Joon and the incompetent Rhee, who exchanged puzzled expressions before Rhee asked, "Time for what, Director?"

Choe tilted his head, his thin lips parted just enough to exhale with disappointment.

Inexperience and incompetence were certainly qualities he could do without during this crisis—a time when Choe desperately needed people who could march in lockstep with him and Pak.

For a moment, Choe contemplated pressing the red button on the desk to summon the guards and have Rhee shot. And he could do the same with Joon since the young officer no longer had the protection of the Supreme Leader.

But Choe's old friend raised his right hand ever so subtly.

Temperance.

As toughly and decisively as Pak drove his troops, carrying out orders from this office with tank-commander ruthlessness, he also had a gift of inner control, of cautious moderation. Choe had seen him use it with the young Supreme Leader on occasion to temper his often-reckless enthusiasm, to help him control short-term urges for the sake of long-term gain.

And this was one such time. As much as Choe wanted to be surrounded with Pak-like leadership now, that short-term urge would have to wait.

Choe took a deep breath and gave Pak a slight nod.

Pak turned to his confused colleagues, who had no earthly idea how close they had come to being dragged away by their feet, and said, "Time to unleash the *Azure Dragon*."

CHAPTER 19
Unlikely Alliance

"This is the work of Japanese agents using Japanese missiles, and I have already reported it this way to Pyongyang."
—Naree Kyong-Lee

BEAR CREEK GOLF COURSE.
DALLAS-FORT WORTH, TEXAS

"Now, *this*, Gus, is what I'd call a *big* fucking problem," Monica Cruz commented, stepping away from the Black Hawk helicopter and starting toward the line of North Korean soldiers.

For a second, Monica felt as if she was a protagonist in some B movie as she faced the foreign soldiers in their tight olive uniforms, each clutching a venerable—but quite deadly—AK-47.

She regarded their blank faces, their menacing stance, standing with their Kalashnikovs ready—across their chests, right hands on the pistol grips, left under the barrels, pointed at the sky,

But unlike the Americans, who held their fingers resting on the trigger guards of their M4 carbines, the North Koreans kept theirs right over the triggers. And although she couldn't tell, Monica guessed that the safeties on those rifles were off.

In all, she counted 22 KPA soldiers plus the pale woman standing in front of them, one hand holding a black pistol and what looked like a satellite phone in the other.

Less than two dozen feet from Monica, the hate in her eyes combined with a mouth twisted in fury, broadcast she probably would take pleasure in shooting everyone dead.

There were four times as many Americans, half Guardsmen and the rest a mix of uniformed state troopers and Dallas PD cops, all armed with a combination of M4s, pistols—mostly Glocks—and a few shotguns. The entire area was bathed in flashing red, blue, and yellow lights combined with the light from the still-burning wreckage—none of the firetrucks had been allowed near the site.

Christ Almighty, what a night.

"So, what's the plan, guys?"

The question was asked by a young helmeted lieutenant from the Texas National Guard in a loose-fitting Army Combat Uniform, the name **KERNS** stenciled over his breast pocket. Apparently, he was in charge of the very young soldiers, who at a glance looked like they could still be breastfeeding.

Kerns was accompanied by a lieutenant from the Texas State Troopers named Gutierrez. Tall, in a heavily-starched, long-sleeved tan shirt, matching slacks, blue tie, black boots, and a tan Stetson over brown eyes in a dark and leathery face, Gutierrez added, "Little fuckers haven't moved an inch since we got here two hours ago. Like a bunch of toy soldiers. Kind of creepy if you ask me."

"No, officer," Monica said. "It has *nothing* to do with being creepy but with being *disciplined*. You're looking at a highly-trained and well-organized military force that won't hesitate to take on your combined forces if provoked."

Monica and Porter had discussed their approach via satellite phone with John Wright, and in the end, it was agreed to let Monica try first since the head of the North Korean contingent was reported to be a woman.

"We requested a translator," Monica added.

"You won't be needing one," Kerns said, motioning toward the woman in front of the North Korean soldiers and adding, "That one. She's fluent in English."

"And also fluent in trouble," added Gutierrez.

"How's that?" Monica asked.

"Threatened to shoot off our balls if we got any closer," the trooper said, his right hand moving to the grip of his holstered pistol.

"Good to know," Monica said. "Now, first thing we need to do is dial this shit down by moving your people out a couple hundred feet. Let's give these folks a little room to breathe."

Kerns and Gutierrez exchanged a look, not expecting that, and both looked at Porter for confirmation.

"The fuck you're looking at me for?" Porter said. "You heard ASAC Cruz. Pull your goddamned teams back, now."

"But," Gutierrez said, "this is our country—our goddamned state—and these fuckers—"

"Just lost their Supreme Leader," Monica interrupted. "And unlike us, they view their leader as a divinity. They're trained soldiers, with fingers on the triggers, in a foreign country, and scared to death because they all grew up being told that we are the devil. So, again, pretty please, with sugar on top, dial it the fuck down and pull back. Now."

Monica said this loud enough for the woman to hear. Her deep-set eyes, hot and bright under black hair falling messily over her forehead, narrowed in a way that seemed to consider what Monica had just ordered the Americans to do.

Monica removed her Sig, using just her thumb and forefinger. And even then, she drew the Kalashnikovs of a half dozen KPA soldiers. But to her credit, the mystery woman waved them down.

She handed the gun to Porter, who motioned the dozen FBI agents to retreat.

Then slowly, showing the North Koreans her palms, Monica approached this woman with vampire-white skin whose weapon was trained on her.

"I'm Assistant Special Agent in Charge Monica Cruz, from the Federal Bureau of Investigation," Monica said.

The woman regarded Monica. There was an air of strength about her that showed in her balance, in the way she held her weapon, in front of the line of KPA soldiers.

Then, slowly, her eyes gravitated to the American troops moving back, before once more burning into Monica.

"Major Naree Kyong-Lee. Korean People's Army," she said with a faint Asian accent.

"Hello, Major. Long way from home to be dealing with this shit."

Naree blinked, apparently not expecting that. "This is correct, yes. I have been instructed by my government to retrieve the remains of our Supreme Leader, his wife, and his sister and fly them home for a proper burial."

Now it was Monica's turn to blink at the woman's fluidity. Kerns and Gutierrez had been correct. She spoke English quite well, especially for someone living in that closed state.

"We can help you with that, Major. But you need to let our firefighters in to put out the blaze."

Her black eyes in that intense, ghostly face seemed to glitter in an unsettling way, reminding Monica of a cornered big cat, ready to strike.

"And then we can look for your people," Monica added. "Okay?"

She looked at Monica, assessing, weighing, then finally coming to a decision. "Okay."

"We also need to retrieve our dead. The Secret Service detail that was escorting your leader, and the pilots were decorated war heroes."

Another pause, followed by, "Okay."

Monica considered her next move carefully, remembering her conversation with Porter on the way here.

"One more thing, Major. We've organized a special cross-agency team to figure out who is responsible, and we invite you to be a part of it since this was an attack against both of our countries."

She tensed again. "We already know who is responsible," she said. "This is the work of Japanese agents using Japanese missiles, and I have already reported this to Pyongyang."

Oh, shit. That's not good.

"How . . . how can you be so certain?" Monica asked

Naree clipped the large satellite phone to her waist and holstered the semiautomatic—to Monica's relief. She noticed the custom, mother-of-pearl grip as Naree secured it with a Velcro strap.

The North Korean woman reached into her pocket and produced a small phone that looked like some iPhone knockoff and showed her pictures of two heavily tattooed men, one of whom was still holding a Type 91 launcher.

"*Yakuza*," Naree added, eyes once more flashing that feral defiance. "And they were enabled by *your* government."

"What? Wait . . . hold on, Major. I get that they're Japanese mafia armed with those launchers, which, by the way were reported *stolen* from a Toshiba warehouse two weeks ago. But that doesn't mean their actions were sanctioned by the government of Japan, and that certainly can't mean the U.S. Government allowed it to happen," Monica said. "I mean, why would we kill our own people, including a Congressional Medal of Honor recipient plus members of our elite Secret Service? This was a terrorist attack, Major, and my job is to find who gave the order. What you have there are the foot soldiers, not the people who conceived it and planned it."

Naree just kept staring at Monica with visible contempt.

"We need to find the people who are responsible, and we can then bring them to justice," Monica added.

The anger dominating her features faded to cautious deliberation.

She replied, "I will have to check with Pyongyang." She put the cellphone away and reached for the larger satellite phone.

"Of course. In the meantime, let us help you find your Supreme Leader so he can be taken home for a proper burial."

Naree once again sized Monica up then turned to the soldiers behind her, speaking in Korean.

The men's stances softened, faces relaxing from defiance to some strange form of reverence toward this woman, a response that proclaimed just how much control she had over her troops—in sharp contrast with what Monica just went through with Kerns and Gutierrez to get them to pull back.

Naree turned back to Monica gave her a single nod.

CHAPTER 20
The Way Home

EAGLE PASS, TEXAS

Mireya drove through the night, staying off the main roads.

Along the way, she had used a payphone in Fredericksburg, roughly 120 miles north of Eagle Pass, to make a collect call to Culiacán, Mexico, where she had been instructed to cross the border and return home by any means possible.

She was also informed that none of the other vans made it out of the ranch, so there was a strong possibility that the make and model of the vehicle she was currently driving could be being watched for by the authorities.

So, she had swapped rides, using her looks to flag down a lone driver in a Jeep Wrangler outside of town, pretending to have car trouble.

Mireya had shot the young man in the face and dumped him in the rear of the van, transferred the three missile launchers to the Jeep, and hid the van in the woods.

She had considered leaving the remaining missile launchers behind but decided to hang on to them for the simple reason . . . well, she might need to use them to get away, especially if she was spotted by a helicopter belonging to the state troopers or Border Patrol.

She had continued on to Eagle Pass, sticking to side roads, and once even drove across a stretch of desert to go around a roadblock, finally reaching the outskirts of town at dawn.

She hid the Jeep behind a cluster of cedars off the access road, about a mile from the entrance, and spent fifteen minutes hiking toward the eastern ranch fence, navigating it, and taking another ten minutes to crest a hill just north of the main house.

The indigo heavens had given way to a sky stained orange and yellow-gold, allowing her to see one state police cruiser and a single dark-blue van sporting the sign FBI EVIDENCE RESPONSE TEAM UNIT parked near the entrance to the tunnel.

She spotted five men roaming the premises, two uniformed state troopers and three agents in matching dark uniforms and caps with the letters FBI ERTU stenciled across their backs.

The FBI men were going in and out of the entrance of the tunnel carrying cases, which she assumed contained equipment to gather evidence.

Her eyes zeroed in on the entrance, certainly the easiest way home.

The ranch was isolated, away from the busy Eagle Pass and its small army of Border Patrol agents.

Mireya spent another thirty minutes observing but saw no other vehicle or anyone else in sight.

And that gave her an idea.

CHAPTER 21
Jade

"Those North Korean bastards fire missiles all the time just for the hell of it. Can't even start to imagine what they'll do now."
—USN Lieutenant Rolando "Speedy" Gonzales.

USS RONALD REAGAN (CVN-76).
THE SEA OF JAPAN

Someone pulled out one of his foam earplugs, followed by, "Jade. Wake up. C'mon, Buddy. Up. Now."

U.S. Navy Lieutenant Commander Jacob "Jade" Demetrius stirred in his bunk, turning away from the bright light suddenly stinging his eyes. The same someone lifted his sleeping mask.

"Jade, C'mon, man."

For the love of . . .

Demetrius tried to bury his head under the pillow.

He had just fallen asleep after a grueling eight-hour joint exercise between the F/A-18E Super Hornets of Strike Fighter Squadron 195 (VFA-195), also known as the "Dambusters," and the Lockheed-Martin F-35A stealth fighters recently acquired by the Japan Air Self-Defense Force (JASDF).

VFA-195 was part of Carrier Air Wing Five (CVW-5) based at Naval Air Facility Atsugi, Japan and currently attached to the aircraft carrier *Ronald Reagan*. In addition to the Super Hornets, CVW-5 also had five F-35C Lightnings, the carrier-based version of the stealth fighter.

Although Demetrius and a handful of other pilots in the Dambusters squadron were certified in the Lightning, a number of quality issues as well as problems with the spare-parts supply chain, kept the advanced fighters mostly secluded in one of the hangar bays instead of performing the duty for which they were designed and built: to replace the Super Hornets.

In addition to running multiple sorties, Demetrius had to spend two hours briefing the American and Japanese strike groups to make sure everyone was in sync, and then another three hours in the debrief.

In fact, the naval aviator had even skipped the hot chow at the cafeteria and headed straight for his bunk at 0700. He was not due to report back until the start of the brief for a joint night exercise at 1700 hours.

Demetrius was exhausted and in dire need of the sleep that his young wingman, Lieutenant Rolando "Speedy" Gonzales, apparently was dead set on denying him.

Slowly, and damn painfully, Demetrius rolled over to face the Mexican-American naval aviator, who had been alongside him through the entire ordeal with the JASDF—soup to nuts.

Demetrius checked his watch and confirmed that he had slept barely three hours. And yet, the short and skinny aviator ten years his junior stood there all bushy tailed, bathed, clean-shaven, and wearing a fresh flight suit, like he'd slept for twelve hours.

He sighed.

Damn kids.

But the commander's eyes gravitated to the cup of steaming coffee Gonzales held like a peace offering, and which Demetrius quickly accepted, yawning and blinking rapidly to clear his vision.

He brought the mug to his face and inhaled the aroma of this drink of drinks, black, strong, and hot, before taking a sip, and once again closed his eyes, savoring the caffeine bullet.

Finally, he asked, "Want to tell me what this is all about?"

"Looks like we're going to war."

That made him blink again.

"Speedy . . . goddammit, get your head out of your ass. We're already at war in Iraq, Syria, and Afghani-fucking-stan."

"Well, it looks like we're adding North Korea to the list, buddy."

Now he was definitely awake, *very* awake, and dumbfounded. He suddenly remembered he was still wearing the flight suit from yesterday, which was starting to smell.

"What—what are you talking about?"

"I guess you haven't heard?"

"No, Speedy, I haven't fucking heard because I was fucking sleeping, or at least *trying* to fucking sleep! Now, what the hell's going—"

"Jade! Goddammit! Get your sorry ass up now, mister! There's a goddamned war out there!"

Demetrius blinked once more, but not at Gonzales. A larger figure loomed behind his wingman, broad shoulders, bald, skin the color of the darkest night, and the fearlessness of a veteran naval aviator. He always came across as someone ready to tear your head off at the slightest provocation. Demetrius considered him to be one of the finest officers he'd served under in his two decades of being catapulted off the bows of aircraft carriers.

Commander Damian "Hound" Bassett, a native of Detroit and squadron commander of the Dambusters.

"Hey, Skipper."

"Don't fucking hey me, Jade. I need every stick up in the ready room in ten, and that includes you!"

"Mind telling me what the hell's going on?"

It took all of sixty seconds for Commander Basset to relate, with plenty of color, what everyone else on the ship apparently already knew: that President Vaccaro had just raised the combat readiness of her military forces from DEFCON 5 to DEFCON 2. Apparently, some madman, or madmen, had decided to assassinate Kim Jon-un, along with members of his inner circle, in Dallas, Texas.

Demetrius nearly spilled his coffee, his mind trying to process what he had just heard.

"So, how about it, Jade?" Bassett continued. "Feel like cutting your goddamned beauty sleep short to join us upstairs? We're within spitting fucking distance of twenty-five million pissed off North Koreans."

Without waiting for a reply, Bassett stormed out of the stateroom like a roaring tornado, leaving Demetrius gaping at his cup of coffee.

"World's going to shit, Jade," Gonzales, said, his satiny brown skin glistening beneath the fluorescent lights. Demetrius hated him for being so young and full of hormones. He was definitely starting to feel the mileage.

"Those North Korean bastards fire missiles all the time just for the hell of it," Gonzales pointed out. "Can't even start to imagine the shit they'll do now."

It seemed that some form of response from North Korea was imminent. And if history gave any indication of the rogue state's likely targets, it would include South Korea and most certainly Japan.

And the *Ronald Reagan* carrier force was smack in the way of the latter.

CHAPTER 22
Tradecraft

"I guess you can take the man out of the Agency, but you can never take the Agency out of the man. And believe me, I've tried."
—Bill Gorman

KARACHI, PAKISTAN

Khalid Raza was a busy man. He was an important man, with nearly twenty-five thousand people working for him across six countries in an oil-and-gas empire worth nearly fifty billion dollars, and he had little time to spare.

Raza loved his wealth and he certainly loved his power, his fast cars, jets, mansions, and yachts. He was a florid man with a florid face who had all of the toys. But above all, Raza loved his women, especially those Western girls with their blonde hair and blue eyes.

The younger the better.

Tonight, it was going to be special. A new shipment of girls from Europe had arrived the day before—virgins all according to the message he'd received from Yasir, his local contact. A dozen school girls had been taken from the streets of Munich, drugged, and brought directly here.

Sitting in the rear of the Mercedes-Benz SUV cruising through the recently rebuilt section of the city, Raza couldn't help but smile in anticipation. Nothing came close to the feeling of taking a scared virgin after another day spent dealing with the massive reconstruction projects along the coast. He needed a distraction from dealing with overpaid architects, stubborn engineers, demanding investors, and the seemingly endless list of corrupt government officials and inspectors he had to pay off.

The address in the message took him to the northern section of Karachi, away from the bustling port, but that was by design. The nature of what he was about to engage in required the highest degree of discretion. To that end, tonight Raza had only taken Maaz, his best, most powerful, and most trusted bodyguard, who currently doubled as his driver.

"The address is coming up, Mister Raza," he said, turning onto a dark side street behind a row of warehouses that was all but deserted at this late hour. Maaz pulled into a narrow driveway that led to the rear of a warehouse.

A garage door came alive, rolling up to reveal a well-lit interior and his man, Yasir. He waved them in.

Raza's heartbeat increased with anticipation as Maaz pulled in and the door closed behind them.

"Wait here," Raza told Maaz, getting out and approaching the local trafficker.

It happened between breaths. One second Raza was walking toward Yasir, and the next, the side of the trafficker's head exploded.

Raza spun around to return to the SUV and heard glass breaking followed by Maaz's head also turning crimson.

Two breaths.

As he stared in disbelief at his bodyguard shot dead through the windshield, Raza heard a noise behind him. But before he could turn around, someone slipped a bag over his head. Someone else tugged his hands behind his back and bound them.

Three breaths.

"Do you know who I am?" Raza shouted.

But instead of a reply, an automobile pulled up next to him. Rough hands picked him up and tossed him inside what felt like the trunk of a car and the lid was slammed shut.

"I see you haven't lost your touch, Billy boy," Harwich said, unscrewing the sound suppressor from his Sig Sauer P220.

Bill Gorman shrugged after closing the trunk and sliding behind the wheel. "I guess you can take the man out of the Agency, but you can never take the Agency out of the man. And believe me, I've tried."

CHAPTER 23
LERNE LEIDEN

"Learn to suffer."
—Colonel Hunter Stark

30,000 FEET OVER THE ATLANTIC

It never got any easier.

There was nothing more difficult in his chosen profession than escorting the mortal remains of fallen warriors on their final journey home.

Colonel Stark could take the violence—both giving and receiving—but he could never get used to the silence of those long plane rides staring at flag-draped coffins.

And today was no exception.

His mourning process had included that spiked drink at KAF, followed by finding a way to get busy again.

That was the key: getting busy.

The quicker the better.

And President Laura Vaccaro, of all people, had provided timely assistance in that critical next step, dispatching Stark and his surviving team to Texas to hook up with no other than Monica Cruz.

Stark sat back in his seat next to Chief Larson's casket and remembered the last time he saw her outside Washington, D.C., after Cruz had not only prevented a terrorist from detonating a suitcase nuke, but then decided to save the taxpayers a whole bunch of money by putting a bullet in the terrorist's head.

The woman was certainly one hell of an operator, but she had been out of the game for almost a year. And Stark knew that the skills that kept him and his team alive had a very short shelf life.

Use them or lose them.

He had considered bringing that up with the President during the conference call at KAF but had decided against it. His commander-in-chief had already plenty on her plate. And besides, Vaccaro had placed him in charge, with the latitude to do as he saw fit to get the job done.

America was once again under attack, and the President was relying on Stark to lead her covert fast-reaction team while overtly, she worked the massive bureaucratic contraption that was the U.S. Government.

He realized there had to be a reason why warriors like Vaccaro ended up leading the nation while warriors like himself remained leading in the trenches.

Stark just didn't know the reason, and he really didn't want to know it. His motto was simple: *Let the politicians do what politicians do and pipe fitters like me do what I do.*

And in this case, the politicians signed me up to do a job, and the job didn't include worrying about the repercussions in Washington. There are certainly far more important things to worry about, like this new mission and preventing more flag-draped caskets on my watch.

So, here we go again, he thought, his eyes moving past the Chief's coffin to Danny Martin and Ryan Hunt, both snoring away across the aisle.

Stark was tempted to shout over to Ryan that they would be hooking up shortly with his former girlfriend—or whatever it was that Ryan and Monica had a year ago. But he decided against it.

Given the shitstorm they were diving into, his surviving operators needed their rest. And to their credit, they had a knack for sleeping pretty much anywhere, one of the few warring skills not in his arsenal, even though it was a critical one.

Sleep is a weapon.

But how could I?

His survivor's guilt was eating at him, and the last word he got before boarding this Boeing C-17 Globemaster Air Force transport, Michael Hagen was still undergoing back-to-back surgeries at Landstuhl.

Stark did what he always had done following an op, but especially the botched ones: he closed his eyes and forced himself to replay events like a video in ultra-slow motion, advancing the frames one by one.

The problem was that every time he relived the final minute on that rooftop, he wasn't sure if he would have played it any differently.

The rooftop was clear—or so he had thought—and that kid was wailing for one of the dead hajis, presumably his father. Plus, the look in his young eyes, a stare he had seen years before in Mexico. Perhaps it was the strange sense of déjà vu that had momentarily knocked him off his game for the second or two it took him to realize the boy was wired.

And if it wasn't for the Chief, who had remained focused and—

The alarm on his G-shock went off.

Stark rolled his eyes and reached in his pocket, producing the Ziploc bag with the meds that kept him in business.

But a sudden and powerful sense of worthlessness filled him when he felt what else was in his pocket.

He closed his eyes, his fingers curled around Larson's bracelet, which he had removed from what remained of the Chief's wrist on that rooftop.

The bracelet in his hand brought back the man's brute yet graceful strength, his balance, his mountainous figure hauling that equally outrageous machine gun—and that same overpowering figure pushing him aside and jumping over the . . .

Christ Almighty.

Sucking in a lungful of courage, Stark inspected the damage on the carbon-fiber surface. The blast had charred part of the lettering, leaving only **LERNE LEIDEN** still legible.

"Learn to suffer," he whispered.

Feeling as if he had aged a decade in the past minute, Stark decided to put it on his right wrist, just as the Chief had worn it. And when he did, he found something centered and reassuring in that hunk of man jewelry; maybe a silent understanding of brotherhood, or perhaps the realization that the best way to honor his sacrifice was to go on fighting the good fight for as long as the Heavens above allowed him to do so.

I'll join you soon enough, Chief.

But not just yet.

Stark took three small pills from the bag and downed them with a swallow of water.

They would be landing at DFW in just two more hours. A U.S. Army escort would meet them there to accompany the Chief's remains to Arlington while Stark hooked up with Monica to work out a plan.

Their target: Ricco Orellana, boss of the Sinaloa Cartel and one of the most wanted—and most protected—men in the world, and whom Harwich believed to be the brains behind the Type 91 missile conundrum—at least according to some Mexican hooker who'd just finished screwing some of Orellana's men.

He shook his head at how damn wet the intelligence was on this op. But on the other hand, and given the tragic sequence of events that had unfolded in Dallas, the weapons were very, very real.

Picking up the satellite phone, which was connected to an outside antenna with line of sight to a military communications satellite, Stark dialed the number provided to him in his briefing.

CHAPTER 24
The Stench of War

"It's a smell like no other . . . a cruel smell."
—Monica Cruz

BEAR CREEK GOLF COURSE.
DALLAS-FORT WORTH, TEXAS

Monica waited patiently with Naree as the firemen doused the wreckage and began the recovery of bodies, which they lined up a couple hundred feet from the crash site.

The first signs of dawn cast a dim glow on a vista that brought back memories from her years in-country.

Even the smell—the reek of burnt flesh. A smell like no other, bringing back the finality of death. And not just for those who had perished, but for the survivors, in this case, the whole of humanity as it awakened to a very different world.

The smell of war.

Unlike the beautiful shafts of yellow-gold projecting skyward along the horizon, there was nothing remotely beautiful about what this new day, or the one after that, would bring.

But the potential severity of the near-future rested in the hands of the North Korean officer standing next to her.

Naree had been quiet, like the soldiers behind her, stoically watching the gruesome scene as firemen hauled body after body out of the wreckage. Most were burnt to a crisp, some still hissing from boiling bodily fluids—all giving off that stench filling Monica's lungs, reaching down to her damn bone barrow.

Ron Castillo, the Dallas Fire Department chief working this macabre scene finally gave Monica a nod.

"Ready?" Monica asked Naree.

"I am ready, yes," she replied.

They approached the dead walking side by side, in silence. Castillo, a big man in his forties, his face smudged with smoke and sweat, raised the first two sheets, unveiling two unrecognizable faces on charred bodies, a male and a female.

"These are the pilots," the chief offered. "They were still strapped in their cockpit seats."

Monica knelt by the man, reaching for the pin on his lapel.

"What is it?" Castillo asked.

Monica removed the small pin in the shape of a five-point star and wiped off the soot.

"MOH," she said. "Please see to it that his family gets this."

Castillo took the pin and nodded solemnly.

"What is MOH?" Naree asked.

"He was a Medal of Honor recipient. The highest military honor in the United States."

"Oh," the North Korean officer said.

They continued viewing the bodies recovered from the main cabin.

"This one's ours," Monica said, pointing at a body still wearing an earpiece with a holstered Glock, marking him as one of the Secret Service detail.

Monica and Naree looked at another ten bodies, which Naree indicated were Kim Jong's staff because of the lapel pins they wore, plus two more that Monica identified as Secret Service from their holstered Glocks.

Then, Naree paused by a body wearing a very unique lapel pin.

Shaped like a flag, it depicted the portraits of Kim Il-sung and Kim Jong-Il, the slain president's grandfather and father. Monica recognized the thick glasses Kim Jong-un wore, which were now fused to his face.

"Now you are an eternal leader," Naree mumbled, before speaking in Korean to her soldiers, four of whom somberly carried the body to a gurney.

As Naree knelt by the next body, this one a woman wearing the same lapel pin, Monica's satellite phone started vibrating.

Naree looked at her.

"I need to take this. Be right back."

The North Korean resumed her work and Monica stepped out of earshot.

"Agent Cruz."

"Cruz, Stark here."

Briefly taken aback, Monica said, "Colonel? How did you . . . get this—"

"We're headed your way with an ETA of oh eight hundred local. That's eight a.m. your time in case you've forgotten. We've been activated to go into Mexico, locate Ricco Orellana, and haul his ass back north of the border to face criminal charges."

"Good for you, Colonel, but why are you telling me this?"

"Because you're part of that team, Cruz."

"Excuse me?"

"You, at this moment, belong to me, and you'd better be fit to keep up with the shit we need to do. Clear?"

"Ah . . . hold on there," she said, looking in the direction of Porter, who was conferring with the other agents by the helicopters while a number of soldiers from the National Guard erected a tent to set up temporary headquarters of the DHS task force. "Yes, I was activated to be part of a special team, but I thought I was already in it, an FBI special team reporting into the Department of Homela—"

"I hate to break it to you, Cruz, but that's the overt team. You're in the covert one."

"But—but I just got reinstated into the Bureau working for Porter and—"

"When was the last time you fired your sniper rifle at anything but a goddamned coyote or whatever critters you have down in Texas?"

Monica paused briefly, recalling the bodies in her front yard. "Just a few hours, actually."

"Don't fuck with me, Cruz. I'm not in the mood for—"

"Eight confirmed kills."

"No shit?"

"Now, you want to tell me what—"

"You tell that FBI boss of yours to hold his shit tight until we get there."

"Sir, look—"

"Don't go anywhere. Don't plan anything. Don't talk to anyone."

"I get it, sir, but—"

"And especially, don't trust anyone."

"Colonel, with all due respect—"

"We're at the brink of war, Cruz. At the very fucking brink of the world going up in goddamned smoke, and you're in the game to save it. Again. So, you sit, do push-ups, sit-ups, clean your gear, take a nap, but just be there. We need you on this one."

"But—"

"And Cruz: You've been out of this game for a while herding goats and—"

"Herefords."

"Come again?"

"Herefords and Red Angus. No goats, sir. This isn't Afghani-fucking-stan."

"Ah . . . sure. Anyway, you might think you're ready but you're really not."

"Colonel—"

"Hold tight, watch your six, and we'll be there in two hours."

"Look, sir, I appreciate—"

The phone went dead.

Monica stared at the blank screen. "Fuck."

CHAPTER 25
The Carrot and the Stick

"What were we thinking?"
—Bill Gorman

KARACHI, PAKISTAN

Bill Gorman could still hear the screams from the road-to-perdition business that had been black ops interrogations in the post-9/11 years.

And while he dreaded the thought of being back in this shithole of a city, he was at least glad that interrogation techniques had evolved from those dark days.

Gorman had witnessed their brutality in places like Gitmo and the Bagram Detention Center, as well as in lesser known locales in Istanbul, Riyadh City, and even outside of Tempe, Arizona—all of them making him question his chosen profession.

But even worse than the screams, the blood, and the broken bones had been the realization that such methods had not worked. The captured enemy combatants were either prepared to endure the ferocity unleashed on them or never had intelligence beyond the execution of their specific mission.

What were we thinking?

The past year in Maine had certainly helped distance himself from the horror he had witnessed back then, before the U.S. intelligence community realized the futility of such methods and transitioned to the approach currently being taken by Glenn Harwich inside the cabin.

Unfortunately, the damage had already been done, scarring him to his soul.

Gorman flexed his shoulders in a lame attempt to shake off the strange weight that always burdened them when he thought about his past transgressions. Perhaps it was his desire to achieve some semblance of redemption that had prompted him to jump on Harwich's offer a week ago, to part ways temporarily with the new life he had made for himself in Maine.

Marrying someone like Maryam Gadai and fathering a child had gone a long way toward bringing him back from a darkness that he feared would never leave him. But late at night, when the demons crawled out of the deepest recesses of his damaged mind and those gut-wrenching screams became so very real, Gorman would find himself walking alone in the frozen woods praying that the bitter cold would somehow smother the flames scorching his conscience.

Although he had not conducted those sessions, he had not stopped them or objected to them, or even reported them. He had gone along with them and knew that one day he would have to answer for that—in this life or the next.

But on the bright side, tonight, Gorman at least, would not be adding yet another regretful memory. Glenn Harwich was using a very different technique in this secluded cabin on the outskirts of Karachi.

Although the methods had evolved, this was still an interrogation—and one conducted completely off the books. And this was precisely why they were alone here tonight, Harwich and him, flying below radar to follow up on a lead extracted from the surviving Taliban chief on that rooftop in Afghanistan yesterday.

And as had been the case in his operational past, Gorman prayed that the ends would justify the means—even this new and evolved means of extracting the truth.

Dressed like a local, Gorman continued regarding his surroundings, recalling with vivid detail the last time he had been here.

Almost one year ago to the date, Maryam and he had run for their lives while American bombs rained on them as part of President Vaccaro's retaliation for the attack in New York City.

Karachi had been in flames then, and Maryam and he had only been spared by their quick reaction to go below ground, deep into the tunnels of the then recently-built subway system linking the downtown area to the large train station connecting the port city to Islamabad.

And just like his last venture in this godforsaken corner of the world, Gorman once more operated without host-government support and—

The door creaked open, and Harwich stuck his bearded face through. "We're ready for the stick, Billy Boy."

Gorman, clutching the UZI submachine gun he hid under his tunic, followed Harwich inside.

The room was illuminated by a single bulb dangling from the end of a cord over the subject, Khalid Raza. Harwich had flex-cuffed him to a wooden chair behind a rustic table.

Images from so many nightmarish sessions once more flooded his senses. But this time around, the subject wasn't bloodied, or bruised, or missing fingernails. Raza's head was not soaked from the aftermath of a waterboarding session, and the room lacked the smell of burnt flesh, or the coppery smell of blood, or the acrid stench of urine. And the man had all of his fingers and toes still attached, as well as his balls.

Raza was physically unharmed, staring at the photos spread on the table in front of him—photos of his wife and two young sons, Fadi and Amir. The former was the spitting image of the heavy-set industrialist: dark hair, honey skin, soft dark eyes—a handsome Pakistani boy of twelve. His brother Amir, however, was completely bald, with the ghastly-white skin and purplish circles around his sunken eyes that signaled a long battle with an illness.

"We can help him, Khalid," Harwich said, taking a seat across the table tapping the image of the boy. "We can help him reach his tenth birthday and beyond. There's a hospital in the state of Minnesota. It's called the Mayo Clinic. They can get Amir better, healthy. Their survival rate for acute lymphoblastic leukemia is almost ninety-nine percent."

Raza hardly seemed to be breathing at all. He continued staring at the image.

"But you need to help us . . . to help him," Harwich added. "He could be on a plane within the hour and start treatments in less than twenty-four. It's all set up and waiting."

Harwich glanced over at Gorman, who took the seat next to him.

"There's this to consider," Gorman said, sliding a sheet of paper across the table. "Your accounts in Geneva, the Cayman Islands, and Costa Rica."

Khalid's damp eyes moved from the photos to the paper, before they grew wide in obvious surprise.

"We know how volatile your government is," Gorman continued. "Political friends today can easily become your worst enemies tomorrow, thus the need for these." Gorman waved at the paper. "A security blanket for you and your family."

"And we can't blame you for having them," Harwich said in tag-team fashion. "I'd do the same in your position. Family *always* comes first."

Gorman tagged in. "But imagine what would happen if all the funds were to be . . . donated . . . to the American Red Cross or to Doctors Without Borders? Or maybe even to the American Cancer Society so they could go on fighting the good fight against all forms of cancer . . . including acute lymphoblastic leukemia, the disease that you would let your son succumb to by refusing our offer to help."

Raza leaned back and closed his eyes, taking a deep breath, then another. "What good is all of this when everyone is murdered?"

Gorman leaned forward, resting his bronzed forearms on the table. "What are you talking about?"

"They *will* know it was me who talked," Raza said. "They will know I was . . . the rat. They *always* know."

Gorman pursed his lips thoughtfully, then said, "We'll protect you, of course. You and your family. Fly you to safety in America. New identities. New life, maybe even in Minnesota, by the Mayo Clinic. Nice house and cars. Legal bank accounts."

Moisture beaded on his upper lip. Capitulation settled on his features, like a conquered king of old forced into submission. Clearing his throat, he said, "What is it you wish to know?"

CHAPTER 26
Young Guns

"I have a small problem."
—Mireya Moreno Carreón

EAGLE PASS, TEXAS

Maverick County Sheriff Deputy Dwayne Turner leaned against the side of his police cruiser and softly massaged the bridge of his swollen nose while his rookie partner, Deputy Frank Navarro, took a nap.

The excitement of the night before had wound down quite rapidly, especially after the FBI and Dwayne's lieutenant had all the vehicles, missiles, and bodies hauled away—though not without giving him a strong reprimand for disrespecting that female FBI agent.

"You're damn lucky she isn't filing any charges against you for sexual harassment," his lieutenant had told him.

The federal agents had returned to their helicopters and flown off to who-knows-where, leaving behind these three FBI characters in matching jackets gathering evidence.

But Dwayne didn't need a degree in criminology to know that the damn perps were connected to the same Mexican cartel smuggling drugs either across the border or under it with tunnels like this one.

The young deputy didn't bother suppressing a yawn. He was tired—no, scratch that. He was *exhausted*, having pulled a full eight hours before his lieutenant decided to punish him by making him stay here last night, never mind it was the end of his shift. And to add insult to injury, the same lieutenant had then ordered him and Navarro to guard the premises overnight until a replacement arrived in the morning.

And without any goddamned coffee.

"And consider yourself lucky," his lieutenant had told him. "I mean, seriously Dwayne? The fuck's wrong with you?"

Dwayne had just shrugged, remembering just how damn difficult it had been to keep his hands off that FBI woman. And it wasn't the angelic, yet stubborn face and swimmer's shoulders, honey skin, and never-ending legs in those tight jeans and combat boots that had somehow drained him of his will for long enough to do something so stupid and career-ending. Dwayne, after all, had had his fill of the beautiful *señoritas* that populated the brothels across the border in Piedras Negras. He could have—and had had—any one of those Latina beauties for the price of a steak dinner without having to risk his career.

No, he decided. *That wasn't it.*

What had pushed him over the edge was seeing her breezing about the kill zone like some mystical warrior wielding that oversized sniper rifle, surveying her prey.

The hell came over me?

The two junior deputies had decided to break protocol and take turns napping since there was nothing to do except watch the very distant, even unfriendly, FBI trio go about their business.

The young guns always get screwed, he thought.

He heard an engine noise coming from the front of the property.

That made him perk up, but not enough to bang on the roof of the car to wake up Navarro.

Fuck it. Let him sleep.

A black Jeep Wrangler steered onto the property, driven by a woman.

"Well, well," he muttered to himself. "What have we got here?"

Two of the three FBI men currently kneeling by the entrance to the tunnel looked up from their work, but Dwayne waved them off as he walked up to the Jeep, which pulled up behind the cruiser and rolled down the window.

"Morning, ma'am," Dwayne said, tipping his hat. He was struck by the realization for the Jeep to make it this far, it would have to have driven through the yellow police tape stretched across the main entrance a mile away.

The woman smiled an embarrassed smile, saying with the cutest Hispanic accent, "Morning officer. I think I am lost."

Dwayne held back his planned scolding for driving into a sealed crime scene. After the long day and even longer night his superiors put him through, another attractive Latina, this one far friendlier than that FBI agent—and in a Jeep—was certainly a welcome sight. And boy, was she pretty, with that long hair that fell in waves past her shoulders framing a narrow face and fine features that seemed a little crooked but in a way that conveyed a fragility he found irresistible.

Oh, shit, he thought. *Here we go again.*

The woman was anything but discouraging, even inviting.

She held that smile and turned her face toward him, revealing a fine scar traversing her right cheek. It held Dwayne's eyes long enough to miss the object in her right hand: a gun with a silencer.

Mireya aimed for the big bruise at the base of the deputy's nose and pulled the trigger once, the sound-suppressed Rugger absorbing the report.

The subsonic ammunition prevented the shockwave or "crack" of a standard bullet as it broke the speed-of-sound barrier, limiting the overall noise to the semiautomatic's reloading mechanism plus the mild sound of the round punching the officer between his eyes.

She moved quickly now, keeping the large cruiser between her and the FBI men by the tunnel, completely unaware of her actions—as was the second deputy, sleeping in the front passenger seat.

Mireya shot him in the face and dropped to a crouch, moving to the front end of the cruiser.

The FBI men were absorbed in their work, gathering footprints from the tunnel's entrance.

From a distance of around twenty yards, she went through her progression, firing three rounds in rapid sequence, and scoring three headshots.

From the time she pulled up, it was over in less than a minute.

Surveying her surroundings to make sure she was alone, Mireya approached the entrance to the tunnel, seeing it was partially collapsed—enough to prevent her from using it.

Mierda.

Kneeling by the closest FBI man, Mireya checked his pockets and produced an iPhone. She powered it up and held the screen in front of the dead man, using the phone's facial recognition software to unlock it. Mireya added her face to the system so she could use the phone later.

Dialing the same number she used in Fredericksburg, Mireya said, "It's me. I have a small problem."

CHAPTER 27
Hard Call

"They're distancing themselves . . . out of pure fear."
—Ricco Orellana

CULIACÁN INTERNATIONAL AIRPORT. CULIACÁN, MEXICO

Ricco Orellana watched them leave one by one, boarding their respective jets for their long flights home.

Akari Tanaka, followed by her accountant and the rest of her entourage, boarded a Tokyo-bound private jet, which was not unlike the one Mireya had shot down the day before, triggering one hell of a ripple effect across the world, and eventually probably across his global operations, which pretty much reached every continent.

Prince Hamid bin Nayef-Darzada was getting on his own jet bound for someplace in Europe, where he planned to lay low for a while.

I mean, what are the damn odds? he thought, still coming to terms with the reality that in ordering the assassination of President George W. Bush, Ricco had inadvertently assassinated North Korea's dictator. And even worse than that, the assassination team didn't get away cleanly—including Mireya, who was now running for her life.

Running towards me.

Ricco was quite aware of the risk he had taken by ordering the hit. It had meant committing a crime on U.S. soil, which had traditionally been enough for the American government to send in troops to retaliate, thus the need to keep it from blowing back on him.

Although he still could not fathom what the consequences of eliminating Kim Jong-un would be, the fact that his so-called business partners had chosen to depart in a hurry was not a good sign.

After all, North Korea was the darling of China and even Russia, two countries that no one in their right mind would consider crossing.

They're distancing themselves.

Out of pure fear.

But the prince and Akari did take his money and released the missiles to his organization, which was another way to put distance between them. Neither wanted to be remotely associated with the missiles.

Transfer from Karachi to the border with Afghanistan was scheduled to start in a few days, and for Ricco it couldn't be soon enough. The quicker he could start taking down American helicopters with those missiles, the sooner he could divert attention away from the fiasco in Dallas.

Ricco had placed his complex security apparatus on high alert and sent word across his network of military officers and government officials at the state and federal level to keep their ears to the ground for anything out of the ordinary coming from the Americans. After all, they had come after his Tío Chapo for far less.

In his Sikorski helicopter for the short ride to his compound, Ricco Orellana began to question if his wealth, power, and influence would be enough to protect him.

Concluding that perhaps his associates were not too far off base for distancing themselves from him, Ricco decided that he should distance his operation from that assassination.

Mireya had already made contact with Ricco's team in Piedras Negras and requested assistance clearing the tunnel. That was currently underway.

A somber look overcame him because what he was about to do went against that which he held most dear—loyalty—Ricco steeled himself to make the hardest phone call of his life.

In the words of the Americans, he thought, *the buck must stop with Mireya.*

CHAPTER 28
Chariot of the Gods

"Little bastards caught us with our pants down."
—USN Lt. Commander Jacob "Jade" Demetrius.

PANGHYON AIRFIELD. PYONGAN PROVINCE, NORTH KOREA

Colonel Mina Kyong-Lee of the Korean People's Army Air Force slowly inched the dual throttle handles along the left side of the cockpit of her Sukhoi-35S.

The twin Saturn 117S engines responded with increased pitch, and the required thrust to steer the multi-role, air superiority fighter out of its underground hangar, in an earth revetment on the north side of the airfield.

She lowered her visor, taxiing across the ramp under a bright morning sun. When she reached the red lines marking the start of the taxiway, which ran parallel to the single concrete runway, she cut back to idle and pressed the soles of her flight boots against the top of the rudder pedals, engaging the hydraulic brakes.

A moment later, her wingman, Major Byung Ko, pulled up next to her.

"Panghyon ground, Haemosu Niner-Six ready to taxi," Mina said through the mic built into her oxygen mask, identifying her jet by squadron name and tail number.

In Korean mythology, Haemosu was the sun god, which came down from the heavens on a chariot drawn by five flying dragons.

"Haemosu Niner-Six, clear to taxi. Runway Three One."

Mina read back the instructions and once more nudged the throttle forward, releasing the brakes, steering the MiG onto the taxiway.

She took a deep breath of cold oxygen as she went over the strange mission, ordered by her *Samchon*, or uncle, General Pak Yong-Gil.

Her eyes were focused on the long concrete taxiway but Mina was thinking about her *Samchon*, the only father she'd ever known.

It was General Pak Yong-Gil, then a young captain, who had rescued the twin baby girls, the only survivors from a landslide that had swallowed their village north of the capital during the week following some of the worst rains her nation had ever seen.

It was her *Samchon* who had adopted the "miracle twins" as they were labeled by the *Chongnyon Jonwi*, North Korea's daily newspaper, and he took them to Pyongyang, raising them as his own.

It was her *Samchon* who enrolled them in the prestigious Kim Il-sung Military University.

It was her *Samchon* who propelled her sister, Naree, into her stellar career with the KPA while launching Mina's in the KPAAF, where she became the first woman certified to fly the venerable MiG-25 right here at Panghyon.

And it was her *Samchon* who dispatched her to Fuzhou Air Base in the People's Republic of China five years ago, where Mina trained for six grueling months alongside the best KPAAF pilots in the Sukhoi Su-35S, the advanced jets that her nation was securing from the PRC.

She kept the Sukhoi on the center line of the taxiway, and Major Ko followed close behind.

Four Su-35S had taken off thirty minutes earlier with orders to remain low, flying a long and wide circle around the northern end of the Sea of Japan, then heading south to rendezvous with Mina in an attempt to confuse the enemy into thinking they were Russian jets from the base in Vladivostok, near the border with North Korea.

Reaching the end of the taxiway, she went through her pre-takeoff list and waited for her wingman.

Mina glanced at her fuel gauges and frowned—barely filled to half, common practice to prevent pilots from defecting to South Korea.

But not today, dammit.

Considering all of the unknowns of what they were about to attempt, anything but full tanks should be considered a crime against the state. And she had registered her complaint with her superior officer, General Yuhn. But the stubborn and aging officer had ignored her.

Stupid old fool.

"Panghyon Tower, Haemosu Niner-Six ready for takeoff," Mina said.

Both Sukhois held short of the runway by the double yellow lines separating the taxiway from the active runway.

"Haemosu Niner-Six, clear for takeoff. Runway Three One."

Mina read back the clearance and taxied into position, smoothly pushing the throttles to the afterburner setting.

And she rocketed down the runway and into a partly-cloudy sky.

"Dambusters Three-Oh-Three, Torchbearer Five-Six, we're showing two bandits at your nine o'clock, one hundred ten miles climbing through ten thousand at Mach one point three."

Commander Demetrius snapped his head to the west, flying the lead Super Hornet in a two-plane section, completing another loop of a wide sweeping barrier combat air patrol (BARCAP) over international waters between North Korea and the *Ronald Reagan* carrier group.

The warning had come from the E-2D Advanced Hawkeye, a twin-engine turboprop from the Carrier Airborne Early Warning Squadron 125, the "Torchbearers," flying at 24,000 feet. Its mission was to provide early warning and command-and-control functions to all airborne aircraft from *Ronald Reagan.*

"Dambusters, copy," Demetrius replied. "But, bandits, not bogeys?" A Bogey was an unidentified contact. A Bandit was a definite threat. Demetrius suspected that being this close to North Korea and given the speed and heading, they had to be the latter. But he still wanted confirmation.

"Yes, confirmed. From North Korean coast."

"Roger," Demetrius said. *What are these bastards up to?*

"Dambusters, turn port, heading zero-eight-zero."

"Eight-zero," Demetrius replied. "Speedy, combat spread."

"Roger," Lieutenant Gonzales replied from the second Super Hornet, banking his jet two thousand feet to the right to parallel

Demetrius as they turned to face the threat head on. *"But, Jade, you don't need me to tell you that we don't have the fuel for this shit."*

Demetrius frowned under his oxygen mask. They had been flying BARCAP for nearly an hour now, depleting their tanks by two-thirds, and they were scheduled for aerial refueling in thirty minutes from a KC-135R Stratotanker from the U.S. Air Force 18th Wing out of Kadena Air Base in Okinawa circling halfway between them and the carrier task force a hundred miles east.

The intercept vector would now take them farther from the tanker.

"Torchbearer, you might want get those alert birds airborne ASA-fucking-P," Demetrius said, referring to the two Super Hornets on the fight deck of *Ronald Reagan* ready to be catapulted in an emergency.

"We're on it. Bandits now at your twelve 'o'clock out of fifteen for eighty."

"Roger," Demetrius replied, glancing down at his radar and finally picking up two bandits coming straight at them, climbing through fifteen thousand feet, eighty miles out. "Speedy, do you have our bandits?"

"Scope only."

"Call visual when you see them."

"Roger."

"Master Arm on," Demetrius added, ordering Gonzales to activate the weapons system controlling four AIM-9 Sidewinder heat-seeking missiles and two radar-controlled AIM-7 Sparrows.

Demetrius continued frowning, consuming oxygen while his jet was drinking the fuel he didn't have, peering into the western skies in search of the incoming jets and wishing he and Gonzales were flying F-35C Lightnings.

The $100-million jet's low radar cross-section, combined with its use of fiber-mat and other radar-absorbent materials, made it pretty much invisible to the enemy.

And at this moment, Demetrius would give anything to be invisible.

❖

"Burners, Byung," Mina ordered her wingman as they closed in on the two American jets that had been circling the space between the coast and the carrier group, and had now turned toward them.

She advanced the throttle to the forward stops, engaging the afterburners, which nearly doubled the thrust of her turbofans—as well as her fuel consumption.

She grimaced at her fuel gauges, already well below half tanks and the battle had not even started.

Damn you, Yuhn!

"I'm with you, Colonel!" replied Major Ko. Mina felt the afterburner kick, propelling the Sukhoi through Mach 2.0, or just shy of the muzzle speed of the 9mm bullets in her QSZ-92 pistol.

"Whoa! Where the hell did they get those jets?" Gonzales shouted when the two bandits emerged on the horizon and a few seconds later flashed by in full burner right between the Super Hornets, heading straight for the carrier force.

Demetrius felt the sonic booms in his control stick. He swung it to the right, entering a tight turn to go in pursuit.

He groaned from the G-forces pounding him. His G-suit inflated, applying immense pressure to his legs to force blood to his head, keeping him from passing out.

Demetrius shared Gonzales' concern. North Korea was only supposed to have ancient MiG-23s and a handful of the more modern but still dated MiG-29s. The Sukhois that just blasted past them were much more advanced, and even a tad more maneuverable than the Super Hornet—and faster.

"Where do you think they got them, Speedy?" Demetrius said after he exited the turn and the G-forces disappeared. "Fucking China!"

Mina cut power and extended her air brakes, slowing down enough to enter a wickedly-tight left turn when she spotted the American jets turning toward her.

Fortunately, the turning radius of the Su-35S outperformed the Super Hornet, allowing her and her wingman to turn inside the radius of the Americans.

She grinned as she came out of her turn directly behind one of the American jets and engaged the infrared seeker of one of her Vympel R-73 air-to-air missiles. But her leer vanished. Her fuel gauges had dropped to the quarter mark.

"Jade! Bastards are right behind me! Got a lock on me!"

"Break to starboard! Now!" Demetrius shouted, tugging the control column toward him while Gonzales broke hard right.

His Super Hornet entered a close vertical loop, vapor streaming around its leading edges from the G-forces that once more shoved him into his seat, tunneling his vision even with the air bladders pressurizing against his legs.

Fuck . . . me . . .

But three seconds later he was back down, attaining a position behind the twin Sukhois tailing Gonzales, halfway through his right turn.

"How did he do that?" Ko shouted as the second Super Hornet performed what had to be the tightest loop-the-loop she had ever seen.

"Focus!" she replied, remaining engaged with the Super Hornet as it twisted and turned across the sky. But she did wonder if her Chinese instructors had been incorrect about the capabilities of the Super Hornet.

Demetrius settled himself behind the Sukhoi pair, for the first time getting a glimpse of the jets' underwing ordnance: four air-to-air missiles each.

You want to dance?

Let's.

And Demetrius engaged the IR seekers of two of his four AIM-9 Sidewinder missiles while maneuvering to achieve a lock on the Sukhois' superhot dual exhausts.

"Dambusters, we now show four more bandits approaching from your eleven o'clock. Might be Russians," the Advanced Hawkeye reported.

"Russians?" Demetrius said. "Where are those Alert Five jets?"

"Cool it, Jade," Basset's voice boomed through his headset. *"We're thirty-five miles out in burner. Be there in a sec."*

"Skipper, we're flying on vapor here."

"And one has a lock on me!" Gonzales piped up. *"Can't shake the bastard!"*

Mina stayed with the Super Hornet through another series of evasive maneuvers, from turns to dives, going in and out of clouds, followed by more tight turns.

Her Sukhoi could easily match each move while maintaining her IR lock and—

A light started flashing on her panel, warning her that the Super Hornet behind her had a lock on her.

"Colonel! The American has a lock on you and on me and—"

"Let him," she replied, her eyes on the tail of her enemy as it entered another tight left turn. "Let's see what's he's made of."

Demetrius achieved IR lock on both enemy birds, but neither broke away as was customary.

Crazy North Koreans.

"Get this bastard off of my tail, Jade! He's all over me!" Gonzales went into an inverted dive, followed by the two Sukhois, and then Demetrius, who mimicked the maneuver, heading straight for the dark ocean, maintaining missile lock.

"Skipper, do I have permission to fire?" Demetrius asked.

"Negative," Basset ordered. *"Do NOT fire unless fired upon."*

Demetrius frowned, glancing at his fuel gauges. Gonzales broke out of the dive, into a climbing turn.

Goddammit.

"We're coming up behind the other four bandits," Basset said. *"Thirty miles out at your six. Bastards are trying to sneak up behind you."*

"Well, Skipper, in another ten minutes it won't matter. Speedy and I will be in the drink. Flying on vapor here."

"Dambusters, break west, go max-endurance straight for the tanker," Basset ordered.

"And the bandits?"

"If they were going to fire, they would have by now. They're just making a statement, and you made yours by locking a Winder on them. Now, scram."

"Copy that. Speedy, follow my lead," Demetrius said, glancing at his radar and turning straight for the KC-135R Stratotanker, easing back the throttles to conserve fuel.

"Cowards," Mina mumbled into her mask when the two Super Hornets broke away from the dogfight.

She considered following, but her gauges were well below the quarter mark. The four Sukhois joined them, along with a second set of Super Hornets that remained a cautious distance back, Mina turned east on a direct vector to Panghyon.

"Max conserve," she ordered reluctantly, wishing to remain engaged with the Americans for a bit longer, to complete the part of the mission to see how close they would let her get to the carrier.

Her instructors had told her that unless she fired first, the Americans would hold their fire—to a point, and then she would be given a warning shot. But no one knew how close that would be, thus the nature of her mission.

But the reality of her fuel situation told her this was as much as she should push things. She was dangerously close to reaching her point of no return.

And besides, she had achieved part of her *Samchon*'s orders: letting the Americans know that North Korea could hold its own in an aerial battle.

Demetrius keyed his mic, approaching the refueling basket on the port wing of the four-engine KC-135R tanker.

"Jumbo Twenty, Dambusters Three-Oh-Three has you in sight."

"Roger, Three-Oh-Three call port observation," replied the tanker operator.

"Roger," Demetrius replied and cut back throttles while Gonzales made his call to approach the starboard refueling basket.

He extended his probe and lined up behind the basket. "Dambusters Three-Oh-Three, port side, switches safe, nose cold, requesting six point five," Demetrius said, indicating his need for 6,500 pounds of fuel and that his weapons systems were not armed, including his nose-mounted 20mm M61A2 Vulcan cannon.

"Three-Oh-Three cleared in for six point five."

Demetrius added a dash of power to nudge his probe toward the basket, smoothly engaged it, and released the breath he had been holding as fuel began to flow into his nearly-depleted tanks.

As the gauges climbed out of the red, Demetrius settled back into his ejection seat.

For the first time since the engagement began, he looked at the photo taped to the side of his cockpit, depicting a young woman of light-brown skin and matching hair and eyes holding a baby girl with blonde hair and blue eyes—Demetrius's eyes and hair.

The woman's name was Ghalia Khan, a Qatari waitress he had met during a long shore leave in that country following the week-long conflict with Pakistan a year ago.

Demetrius had been alone at the oceanside bar of the InterContinental Doha Hotel, too tired to go partying with Gonzales and the rest of the younger aviators. After the week he'd had and the countless sorties, all he had wanted was a couple of Old Fashioneds and a good night's sleep. But the waitress had been friendly, beautiful, and had an irresistible British accent, striking up a conversation that ended in his room with some of the best sex he'd had in years.

The days that followed were as memorable as Demetrius ever had, spending every waking—and sleeping moment—with Ghalia until it was time to ship off.

He had promised to write to her and even find a way to have her visit him stateside after his rotation. But two months later he'd gotten the phone call that forever changed his life: Ghalia was pregnant—in a country that didn't tolerate pregnant women out of wedlock.

So, he had done the right thing, getting her out of Qatar and flown to Abu Dhabi, a more tolerant country, where he had set her up in an apartment until he could marry her after he finished of his rotation and bring her home to New York.

Unfortunately, the Navy had other plans.

Demetrius was stop-loss due to a shortage of carrier-qualified pilots, and redeployed right here, to the Sea of Japan, for an additional six months. He was due to rotate home next month.

But now we're at war, he thought, wondering when he'd be able to see her and meet his daughter, Jasmine, who had turned four months old last week and—

"Good to go, Three-Oh-Three," the tanker operator reported, pulling Demetrius out of his reverie. *"You're cleared down and to the left."*

He looked at his fuel gauges, verifying he had received the amount of fuel requested.

"Jumbo Twenty, appreciate the drink."

Giving Ghalia and his daughter another glance, Demetrius retracted the probe and eased the Super Hornet down and to the left of the tanker to wait for Gonzales to finish his refueling.

He then shifted his gaze to the west while wondering what kind of crazy game of chicken the North Koreans were trying to play.

CHAPTER 29
Battlefield Promotion

"There is seldom a need for words. But there is always a need for actions."
—General Pak Yong-Gil

PANGHYON AIRFIELD. PYONGAN PROVINCE, NORTH KOREA

Helmet in hand, Mina walked away from her fighter and straight into the briefing room.

Although tired and thirsty, she was still feeling the adrenaline rush of close aerial combat, plus she was enraged that her government didn't trust her enough to fill her damn tanks to confront the enemy.

When she stepped inside the briefing room, she was initially taken aback by seeing only one person there instead of the base commander and his staff, especially given the nature of her sortie.

But what made her drop her helmet was recognizing the man in the olive-green uniform: General Pak Yong-Gil, and he was smiling while removing his peaked cap and setting it on the table.

"*Samchon!*" she said, not expecting to see him there. The supreme commander of the armed forces only visited the base on special occasions, such as the week of Military Foundation Day, which marked the birth of the Korean People's Army, when he toured military bases around the country. And when he did, it was always with an entourage of officers and aides.

But the initial surprise gave way to concern. It had been at least a year since she had last seen him, and his salt-and-pepper hair was now almost white, and with deeper lines across his forehead and cheeks. And his eyes . . . they seemed sunken, tired, conveying the stress of his position, and more so now given the extreme circumstances.

Mina saluted him, then hugged him, then kissed him on the cheek, then hugged him again.

It really didn't matter how many commendations, military ranks, or fighter-jet certifications she received, there was something about seeing General Yong-Gil that always made Mina feel like that little girl he took by the hand on her first day at school a lifetime ago.

Pak held her at an arms' length, giving her a good look, his eyes softening, filling with paternal pride. He pointed at the holstered QSZ-92 with the mother-of-pearl handle on her chest. "That old Chinese thing still works?"

Mina placed a hand over it. The 9mm pistol was one of two that the general had custom made and engraved for the twin lieutenants upon their graduation from the Kim Il-sung Military University.

"It's my most valuable possession. I keep it close to my heart . . . as I do you."

Pak's face softened and he hugged her again, whispering, "As I do you, my dear."

Mina then became serious. "*Samchon*, when did you—"

"Thirty minutes ago, and I'm afraid I can't stay long," he said, as he guided her to the briefing table, where they sat side by side. "I'm needed back in Pyongyang this afternoon. Tell me, did the Americans get a good look at your new jets?"

Mina sat back, drew a deep breath, and then took all of five minutes to relate everything that took place that morning, including her inability to get close to the carrier due to the fuel situation. When she was finished, she waited expectantly.

"So . . . you could have taken them?" he asked.

"The tactics work. We caught them by surprise. We can do it again, and shoot them down too . . . with enough fuel. There will be losses on our side as well . . . but that's the nature of war, yes?"

Pak regarded her, then stood and placed a hand on her shoulder, giving it a soft squeeze. "Sacrifices must be made by each generation to preserve our independence."

"I am always ready to do my part, *Samchon*."

"Then get some rest, my dear. Because you are in charge here."

She blinked and stood. "In *charge?*"

He clapped his hands twice, and the rear door of the briefing room swung open. Two soldiers were holding the elderly General Yuhn, his face bloody.

Although Mina was angry at the old officer, she didn't think—

"Take him out back and shoot him."

The door closed and they were alone again.

Mina forced a composed face.

"That old imbecile," Pak added. "He won't be troubling you again."

"How did you . . . I just told you what happened and—"

"It is my job to know everything, my beloved."

She didn't know how to reply to that.

"Now, get ready," he said. "We start at dawn."

"What happens then?"

"Phase One of the *Azure Dragon.*"

Mina's eyes widened and a chill crawled up her spine.

One of the first things she had become privy to after her promotion to colonel two years ago was the existence of a strategic attack plan for Japan, codename *Azure Dragon*. She learned how the plan had changed over the years, as her nation's military capabilities grew, including its nuclear weapons program and its ballistic missile technology.

"Yes," Pak added, filling the silence as Mina began to consider the possible repercussions of such an attack, even if it was just the first phase. "The Japanese were behind the assassination of our Supreme Leader. Your sister has confirmed it. She has recovered his body."

Mina stood there surprised yet again. "Naree? Is—is she okay?"

"She witnessed it."

"What . . . what is going to happen to her over in—"

Pak put a hand on her shoulder once more. "You are now the commanding officer at Panghyon and must remain focused on the execution of *your part* of this plan of plans. Naree is doing *her* part over there, and trust me, it is very significant. She is our eyes and ears in America—has been for some time, and will be more so in the coming days and weeks. Are we clear?"

Her jaw firming, Mina bobbed her head once.

"Good." Pak then presented her with a small box. "For your new role."

Mina took the box and opened it. Inside were a pair of shoulder bars, each depicting the single silver star of a major general of the KPA Air Force.

"*Samchon* . . . I don't know what to say and—"

"There is seldom a need for words. But there is always a need for action. Is that understood?"

"Yes, sir."

"Good, good. I know you will live up to those," he added, pointing at her new insignias. "Now, I must leave you to it. Good luck, my dear."

Pak pressed a button on the side of the table, and a host of colonels and lesser officers stormed the room. That included Yuhn's staff, who arrayed themselves around the table, their inquisitive faces turned toward Mina, the first North Korean pilot to directly confront American forces since July of 1953, when her country was broken in two by a prior generation of Americans.

"I present to you, General Mina Kyong-Lee, your new commanding officer," Pak said, pointing at the shoulder bars in her left hand.

Everyone stood and snapped to attention, eyes on her.

But Mina's eyes remained on her *Samchon*. He gave her a quick salute before turning around and departing the hangar, tailed by his aides.

As he left, Mina placed her right hand on the holstered QSZ-92 pistol.

CHAPTER 30
Protection

"You use no protection on a complete stranger you picked up at a bar? Ever heard of STDs, Jade? I mean, what are you, sixteen?"
—USN Lieutenant Rolando "Speedy" Gonzales.

USS RONALD REAGAN (CVN-76). THE SEA OF JAPAN

Demetrius dropped off his flight gear and headed straight to the Dambusters ready room on Level O3, which was right below the flight deck.

The room trembled, marking the controlled-crash landing of another jet.

The sound and vibrations reminded Demetrius of the "great deal" he'd gotten on his apartment in New York City, which he'd leased in a hurry in between deployments with the intent of moving Ghalia and the baby there following their marriage. Unfortunately, in his haste to lease it, he'd failed notice that it was located right above a subway train track.

The ready room wasn't the best place to hang during combat operations, which typically involved upwards of 120 sorties every twenty-four hours. That meant endless clanging and tremors marking the launch or recovery of another Navy jet. But this happened to be the location of the best espresso machine aboard *Ronald Reagan*, a gift from Bassett to his pilots.

Priorities.

Demetrius fixed himself a triple-shot latte and sat at one of the tables in the rear of the room, behind the five rows of airline-style armchairs facing the briefing board.

A pilot wearing noise-cancellation headphones currently occupying a chair in the front row was engaged in a Skype conversation with some woman, presumably his wife or girlfriend. This was another reason to visit the ready room even on days like today: it was a Wi-Fi hotspot reserved for naval aviators.

But Demetrius couldn't call Ghalia since it was almost 3:00 am in Abu Dhabi, so he settled for the picture he removed from the cockpit before deplaning fifteen minutes ago.

He set it in front of him, wondering when he would see her again in this world that was quickly turning to shit.

But the way he figured it, every generation was destined to deal with war. His great grandfather fought the Germans in World War One, his grandfather was a pilot in the Second World War, where he fought alongside Royal Air Force pilots in Spitfires, and his father was a "Hun pilot," flying F-100 Super Sabers in Vietnam, until he was killed when Demetrius was five years old.

Demetrius grew up listening to his grandfather's stories, especially the ones during the height of the German V-1 missile attack against London. Demetrius was fascinated by how Spitfire pilots would kill the slow-flying V-1s.

The technique was simple: maneuver one of the wingtips of a fighter beneath the missile over the English Channel. Then work the ailerons to lift the wing quickly, upsetting the gyro inside the missile, forcing it off course, and—

"Hey, Jade."

Demetrius looked up and glared at Gonzales for interrupting his alone time.

"The hell's eating you?" His wingman asked, heading for the espresso machine. He joined Demetrius a couple of minutes later armed with a straight espresso.

In addition to hot milk, Demetrius proceeded to pour a healthy amount of sugar into his latte, earning a raised eyebrow from his wingman.

"You drink coffee like a girl, man."

"And you can go fuck yourself."

"Copy that," Gonzales replied. "Speaking of girls, tell me again how you know that kid's yours?"

Demetrius pocketed the picture. "Don't you have someplace to be?"

"Seriously, Jade," Gonzales said. "I mean, I get the baby's blue eyes and blond hair, man, but, shit, look around. There must have been at least a couple thousand American swinging dicks with blond hair and blue eyes that week in Qatar. Pretty good chance someone else boned her."

Demetrius closed his eyes.

"Just saying. And now you're supporting this girl that you only met for that one week, plus a baby she claims is yours?"

Demetrius frowned.

"And you said you met her that night waiting tables? And an hour later you were doing the nasty in your room?"

"Speedy, you have no idea how much I regret having told you that."

"It's my fault, Jade."

Demetrius dropped his brows at the comment. "How's that?"

"Should have never left you alone that night, man," Gonzales said. "You're a goddamned romantic fool."

Demetrius tilted his head, too tired to argue.

"And by the way, you ever heard of a rubber?"

"I know what I'm doing."

"Obviously not. You use no protection with a complete stranger you picked up at a bar. Ever heard of STDs, Jade? I mean, what are you, sixteen?"

Demetrius realized how bad it looked when put like that. But that night with Ghalia, and the rest of the week for that matter, had felt very, *very* real to him—still did. And yes, he had used protection for the first night, and the second night, but he had run out somewhere on the third . . . and well, there it was.

"Seriously, Jade, I'm really worried about you and—"

"Where the hell's Hound?" came a deep voice from the back of the room.

Demetrius, Gonzales, and the pilot Skyping snapped to attention.

Captain Jared "Mucker" O'Donnell, commander of Carrier Air Wing Five, came in, room followed by the commanders from the Diamondbacks, the Royal Maces, and the Eagles, plus O'Donnell's aide, a petty officer second class.

"As you were," he ordered, waving them down. Also known as the CAG, short for Commander Air Group, O'Donnell was originally from Boston. He was a man of medium stature, but thickly built, with closely-cropped orange hair, a pair of ice-cold blue eyes, and skin sprinkled with freckles.

O'Donnell earned the callsign from a rumor that he was a descendant of a laborer who worked to fill the Back Bay of Boston in the 19th century, a "mucker."

"Hound's still flying BARCAP," Demetrius replied. "Just relieved us after the little dance we did with the North Koreans."

"Goddammit!" O'Donnell hissed, turning to his aide. "I need *all* of my squadron commanders in my quarters ASA-fucking-P! Shit has officially hit the fucking fan!"

The aide took off in a hurry, presumably to the CATCC, the Carrier Air Traffic Control Center, to get word to Bassett.

"So, Su-35s? Confirmed?" O'Donnell asked. Although the man certainly possessed quite the intimidating physique, not to mention a colorful, drill-sergeant language, Demetrius decided that O'Donnell's real power resided in that damn cold stare. It bored holes through the toughest personality.

"Confirmed," Demetrius replied. "They were the real thing and they flew them like they knew what they were doing."

"Fucking Chinese motherfuckers!" O'Donnell cursed.

"Yeah," Demetrius said. "Why don't you direct some of that love toward Lockheed-Martin? Could have used Lightnings up there today."

O'Donnell shook his head, and left, still cursing

Demetrius shrugged and returned to his latte.

"That's one pissed off sailor cursing like a sailor," Gonzales said. "Looks like shit has indeed hit the fan, huh, Jade?"

Demetrius said nothing, well aware that in the United States Navy, like in any other large organization, shit *always* rolled downhill.

Problem was, at this particular instance in history and in this particular corner of the world, the bottom of the hill meant the pilots of Carrier Air Wing Five.

CHAPTER 31
FNG

"I need a Fucking New Guy, and I need him right now to do a job no one wants to do, few can do, no one will know you did, and as you just saw, a job that can easily get you killed even if you're the very best."
—Colonel Hunter Stark

DALLAS-FORT WORTH INTERNARTIONAL AIRPORT, TEXAS

There were few things in life that Stark savored more than stepping off a U.S. Air Force transport and onto American soil following a deployment. And it didn't matter where that soil was, as long as it was in the good old U.S. of A.

Although the circumstances were far from ideal, the colonel did take a moment on the tarmac to fill his lungs with the hot, humid air of a central Texas summer day.

It was glorious.

Until reality sank back in.

Ryan and Danny followed him, flanking the gurney bearing the mortal remains of Chief Evan Larson, to be handed to an Army volunteer who would escort him to Arlington for a military burial in the near future.

Normally, fallen troops returning home entered the U.S. through Dover Air Force Base in Delaware, where they would be greeted and transferred with great dignity by hearse to the base's Air Force Mortuary Affairs Operations Center. The remains would then undergo all of the required burial preparations prior to being transferred to the assigned fallen hero escort.

Each fallen warrior received a personal escort to his or her final resting place in the form of a volunteer from any of the branches, though typically the escort would be from the same branch as the fallen hero and, sometimes, it would even be a war buddy.

Stark wanted nothing more than to do this honor himself, but President Vaccaro had preempted that.

The colonel didn't like it—actually *hated* it—but he understood it and accepted it. The nation was at the brink of opening a war on another front, and this time against a rogue nation with nuclear capabilities.

Honoring the fallen, at least for him and what was left of his team, had to take a very unfortunate back seat to preventing the deaths of thousands, if not more.

Stark had no choice, so he walked toward the hangar, his eyes drawn to the big and ugly North Korean jetliner parked two hangars down. He could see a number of people rolling a line of silver caskets on gurneys. At least twenty of them.

Goddammit.

He paused to observe the procession, and so did Ryan and Danny behind him.

What a damn mess.

Like Chief Larson, each of those caskets was likely headed for some national cemetery.

Stark regarded the North Koreans as they loaded their dead in their jet, but in his mind, he saw the endless rows of crosses at Arlington, where Chief Larson was headed. And that was the thing about such places. When people visited them, especially tourists, all they would see were crosses and names. Ditto for the Vietnam Veterans Memorial Wall. Names, albeit etched in stone, but still just names.

Stark saw faces.

He heard their voices—even felt the heat of the desert or the humidity of some jungle as they died in his arms.

And in the case of Chief Larson, Stark knew he would not only see the big man's face and hear his stupid jokes, but be overwhelmed by the smoke and the dust on that rooftop, and he would hear that deafening blast and feel the spray of the warrior's bloody fragments peppering him.

Stark continued to his assigned hangar to deliver his own dead.

He was met by not one but two men in Army Service Uniforms who he assumed had volunteered to escort the Chief's remains to Arlington. Behind them stood a third man, taller than the others, muscular, and with the honey skin of either a Hispanic or Mediterranean under closely-cropped dark hair. But it was the eyes that caught his attention. There was something profane about them, a glimmer of irreverence Stark only saw in the toughest, battle-hardened souls, like those Taliban commanders who would laugh while cutting off your balls—or the American warriors who paid them back in kind.

As the Army men saluted the colonel and took possession of the coffin, Danny walked around them and went to the big stranger, hugging him in a way that signaled he was part of the brotherhood.

"The fuck you doing here?" Danny whispered, but Stark could hear him.

"Saw the Chief's name come up on the bulletin at Coronado," replied the stranger. "Flew in an hour ago to pay my respects."

Stark had to blink at that, but he let them have their moment of camaraderie while he signed the required transfer document.

"Will catch up to you soon enough, Chief," Stark murmured. The fingers of his left hand toyed with the carbon fiber bracelet hugging his right wrist.

"Till Valhalla," Ryan added.

"Rest in peace, brother," Danny said, already snapped to attention.

"*Vaya con Dios, hermano,*" said the stranger, saluting the departing coffin, tears in his eyes.

And just like that, Chief Evan Larson went off to join the many other fallen warriors that Stark had known and loved through his decades serving in and out of uniform.

I'm getting way too old for this shit, he thought. Once again he felt as if a part of him had died along with Chief Larson.

Taking a deep breath, and mustering the visceral fortitude required to turn the page, Stark faced the stranger, who seemed in his forties, around Danny's age.

"Colonel," Danny said. "This is Master Chief Petty Officer Juan Vazquez. He was in my BUD/S class back in Oh One."

"A pleasure, Colonel."

"Pleasure's all mine. You knew Chief Larson?"

"Three tours," Juan said in a booming voice, "before I got my trident with the Little Guy."

Stark shook hands with Juan, who wasn't quite as tall as Larson but just as wide, strong, pressing against the fabric of his navy-blue long-sleeve T-shirt sporting white lettering over his right pectoral spelling:

BUD/S INSTRUCTOR
NAS NORTH ISLAND

Vazquez was a Basic Underwater Demolition/SEAL instructor at the naval air station on the Coronado Peninsula in San Diego Bay, California.

"That's right, Colonel," Danny added. "Me and my BMF here were two of the six graduates on that BUD/S class. Everyone else washed out."

Stark thought he knew most modern-day acronyms, including BFF. But he never heard of BMF. But Ryan beat him to it.

"The hell's BMF?"

Juan frowned and raised his eyebrows.

"Bad motherfucker," Danny explained. "BUD/S's nicknames . . . earned by giving the cruelty our instructors dished out right back to them. And he continued to earn it by being particularly cruel to the Taliban—to the point that there was a bounty on his big Mexican head."

Stark and Ryan exchanged a glance. Danny fist bumped Juan who said, "I'll take BMF any day over *Little* Guy," and proceeded to spread the thumb and index finger of his right hand about two inches, looking pointedly toward Danny's groin. "But hell," he added, "That was an asset in-country."

"How so?" Ryan asked. Danny closed his eyes and shook his head.

"Tough for the Talis to cut off something that's hardly there."

Stark had to smile at that.

"Missed you, bro," Danny said.

"Right back at you," Juan said.

"And you served together?" Stark asked, an idea forming in his mind.

"SEAL Team Two," Danny said. "Helmand Province. Three tours. Best goddamned operator in the teams. Did over ninety raids and multiple HVT hits in our last one, before you pulled me into your world. Juan stayed on for another decade, before deciding to dedicate his sorry ass to torturing BUD/S candidates . . . when was that?"

Juan tilted his head. "Two years ago."

"A waste of your talent if you ask me."

"Somebody's gotta help separate the men from the boys, bro, and God knows we're always in need of operators. More so given the shitstorm headed our way."

Stark had three rules when hiring operators.

1. Never hire an operator with whom you have not personally served.

2. If you must hire an operator that you have not personally served with, he or she must have served with the person making the recommendation, and that person had to be a current member of the team.

3. Due to the nature of their back-to-back missions, only hire operators without families, especially spouses and kids.

It was all about competency, trust, and complete detachment from anything not associated with the mission.

Stark looked at Ryan. "Romeo?"

No more words were necessary. The former Delta sniper understood and without hesitation gave Stark a nod.

Then Stark looked at Danny.

"Hell yeah," he said.

Juan shifted his gaze between them, apparently confused.

"You married, Juan? Kids? Maybe a girlfriend somewhere?"

Juan frowned and shook his head. "Never worked out, Colonel. Hard to start something when you're away all the time. And then, there's the bag of shit we bring home after each mission. So, no."

"You're fluent in Spanish?"

"Ah, yes, sir. Kind of comes with being Hispanic. But I speak a little German."

"How come?"

Juan lifted his big shoulder a trifle. "Army brat, sir. Born and raised in El Paso. Mexican mother from Juarez married to a Mexican-American GI, Colonel Roman Vazquez, First Armored Division out of Fort Bliss. Spent plenty of time in El Paso, Juarez, and in Germany—mostly in Katterbach and Zirndorf—when Dad was with NATO's Central Army Group back in the Eighties, up to the Gulf War."

Stark had to decide if this guy was someone he could trust to get the job done and watch his back and that of his team. Danny had already vouched for him, and the fact that he had dropped everything to fly here just to receive Chief Larson and watch his coffin for what amounted to a minute, spoke volumes about his character and love for the brotherhood.

And that went a very long way in his mind—in fact, even longer than any military pedigrees, awards, or even foreign languages.

"Well, Juan," Stark finally said. "I can a think of a place where you can spend your time and serve your country in a higher capacity than screaming at BUD/S candidates while they freeze their asses off in the surf. And as you can see, I'm a man down—two actually—so I need a Fucking New Guy, and I need him right now to do a job no one wants to do, few can do, no one will know you did, and as you just saw, a job that can easily get you killed even if you're the very best."

Juan's brown eyes grew wide, understanding what Stark was proposing.

"Colonel, I want to help, but my assignment at Coronado doesn't end for another—"

"That's just one phone call, Master Chief," Stark said, tapping the satellite phone strapped to his utility belt, opposite his Colt 1911. "Say the word and it's done."

Juan looked at Danny for confirmation that Stark was on the level.

Danny said, "Best decision you'll ever make, bro."

Looking Stark in the eyes, Juan said, "Alright, Colonel. I'm in."

"Good man," Stark said, patting him on the shoulder. He turned to Ryan and Danny, adding, "Brief him."

"Where are you going, sir?" Ryan asked.

Stark shouted over his shoulder, "To find your goddamned girlfriend, Romeo."

As he walked away, he heard Juan asking Ryan, "So, why they call you Romeo?"

"Because," Danny said, "he's a horny dumbass."

Stark grinned and walked into the hot Texas sun.

CHAPTER 32
We the People

"There are some on Capitol Hill who feel that the power of this office was not used in a manner consistent with our Constitution a year ago."
—Congressman Wes McDonald

WHITE HOUSE. WASHINGTON, D.C.

"What the president is trying to tell you, Ambassador Jing, is that having *their* jets in such close proximity to *our* jets . . . I don't need a degree in combat strategy to tell you that's a recipe for *disaster.*"

Vaccaro sat against the edge of her desk observing John Wright, on one of the sofas in the center of the room, crossing swords with Xiao Kwan, the ambassador from the People's Republic of China, sitting across from him.

Kwan was a slim man with a haggard face under a full head of dark hair, and, like prior ambassadors from the PRC, he had little power to do anything but pass messages to and from Beijing. And in this case, probably even less, since the jets belonged to North Korea, not China.

Shifting uncomfortably in the sofa, adjusting the knot of his tie, Kwan said, "I will convey the sentiment, Mister Wright, but I would point out that the actions of North Korea are not a reflection of the views of Beijing."

"What about those advanced Sukhoi jets, Mister Ambassador? Are they not a reflection of Beijing?"

Vaccaro nearly laughed at the way her chief of staff told the PRC about the damn fighters that engaged the Super Hornets of *Ronald Reagan.*

Kwan once more squirmed on the sofa. "I . . . I do not know about that."

"Is there anything you *do* know about, Mister Ambassador? You realize that there is an agreement between your nation and ours, that North Korea's air force was to be limited to MiG-29s. And yet . . ."

"Perhaps you should be having this discussion with the Russian ambassador?"

"Is that the official position of Beijing, Mister Ambassador? That President Putin sourced those Sukhoi-35s to the North Koreans?"

Kwan sat back, reached inside his pocket, produced a handkerchief, and wiped the perspiration forming over his upper lip even though Vaccaro kept her office at a constant 65 degrees year-round.

"No, Mister Wright. Of course, not. It was just . . . a thought."

Under different circumstances, Vaccaro would had felt sorry for Kwan, who was little more than President Xi Jinping's errand boy. But the scrambling of North Korean fighters in a direct and quite dangerous challenge to the jets of the United States Seventh Fleet felt like throwing fuel into an already explosive situation.

Vaccaro certainly understood the desire by the surviving North Korean government to do *something* in the wake of the assassination of Kim Jong-un, but she would have expected China, which pretty much controlled North Korea, to have tempered the enthusiasm of its puppet nation.

Unless, of course, Beijing being Beijing was using the crisis to advance its own long-term global agenda, which Vaccaro believed was nothing short of total world domination, starting with the Pacific Rim nations.

China was already a military superpower, second to none but the United States in annual military spending. The U.S. hovered at around $650 billion while China had reached almost $300 billion. By comparison, Russia was in sixth place at $62 billion behind Saudi Arabia, India, and France.

China had already passed Russia in the number of satellites deployed, had a navy that included aircraft carriers and quite the fleet of ballistic missile submarines. Plus, it had an air force to be reckoned with, enough land-based ICBMs to wipe out America many times over, and an army already topping two million soldiers.

In addition to its military and economic might, China was expanding in the Western Hemisphere via Cuba, just 90 miles off the coast of Florida. It was providing the rogue island with everything from brand new city buses to mobile phones and the IT infrastructure to use them, plus the construction muscle to kick off a massive reconstruction project across Havana. In addition, China had taken over the massive tunnel system excavated under Havana by the Soviets during the 1980s for a subway system that would be connected to the planned high-speed trains that would link the island by 2030. It was only a matter of time before China transformed Cuba into a true tropical paradise reminiscent of the 1950s, and in the process, its government would fall under the control of Beijing, like North Korea.

Wright continued grilling the ambassador to make absolutely certain that the right messages would be delivered to Beijing. They had to get President Jinping to drag North Korea to the negotiation table and prevent a crisis already escalating into—

"Madam President?" Wright asked.

Vaccaro looked up.

"Would there be anything else for the ambassador today?"

She shook her head and pressed a button on her desk.

Ambassador Kwan stood, went to Vaccaro and shook her hand. "Thank you, Madam President. I will speak to Beijing immediately."

"Thank you, Mister Ambassador. Please pass on my personal request to President Jinping to help us bring this unfortunate situation under control before it gets away from us. The United States will not condone any form of reprisal against our allies in the region, including Japan and South Korea. As you're aware, I have increased the alert status of our armed forces to DEFCON Two. This would *not* be a good time to test our resolve."

"I understand completely, Madam President." The ambassador departed.

"What's next, John?"

Wright checked his tablet. "Homeland is kicking off the taskforce in the Situation Room in fifteen, followed by the joint chiefs, and the defense secretary an hour later. But first, Congressman McDonald. He's been waiting outside for over an hour."

Vaccaro let out a resigned breath.

She was in the middle of a crisis that could easily lead to a global armed conflict if not properly handled, yet, she had to find the time to deal with the House Minority Leader.

"Five minutes, John. Not a goddamned second more."

An aide escorted the congressman through the door.

The first impression of Congressman Wes McDonald was that of a mild, aging statesman. Silver hair, a face lined with the stress of two decades on Capitol Hill, and a voice raspy from a lifetime of smoking, McDonald walked slowly, talked slowly, and ate slowly. Nevertheless, the seventy-year-old congressman—today in a brown tweed suit, a white shirt, and a maroon bowtie that made him look like a college professor—was quite the unrelenting legislator.

And in Vaccaro's opinion, quite the political agitator.

The man just would not stop rallying Congress to find a way to bring articles of impeachment against Vaccaro for the way she handled the crisis a year ago.

The aide led him to the sofa just vacated by Ambassador Kwan, across from Wright, while the president remained sitting against the edge of her desk facing them.

"Madam President."

"Congressman."

"I will be brief, ma'am," he said, "I realize you have a great deal on your plate."

Vaccaro just kept his gaze on him.

Clearing his throat, McDonald said, "Our Constitution was written by the people and for the people in order to create a more perfect—"

"Tick tock, Congressman. Get to the point," Wright interrupted.

Vaccaro raised a hand. "That's alright, John. It's the congressman's time. He can use it any way he pleases."

"Thank you, Madam President," McDonald said. "Like I said, I intend to be brief. Our Constitution was created to provide our nation with checks and balances. Our forefathers' intent was to prevent the unbridled use of power by any individual occupying the executive or judicial offices. And yet, over the years, we have seen elected officials abuse that power and get impeached, including nineteen federal judges and even three presidents, Andrew Johnson in 1868, Bill Clinton in 1999, and—"

"And they were later acquitted by the Senate," Wright interrupted again. "Get to your point, please."

This time Vaccaro said nothing.

McDonald cleared his throat again. "There are some on Capitol Hill who feel that the power of this office was used in a manner not consistent with our Constitution a year ago. And yet, the majority on the Hill continues to turn a blind eye to it, even after the sworn testimony of Mister Hollis Gallagher."

"And your question, Congressman?" Wright pressed.

Vaccaro held back a smile. Wright had transitioned into full USMC platoon leader mode.

"Tic tock, Congressman," Wright pushed, tapping his watch.

McDonald gave him a resigned nod. "While I will continue to fight to protect the Constitution of the United States against all enemies, foreign and domestic—even if doing so places me at odds with the majority of my colleagues, and arguably with this office—I would like for the president to consider the great . . . *opportunity* that this new crisis presents to her office."

"Opportunity?" Wright pressed. Vaccaro already knew where the old man was headed.

"Yes . . . to do the right thing. To handle this crisis in a manner that is, without question, fully consistent and compliant with the highest law of the land, our Constitution."

"Thanks for stopping by, Congressman," Vaccaro said, and pressed the same button on her desk. "Your directness and candor is always appreciated."

"Madam President," McDonald said, standing slowly and walking out even more slowly.

Wright waited for the door to close, then he turned to face her, tall, steady, like a ship's mast. "Madam President, we must be cautious in how we—"

"Has Stark reached Dallas yet?"

"Ah, yes . . . about an hour ago, and—"

"Anything he needs, John. *Anything.*"

"Yes, Madam—"

"What's next on my agenda?"

"We are, Madam President," Wright replied. Lisa Jacobson entered the office from another door.

"Hey, Lisa. What's up?" Vaccaro said, and Jacobson proceeded to update her on the situation in Karachi, where Harwich and Gorman apparently had a breakthrough in locating the missiles.

While that was good news, in order to act on that information, she would have to task a SEAL team to that location as soon as practicable because there was no telling how soon those missiles would be smuggled from their staging point into Afghanistan.

"This is the slippery slope, Madam President," Wright pointed out. "Harwich and Gorman are part of our team with no name, but now we would have to bring in SEAL operators, who report to Admiral Kent Olson, who reports to Kaminski. Sooner or later someone *will* ask how we obtained that intelligence and—"

"I'm well aware of that, John," she replied.

The Navy SEALS were part of the United States Special Operations Command, or USSOCOM, which oversaw the various special operations components of all branches of the U.S. Armed Forces, and it fell under the umbrella of the Department of Defense headed by Secretary Art Kaminski.

"Madam President, the question *will* be asked," Jacobson added, "and it *will* lead to another Congressional inquiry that *will* be led by Congressman Mc—"

"I'm aware of that as well, Lisa. And we *will* deal with that . . . later. Right now, I need to do everything possible to keep any more of those missiles from getting across the border."

Vaccaro could read in their faces just how concerned they were about once more circumventing established processes.

"Lisa, John, I know you know this, but I need to say it to clear my head and the air. I did what I did a year ago because I was convinced that our government could not stop that nuke from going off. Everything in my life up to that moment and after coming out of that first fucking briefing, told me our bureaucracy was too large, too set in its ways, and incapable of making decisions fast. Nothing has changed my mind. I'm responsible and accountable to Congress for what I did a year ago, and for what I'm doing again. I will answer for that, I have no doubt. But before that day comes, we have another world emergency to handle. So, get on the horn and get those SEALs hooked up with our CIA contingent on the ground. Then pipe everything to me."

"Yes, Madam President," Wright said. "We—"

"About the SEALs," Jacobson interrupted, before pointing at the satellite phone in her right hand. "Gorman had an idea."

As she left the Oval Office five minutes later, Lisa Jacobson made a mental note to tell Jason Savage, whom she had dispatched to hook up with Gorman and Harwich, to do a deep dive into Congressman McDonald. Anyone who was that self-righteous had to have a few things in their lives that would turn out to be harmful when exposed to the light of day.

CHAPTER 33
Shiraki

"It was a damn boy wired up, and we all missed him . . . I fucking missed him."
—Colonel Hunter Stark.

**BEAR CREEK GOLF CLUB,
DALLAS-FORT WORTH, TEXAS**

The very hot and very bright mid-morning Texas sun made Monica wish for a cold beer, a hot meal, and a hot shower—in that order.

Instead, fate presented her the very imposing Colonel Hunter Stark.

Oh boy.

"Cruz!" Stark shouted from almost fifty yards away looking like he had just stepped off the battlefield in Afghanistan.

Monica was currently alone. Naree was dealing with the loading of bodies aboard the Ilyushin. FedEx mechanics had returned it to full functionality by repairing a couple of leaky fuel connections. Porter and the rest of the Feds were holed up over in the newly-erected FBI operations tent engaged in some interagency taskforce conference call.

Monica had lasted thirty minutes listening to some assistant deputy from the DHS up in Washington outlining his grand scheme to bring together America's law enforcement agencies in collaboration with Mexico's Federal Police as well as with the police from Sinaloa to go after Ricco Orellana.

Given the choices, Monica preferred to deal with Stark. At least with the colonel she always knew where she stood.

Stark removed his glasses, revealing a pair bloodshot eyes signaling a definite lack of sleep.

"Good morning, Colonel."

"Not for us, Cruz, and certainly not for them." Stark pointed the phone's foot-long antenna at the row of black body bags being hauled into a waiting Chinook for their short trip to Fort Hood, where they would be processed and released to the next of kin.

Monica didn't know how to answer Stark's comment, so she said, "Damn, sir, your eyes look terrible. Gotten any sleep lately?"

Stark frowned and slipped the glasses back on. "Just finished talking with Wright," he said, "who *assured* me that our ride and gear would be here when we got here. And yet, it's *still* not here. And where's the rest of the feds?"

Monica pointed at the tent. "Interagency conference call. They're going to coordinate with the *Federales* and also with the Sinaloa State Police."

"Jesus H. Christ," Stark hissed. "When will they learn?"

Monica raised her brows a bit.

"And they didn't rope you in like the last time?" Stark asked, referring to the disaster in Monterrey, Mexico a year ago, when a planned raid on the compound of then Cartel Boss Miguel Montoya by the FBI and the *Federales* had gone sideways. Monica had been the only survivor of a Cartel ambush on an FBI convoy, and only because of Stark's timely intervention.

"Screw that," she replied. "Don't feel like having my head on a stick."

"You're learning, Cruz."

"Yeah. Fool me once, shame on you. Fool me twice . . ." Monica looked beyond the colonel but didn't see anyone else.

"So, where's the crew? I missed those guys."

"Yeah," Stark said, removing his sunglasses again. This time Monica saw something deeper, sadder than those red capillaries. "About that. We had an incident . . . in-country. The Chief's gone."

She felt like she had been kicked in the gut.

"Wh-*WHAT?* Chief Larson is—"

"Some haji kid lit up his s-vest. The Chief jumped on him. Saved Romeo and me. Mickey's in Landstuhl. Lost the bottom of his leg."

"Oh, my God!" Monica said, covering her mouth.

"Wasn't the Almighty, Cruz. It was a damn boy wired up, and we all missed him . . . *I* fucking missed him, so now the Chief's dead and Mickey is all fucked up in Germany." He looked past Monica, staring at nothing, shook his head and said, "You know the deal, Cruz."

Monica did know the deal.

"And Danny?"

Stark pointed the antenna of his phone over his right shoulder to the airport. "Over in that hangar with your boyfriend."

Monica crossed her arms. "Goddammit, Colonel, he's not my—"

"Oh, and we also have an FNG."

"An FNG?"

"Juan Vasquez."

"Who the fuck's he?"

"Badass SEAL, or so I hear. Danny vouches for him. Just signed him up. He has the quals and the timing is perfect. You're gonna love him," Stark said, before looking about him.

"Expecting someone else, sir"

"Yeah. Wright said something about babysitting some North Korean officer?"

"Yeah . . . that would be Major Naree Kyong-Lee. She's the ranking officer of the survivors. She has a direct line to Pyongyang. The quicker we can prove that this wasn't us or Japan, the better."

"Cruz, you of all people know what happens when non-operators tag along with us: they get *killed* and sometimes they get *us* killed. Hell, we even get killed *without* them. That's how damn dangerous this shit is, and I expressed this very concern to Wright. But I think the years away from the trenches may have caused his head to be up his ass."

"Well, sir, from what I've seen, this Naree woman is quite capable of holding her own."

"Great. Just what we fucking need. Not one but *two* FNGs." He looked around. "So, where is she?"

"Over by their jet. Everyone but her is scheduled to leave shortly. Heading back to North Korea."

All the silver caskets were gone, meaning they were inside the big Soviet-era jet. The engines spooled up to a deafening whine that echoed down the tarmac.

"Damn," Stark said. "No wonder they lost the fucking Cold War. You can hear those piece-of-shit engines from half a world away."

The big jet loudly taxied to the runway, spewing a bluish haze.

"Let's go," he added, starting back to the airport through the broken fence.

But they didn't need to walk far.

A lone figure in an olive-green uniform stood a short distance from them near the edge of the tarmac, staring at the jet taxiing noisily away.

Naree was used to being alone.

She had been operating on her own in America for the better part of a decade. But there was something about seeing that jet leaving for home that gave her a sudden pang of nostalgia.

She touched the mother-of-pearl grip of her pistol.

I miss you sister . . .

The jet reached the end of the runway and was cleared, its four engines roared, sending a shockwave across the tarmac that Naree felt in her chest.

And I will see you again.

But not yet.

Not yet.

Breathing in a lungful of determination tinged with the smell of burnt jet fuel, Naree watched the big jet lumber down the runway, liftoff and begin turning west.

She turned her attention to the two people approaching her.

One was the FBI woman, Monica Cruz. She was accompanied by a big and bald man that reminded her of—

Impossible!

It can't be . . .

Monica sensed something was terribly wrong the instant Naree turned around.

And froze.

The North Korean's lips parted, but she said nothing. Her cat-like eyes widened in a mix of obvious surprise and something Monica had not yet seen from her: dark amusement, perhaps with a tinge of wariness.

It happened very quickly, evoking images of gunslingers at high noon.

Stark reached for his Colt, an action that prompted Naree to draw her weapon. By the time Stark freed it from the holster and aimed it at the North Korean woman, she had aimed hers at him.

"*NO!*" Monica shouted, getting between them, her back to Naree. She held up an open palm toward Stark, whose face was twisted with an anger she had never seen in him before.

"Out of the way, Cruz! She's a goddamned North Korean agent!"

"Yes! I know! That's the whole *fucking* point of having her with us!"

Three distant figures started running towards them from the hangar.

"You fucking tricked me, Seung!" Stark shouted past Monica.

"Who the hell's Seung?" Monica asked. "Her name is—"

"It was the job, *Shiraki*. Yes?" Naree replied.

"Don't fucking *Shiraki* me! Goddamn you!"

Monica was utterly confused now, but she held her ground as both still had their weapons out.

"And who the hell's *Shiraki*?" Monica pressed.

"Hunter," Naree said calmly behind her. "In Korean. That's what he liked to be called when we sipped tequila . . . and *fucked*."

Monica gaped at Stark.

"Goddammit!" Stark shouted, lowering his weapon. "The hell you doing here?" he added, removing his glasses and glaring with obvious anger.

"Damn, *Shiraki*. You look like shit. You need a vacation or something? Maybe a hug?"

Before Stark could answer, the whirring of helicopters reverberated across the tarmac.

At the golf course, FBI agents and the detachment of National Guard soldiers were running toward the two Black Hawks.

"What the . . . *Cruz?* Where the hell are they going?" Stark said.

Monica hit the speed dial on her phone, putting it on speaker so everyone could hear. Porter answered on the second ring, just as Ryan, Danny, and Juan reached them.

"Gus? What's happening?"

"Can't talk now! Trouble at your . . . place in Eagle Pass!" Porter shouted, sounding out of breath. The helicopter blades were in danger of drowning him out.

"What are you talking about?"

"Radio silence . . . team down there!" he replied. *". . . one of their phones was used two hours ago to call Culiacán . . . ranch . . . check it out."*

"Bad idea, Mister Porter!" Stark screamed into the phone.

A pause, then, *"Colonel Stark?"*

"We need to talk! NOW! Stop the goddamned helos!"

"No time, Colonel! Need to . . . there . . . apprehend anyone . . ."

"No, Mister Porter!" Stark shouted back. "You're going into an unknown with no eyes on the ground! Like I said, a bad idea and—"

"He hung up, Colonel," Monica said.

Stark glared at the departing Black Hawks, then turned to Naree, who stood there, arms crossed, her lips twisted into something that fell somewhere between amusement and trepidation.

He jabbed the satellite phone's antenna at the North Korean. "I'm going to deal with you later."

"Not going anywhere, *Shiraki*," she said, blowing him a kiss.

"Fuck me," Stark muttered.

"Need some Cava de Oro first, *Shiraki*. Remember?"

Stark shook his head and hastily walked away. He pressed the satellite phone against his ear and started shouting obscenities until he was out of earshot—something about their helicopter and gear not being there as promised.

"What was *that* about?" Monica asked Naree. Ryan, Danny, and Juan stopped as one and waited to hear her reply.

The North Korean officer tilted her head and said, "Men. They're all the same. So predictable."

Ryan Hunt, flanked by Danny and Juan, just stared at Monica.

Why do you have to be so damn handsome?

Ryan winked and gave her a smile that was strangely reassuring. It had attracted her to him a year ago, chasing nuclear terrorists across two countries.

"You've got that right, Sister," Monica whispered to Naree, determined not to fall under his damn spell again. "They're all the *fucking* same indeed."

CHAPTER 34
Handy Work

"*What are you trying to do, Flaca? Start a war with the gringos?*"
—Francisco Navarro, Sinaloa Cartel *Sicario*.

EAGLE PASS, TEXAS

Even from inside the tunnel, Mireya heard the distant purring of helicopters.

She knew they would come eventually but didn't think it would be this soon.

She grimaced, wondering if the American phone in her pocket—the one she had used to call in Ricco's people to remove the debris from the tunnel—had brought them here.

Mireya could also hear the *mineros*, the miners, on the other side of the collapse, trying to punch through.

The *mineros* were close, as signaled by the increased vibrations and noise of their hardware.

But they needed a little more time.

Which meant *she* had to buy them a little more time.

Mireya ran to the mouth of the tunnel and saw the distant shapes—two of them, side-by-side—just over the horizon.

Making her decision, she slid the Ruger between her jeans and her spine, and sprinted to the Jeep.

She yanked all three launchers from their cases, powered them up, and set them side by side at her feet.

The helicopters were probably no more than a mile away now, flying at roughly three hundred feet.

She brought up the first launcher, activating the IR seeker and aiming it just below the rotors, on the super-hot turbines.

The lock was almost immediate, rewarding her with a high-pitched whine.

Exhaling slowly, she squeezed the trigger. The missile shot out in a plume of white smoke as the first stage rocketed it away from the launcher. The second stage ignited some distance away, tracking beautifully all the way to the closest helicopter.

The pilot tried an evasive maneuver. But to her pleasant surprise—and like the Embraer last night—the helicopter didn't disperse any defensive flares.

The blast was as bright as it was loud, and powerful—very powerful. The shockwave reached her at the same time the fuselage separated from the main rotor. It tipped, slicing through the middle of the aircraft on its way to the ground. The crash was followed by another explosion, red and yellow flames reaching to the sky.

Mireya was already raising the second launcher, again achieving a lock in seconds on the other helicopter. It made a hard left turn.

She fired and the missile streaked after the departing rotorcraft, scoring another direct hit.

But for some reason, the helicopter remained airborne, trailing smoke and flames from its turbines.

Reaching for the third and final launcher, Mireya brought the wounded bird into the sight assembly and engaged the IR seeker, achieving another lock.

She fired, and this time it was different. The missile tracked into the center of the plume of fire, detonating in a ball of flames that engulfed the helicopter, which detonated in an even larger explosion at an altitude of about two hundred feet.

The expanding cloud of smoke and fire began to rain fiery debris.

Mireya watched, transfixed—

"Hey, *Flaca! Vamonos!*"

She turned and saw Francisco Navarro, one of Ricco's *Sicario*s, a heavily tattooed man slightly shorter than her, holding an AK-47.

"The hell's that?"

She shrugged, still holding the empty launcher. "One of their helicopters."

"And *that?*" Francisco asked, pointing at the fire off to their right, where the first helicopter had crashed.

"Another one."

"What are you trying to do, *Flaca?* Start a war with the gringos?"

"Little too late for that," she said, giving her handiwork a final look, then following Francisco into the tunnel, where she discarded the launcher.

CHAPTER 35
Frogmen

"Nothing warms up little frog hearts like being called by you guys in the middle of the night, asked to keep this op under wraps from the powers that be, and then get to ride on your fancy jet for two hours to this shithole."
—USN Chief Special Warfare Operator (SEAL) Scott Kelly

KARACHI, PAKISTAN

There was a big difference for Gorman between meetings with regular assets—like a government official they had turned, or a village chief they paid to cooperate—and meeting with a U.S. Navy SEAL.

It truly was night and day.

Hell, thought Gorman, *pretty much anyone is completely different than meeting with a SEAL.*

He had worked with Scott Kelly before and they were inclined to trust each other, though always with the thought to "trust but verify" what the other was saying.

In the dining room of a CIA safehouse in a neighborhood just north of their target, these two men knew what few did: that lives always depended on these meetings.

Chief Kelly was the senior operator from SEAL Team Six's "Blue Team." He and his team had been doing up to two missions a day in the Kabul region for the last forty-five days. So, as much as they loved what they did, rolling up on compounds by truck or helo at night and capturing or killing very bad people did get a little stale.

"We got this intel yesterday," said Gorman, dressed in local garb and sitting across from Kelly, similarly attired.

Harwich covered the house from across the street along with the six members of a Special Operations Group team he had flown in from New Delhi to go in after the SEALs and deal with the missiles and any intel.

But the SOG team's current duty was to make sure the safehouse remained safe.

"It's actionable," Gorman added, which meant the intel had to be acted on within twenty-four hours, and they were currently at hour sixteen since the kidnapping of Raza. "So, we asked for you guys to help us out."

Kelly, a man as tall as Gorman with a short dark beard, broad shoulders, and a waistline that signaled insane fitness, grinned. "Nothing warms up little frog hearts like being called by you guys in the middle of the night, asked to keep this op under wraps from the powers that be, and then get to ride on your fancy jet for two hours to this shithole."

Gorman opened his mouth but Kelly cut him off. "*Especially* when the objective is to keep a bunch of goat fuckers from getting their dirty little paws on a shitload of SAMs."

Gorman waited until Kelly was done. Then he said, "And we're grateful you're here, Chief. We'll have you back in Kabul by breakfast."

"That's the thing, Bill. We're really not here, are we?"

"Nope. Never were. And the president thanks you for that."

"Well, the boys are staging in your warehouse and rehearsing based on the information you gave us en route. So, what else do you have for me?"

Gorman waved over a person waiting patiently in the back corner of the room.

Kelly raised an eyebrow at the skinny little woman in black holding a tablet computer. Looking more like a rebellious teenager than a SAP operator, she regarded them with a pair of heavily mascaraed dark eyes that matched her dark lipstick. She passed the tablet to Gorman and returned to her corner.

"Who the hell was that?" Kelly asked.

"She's you, Chief."

Kelly blinked.

"In the cyberworld," Gorman added. "Someone you never want to piss off if you value your bank accounts and your identity."

"Oh."

"She's worked ISR on the tanker," Gorman said, meaning intelligence, surveillance and reconnaissance, "since we pinpointed the location yesterday. You can scroll through the last set of sat photos, some audio and still pictures."

Kelly spent a couple of minutes browsing through the information.

"Well, Bill, this makes me a fucking proud American to know you haven't wasted our time. But I need access to the real-time streams of your aerial asset," Kelly said, referring to the Global Hawk UAV circling off the shore of Karachi at 40,000 feet.

"This is a takedown with minimal information and even less rehearsal time so help me help you and give me everything you got," Kelly added.

Gorman made a single call on his satellite phone, and within a minute the real-time infrared and night-vision feeds from the Global Hawk appeared on Kelly's phone.

Kelly reviewed the images then checked his digital watch. "See you at the staging area in forty," he said, glancing at the slight figure standing in the corner and nodding on his way out

Harwich came in, holding an AK-47. "Well?"

Gorman tilted his head. "We're in business."

CHAPTER 36
Dead Presidents

"There comes a time where strength is demonstrated through restraint, not by foolish shows of force."
—President Laura Vaccaro

THE WHITE HOUSE. WASHINGTON, D.C.

In the Treaty Room, Secretary of Defense Art Kaminski gave the President a private briefing on possible attack scenarios by North Korea.

Like earlier presidents, Vaccaro used the historical room as her unofficial study, away from the endless activity surrounding the Oval Office.

Kaminski was an *Iraqi Freedom* and *Enduring Freedom* veteran awarded three Purple Hearts for wounds sustained during his six combined tours, two in Iraq and four in southern Afghanistan. Vaccaro had even placed the Congressional Medal of Honor around his neck a year ago for exemplary courage under fire while rescuing a platoon of ambushed Marines in Afghanistan. In the process, Kaminski had gotten both of his legs blown off below the knees, forcing him to rely on the graphite and titanium prosthetics on which he stood next to a large LED TV on rollers.

A high-definition screen depicted a map of the Sea of Japan and surrounding countries that included North and South Korea, Japan, and parts of China and Russia. Army and air force bases in the Koreas were marked as well as joint American-Japanese bases in Japan, plus the closest People's Liberation Army Air Force bases on mainland China and Russian Federation bases near their border with North Korea. And in the middle of it all cruised the U.S. Seventh Fleet.

"For some time now," Kaminski said, looking very much the aging jarhead but still quite fit in his tight dress blues, and sporting a chest full of ribbons and medals. "North Korea has two standing strike packages, one for South Korea and another for Japan. They're codenamed from Korean mythology. South is the *Red Phoenix*, a complex plan to strike Seoul and reunite the Koreas. This is the scenario for which we've spent most effort devising defensive strategies. Though in all honesty, nothing we've worked out will prevent significant destruction in Seoul, given its proximity."

Kaminski paused to see if Vaccaro had any questions.

"Please, continue," she said.

"The *Red Phoenix* is basically a ground assault, primarily tanks and infantry supported by artillery units and fighter jets designed to overwhelm defenses south of the DMZ before razing across Seoul in Blitzkrieg fashion. Pyongyang's belief is that once Seoul falls, the rest of the country will capitulate, plus we would be in a difficult position trying to root them out of the capital without incurring significant civilian casualties. But there's a strike package designed for its eastern war theater, meaning Japan and anyone stepping up to its defense, namely us. It's called the *Azure Dragon*, and unlike the *Red Phoenix*, we believe it would be primarily an air assault, a combination of missiles and air strikes."

"To what end? Terror?" Vaccaro asked. North Korea could never invade Japan. The KPA Navy was considered a "brown water navy" meaning its fleet was designed to operate near coastal waters, mainly within its 30-mile exclusion zone.

Kaminski grimaced. "I'm afraid so, Madam President. And that's what we think was the intent of yesterday's air skirmish: testing our defenses in preparation for a large air assault."

"When?"

Kaminski bit his lower lip, then said, "*Technically*, I believe they could launch it at any time. We've seen how much they've improved their rocket technology over the past decade, and yesterday we got a look at their advanced fighter jets. But whether or not they'll pull the trigger falls outside the scope of this briefing."

One of the things she admired about Kaminski—and a key reason she appointed him to the job—was the secretary's keeping strictly to what he knew: military matters, staying clear of all politics, foreign or domestic.

"Where do we stand on our defenses against this . . . *Azure Dragon?*"

"We have over fifty thousand military personnel stationed in Japan, including the Seventh Fleet based in Yokosuka and the Third Marine Expeditionary Force in Okinawa. Between our airbases at Misawa in Aomori, Yokota in Western Tokyo, and Kadena in Okinawa, we have over two hundred fighter jets—a combination of F-22 Raptors, F-16 Falcons, and a squadron of the new generation of stealth fighters, the F-35B Lightning. In addition, *Ronald Reagan* is in the Sea of Japan with four squadrons of Super Hornets and a handful of Lightnings. And on top of that, we have joint-trained with the Japan Self-Defense Air Force, which has a large inventory of F-15E Strike Eagles and F-35As."

"Is that enough?"

"I believe so . . . barring any intervention from China. There are over a dozen air bases in the Nanjing Military Region around Shanghai, most of which are within striking distance of our bases in Japan. The PLA Air Force is, of course, armed with the latest fighter jets, including their new Chengdu J-20, a stealth multirole fighter designed to combat our F-22s and F-35 stealth fighters. Plus, we have intelligence that China has purchased over fifty of the advanced Sukhoi-57s, Russia's most advanced single seat fifth-generation fighter with stealth capabilities matching those of the F-35."

Vaccaro frowned. She hoped that in her upcoming conversation Xi Jinping would prevent the situation from degrading into a multi-country armed conflict.

"Anything else?"

"Yes. There's another . . . development."

"Development?"

"Yes, Madam President, in Russia."

Vaccaro motioned for him to continue.

"As you know, there are half a dozen Russian bases in the region, near their border with North Korea," he said, pointing at the TV screen. "That includes Chuguyevka and Uglovoye Air Bases, both near Vladivostok, where they keep a few squadrons of Sukhoi-35s and also MiG-29s. But in the past twenty-four hours, our high-assets

assets—Global Hawks and Tritons—spotted a squadron of Sukhoi-57s landing at Chuguyevka, and a squadron of the new MiG-35s at Uglovoye. For a short while yesterday, we even thought that four of the Sukhois dancing with our Super Hornets might have come from one of those bases, but it turned out to be the North Koreans circling in to make us think that."

"How did we figure it out?"

"Visual markings, but one of the Tritons confirmed it."

The Northrop Grumman RQ-4 Global Hawk was an advanced unmanned surveillance drone capable of flying at altitudes of up to 60,000 feet with a range of over 14,000 miles. The Triton basically built on the Global Hawk technology with deicing systems for its wings plus lightning protection, essentially turning the Triton into an all-weather surveillance platform capable of operating in storms.

Kaminski added, "The thing to remember about Russia is that it keeps most of its fifth-generation fighter jets closer to Moscow, so we can only interpret the move as Moscow flexing its muscles in light of the crisis."

"But, so far they haven't scrambled them?"

"No, Madam President."

She stared at *The Peacemakers*, the 1868 painting by George P.A. Healy. In it, President Abraham Lincoln conferred with General Ulysses S. Grant, General William T. Sherman, and Admiral David D. Porter aboard the steamer *River Queen* during the final days of the Civil War.

Vaccaro had the painting returned from the Oval Office Dining Room, where the previous administration moved it. With that exception, it had hung in the Treaty Room since the Kennedy Administration.

She often wondered the level of visceral strength, the utter determination and resilience that Lincoln must have had to get through that unique and terrible war. Never before—or after—did Americans fight Americans, tearing the country apart in so many bloody encounters over so many years.

The nation actually emerged whole, and in a short time was stronger than ever, cementing the people's belief in the Constitution.

As a whole, Vaccaro thought that America had emerged stronger after the New York attack a year ago, but she wondered how it would fare after this crisis, as competing superpowers, namely China and Russia, took advantage of the situation to further their own agendas.

"Keep a close eye on the North Koreans, but a *closer* eye on the Chinese *and* the Russians, okay?"

"Yes, Madam President."

When Kaminski left the room, Vaccaro got up to look at the other painting in the Treaty Room: Aaron Shikler's official portrait of President John F. Kennedy.

She admired the somber artwork commissioned by Jacqueline Kennedy after his assassination. JFK had his arms folded and eyes down, clearly deep in thought about some dark global event, perhaps the Cuban Missile Crisis or the onset of the Vietnam War.

Vaccaro was dealing with a crisis that had elements of both.

"What would you do, John?" Vaccaro asked the portrait.

"Do what, Madam President?"

Vaccaro managed not to jump. She turned around to see John Wright and Lisa Jacobson, each holding a tablet computer.

Vaccaro checked her watch. "When am I speaking with President Jinping?"

"Ambassador Kwan scheduled it four hours from now," Wright replied.

"And Putin?"

"Right after Jinping."

Vaccaro felt as if she was struggling to remain afloat, playing the reactionary game. She needed to get in front of this freight train, to make North Korea—and even China and Russia—react to her. But to even have a sense of how to go about achieving that, she, at a minimum, had to speak directly to Jinping and to Putin, and make an assessment of where their heads were.

And every minute that passed was another minute closer to North Korea doing something stupid again.

Or even stupider.

Wright and Jacobson stood to execute her orders, and their phones dinged simultaneously.

"Oh, damn," Wright said, staring at his screen. Jacobson pressed a palm against her forehead.

"What is it now?" Vaccaro said.

Wright replied, "The DHS task force down in Eagle Pass . . . we've lost contact with them."

"How?"

"Unclear," Jacobson replied.

"Is that why Stark called screaming an hour ago?" Jacobson asked.

"Yeah," Wright said, "and also because the hardware he requested hadn't—"

"Stark called *screaming* and I *wasn't* notified? What the hell, guys?"

"Madam President," Wright said, "you were tied up in the Situation Room with—"

"Goddammit."

Vaccaro counted to ten, her eyes returning to the portrait of Lincoln, whom she considered the master of the art of patience.

"Look," she began. "The whole point of me risking getting impeached by the likes of McDonald is to gather actionable intel quickly and then act on it even faster. And you two are my eyes and ears, and I do not expect to be uninformed ever again. Is that clear, John? Lisa?"

"Yes, Madam President," they replied in unison.

"Where is Stark now?"

"His gear was just delivered to Dallas," Wright replied. "Took a while to source *everything* on his list."

"Why? Don't we have at least a dozen bases in Texas?"

"Yeah . . . it's just Stark was being . . . well, Stark. Requesting serious hardware."

"Like I told you, John, *anything* he needs."

"Yes, Madam President."

"Are they headed to Eagle Pass now?"

"Yes, ma'am," said Jacobson.

"And the situation in Karachi?"

"Gorman managed to move Blue Team from SEAL Team Six, who were operating in Afghanistan, into the target area. They're going in within the hour."

"Good. Very good. Now, get me the Secretary of Homeland Security on the horn," she said. "Let's figure out what the hell happened to his task force down there."

The silence from the DHS task force could only mean they were compromised. For a moment, she wondered if the DHS's attempt to collaborate with Mexican authorities had backfired, as it had in Monterrey a year ago.

The president hoped—no, *prayed*—that China and Russia would be able to temper North Korea's impetuousness until Stark's team was able to gather the proof required to vindicate Japan and the United States.

She had to follow the example of JFK during those thirteen days of the Cuban Missile Crisis, when the world came so damn close to a global nuclear war.

There comes a time where strength is demonstrated through restraint, not by foolish shows of force.

But Vaccaro had a feeling that Pyongyang was just getting warmed up.

CHAPTER 37
CEP

PANGHYON AIRFIELD. PYONGAN PROVINCE, NORTH KOREA

In the predawn hours, Major General Mina Kyong-Lee observed the convoy of ten Astrolog transporter-erector-launcher 8x8 trucks from the KPA's missile brigade driving out of their vast underground housing and onto the airfield's main ramp.

Each of the long Russian-made vehicles carried a single 9K720 Iskander-NK short-range ballistic missile capable of climbing up to 80 miles to reach targets as far as 700 nautical miles with a circular error probability (CEP) of 100 feet. That meant that 50% of the targeted missiles would fall within fifty feet of the target, 43.7% within a hundred feet of the target, and the balance within three hundred feet of the bull's eye.

The "NK" was the version improved by North Korean scientists, based on a single shorter-range Iskander-E secretly borrowed from the Armenian government—improvements that her *Samchon* had confided were in part the result of her sister's covert work in America.

One by one, the trucks turned to face the eastern horizon and stopped, lifting their individual 24-foot-long missiles into the launch position.

The road-mobile Iskander was the brainchild of rocket designer Sergey Nepobedimy of the Russian Federation, who were prohibited from exporting it under the Collective Security Treaty Organization. But in 2016, Armenia, a Russian ally and member of the CSTO, became the first foreign country to operate it. And after secret negotiations between the late Kim Jong-un and the Armenian president, an agreement was reached in the spring of 2017 to loan one of its

Iskander-Es to North Korea for a period of one year. In that time, North Korean scientists were able to reproduce the missile and even improve it.

Her nation's NK version could be fitted with a variety of warheads, including high explosive and fragmentation for infantry units, penetration to go after bunkers or ships, or EMP, to disable the enemy's electronics in a fifty-mile radius, and last but not least, a single 50-kiloton thermonuclear bomb.

Mina continued supervising the ordnance for another hour, until she was satisfied that each Sukhoi carried the weapons required for this initial phase of the *Azure Dragon*.

She began the exterior preflight of her own Sukhoi. The other seven pilots in her squadron did the same, including her wingman, Major Byung Ko.

Her new rank and position gave her the option to coordinate the strike from the safety of the base's bunker-like operations center, like her predecessor. But unlike General Yuhn, now buried in an unmarked grave behind the airfield, Mia was qualified to lead her squadron into combat. And given the critical role her Sukhois played in the first phase of the *Azure Dragon*, she could not conceive delegating this morning's mission to a less experienced pilot.

And besides, Mina was a disciple of the teachings of Sun Tzu, who believed that the best leaders were those who led from the front lines.

She checked her watch and gave the cloudy skies to the west a concerned look. The breeze from the Sea of Japan was picking up strength, tossing the airfield windsock around, a warning of windshear—when the wind's direction and speed change rapidly, making it difficult for pilots to take off and land. Windshear was also an indication of turbulence up in the flight levels as well as the likelihood of rough seas.

Deciding that days like today were *precisely* why the engineers at Sukhoi Aircraft called the Su-35 model an all-weather air superiority fighter, she climbed inside her cockpit, settled behind the controls, and continued her preflight. Thirty minutes later, Mina fired up the dual Saturn turbofans.

But as she scanned her flight instruments and verified that all was nominal, including full tanks, Mina once more glanced at the grey skies as a single thought entered her mind: even at the command of this advanced jet, it still looked like a lousy day to fly.

CHAPTER 38
A Beautiful Day in the Neighborhood

USS RONALD REAGAN (CVN-76).
THE SEA OF JAPAN

What a lousy day to fly.

Commander Demetrius sat in the cockpit of his F/A-18E Super Hornet as the massive carrier bounced in the angry seas. Powerful swells crashed against the hull in explosions that spewed surf and mist across the flight deck.

At least he was safely tucked inside a 50,000-pound jet, unlike the helmeted flight deck crews in their duty-specific, different colored jerseys fighting the elements head on.

Under normal conditions, all aircraft would have been secured in the cavernous hangars belowdecks until the storm pounding this corner of the world abated.

But the situation was far from normal.

Being at DEFCON 2, combined with yesterday's close encounters with the North Koreans, had everyone aboard on edge. It kept all twelve of the Dambusters' Super Hornets flying constant sorties—as were the other three Super Hornet squadrons, the Eagles (VFA-115), the Diamondbacks (VFA-102) and the Royal Maces (VFA-27).

Demetrius didn't like it because the storm added another degree of danger to the already dangerous process of launching and recovering aircraft. But he understood it and accepted it.

Swirls of steam rising from the twin bow catapults—Cat I and Cat II—joined the spray, creating a ghostly scene as crewmembers darted about preparing for an upcoming launch.

A helmeted figure emerged through the haze to secure his jet's nosewheel launch bar to the Cat I shuttle. Another crewmember did the same to Gonzales' jet, linking him to Cat II. They were getting ready to relieve two Super Hornets from the Diamondbacks currently flying BARCAP-1 a hundred miles to the east.

Captain O'Donnell, after his meeting with the squadron commanders, ordered four Barrier Combat Air Patrols, spaced 50 nautical miles apart along a two-hundred-mile imaginary line a hundred miles off the coast of North Korea. The intention was to give the *Ronald Reagan* carrier task force a little more room to maneuver, currently cruising 220 miles from the coast.

In addition to adding another 240 miles to the BARCAP missions, eight Super Hornets had to be in the air at all times, in three-hour shifts.

As his two-plane section was readied to be catapulted off the bow, a pair of Super Hornets belonging to the Royal Maces taxied up to the jet blast deflectors already raised behind Demetrius and Gonzales.

The yellow-jerseyed flight director signaled Demetrius to increase power.

He advanced the throttles to the military setting, moving his flight controls for continuity. The jet blast deflectors redirected the dual scorching plumes from his engines skyward, and most importantly, away from the F/A-18E and the flight deck personnel staged behind him.

Giving his control panel a final scan, Demetrius flicked on his external lights, signaling the catapult officer, who also wore a yellow jersey, that he was ready.

The cat officer, vapor wisps lazily curling about him, looked left, then right, dropped to a deep crouch and gave the forward signal to release the catapult.

Demetrius selected the afterburner setting for both engines just as the sudden acceleration pinned him into his ejection seat.

The immense force of the catapult nearly took his breath away. The Super Hornet, a frightful beast with slippery gray skin, violently agitated this milky-white, surreal world, hurtling to 150 knots in two seconds, tearing through the stormy skies.

Ignoring the scene outside, intent on his instruments, Demetrius throttled back to the military setting, killing the afterburners when he achieved a positive rate of climb over the dark swells and raised the landing gear.

He inched back the control column and climbed into the zero-zero visibility inside the thick blanket of clouds at eight hundred feet.

"*Coming up to you, Jade,*" Gonzales reported as he shot off Cat II five seconds behind him.

Demetrius keyed his mic twice.

"*Dambusters Three-Oh-Three, Torchbearer Five-Six,*" came the voice from the Advanced Hawkeye controller. "*Zero niner five on the nose. Climb and maintain flight level two one. Tops at one seven.*"

"Zero niner for two one," Demetrius replied, turning the jet to the prescribed easterly heading and shooting up to 21,000 feet.

He broke out of the clouds at 17,000, as predicted by the controller, and continued climbing into a pristine morning, a sharp contrast with the greyish muck he'd just slogged through.

The sun was breaking on the eastern horizon, staining the irregular and undulating cloud surface with deep hues of burnt orange and blood red, making it look like an alien landscape.

"*Damn, Jade,*" Gonzales commented, settling behind his right wingtip. "*This is something.*"

"Yeah, it's something alright," he said, leveling at 21,000 feet and holding their assigned heading for another ten minutes, listening to the Advanced Hawkeye vectoring the current BARCAP-1 jets to the tanker.

"Speedy, let's go to max conserve," Demetrius said.

"I'm going to pull away a little," Gonzales replied, easing his jet a hundred feet off Demetrious' starboard wing. "Relax a bit."

"Don't go catching any Z's on my watch," Demetrius warned.

He glanced at the picture of Ghalia and Jasmine in his cockpit, and he recalled the short Skype conversation he'd had with her a few hours ago.

"Wotcher, love. How're you holding up?" Ghalia had asked, staring into the camera with those incredible green eyes under eyebrows that evoked images of Actress Brooke Shields.

"Hanging in there, baby," he had replied. "You?"

Her well-formed mouth twisted in a scowl. "Day by day. This place is better than Qatar, but not by much. I still get the occasional *look*, even with the decoy wedding band."

"As soon as I can get away, I promise. I'll get you an official ring, marry you, and bring you both home."

"I know, love. I know. Still, it's hard. And I miss you."

Demetrius had forced his best possible smile even though he just wanted to scream at this quite ill-timed and quite nasty little war getting in the way of his personal life.

"I miss you too. How's my baby girl?"

Ghalia had run a hand through her tousled brown hair. "Asleep. Finally. Little bugger's quite the bloody fighter, like his father. She definitely has your eyes and *not* my hair." She wound a lock of hair around her index finger.

He chuckled at that, but Gonzales' words had echoed in his mind.

There must have been at least a couple thousand American swinging dicks with blond hair and blue eyes that week in Qatar. Pretty good chance someone else boned her.

Demetrius pushed the thought away and said, "Soon, baby. Trust me."

"I know," she replied, covering a yawn with her hand.

"Soon and I'll—"

A cry had made Ghalia turn to her right and frown. She muttered, "Bollocks. Here we go again." Then she said, "Gotta run, love. Feeding time. Cheerio," blew a kiss at him, and terminated the call.

For the first time ever, Demetrius began to wonder if he was getting too old for this.

CHAPTER 39
Tunnel Rats

EAGLE PASS, SOUTH TEXAS

I'm getting too old for this shit, Colonel Stark thought. He had Danny Martin set their Black Hawk two miles from the main house, at a spot Monica had indicated would lead to a hill with a great vantage point to search for threats.

At his request, law enforcement had formed a three-mile cordon around the kill zone just east of them, where the two Black Hawk wrecks still burned, presumably shot down by more of those damned surface-to-air missiles. A single emergency team had been allowed in but had reported no survivors.

Stark jumped out first, followed by Monica and Naree, then Juan Vazquez and Ryan.

They moved single file. Stark, Monica, and Naree were armed with MP7SDs; Vazquez had opted for an M249 Squad Automatic Weapon, or SAW, a machine gun not as powerful as the .50-caliber Chief Larson hauled around, but still with plenty of bite. And Ryan had his big Barrett. Everyone was equipped with assorted grenades, back-up pistols, MBITR radios, body armor, throat mics, and helmets with integrated earphones.

Danny stayed with the helo.

They trotted at a pretty good clip for almost two miles. Toward the final stretch, Stark started feeling his fifty-four years, but he sucked it up and stayed with the team.

At the bottom of the hill, he said, "These are your stomping grounds, Cruz. Get up there and take Romeo with you. You're on spotting duty." Stark produced a Leupold M151 spotting scope from his rucksack and handed it to Monica.

She took the gadget and gave it the once over, nodding.

"And no screwing around up there, guys. Keep your minds in the game and your hands to yourselves."

"Seriously, Colonel?" Monica said. Ryan grinned.

"Yeah, very fucking seriously. Now, scram."

Monica mumbled something Stark couldn't make out and scrambled up the hill with Ryan behind her, hauling his Barrett and a rucksack of .50-caliber ammunition.

Turning to Juan, Stark pointed to a rocky outcrop on the right side of the hill and added, "I want that SAW up on that ridge and—"

"Something I need to know?" Juan interrupted, stretching a thumb over his shoulder toward Monica and Ryan.

"Yeah," Stark said, "I need some goddamned covering fire. Go, soldier."

Juan took off in a hurry.

"And you," he told Naree, "with me. We're going around the hill."

"No lecture for me, *Shiraki*?" she said, giving him a sidelong look, her eyes gleaming with bold intelligence, and something Stark didn't want to think about.

So, he ignored her and took off, down a trail that wound around the hill. Monica and Ryan had already crested it like a pair of damn mountain goats, and Juan was two thirds of the way up the next ridge.

Damn young guys, he thought just as Naree passed him.

Looking over her shoulder, she said, "Keep up, *Shiraki*."

"Stop . . . calling me . . . that," he said, kicking harder to stay with the nimble North Korean.

"You didn't mind it so much back then," she said.

"That's right, *back then*."

"It wasn't personal. I had a job and so did you. And I'd have to admit, you did it better than me."

Stark didn't respond, saving his breath to maintain pace, keeping his eyes and his MP7SD on the trail.

"And for what it's worth," she added, "I did enjoy the time we spent together."

"Sure, you were pumping me . . . for intel."

"Among other things."

Stark stopped. "Goddammit, Naree, do you think this is a fucking game?"

She stopped and turned around.

"*Shiraki*," she said. "My Supreme Leader was assassinated, along with his wife, sister, and key members of his inner circle. Right now, my nation is of the belief that this was the doing of Japan with *your* help. Unless *I* am convinced otherwise, *they* will not be convinced otherwise, and I hope you know what that would mean. At the moment, all I've *heard* is that your CIA *heard* from some Mexican whore who *heard* from some cartel men talking that their boss might be behind this. The word of a hooker relayed to me by an agency that lies for a living is hardly proof, is it?"

Stark studied her and said, "Then let's go get you the proof you need."

They continued in silence for another five minutes, slowing down as they approached the final bend before the clearing and the main house.

Glad to be taking a knee, Stark inhaled deeply through his nostrils and exhaled slowly through parted lips, inspecting the picture ahead. He spotted a Maverick County Sheriff's Department cruiser next to a black Jeep wrangler, as well as the bodies of two uniformed deputies and three FBI forensics technicians.

"Looks clear," Naree said.

Stark spoke in his throat mic. "Romeo? Juan? How are we looking?"

"All clear up here, colonel," Ryan replied.

"*Ditto,*" Juan reported over the squadron frequency.

Monica surveyed the grounds through the M151, which had a much wider viewing angle than the sniper scope on Ryan's Barrett.

They lay side by side under an early afternoon sun, spotter and sniper, immersed in their respective duties.

"So, this is home, huh?" Ryan said.

"Yep," she replied, panning over her house. "Home-sweet-fucking-home."

"Very sorry about your brothers."

Monica shook her head, not wanting to think about that.

"I meant to call," he said.

"Fuck off, Ryan. You're a piece of shit."

"Hold on there, little lady," he said. "You're the one who took off without saying goodbye."

Monica raised her right eyebrow but said nothing.

She did leave, and quickly, right after terminating the last terrorist outside Washington D.C.

At the time, Monica had had enough of the violence and had wanted nothing more than to put as much distance from her former life as she could. And Ryan, as attracted as she was to him, represented that life she so desperately wanted to leave behind.

But still, a part of her wished that he had wanted to leave that life and follow her here, to this desolate, but, at least as of yesterday, peaceful corner of the world. But Ryan being Ryan, had chosen to remain with Stark doing what she no longer wanted to do.

Now, she wondered if she had made a paramount mistake by walking away, bringing home the very violence she had sought to escape.

And in spite of her better judgment, especially given Stark's parting words, Monica said, "I think . . . I think it's my fault they're dead."

"What are you talking about?" he asked, glancing at her then resuming his watch.

"My brothers . . ."

He scooted closer to her and put his hand on her shoulder, giving it a soft squeeze, sympathy in his green eyes.

"The way I see it," he said, "There was nothing anyone could have done to prevent what happened. The cartel was going to dig that tunnel whether you were here or up in D.C. doing the FBI thing or with us doing Stark's thing."

"This ranch has been in my family for three generations, and there was never a problem. Ever. I'm here for less than a year and everyone is killed. Until we get to the bottom of what happened, it's hard for me not to assume that—"

"Don't," he said, moving the hand from her shoulder to the side of her face, and she briefly closed her eyes at his touch. "This isn't on you," he added. "Okay?"

Monica wanted to believe that more than anything.

Unfortunately, two decades of law enforcement had taught her that there were no coincidences. And until she could unravel what was happening, she couldn't discard the possibility that her being at the ranch had something to do with the cartel being here; she'd killed so many of them in Monterrey.

This had to be connected.

Somehow.

Monica chose to kill whatever it was that was starting to happen. "You heard the Colonel. Let's stick to business."

"That's my girl."

"Fuck you," she replied, pressing her right eye against the rubber cup of the spotting scope. "I'm not your goddamned girl. And you're still a piece of shit for not—"

Distant shots echoed from the direction of the border.

"That can't be good," Ryan said.

"No shit," she replied.

"You're hearing that?" Stark asked.

"Ah, affirmative," Ryan replied.

"Yep," Juan concurred. *"Shit's definitely going down beyond the wall."*

Well, *Shiraki*? You needed proof? That just might be it."

Multiple reports echoed from the shaft, a macabre, unharmonious musical tempo.

Stark let go of the breath he had been holding, certainly not relishing the thought of walking into a firefight. That hadn't worked out for the FBI continent, they were burned to a crisp under the hot Texas sun.

But she was right. They weren't going to find anything staying put, so he moved out, leading the two-person stack. Naree handled their left flank. Their right flank and rear were being covered by his team on the hill.

They reached the dead deputies behind the cruiser. "Not much of a fight here," Naree said.

"More of an execution," Stark agreed, noting the headshots from a small-caliber gun.

At the tunnel mouth, Naree crouched next to the FBI techs.

"More headshots. Small caliber . . . I think a twenty-two," she said.

"Yeah."

"Looks like not just North Koreans hate your FBI."

"Yeah," Stark repeated, studying the spent launcher tubes.

Naree joined him. "Same kind used in Dallas. Japanese."

"Well, that should tell you something, right? It makes no sense that we would take out two helicopters packed with American federal agents and National Guardsmen. It makes no sense at all."

"*Shiraki*," she said, looking up into his eyes and touching his cheek. Something inside him stirred at her touch, and he didn't resist as it reminded him of their time in Seoul.

"This proves *nothing*," she continued. "And besides, George W. Bush was *not* the first president Americans tried to kill, yes? The list of assassination attempts is very long, almost every single one of your presidents. And there is the shorter list of successful assassinations, including John F. Kennedy, which allowed America to start the Vietnam War, yes? And as far as sacrificing Americans, how many did George W. Bush kill staging the attacks on your World Trade Center to have an excuse to attack Afghanistan and Iraq, yes?"

Oh boy.

"This could be the same. A reason manufactured to give you a reason to attack North Korea. No. I need irrefutable proof, *Shiraki*. Not this. And we're running out of time."

Stark sighed. There was no fast way to undo the indoctrination. She believed the warped version of history she was taught in that communist regime. So, he would pursue the one thing that would convince her: proof that the Mexican cartel was behind the attack in collusion with the *Yakuza* and al-Qaeda.

He reconnoitered the tunnel mouth and found it quiet now. Naree picked up another one of the spent missile launchers.

And that's when he spotted movement—a shadowy figure shifting from behind a pile of rubble.

The figure swung an AK-47 toward them, catching Stark with his weapon down and Naree still holding the missile launcher.

Stark reacted instinctively, throwing his body in front of Naree and firing his MP7SD at the silhouette, who returned fire, the muzzle flashes lighting up the tunnel like a strobe, punctuated by the amplified reports bouncing off the walls.

The shooter went down from a head shot with a final volley that carved a track on the roof of the cave.

But one of his rounds punched Stark's center mass when he dove in front of Naree.

The 7.62mm slug struck the titanium plate over his sternum. The plate did its job, stopping the slug and dispersing its energy across his chest.

But it felt like the devil himself punched him with supernatural might, knocking the wind out of him and shocking him to his core, ramming him against the wall of the tunnel. Hard.

Naree was on top of Stark before he even realized what had happened.

"*Shiraki!*" she shouted, straddling him. He lay there with his mouth gaping, resembling a fish out of water. "Breathe!"

But it became evident very quickly that he was in shock, unable to draw a breath. Possibly with collapsed lungs from the force of the bullet. His eyes were vacant.

She pulled open his vest and verified that the bullet had been stopped by the body armor. She got back in his face, trying to get him to look at her.

"Goddammit! Breathe!"

She slapped him. Nothing.

Naree took a deep breath, and, leaning down, she pinched his nostrils closed and locked her lips over his. Exhaling hard, she forced air inside his lungs.

It only took one strong breath, and Stark started coughing.

She straightened, still straddling him, a hand on his shoulder, the other on the side of his face. He coughed, gasped, and coughed again.

"That's it, baby . . . *breathe*," she said as his chest expanded and contracted. "Good. Now, look at me. Look at me!"

He looked up at her, still dazed but aware of his surroundings.

"Hey," he said. "You . . . okay?"

"Goddammit, *Shiraki*," she whispered, cupping his face. "Of course, I am okay! Yes!" Then she leaned down and kissed his cheek, her hands on his chest.

Stark wrapped his arms around her, and for a moment he was transported to that hotel room in Seoul a lifetime ago.

His chest was on fire, and so was his head, even his mind, but somehow, he managed the energy to embrace her, acknowledging just how much he had missed this damn woman, even if it was wrong to feel that way.

However beautiful, Naree was the enemy, a devil in angel's skin. She had tricked him in Seoul, humiliated him, and yet, he had thrown himself in harm's way to protect her.

"Thank you," she whispered in his ear. "Thank you for—"

"You two need to get a goddamned room," Monica said from the entrance of the tunnel. "What the fuck?"

Naree got off of him, looking furtively at Monica, then at Stark.

"And you were lecturing *me?*"

"He got shot," Naree said. Stark sat up and took another deep breath. "By that asshole over there." She pointed at the dead lookout the cartel left behind.

Stark got onto one knee, then stood, running a hand under his body armor to massage his chest. Flinching at the sharp pain, he gingerly used his fingertips to make sure nothing was broken.

"You abandoned your post," Stark said to Monica, walking over to inspect the man who had managed to sneak up on them.

"Yeah, well," Monica replied, "we heard the shots and you didn't reply, so Ryan stayed up there, and I came running to check on you two . . . lovebirds."

"That's enough, Cruz."

His earpiece was dangling from a coiled wire down his chest. Frowning, he plugged it back into his right ear.

He tapped his throat mic and said, "Alright, everybody, looks like someone punched a hole through the debris in the tunnel Cruz had collapsed."

"*No shit?*" Ryan replied through the squadron frequency. *That quick?*

"Apparently. Get your butt down here, Romeo," Stark said. "You too, Danny and Juan." Stark peered into the darkness of the tunnel and added, "And we'll need goggles."

"*Roger that, Colonel. On my way,*" Danny said.

"*Ditto,*" Juan replied.

"*Be right down,*" Ryan said.

The whop-whop sound of the Black Hawk helicopter started in the distance. Stark turned to Naree. "You know what a tunnel rat is?"

"A tunnel rat, my sweet *Shiraki?*" she said, with the devilish smile that took him back to those nights he'd tried so damn hard to forget. "How do you think we get across the DMZ?"

CHAPTER 40
Pacific Sun

"A simple plan, violently executed, always beats the shit out of a complicated plan conceived by some asshole who wouldn't be there when his plan was executed."
—USN Chief Special Warfare Operator (SEAL) Scott Kelly.

KARACHI, PAKISTAN

To the uninitiated, the seaport resembled a massive traffic jam.

Hundreds of the most obnoxiously-painted midsize trucks you could ever imagine in colors only a drug-addled brain could have conceived, adorned with bells and beads, lined up on the approaching road.

As your eyes adjusted to this psychedelic parking lot, they began to water from the fumes and oil permeating the air like a living thing.

And as you drove deeper into the port, the volume of shipping containers staggered the mind, projecting as far as the eye can see. They were all under an army of cranes moving them around between trucks and ships with a speed and certainty that drove home the point that this was not only a major seaport, but one that thrived on organized chaos.

Chief Kelly, Gorman, and Harwich along with the Blue Team studied a mockup of the port that the team planned to hit. The SOG team remained outside the warehouse, providing security.

Mockups could be as simple as sandbags, tables, maps or pictures, or even chess pieces. The rehearsal was to ensure that everyone involved in the mission from operator, to truck drivers, to intel providers—every goddamn body—knew the plan and their part in it.

The drill was where the what-if questions got asked. For this one, the short prep and the paucity of intelligence would ordinarily have caused Chief Kelly to say, "Hell no." But with this mission, the future of the world was truly at stake.

So, fuck everything else.

The worst part of these types of ops was the presence of the local police or military, or both, during the assault. No one in the world was better trained to do a takedown of a vessel than SEAL Team Six, but they still needed a little elbow room to operate.

So, the decision was made to use the local police to shut down access to the target pier, accomplished by having a SEAL operator stage an accident near the entrance.

Once the assault was completed, Gorman, Harwich and their SOG team, which doubled as the site exploitation experts, would come aboard, verify the missile count claimed by their source, and take charge of any and all evidence.

Kelly did not envy the CIA's clean up job. If their intel was accurate, there were north of 250 missiles on the ship plus all the computers, cell phones, and hard drives that had to be recovered and scrubbed for intel.

The plan called for Kelly to secure the cargo until Gorman and Harwich took over.

"Guys, we need to be gone once we secure the site," Kelly said. "I'll need four minutes to do my thing, max, leaving you no more than another four or five to do yours. After that, well . . ."

"Chief, our speedboats will pull up to the pier and we'll be done in half that time," Gorman replied. "Then we're on the jet to Qatar and you guys are on your way back to—"

Gorman's secure sat phone vibrated with the White House code.

Frowning, he answered. "Yes?"

"Sir, this is Jason Savage from Miss Jacobson's staff. I've been hired and read onto your program, and I'm calling to inform you that we have a Global Hawk in orbit for your use for the next two hours, should you need it. I've sent the feed to your location."

Gorman narrowed his eyes and said, "Savage, if that's is your real name, I will personally skin you alive if this is a bullshit call. If it's real, I'll buy you a bottle of the best whatever-you-drink when I'm in town next."

"That'd be Qatar," Savage replied. "In . . . four hours?"

"Excuse me? How the fuck do you know—"

"Like I said, sir, I've been read onto your—"

"I heard you the first time," Gorman said and hung up.

"Problem?" Kelly asked.

"Not really . . . we just got some unsolicited support from the NSA—a Global Hawk. So, we're not totally fucked on this op."

"You know, guys," Kelly smiled as he left the hangar. "When it's done, no pictures or autographs."

A simple plan, well and violently executed, always beat the shit out of a complicated plan conceived by some asshole who wouldn't be there when *his* plan was executed.

One of the reasons SEAL Team Six had earned its reputation as being the very best in the world at what it did was because it *only* executed its own plans, never someone else's.

The *Pacific Sun* was a 300-foot tanker transporting oil within the sea borders of Thailand. It was built and owned by the Thai Army but flagged out of Panama.

It currently occupied one of the docks at the end of Creek Road Pier in Korangi, a suburb east of downtown Karachi and south of the Jinnah International Airport, where two Agency jets were currently parked at a private hangar.

The ship's relatively small size and current location made the takedown planning much easier.

Kelly, staged with his team behind a colorful truck fifty feet from the gangway, checked his G-shock watch, then the small phone displaying the infrared view from the Global Hawk Gorman had somehow secured.

The time was 0425 hours, and as he had hoped, the port was quiet. No crane activity. No trucks loading or unloading. No ships moving about. The port was shut down from 2:00 am until 6:00 am, when the morning shift arrived.

He put the phone away and spoke into his throat mic.

"You're up, Jimmy."

A quarter of a mile away, near the entrance to the pier, Seal Operator James "Jimmy" Johnson, from Wilmington North Carolina, steered a twelve-foot rowboat, stolen from a local merchant, into the narrow space between two merchant ships, and under the pier, stopping in the middle.

Wearing a set of night-vision goggles, Johnson inserted a fuse into five sticks of Semtex and connected it to a remote timer.

Then, quietly, he lowered a cinderblock anchor into the water and swam back to the end of the pier to join Kelly's team.

The time was 0430 hours.

Johnson climbed a rope ladder hanging from the pier and rolled onto the dock, took off his fins and diving mask, and secured them to his utility vest.

Removing the plastic wrapper from his sound-suppressed M4 carbine, he scrambled across the hundred feet separating him from his team.

He handed the remote control to Kelly, who patted him on the shoulder and pointed to the end of the line of SEAL operators huddled behind the truck.

Kelly tapped his throat mic twice, signaling to Gorman that the op was about to commence.

He received two clicks back, confirming the CIA contingent aboard two large speedboats were on their way from the staging area, a mile away.

Time: 0435 hours.

At precisely 0436 hours, Kelly pressed the button of the remote for five seconds and the rigged boat exploded beneath the front of the pier in a gaudy shaft of fire.

The blast twisted the metal and concrete substructure, ripping through the heavy wooden planks surfacing it, and took down two cranes, which toppled with a crash onto a half-dozen parked trucks.

Kelly got the tap on the shoulder—the team was ready—and he led them toward the *Pacific Sun*'s gangway.

SEALs practiced attacking ships countless times. They practiced taking down big ships, small ships, ships sitting still, ships moving—all of it.

They preferred to attack with every advantage, time-of-day or -night, superior weapons, speed of the assault, violence of the strike, and intimate knowledge of what and who they were hitting.

Kelly's team had limited intelligence on the *who* part of the equation and decided to use their speed and firepower to overwhelm and kill any and all obstructions.

The intelligence they did have indicated that there were a lot of very bad things on this tanker that needed to be stopped.

Now, *that* was a mission everyone could sign on to.

Chief Kelly, as any good leader would, led the stack, walking quickly, heel-to-toe, a sound-suppressed M4 carbine held firmly against his right shoulder, pointed ahead, and moving with his eyes.

SEAL Operator Johnson had shifted to the number two spot in the stack, covering Kelly from his right shoulder to approximately Johnson's three o'clock position. The next in line operator, Petty Officer Second Class Art Warren, pointed his light machine gun to Johnson's left. The remaining six operators covered the other angles, plus the rear, utilizing the same assault posture as those in front of them.

Moving as one, the stack dashed across the pier and up the gangway.

Kelly stepped onto the deck and was proceeding to the bulkhead just behind the bridge when a man dressed like a local and armed with an AK-47 stepped out, probably to see what the explosion was all about.

Kelly shot him twice, placing two 5.56mm rounds in the center of his chest, the bulky sound-suppressor absorbing the report.

The team followed Kelly in, stepping over the dead haji, except for Warren, who stayed behind to secure the approach to the bulkhead.

The time was 0439 hours.

Kelly threw two concussion grenades down the stairs, which, according to the intel, led to the ship's main storage area.

The flashbangs, set for two seconds from release to blow, allowed Kelly and his team to be on top of anyone at the receiving end of their brain-scrambling violence.

He waited for the two detonations before moving down the stairs, where six men crawled on the floor, their weapons scattered haphazardly around them.

Two had their hands over their ears. Three were screaming. One was trying to stand.

In three seconds, all were dead. Two shots to the chest and one to the head.

As his men dispersed to secure the area, Kelly tapped his throat mic and said, "Boston."

Time: 0441 hours.

"Here we go, Billy boy," Harwich whispered as he and Gorman jumped off the lead boat, clambered up the rope ladder and onto the pier, racing across to the gangway.

Gorman glanced up the long pier toward the fire and commotion. Distant sirens heralded emergency vehicles descending on this part of the port.

The sound brought back images from a year ago, when he and Maryam had narrowly escaped the ferocity unleashed upon this port city by President Vaccaro in retaliation for the New York strike.

At the bulkhead, he glanced at the SEAL operator guarding it, and trotted down the stairs, where he found Kelly and his crew standing over six dead men.

"Merry Christmas, Bill," Kelly said, pointing at the stacked hardware behind him and the small pile of laptops and phones gathered by the stairs.

Gorman checked his watch as the rest of the SOG team reached the storage area hauling large backpacks. "A little slow, Chief? About five minutes?"

Kelly checked his watch.

The SOG operators started opening cases. Some photographed missiles to record serial numbers, others began to set up their Semtex charges.

The plan called for blowing it in situ since it would be impossible to haul out that much hardware before half of Karachi's law enforcement descended on them.

"Four minutes and forty-two seconds, actually," Kelly informed him. "So yes, we'll have to work on it."

It took the SOG team less than two minutes to record the evidence and finish rigging the charges in their backpacks, nearly fifty pounds of Semtex—plenty to vaporize the missiles, but not so much as to seriously damage the adjacent vessels.

Gorman ordered four of the missiles hauled out, plus all of the tech gathered by Kelly's team.

"Two minutes . . . told ya," Gorman said, tapping his watch at Kelly.

The combined teams mustered out of the ship, down the rope ladder, and onto the waiting boats.

Gorman enjoyed the sea breeze and mist in his face as they accelerated back to their wharf. It was a beautiful night; the stars were out and the outboards drowned out the sirens from the emergency vehicles crowding the pier.

He turned to see the commotion and thought, *Here we go.*

He pressed a button on his phone and sent a text to the phone wired to the detonators in the Semtex.

Even from half a mile, the blast was impressive, dwarfing the smaller blast set by Johnson, and lighting up the surrounding bay, piers, and moored ships.

"Where's the girl?" Kelly asked.

"Back at the jet," Gorman replied. "This isn't her world."

"Ones and zeroes, huh?" Kelly said.

Gorman nodded. "Ones and zeroes."

"Well, you tell her that she—and the rest of you—saved lives today, Bill," Kelly said. "*American* lives."

"Thanks, Chief, but we were never here."

CHAPTER 41
Incoming

"What the hell are those, Jade?"
—USN Lieutenant Rolando "Speedy" Gonzales.

PANGHYON AIRFIELD. PYONGAN PROVINCE, NORTH KOREA

Mina gave the order and taxied her Sukhoi onto the runway, pushing the dual throttles to the forward stops.

As she gathered speed, she watched the synchronized ignition of the row of parked Iskander-NK missiles. Ten blazes cast a yellowish glow on the runway, reflecting on her canopy.

The missiles shot up into the cloudy skies on independent courses to targets in the Sea of Japan and beyond, identified by the base's radar operators tracking them.

"What the hell are those, Jade?"

Ten missiles broke through the cloud layer and streaked away, into the clear skies.

"Torchbearer Twenty, Dambusters Three-Oh-Three, are you seeing this shit?"

"Roger, Oh-Three. Already tracking them and . . . Dambusters we're showing two bandits at your ten o'clock, ninety miles climbing through seven thousand at Mach one point one—wait, make that four bandits—no

eight bandits. Repeat. Eight bandits in four pairs. Eighty miles through ten thousand holding Mach one point one."

"Roger. Eight bandits, eight zero at ten," Demetrius replied sounding much calmer than he felt.

"Dambusters, go starboard, heading zero-niner-zero."

"Niner-zero," Demetrius replied. "Speedy, let's go combat spread."

"Roger."

The Super Hornets turned toward the threat still somewhere in the clouds. But his eyes were drawn to the vertical contrails left by the ballistic missiles, already out of sight.

Concentrate on your part of this, Demetrius thought.

The controller in the Advanced Hawkeye vectored the other three pairs of fighters flying BARCAP.

Demetrius had to give Captain O'Donnell credit. By forcing the carrier air wing to fly so many simultaneous BARCAP missions, the CAG had given them a better than average chance of coming out of this in one piece.

He could only hope that the folks in charge of missile defenses were equally ready for the shitstorm headed their way.

Eight of the Iskander-NK missiles climbed to an altitude of thirty miles on a quasi-ballistic path, reaching the transitional speed of Mach 4, or four times the speed of sound. The other two surged through the stratosphere on a true parabolic ballistic path reaching the hyperspeed of Mach 6.

In the control center, radar operators tracked their moving targets in the Sea of Japan and used encrypted radio transmissions to manage the gas-dynamic control surfaces of the missiles to keep them on their assigned courses.

CHAPTER 42

Vampires

"Track 'em and splash 'em."
—USN Commander Joanna Watson.

USS ANTIETAM (CG-54). SEA OF JAPAN

On the bridge of the Ticonderoga-class guided-missile cruiser escorting *Ronald Reagan*, Commander Joanna Watson, the ship's executive officer, stood next to the phone she had just used to call her commanding officer.

Dressed in a Navy Working Uniform Type I, a pixelated grey and dark garment, Joanna took a deep breath, forcing her mind to remain focused.

The warning from Torchbearer Twenty had prompted her to place *Antietam* on general quarters, getting the operators of the multi-mission Aegis weapons systems to track the incoming missiles, or "vampires."

"There's ten of them, ma'am," one of the operators reported, Petty Officer Third Class Carla Martinez, her long fingers working the system's oversized keyboard.

Joanna leaned down to get a better look over Carla's shoulder as the radar operator used the mouse to draw a circle around the red dots on her screen.

"Ten?"

"Yes, ma'am. Confirmed."

Antietam cruised two miles east of the carrier, meaning it was a tad closer to the incoming vampires. But the carrier task force included two Arleigh-Burke guided-missile destroyers, USS *Ramage* (DDG-61) and

USS *Decatur* (DDG-73), currently three miles ahead of and behind *Ronald Reagan* respectively.

Unfortunately, the destroyers were armed to protect the carrier task force against low-flying cruise missiles, and enemy surface ships or submarines, not ballistic missiles dropping on them from the lower atmosphere.

"Track 'em and splash 'em," Joanna ordered.

Captain Jake Taylor, the commanding officer of *Antietam*, burst onto the bridge trailed by two junior officers. Taylor was a thin man with grayish hair who cut his teeth during Operation Iraqi freedom firing volley after volley of cruise missiles in support of the ground troops.

"Talk to me, JW."

"Skipper, we have ten ballistic vampires headed our way."

"Goddammit."

"Got missile lock on eight, but they're still not in range," Carla reported.

"Eight? What about the other—"

"Still climbing into the stratosphere. Too high to engage. One could still hit us. The other already overshot our position . . . looks like it's headed for the island."

"Stay on the eight plus one, JW," Taylor ordered, turning to a sailor manning a radio panel. "Get me Matsumo on the horn." General Isoruku Matsumo was the Chief of the Air Staff of the JASDF, the Japan Air Self-Defense Force.

Focus, she thought, letting Taylor and the Japanese worry about the last vampire while she handled the threat to the carrier group.

"Splash them when they're in range," Joanna ordered the operator.

"Yes, ma'am."

Although that was all good, Joanna was painfully aware of the probability of hitting a missile flying at twice the speed of a bullet *with* another bullet.

You got this.

"The first eight are in range," Carla reported as the incoming missiles dropped below the 20-mile ceiling of *Antietam*'s load of the RIM-174A Standard Extended Range Active Missile (ERAM).

"Cut them loose," she ordered.

She held her breath as twenty-one ERAMs blasted into the cloudy sky from their Vertical Launcher Tubes on solid-propellant boosters.

Twenty-one against eight, she thought. For an instant, their plumes rippled like sheet lightning across the base of the gray clouds.

Eight Iskander-NKs entered the terminal phase of their shallow flight, still slaved to encrypted radio transmissions from operators on the mainland.

Screaming up to meet them, the ERAMs second stages ignited, accelerating them to Mach 3.5.

"Five seconds to impact," Carla warned. "Ninth missile still in the stratosphere. Too high to engage."

Joanna felt tremendous pressure on her chest and realized she'd stopped breathing. Booms, like distant fireworks—the ERAMs proximity targets.

"Oh, shit," the operator reported.

Seven red dots disappeared, but the eighth one fell toward the carrier group at blinding speed.

It was all in the probability of matching ballistic trajectories. The ERAMs reached the Iskander-NKs at an altitude of fifteen miles with a closing velocity of nearly seven times the speed of sound.

It was over in a very loud and fiery second. The ERAMs' warheads detonated in overlapping circles of sizzling shrapnel intended to envelop the Iskander-NKs.

In theory, even lacking a direct hit, the fragmentation debris was supposed to damage an incoming missile enough to, at a minimum, knock it off course.

But one missile managed to pierce the barrier of high explosives with only surface damage and remained locked on its target.

In its final seconds of the terminal phase, the missile's onboard computers made minute adjustments plunging through the clouds, emerging a moment later below the base.

And that's when the targeting system transitioned from radar to its electro-optical guidance software with self-homing capability. In less than a thousandth of a second, the onboard computers locked onto the target, bobbing in the waves.

The 1200-pound bunker-buster warhead punched through the target, piercing four levels of the ship before its high-explosive warhead detonated.

"Oh, Dear God," Joanna breathed at the column of fire billowing northwest of their position. A few seconds later the shockwave rattled the armored glass windscreens of *Antietam*'s bridge.

"It hit *Decatur*," Carla reported.

As Joanna tried to process that, the operator added, "The other missile is beginning its descent."

"Engage when able," Joanna said.

"Tracking," Carla reported. "Forty miles high. Mach five point nine. It's headed for the center of the carrier group."

"The *Reagan*," Joanna whispered. "Fire at will."

"Missile lock," Carla replied, pressing a button on her console.

A moment later a volley of six missiles blasted into the morning sky.

Joanna held her breath once more when the green dots appeared on the radar screen and tracked toward the incoming missile.

"The tenth missile," Carla said. "It's dropping over—"

"Tokyo," Captain Taylor finished, joining her behind Carla, who was using Aegis to track the parallel trajectories overlaid on a map encompassing the carrier strike group and central Japan.

"Matsumo over at Iruma has the place on high alert already," Taylor said. The tenth missile on the screen was already cruising over land.

Iruma Air Base was a JSDAF military complex northwest of Tokyo, charged with defense of the capital, specifically missile defense, against attacks from North Korea. It was adjacent to Yokota Air Base, Headquarters, U.S. Forces, Japan. "They're getting ready to—"

Dozens of green dots blinked to life on the screen from and around Tokyo. "Way to go, Iruma!" Carla shouted.

Relief swept through Joanna as she watched the green dots progress, a hundred miles away over central Japan. But before the volley of anti-missiles broke through fifty thousand feet, the two red dots, still dropping through the upper layers of the stratosphere, vanished at an altitude of thirty miles—over them as well as over the bases west of Tokyo.

The two Iskander-NKs detonated their twenty-kiloton warheads at an altitude of twenty-nine miles, too high for fireballs, radiation, or shockwaves to cause any damage to the ships or the bases. But gamma rays from the detonation unleashed high-energy electrons that interacted with the Earth's magnetic field, triggering localized electromagnetic pulses, each over an area of roughly fifty square miles.

A fraction of a second after the red dots vanished, the green dots of the ERAMs scattered in a random fashion.

"What's happening?" Carla asked.

Before anyone could answer, a powerful shockwave rattled the bridge. The overhead lights, control panels, LED screens, and radar stations flickered, like there had been a power surge. Most screens went out, but came back on, rebooting.

"Whoa!" Carla said, working her keyboard. "My system is restarting."

"EMP," Joanna said.

"Yep," Taylor concurred. "Bastards tried to knock us out of business with a fucking EMP."

"Does that mean that those two missiles were . . ."

"Nuclear tipped," Taylor said. "Had to be."

"That's the only way to trigger that kind of a pulse," Joanna concurred.

"How long before we're back online?" Taylor asked.

"About ten minutes," Carla replied. "System needs to come back up, and then I need to run diagnostics."

"Get me back on line, JW! And get me a full damage report!" Taylor fumed. "I'm calling the fleet to change our goddamned rules of engagement!"

Joanna got on the horn to get an assessment of the damage incurred from the electromagnetic pulse. But at least on the bridge, the Navy's efforts to design and manufacture EMP-hardened equipment were paying off.

As she watched Carla and the operators work, she hoped to God that no more missiles would come for at least ten minutes.

Antietam may have survived the EMP, but until its defensive systems could come back online, the missile cruiser was a sitting duck.

CHAPTER 43
Rules of Engagement

"Evasive! Countermeasures! Burners!"
—General Mina Kyong-Lee

USS RONALD REAGAN (CVN-76).
THE SEA OF JAPAN

"Damage report!" shouted Captain O'Donnell from the Carrier Air Traffic Control Center.

A moment ago, just after *Decatur* took a direct hit, the radar screens had gone into forced reboots, interrupting the dozen air traffic controllers coordinating the jet traffic to and from BARCAPs with the Advanced Hawkeyes, plus the circling tankers.

The CATCC team worked to recover from the EMP.

Rear Admiral John Kostas arrived. He was the ISIC—Immediate Superior in Command of the *Ronald Regan* carrier group. O'Donnell figured Kostas had been holed up in the carrier's bridge atop the island with the *Reagan*'s skipper watching the fireworks and was now coming here to check on the carrier air wing.

"What's the word on our fighters out there, Mucker?"

O'Donnell took a deep breath and said, "John, those fuckers just fired two nukes at us plus *eight* other goddamned missiles, one of which hit *Decatur*, which is in fucking flames! I lost two birds. One that had just launched and another about to be recovered. Both in the drink, but the pilots punched out. Sending a helo to pick them up. And now the Torchbearer is reporting eight bandits headed for our BARCAP fighters, and our goddamned systems are in reboot mode!"

"Your recommendation?"

"Can't let those bandits anywhere near the fleet. Not now."

"What are you saying, Mucker?"

"I'm saying the rules of engagement call for holding our fire until fired upon. Well, those fuckers turning *Decatur* into a goddamned bonfire and forcing two Super Hornets in the drink certainly qualifies as—" O'Donnell made air quotes, "getting fucking fired upon."

Kostas, a large African-American with a pockmarked face under thick greying hair looked around, his heavily lidded eyes taking in the controlled chaos in the CATCC room.

Operators worked at their respective keyboards with a visible urgency to get their systems back online although a few seemed to be functional.

The admiral's gaze landed on O'Donnell as heavy as a sledgehammer pounding a high striker lever. "Fine, Mucker. Splash them. Fucking splash them."

A hundred miles east of *Ronald Reagan*, Demetrius and Gonzales maintained an intercept course.

The other two-plane sections flying BARCAP to their north and south were heading this way, but unfortunately not before he and Gonzales reached the incoming bandits.

He wondered how in the world the two of them would keep *eight* Su-35s entertained for the two or three minutes it would take for reinforcements to arrive. The answer came from the Advanced Hawkeye.

"*Dambusters Three-Oh-Three, Torchbearer Twenty, eight bandits at your twelve o'clock, forty miles at sixteen thousand. Fire at will.*"

Demetrius keyed his mic. "Torchbearer, Oh-Three, did you say *fire at will?*" he asked, dreading to know what damage those ballistic missiles had caused that prompted the change in his rules of engagement.

"*Roger, Oh-Three. Confirmed. Splash the bandits. Repeat. Splash the bandits.*"

"Copy," he replied, adding, "Speedy, Master Arm on. AMRAAMs."

"*Copy, Master Arm on. AMRAAMs,*" replied Gonzales.

With the cloud tops at sixteen thousand feet, the North Korean fighters were choosing to remain in the clouds.

But that wouldn't matter.

Demetrius powered up the Super Hornet's APG-79 Active Electronically Scanner Array (AESA) radar, capable of tracking and engaging multiple targets. He immediately picked up all eight bandits and began to paint them with radar energy. The downside of doing that was that the bandits could zero in on his radar signal.

But that also wouldn't matter.

The APG-79 assigned a target for each of Demetrius's four missiles, achieving a lock almost instantly. The system showed him that Gonzales had picked up the remaining four bandits and had achieved a lock on those targets.

At a distance of just thirty miles, Demetrius said, "Fox Three!" and released the AMRAAMs.

The all-weather, beyond-visual-range missiles streaked away, accelerating to Mach 4.

A moment later, Gonzales released his missiles, which fired away into the grayish layer below them.

In the clouds, General Mina Kyong-Lee's panel lit up with warning lights. The Americans had fired a radar-guided missile at her.

Fifteen seconds to impact, she thought, checking her range to target for the two Zvezda KH-35 anti-ship missiles she carried.

She frowned, her assigned surface targets were still over 150 nautical miles away, barely inside of the 160-nautical-mile range of the sea-skimming missile. In an ideal situation, she would have waited for the planned 120-nautical-mile release, but having a missile locked on her bird was far from ideal.

She was out of choices, especially because she could not start evasive maneuvers hauling the two very heavy cruise missiles.

Ten seconds to impact.

"Fire when able!" she ordered, releasing the two KH-35s from their undercarriage mounts.

The Sukhoi pitched up from the sudden release of over two thousand pounds of ordnance. The heavy missiles tore away from the jet under the power of their turbofans, dropping out of sight and accelerating to just under the speed of sound toward their assigned targets now 147 nautical miles away.

Cutting hard right to position the Sukhoi at ninety degrees from the incoming missile, Mina started dispensing chaff in an attempt to confuse it.

"Evasive! Countermeasures! Burners!" she added.

Six seconds to impact.

She pushed the throttles to the forward stops, engaging the afterburners and shoving the control stick away from her, forcing the Su-35 into a steep dive.

The twin turbofans ignited and the combination of the extra thrust and the steep descent, rocketed her through Mach 2.4—the very limit of the Sukhoi's structural velocity.

As she dropped with sickening speed, Mina engaged the Khibiny L-175V electronics countermeasures system, releasing more chaff. The ECM began to plaster her surroundings with energy designed to fool the radar-homing head of the incoming missile.

Three seconds to impact.

She shoved the control column to the right, flooring the right rudder pedal, forcing the Sukhoi into a wickedly-tight turn. The G-forces slammed her into the ejection seat. She broke from under the clouds and faced an ocean of white-capped swells just as a series of loud explosions reverberated over the noise of the afterburners.

Exiting the turn and leveling off right above the waves, she released a third load of chaff and the missile warning light went out.

Mina eased back on the throttles. A second Sukhoi dropped below the clouds in full burner, dispensing chaff and decelerating.

"I'm with you, general!" Major Byung Ko said, coming up behind her.

A third Sukhoi appeared, this one trailing smoke.

"Mayday! Mayday!" the pilot shouted. The jet failed to pull out of its dive and plunged nose-first into the ocean.

A fourth Sukhoi, in flames, dropped from the clouds in a flat spin.

A fifth jet in full burner joined Mina and Ko, apparently unharmed.

Mina saw no one else exit the cloud.

"Radio check," she said, getting replies only from the two jets trailing her.

"Goddammit," she said, for the first time since the missile attack looking down at her radar. Only three of them were heading back to base—the other two jets in the vicinity had to be the Americans who fired on her squadron. They were flying in the opposite direction.

Mina's heart leapt when she saw the red dots, eight of them, moving away at just under the speed of sound. At least four of the eight Sukhois had managed to fire their cruise missiles.

CHAPTER 44
Twelve Busy Minutes

"That was a Navy pilot, Skipper. A goddamned Navy pilot."
—USN Commander Joanna Watson.

USS ANTIETAM (CG-54). SEA OF JAPAN

"Incoming vampires. Eight. Range one-one-zero nautical miles. Altitude two-five feet. Speed six-niner-zero knots. Time to impact, niner minutes twenty seconds," Carla Martinez reported.

"This isn't fucking happening," Captain Taylor mumbled.

The radar operator had just reported eight incoming cruise missiles skimming the ocean at nearly the speed of sound. Unfortunately, all she could do was track them until the rest of the systems came back online.

"How long till we're back up?" Joanna asked.

"At least eight more minutes. Maybe ten."

In addition to the ERAMs, *Antietam* had 60 RIM-66 medium range missiles that could be used against other ships or aerial targets, including incoming cruise missiles.

Unfortunately, the RIM-66s, which had an operational range of up to 90 nautical miles, were controlled by the Aegis missile system.

"Goddammit," Taylor cursed. "What about the CIWS?"

There were two Phalanx Close-in Weapons Systems (CIWS) designed to protect against enemy surface ships and airborne threats like anti-ship missiles. The CIWS was basically a radar-guided 20mm six-barrel Vulcan cannon mounted on a swivel base. It had a maximum range of just over four miles, meaning *Antietam* would have to sit tight and wait for the cruise missiles to get in range instead of splashing them from tens of miles away.

The CIWS operator gave them a thumbs-up. So, at a minimum they had the gun system.

"What's the situation on *Ramage* and *Reagan*?" Joanna asked.

"Same. CIWS up all around. The rest are in a goddamned reboot cycle, and we just heard from *Decatur*. Missile took out the bridge. Surviving crew's putting out the fires. No word on casualties yet."

Joanna frowned, feeling like a failure. Taylor was a man of few words. The status report on *Decatur* was his way of warning everyone what could happen to *Antietam* if they didn't get their act together in the next few minutes.

"Incoming vampires. Eight. Range niner-eight nautical miles. Altitude two-five feet. Speed holding at six-niner-zero knots. Time to impact, eight minutes fifty-two seconds," Carla updated.

The report gave Joanna an idea, and she shared it with Taylor, earning a scowl.

"JW, that's the craziest fucking thing I've heard today, plus it's never been done before, to my knowledge."

Joanna shrugged, palms up. "Well, skipper, what the hell do we have to lose?"

"Dambusters Three-Oh-Three, Torchbearer Twenty, eight vampires bearing zero-niner-two, fifteen miles at twenty-five feet and six-niner-zero knots. Intercept and splash."

Commander Demetrius did a double take at the radio panel. The Advanced Hawkeye controller had just given him the order to go after the cruise missiles headed for the fleet. Something was seriously wrong, because the fleet could easily handle eight cruise missiles with their combined load of literally *hundreds* of defensive missiles.

The controller added, *"Dambusters, go starboard, heading zero-eight-two. Burners."*

"Oh-Three copy, eight-two and burners," Demetrius replied. "On me, Speedy."

"Roger!"

Demetrius put the Super Hornet in a steep dive and turned to his assigned heading, engaging the afterburner.

The F/A-18Es dropped from the heavens like a pair of flaming comets, and punched into the layer of thick, gray muck at almost Mach 1.6, near their maximum structural limit.

The clouds came and went, and at a thousand feet, Demetrius started pulling back on the control column. The Gs slammed into him until he leveled off at just fifty feet from a very pissed off ocean, Gonzales on his wing.

Their supersonic booms stirred the already angry swells behind them, parting them like the Red Sea. The two-plane section careened directly toward the cruise missiles now ten miles away.

With a closing speed of almost Mach 1, they reached them in under a minute.

Demetrius throttled back and engaged the infrared seeker for his Sidewinders.

Settling about a mile behind the hot plumes marking the sea-skimming cruise missiles, he got dual locks in a few seconds.

"Fox two!" he said and fired them.

The twin ten-foot-long missiles shot out from under him, propelled by their Mk. 36 solid-fuel rockets, reaching Mach 2.5 in a flash.

Twin bright explosions confirmed the kills.

I'll be damned, he thought. "Your turn, Speedy."

"*Copy,*" his wingman replied, and released his two Sidewinders.

Their bright exhaust plumes ripped through the haze. Two more hits.

Four down. Four to go.

"*Dambusters Three-Oh-Three, Torchbearer Twenty, four vampires bearing zero-niner-two. Range to the fleet six-eight miles. Time to impact, five minutes eight seconds.*"

"Torchbearer, we're fresh out of missiles. What's the word on the other BARCAPS?"

"*Closest pair is still eighty miles out. Use guns.*"

"Copy. Guns," Demetrius replied.

They had taken out the center missiles. The remaining four were in two pairs, two miles apart.

"Take the two on the right, Speedy," Demetrius said and peeled left to position himself behind the northernmost missiles.

The Super Hornet came armed with a single 20mm M61 6-barrel nose cannon, similar to the one in the Phalanx, but his bird only had 412 rounds. With a rate of fire of 6000 rounds per minute, Demetrius had a little over four seconds of continuous firing time.

Simultaneously working the throttle, control column, and rudder pedals, he positioned the F/A-18E three hundred feet behind the hot plume, dropping from the safer fifty feet to match the missile's twenty-five, barely above the whitecaps.

Unlike an enemy jet, which would be diving and rolling to evade him, the cruise missile remained steady in its course and speed. That was the good news.

His proximity to the ocean meant he was enveloped in mist, making it difficult for him to get a good enough visual through the heads-up display to take the shot. And to put a cherry on this shit cake, he was only one slight twitch of the control column from going in the drink.

"Dambusters Three-Oh-Three, Torchbearer Twenty, four vampires bearing zero-niner-two. Range to the fleet four-eight miles. Time to impact, four minutes eleven seconds.

"I know, Goddammit. I know!" he snapped, trying to work out an angle. He keyed his mic and calmly replied, "Working on it."

"Me too," Gonzales echoed.

"Alright," he told himself. "Here we go."

Through his heads-up display, he could just see the yellow plume. The problem was, he could only make very minor adjustments without plunging into the ocean at 700 knots. At that speed, the water was pretty much a brick wall.

The yellow target moved into the crosshairs, and he fired a burst.

The Super Hornet rocked from the powerful recoil, which forced the nose up, sending his shots high.

Dammit.

"Dambusters Three-Oh-Three, Torchbearer Twenty, four vampires bearing zero-niner-two. Range to the fleet three six miles. Time to impact, three minutes five seconds."

Christ.

It took almost another thirty seconds to settle behind the missile so he could fire. This time he anticipated the recoil and remained level, but the missile moved out of the crosshairs.

He glanced at his ammo count display, which read 197. In the two-plus seconds of firing time, he had consumed over half his load.

"Speedy, how are you making out?"

"Nearly out, Jade. This isn't working."

"No shit."

"Dambusters Three-Oh-Three, Torchbearer Twenty, four vampires bearing zero-niner-two. Range to the fleet, two-three miles. Time to impact one minute fifty seconds."

"Goddammit, we know!" Demetrius cursed, keyed the mic, and replied, "Roger."

But he couldn't get an angle and wasted another hundred rounds.

And just when he thought things couldn't get worse, the missiles, which had been flying in tandem, entered their terminal phases and separated toward their individual targets.

"Torchbearer, Dambusters Three-Oh-Three, vampires are breaking away. Low on ammo. Which one should I follow?" he asked, hoping the carrier task force had their own defenses.

"Oh-Three, stay with the rightmost vampire. Its new bearing puts it on course for Decatur, which is currently disabled."

Disabled?

Demetrius shook his head. "What do you mean, disabled?"

"Decatur took a direct hit from a ballistic missile. Crews are putting out the fires, but she's a sitting duck."

"Roger," Demetrius said, and followed his assigned missile.

Once more, he tried to maneuver into a shot, holding as steady as he could, waiting for the plume to move toward the crosshairs and—

He fired again as the missile's exhaust centered in the heads-up display, but a gust pushed the Super Hornet aside, and his final volley went wide.

Dammit!

"Dambusters Three-Oh-Three, Torchbearer Twenty, vampire bearing zero-six-three. Range to the fleet, two-one miles. Time to impact, five-two seconds."

"Copy," he replied, wondering how in the hell he would keep the damn missile from hitting the wounded destroyer with no weapons.

Then he remembered.

His grandfather. The Royal Air Force. The Spitfires.

Easing the throttle forward and nudging the control stick up, he accelerated the Super Hornet parallel to the missile, still cruising at just under the speed of sound.

It worked then, it should work now, he thought, inching his right wingtip under the front of the missile.

"Oh-Three, vampire bearing zero-six-three. Range to target, thirteen miles. Time to impact twenty-one seconds."

"A little busy here," he replied. A thick inky column appeared straight ahead, rising into the overcast skies.

In a single motion, Demetrius pushed left rudder and yanked the control column in the opposite direction, keeping the Super Hornet parallel to the missile but swinging the left wing up.

The missile pitched up and momentarily gained altitude, then resumed its original path toward the destroyer.

"Oh-Three, vampire bearing zero-six-three. Range to target, six miles. Time to impact, eleven seconds."

Seriously?

Demetrius moved toward the missile, but this time he positioned the wing over it, not under it. And with the destroyer getting large in his windscreen, he swung the control stick toward the missile, hard, pushing right full rudder.

The Super Hornet juddered as the wingtip smacked the cruise missile, slamming it into the waves.

The vampire plunged beneath the breakers.

Decatur's hull and the huge column of smoke filled his windscreen, and for an instant, he saw the faces of dozens of sailors gaping at him. The Super Hornet screamed over the deck of *Decatur*, just missing the superstructure, on its way back into the clouds.

He looked at the timer and realized that just twelve minutes had elapsed from the moment he was ordered to splash those Sukhois.

❖

"JW! Who the hell was *that*?" Captain Taylor asked.

They had just witnessed the impossible: A Super Hornet had used one of its wings to slam a cruise missile into the drink less than a mile from *Decatur*, and just seconds after *Antietam*'s CIWS had splashed one of the other incoming cruise missiles. *Reagan* had handled the last two.

"That was a Navy pilot, Skipper," Joanna said. "A goddamned Navy pilot."

CHAPTER 45
Unquestionable Proof

"The United States' presence in the Sea of Japan is in China's best interest."
—President Laura Vaccaro

THE WHITE HOUSE, WASHINGTON, D.C.

"My fleet was attacked by ten ballistic missiles, Xi. At least two of them were nuclear-tipped, triggering EMPs over my fleet and military bases in Japan. One of my damned destroyers is on fire and I lost two Super Hornets. I have *fourteen* dead sailors, times three wounded, and you're telling me this isn't the time to retaliate? Are you out of your fucking mind?"

Vaccaro pressed the mute button on the speaker phone in the Treaty Room. Wright and Jacobson gave her deer-in-the-headlights looks at her conversation with President Xi Jinping of the People's Republic of China.

But she knew what she was doing, or at least she hoped she did. There were a number of weapons in the arsenal of a seasoned negotiator, one of them being the right time to use anger—and it was best used when you had some capital, such as an Arleigh-Burke class destroyer burning from a North Korean missile strike in international waters.

"You know, Madam President, we *did* shoot down five of their new Sukhois," Wright pointed out.

"I realize it doesn't quite even things out, but . . ." Jacobson added.

Fourteen dead American sailors and another fifty-three wounded vs. five dead North Korean pilots was *nowhere* close to evening things out. On top of that, those Sukhoi-35ss went for around $50 million each vs. a $1.8 billion Arleigh-Burke class destroyer plus the two $70-million Super Hornets that had fallen out of the sky after the EMP. And, there was that little fact that America was attacked first—and with nukes.

But Jinping replied before she could give Wright and Jacobson a piece of her mind.

"I'm merely suggesting, Lau, that striking back could result in . . . an escalation that neither of our two nations want."

Vaccaro hated the way Jinping shortened her name, like they were old friends. The Chinese president was anything but. He was the enemy, and in many ways more so than Russia or even North Korea.

"Let me ask you this," Vaccaro said. "What would you do if that was one of *your* destroyers and your dead and wounded sailors?"

"That's not a realistic question because I would not order my fleet so close to their waters. I have not spoken to Pyongyang, but I can only assume they didn't appreciate your fleet being so close to their waters any more than you would appreciate my fleet cruising the international waters off the coast of California."

What Vaccaro didn't appreciate was President Jinping's veiled threat.

"Xi, the United States' presence in the Sea of Japan is in China's best interests."

There was pause there as the Chinese president apparently tried to figure out what that meant, as did Wright and Jacobson, whom she saw out of the corner of her right eye exchanging glances.

"Lau . . . I'm afraid I do not understand what you mean."

Vaccaro said, "Then allow me to explain. At the end of World War Two, the United States made Japan sign an agreement that would keep its military power limited to a size proportionate to that required for internal security. This was done to protect China and the other nations in that hemisphere from another Japanese invasion. As a result, the United States has an obligation to protect Japan since it can no longer defend itself from foreign attacks. This is the primary reason for American presence in the Sea of Japan and for its military bases spread across its islands. North Korea's actions three hours ago is a declaration of war against the United States—a war that North Korea cannot possibly win."

"Please understand that Pyongyang is without a leader at the moment," Xi replied, "Seeing your fleet maneuvering so close to their shores in the wake of the assassination of Kim Jung-un by Japanese agents—"

"Mafia. Japanese *Mafia*."

"Yes, of course . . . but Japanese nevertheless, and on American soil. It has apparently unsettled them."

"On top of attacking our fleet," Vaccaro said, "they detonated another high-altitude nuke over our military bases near Tokyo, triggering an EMP that shut down our bases and the surrounding areas." Her eyes landed on the large TV screen between *The Peacemakers* and Kennedy's portrait. It showed images of Yokota Airbase twenty miles west of Tokyo. In reality, as bad as it looked, the EMP would have been a far worse disaster had it gone off over Greater Tokyo. At least most systems at the base, including airplanes and helicopters, were EMP-hardened, like the Seventh Fleet. An EMP over downtown Tokyo would have thrown the city into a modern-day stone age.

Still, communities near the base had been affected, probably fifty thousand people without electricity, phones, TV, cars, trains, pacemakers, and anything else that had been powered up at the time of the pulse. She had yet to get a death toll from that.

"Yes, we know," Xi replied. "Li has already contacted Shinzo to assure him we will find a way to address that." Li Keqiang was the vice president of the PRC. Shinzo Abe was Japan's Prime Minister, whom Xi had personally engaged in recent years to find ways to improve the legacy trade wars between Japan and China.

But Vaccaro knew that was little more than lip service, as was the attempt to repair relations between Japan and China, which were still quite strained, especially because the populations of each country pretty much hated each other.

Japan had, after all, committed appalling atrocities across China and the Pacific Rim countries during World War II. And China in particular, who lost over fourteen million people during that occupation, was not one to forget so easily.

And who could blame them? Vaccaro thought. She was one step short of going to DEFCON 1 after fourteen American sailors were killed. What would she do if the number was fourteen *million*?

Adding insult to injury, to this day, Japan refused to issue any apologies for those widespread war crimes, which began as far back as 1937 with the infamous Rape of Nanjing, when soldiers of the Imperial Japanese Army raped and murdered almost 300,000 Chinese civilians and disarmed combatants.

"Like I said, Lau, as tragic as this attack was, this is a time to show restraint, not to escalate. Please understand how bad the optics are, especially from the perspective of Pyongyang. Kim Jong-un was assassinated by—"

"Neither my government or the government of Japan had *anything* to do with that."

"I hear you, but we need incontrovertible proof that this was not staged by your government to provoke a war . . . like your President Johnson did in the Gulf of Tonkin in 1964."

Vaccaro felt a blood pressure headache worming in.

"Perhaps," Xi suggested, "there might be an opportunity to offer . . . reparations, to Pyongyang?"

Vaccaro tightened her fists. "What about reparations to the families of the sailors Pyongyang murdered this morning, Xi? And who's going to pay to repair my expensive destroyer and replace my lost aircraft?"

Wright and Jacobson signaled her to calm down.

Maybe they were right.

As much as she wanted to pound North Korea like she had Pakistan a year ago, she had to find a way to handle it without putting her troops and civilians in the line of fire from future attacks.

Vaccaro needed to find a way to temper North Korea's actions until her covert team dug up the proof she needed.

"But I'll take that under advisement, Xi," she added. "Meanwhile, please understand that any further attacks against my fleet or against Japan will *not* be tolerated, so whatever you have to do to control Pyongyang's emotions, whoever you have to call or wine and dine—or even beat into submission—I suggest you do it sooner than later."

"Understood, Lau," Xi replied. "And again, any proof that can be obtained will go a long way to help me defuse the situation."

"I'll be in touch," Vaccaro said and pressed the button to terminate the call, wondering if there was a way to stop the North Korean war machine without blowing them off the map.

"Lisa," she said, "get me Secretary Kaminski."

As Jacobson headed for the door, Vaccaro asked, "Hold on. What's the situation with Stark?"

"The last message I got, they went in the tunnel under the border," Wright replied. "I'm waiting for an update. But we did get confirmation on the wrecks from local authorities and a new contingent from DHS out of San Antonio. The two helos were indeed shot down, as Stark reported, and we lost everyone aboard."

"Just got an update from Karachi," said Wright, looking at his iPad. "Done. Blew up the missile stash plus collected a lot of hardware, laptops and phones. He said that the new guy, a Jason Savage, was very helpful."

"Jason who?" Vaccaro asked.

Jacobson said, "Harwich and Gorman have a very competent but very young tech in his SOG, a woman—a girl, really—named Sally Kohl. So, I wanted to complement that with a more seasoned tech guy, and Jason Savage is the best I've seen. We worked together back when I was with the Agency. He assisted Harwich and Gorman in Qatar, first covertly tasking a Global Hawk to provide aerial IR coverage, and he'll decipher the captured hardware."

Wright and Vaccaro looked at Jacobson with identical blank stares.

Vaccaro was about to lecture her National Security Advisor about being uninformed, but reminded herself she could not micromanage every last aspect of this hairball. She had to trust and rely on her team.

She settled for letting out a heavy sigh. She could only hope the CIA team would extract enough evidence to vindicate the government of Japan and her own.

"According to this, Gorman and Harwich, plus their team, landed in Qatar an hour ago," Wright said.

"Why Qatar?" Vaccaro asked.

"Because," Jacobson explained. "Savage and Kohl are scrubbing the hardware real time, and they're not sure yet where that's going to lead them."

"Oh," Vaccaro said, tilting her head.

"And Gorman says the SEAL team was back in Kabul before breakfast," Wright added, reading from his tablet. "Says here that the SEAL chief is going to play ball, keep this one under wraps."

"Yep," Jacobson concurred. "All tied up nice and pretty."

Vaccaro nodded. Her thoughts drifted to the border, to the dangerous place Stark and team were headed, and covertly, *without* notifying the Mexican government—at Stark's request.

"Madam President, as one soldier to another, in Mexico there are two kinds of police officers, military personnel, or government officials: those in the cartel's payroll and those who don't know they're in the cartel's payroll."

CHAPTER 46
Margaritaville

"Few things in this world bother me more than fighting in a goddamned tunnel."
—Monica Cruz

TEXAS-MEXICO BORDER

They moved as one through the pitch-black tunnel wearing their ATN PS15-4 night-vision goggles.

Stark led the stack, followed by Monica, then Naree. Juan brought up the rear.

Somewhere overhead, Danny was hovering the Black Hawk over the wall waiting for Stark's orders. Ryan was with him manning one of the helicopter's .50-caliber side guns.

"You know, Colonel," Monica whispered behind him, "few things in this world bother me more than fighting in a goddamned tunnel."

Stark ignored her, wishing for his old team, for the Chief and Mickey—especially Mickey since he kept his mouth shut all the time and just did his job.

"What is so bad about a tunnel?" Naree asked.

"Well," Monica replied, "fighting in a tunnel presents a number of difficulties."

"Such as?"

"Number one, you're fighting in a fucking tunnel."

Stark stopped and turned around, glaring at his new team, painted in shades of green.

"Number two," Stark whispered, "sound carries a long fucking way, so zip it."

"Permission to shoot them now, Colonel?" Juan asked. "Put us out of our misery?"

Stark liked that.

A lot.

Juan is going fit just fine with Danny and Romeo—Mickey too—if he ever gets back on his feet, literally.

Monica and Naree turned to stare at the big warrior, who pointed toward the other end of the tunnel. "Mexico's *that* way, ladies, so ándele and hush hush."

Ten minutes later, they reached the other end of the tunnel.

And this is where things could get tricky, thought Stark.

Stark reached the wide mouth, which opened into a large covered area, a sort of open-air warehouse, stepped outside and shifted right scanning the place.

"Clear right," he said, as Monica stepped up to him.

"Clear center," she said.

"Clear left," from Naree.

"So this is what we heard," Juan said, moving ahead of them, a towering dark figure surrounded by a field of fresh death.

"The hell's all this?" Monica asked.

A dozen dead men were scattered on the dirt floor around tools and equipment, mostly compact excavators, plus tons of picks, shovels, and wheelbarrows.

"Tunnels don't dig themselves, Cruz," Stark said, "and I'm guessing those are the tunnel diggers. And that metal roof's there to protect it from rain and from our aerial assets."

The clothes on the dead men were plain, and all wore weathered working boots, like the man who shot him at the other end of the tunnel.

But one of the bodies looked like a cartel gun, perhaps even a *sicario* based on the horrifying tattoos covering both arms and up his neck, a macabre mélange of skulls, thorny roses, and assault rifles designed to intimidate.

"Lot of good all that shit ink did him," Monica said.

Stark took note of the expensive-looking snakeskin boots, designer jeans, silk shirt, and a large gold watch.

Monica and Juan took up defensive positions by the entrance.

Naree knelt by the dead cartel man, who had a bullet hole between a pair of dead eyes staring at the corrugated metal roof.

"Small caliber, *Shiraki*," she said.

"Like the FBI agents and the deputies," Stark said.

Naree ran a gloved finger through the blood pooled around his head and said, "Still fresh. Definitely what we heard."

"Yeah," Stark concurred. "But the question's why?"

Naree raised her eyebrows and said, "Why is a cartel man killed at this end of the tunnel along with the labor force? The way I understand these drug operations, the assassins are here to protect the laborers digging their tunnels."

"Precisely," he replied. "And it looks like one managed to escape by running into the tunnel."

"Until he ran into us," Naree said.

Gunfire started, from the direction of Piedras Negras.

Stark tapped his phone, then spoke into the throat mic connected to his MBITR. "Danny, the tunnel leads to some warehouse. Just sent you a pin. Come get us. And we hear gunfire in the vicinity. You have eyes on that?"

"*Got the pin, Colonel. You're just a klick away, and you won't believe what else just showed up on my screen.*"

CHAPTER 47
A Day in the Life

"I will make each bastard willing to collect the reward on my head pay for the attempt to do so . . . in blood."
—Mireya Moreno Carreón.

NORTH OF PIEDRAS NEGRAS, MEXICO

Her reaction had given her a running start.

Mireya raced across the dusty clearing beyond the metal roof erected at the mouth of the tunnel, where Francisco had turned his gun on her shortly after getting a message on his phone.

It had happened fast. One minute they were headed for the SUVs that would take them to the Piedras Negras Airport for the flight to Culiacán. Then the vehicles suddenly took off and Francisco tried to shoot her in the back of the head.

Mireya survived because her instincts prompted her to drop when the SUVs raced away. Reaching behind her for the Ruger, Francisco's kill shot went high, just above her head.

At that moment, Mireya had been thankful for all the range training, all the impossible shooting and disarming drills. The skills she had learned with Los Zetas and again under Ricco Orellana were life-threatening hard, and they just saved her life again.

For better or for worse, Mireya was used to these life-threatening moments, kind of like "a day in the life of a *sicario*."

And she had not given Francisco another chance to shoot.

She dropped him with a single headshot, ignoring the blood spattering on her as he fell. She'd had just a few seconds to pull the Kalashnikov from his dead hands. The *mineros* had come at her with picks and axes. She killed them with a single sweep at waist level, except for one, who'd managed to escape into the tunnel clutching an AK-47.

Mireya let him go, and went for Francisco's phone, only to find the shocking and totally unexpected message that drove a dagger through her heart.

KILL LA FLACA AND THE MINERS. LEAVE NO TRACE THAT CAN CONNECT THE ATTACK TO ME.

The message was from Ricco Orellana.

So, she had taken off, removing two extra magazines for the Kalashnikov from Francisco's back pockets.

When she reached the road to Piedras Negras, she spotted three additional gunmen staged there to make sure the job was done right.

Fortunately, they had been hired guns, not *sicarios*, resulting in another short firefight.

Mireya thought about Antonio, her nine-year-old son at Ricco's Sierra Madre compound.

She wondered what Ricco had done with him. She hoped that the cartel boss might let her youngster live, but the *sicario* in Mireya told her that was a foolish wish.

Ricco Orellana was, above all, a businessman, and leaving a child like Antonio alive after ordering his mother killed was bad for business because it left the door wide open for a future vendetta.

No. In order to move forward, Mireya had to assume that Antonio was already dead, and the thought scorched her to the core.

Goddammit, Ricco! Why me? I've been loyal to you. Loyal! her mind screamed. She tossed the spent magazine and inserted a fresh one.

If in fact Ricco wanted her dead to distance himself from the assassinations in Dallas, then south was most certainly the wrong direction to run.

Mireya actually needed to go north, back into the United States, where, if she could reach Los Angeles, the place where she grew up, she at least had a chance. Her skills might allow her to join a rival gang.

Her other option was to head east, toward the state of Nuevo Leon, which was controlled by her old cartel, Los Zetas, where she just might be able to talk her way back in—assuming Ricco had not thwarted that by placing a hefty price on her head.

But I don't have the resources to get to either one.

In her hands, Mireya had two phones. The one she had stolen from the dead American federal agent and the one she had just taken from Francisco. Both were powered off to prevent anyone from tracking her movements.

As she considered her very limited options, Mireya chose the lesser of two evils and turned on the American phone, in essence broadcasting her location to the same government, a number of whose citizens, including federal agents, police officers, and probably military personnel she had just killed.

She pocketed the phone and looked at the sky, hoping for a helicopter that would take her away to some secluded jail or black-ops site, where she might be able to land a deal. Or perhaps the phone would draw a missile from a drone, putting her out of her misery.

Either of those possibilities, or whatever else the Americans might throw her way, would be child's play compared to what Ricco would do now, after she had killed the men he had sent to terminate her mercifully, with a bullet to the head. The next round of assassins would not be so compassionate.

Mireya took a trail rising from the main road, following it for the better part of an hour until it reached a rocky hilltop overlooking the eastern edge of Piedras Negras, the capital city of the Mexican state of Coahuila.

A large expanse of one-story structures hugged the southern shore of the Rio Grande for a couple of miles. Piedras Negras was connected to the United States by two heavily guarded bridges—or by the many tunnels dug beneath the slow-flowing river.

Here, high above Piedras Negras, Mireya planned to make her final stand.

She had two magazines left, each with thirty rounds, plus another six in the Ruger. Mireya had sixty-six shots left to defend herself against the fury of the Sinaloa Cartel.

Make that sixty-five, she thought, because the last one would be for her.

She settled behind a thicket of cedars and looked around for alternate firing positions, rubbing dirt all over her clothes and in her hair and face, camouflaging, blending in, giving herself every advantage possible.

With her back against a sharp cliff overlooking the Rio Grande, Mireya rested the barrel of the AK-47 on a branch.

A wispy trail of dust marked a short caravan of vehicles leaving town headed this way.

And so it begins.

Ricco Orellana was apparently not wasting any time, likely posting an online reward that had stirred a wave of hungry bounty hunters fighting for a chance at the grand prize.

She wondered how much her old boss had offered for her head. And in the end, it really didn't matter.

I will make each bastard willing to collect the reward pay for the attempt to do so . . . in blood.

The vehicles, more than ten of them, headed in different directions as they got closer. Some drove straight for the kill zone by the tunnel, blocking her way back north. Others took strategic vantage points in every direction, in essence cutting her off to the interior.

And that told her this group was coordinated, not a collection of bounty hunters, but an organized force deployed with the sole purpose of finishing the job that Francisco had failed to do. That was reinforced a moment later when she spotted a half dozen dark blue pickup trucks belonging to the Coahuila State Police, which remained a safe distance behind the posse Ricco had deployed to locate her.

A grey truck ventured up the goat trail, presumably because it was a great observation post.

Four men jumped out of the bed, two more climbed out of the cabin, all armed with Mac-10 pistols or 9mm Uzi submachine guns.

Six against one.

She frowned at the unfair math.

The men spread out across the top of the hill to cover every angle. And as luck would have it, two paired up to head her way, both clutching Uzis.

Here we go, she thought, regretting what she had to do, because it would telegraph her position to every cartel gun in northern Mexico.

Pressing the stock of the AK-47 against her right shoulder and gazing through the iron sights, Mireya waited until the other men were out of sight.

She lined up the man on the right and held up to the last possible moment, hating to give away her position, but the bastards were almost on top of her.

Mireya had considered using her sound-suppressed Ruger, which still had six rounds left, but sooner or later she would have to use the Kalashnikov, so it might as well it be now.

Firing once, Mireya scored a direct hit to his face, the report echoing loudly.

As he dropped, she switched targets and fired again, scoring a second kill.

She cut right, running in a deep crouch, along the edge of the bluff to a clump of boulders and settling behind it, out of sight of the cartel men.

Inching her way around the outcrop, Mireya saw them surveying the hilltop with their weapons, apparently trying to figure out what had happened. One pointed in the direction of the cedar grove where she just put two of them down.

In that moment, all four assassins were clustered in the center of the clearing, by the Tacoma.

Setting the AK-47 to full automatic mode, she opened up with short, controlled trigger-pulls. This was a speed shooting contest that she had to win.

The rattle reverberated across the hill. She forced the stock deep into her shoulder, like she had done with the *mineros*, fighting the weapon's natural tendency to pitch up.

Two men went down right away, but the other two were able to jump over the hood and seek cover on the other side of the truck.

"*Mierda*," she cursed when one of them returned fire, forcing her to duck behind the rock formation as a volley of 9mm rounds hammered the outcrop.

Then the other man fired while the first reloaded, forcing her to remain hidden.

She glanced over her shoulder at the steep hill and decided it would not only be suicide to try to get down that way, they would likely spot her if she tried and get her from above.

And now, more vehicles had started toward the hill, and she could hear the distant sound of a helicopter.

Really, Ricco?

A goddamned helicopter?

Her heartbeat rocketing, realizing that they had her, Mireya did the only thing she could do: take as many of the bastards with her as possible.

Because the men had concentrated their fire toward the left side of the formation, she rolled away to the right, catching one man reloading as the other emptied his Uzi.

She fired low, two short bursts from a distance of a hundred feet, ripping into a few shins before her Kalashnikov went dry.

The two men rolled on the ground screaming as more vehicles raced into the clearing trailing clouds of dust. The noise from the helicopter grew louder, but she could not yet see it.

Last mag, she thought, running toward a new cluster of boulders, dropping the spent magazine and inserting the last one. *Make it count.*

She waited until the vehicles stopped and she heard footsteps crunching gravel. Peering around the boulders, she tried to get a sense of the threat she now faced.

Too many, she thought. *Way too many.*

"But you gotta die of something."

Mireya aimed the Kalashnikov at the men as the helicopter rose ominously behind her, like a beast from hell, dark, loud, and menacing.

And as her mind registered the imposing aircraft looming over her, she saw the bright flash beneath one of its stub wings.

Mireya reacted instinctively, diving behind the boulders.

The hilltop vanished in a cloud of fire.

"*Hardly a fair fight, Colonel!*" Danny Martin had shouted over the squadron frequency as he surged the Sikorski up to five hundred feet after hugging the desert floor at 200 knots for the past few minutes. "*But she's giving them hell.*"

Stark had already anchored himself behind the port side-mounted .50-caliber M2 Browning, aiming it at the men in the clearing. Ryan knelt next to him with his Barrett. Monica handled the starboard gun and Naree and Juan angled a pair of M247 machine guns.

Danny had detected the GPS signal of the stolen FBI phone, and Stark was determined to capture the owner because whoever stole it had to be in on the operation in Dallas. But little did he expect the current owner of the FBI phone to be a woman being attacked by at least fifty cartel men. And he certainly didn't expect to see a dozen of them already dead or dying.

"We need her alive, Danny!" Stark shouted. The woman huddled behind a cluster of large boulders at the edge of the bluff still firing with a Kalashnikov. The realization that the cartel wanted her dead elevated her importance, kindling his desire to take her alive.

"I've got this!" Danny replied, releasing an AGM-114 Hellfire from a pylon on the starboard External Stores Support System. The ESSS stub wing system projected over both side doors of the Black Hawk and sported two pylons per wing. The inner pylons held a Hellfire missile each. Stark had dedicated the outer pylons to haul two 450-gallon tanks, extending their range to almost a thousand miles.

The missile streaked toward the middle of the hilltop. Its 18-pound blast fragmentation warhead—the equivalent of forty hand grenades going off at once—swallowed men and vehicles in a brief moment of complete conflagration.

It was powerful. It was blinding. And it was damn loud.

And when it was over, Danny swept over the burning wrecks and what remained of the posse, a handful of figures on fire.

Stark jumped off first. Danny kept the Sikorski in a hover a foot off the ground, ready for a quick egress.

"Juan! Romeo! Monica! Stay put and cover us! Naree, on me!"

Monica settled herself behind the portside Browning. Juan stayed put on the starboard gun. Ryan remained on station scanning the area with his Barrett. Stark raced across the kill zone trailed by Naree.

The smell of cordite and burned flesh assaulted his nostrils. The column of inky smoke was a damn beacon for everyone from miles around.

Stark frowned at the 4x4s careening up the goat trail followed by the dark-blue trucks of the state police.

"The police!" Naree shouted. "They're after them!"

"Hell no!" he replied, sprinting toward the mystery woman's hideout. "They're *with* them."

"With them?"

"Welcome to fucking Mexico."

They covered the two hundred-some-feet to the rocky formation where he had last seen her.

As they approached it, Stark motioned Naree to go around the right side of the wall of boulders while he went left and—

Stark spotted the woman on the ground, smeared with sweat and dust, dark hair matted with blood. She drew a Ruger from her waist and Naree instinctively swung her MP7A1 around.

"Don't shoot her!" Stark warned. He dove at the woman just as she aimed the Ruger, not at Stark or Naree, but at her own temple.

He swatted the pistol away an instant before she pulled the trigger.

"*Mierda* . . . no!" she hissed as Stark pried the pistol from her fingers and put it in his belt.

"Easy there," he said. She looked around wildly, her pupils dilated, breathing hard.

"Concussion," Stark said glancing up at Naree who was covering him. "She'll be in and out for a while."

He tossed her over his left shoulder while keeping the pistol grip of the MP7A1 firmly clutched with his right hand.

"Move! Now!" he said, and started running to the Black Hawk.

A truck crested the hill.

But it didn't get far.

Monica opened up the Browning in a deafening display of power, and it was soon on fire, blocking the trail, forcing the occupants of the vehicles behind it to continue on foot.

Stark and Naree deposited the semiconscious woman on the floor.

Danny lifted the helo's collective, twisting the throttle handle and pushing the cyclic forward as soon as Stark, Naree, and the *sicario* asset hit the floor.

The Black Hawk surged skyward in a whirl of dust and gunfire as everyone unloaded their weapons to cover their quick egress.

As they left the kill zone and accelerated back over the border, Stark knelt by the woman, still in an obvious daze.

❖

Hot and humid air seemed to congeal in front of Mireya, and through it emerged a bald head on a powerful neck that poured into wide muscular shoulders, chest, and arms ripped with tight muscles. This real-life bronzed Adonis wearing dark sunglasses hovered above her like some mythical figure, but she couldn't focus on his face, plus her arms and legs would not respond. She lay there completely at his mercy.

But he was not beating her, or torturing her, or raping her. As far as she could tell, Mireya still had her clothes on, which in her tired and confused mind could only mean she had succeeded in getting captured by the Americans.

A chance, she thought, her mind getting cloudier, fuzzier, like her eyesight. *A chance for me . . . maybe for Antonio.*

"She's lucky to be alive," the man said, a tenor voice matching his imposing physique. "and she's damn lucky to . . ."

His voice faded away, as did the rest of him and the whirring of the helicopter . . . Complete blackness engulfed her.

CHAPTER 48
Softening the Blow

"China needs a country like North Korea, where it can indirectly do to this region, and wherever else it wants, what it cannot justify doing directly."
—General Pak Yong-Gil.

RYONGSONG RESIDENCE. PYONGYANG, NORTH KOREA

The current supreme leader of North Korea hung up the speakerphone after a conversation with President Xi Jinping, who had suggested that Pyongyang suspend acts of aggression against Japan and the United States until a thorough investigation could be conducted.

"What do you think?" he asked General Pak Yong-Gil, who had listened to the exchange standing stoically next to him.

"I know we depend heavily on their support," Pak said. "But on the other hand, China needs a country like North Korea, where it can indirectly do to this region, and wherever else it wants, what it cannot justify doing directly. So, whatever they're going to offer, it needs to be . . . significant, not just to compensate for our loss, but as a deterrent against future attacks."

Choe nodded. The crucial role that his country played in the balance of power in the region and in the world, was not lost on him—China needed North Korea, though certainly not as much as North Korea needed China.

His country did have some leverage when it came to negotiating with Beijing. And in this case, Choe had agreed to consider suspending the hostilities in exchange for a military and economic package that President Xi indicated would be of such magnitude as to lessen the pain experienced by North Korea in the past forty-eight hours.

"So, are you suggesting we wait?" Pak asked, his dark eyes flickering warily.

Choe read the apprehension, and he shook his head. "How long until phase two is ready to launch?"

The uneasiness was replaced by an almost imperceptible smirk signaling his approval of Choe's desire to stay the course. "Eighteen hours . . . a day on the outside."

"Good. I want it ready to launch on my command."

CHAPTER 49
New Orders

"I'm getting this nasty little feeling that shit's once more about to roll downhill . . . straight for us."
—USN Lt. Commander Jacob "Jade" Demetrius.

USS RONALD REAGAN (CVN-76).
THE SEA OF JAPAN

Demetrius was on the flight deck just outside the carrier's island staring at the sea of stars from horizon to horizon.

It was spectacular, reminding him of the stars over Qatar the night he'd met her.

The entire U.S. Navy was thrilled with his heroic performance earlier. There were even rumors of a possible Medal of Honor. But all he wanted was to be with his family.

It wasn't that he didn't appreciate the accolades that started the moment he stepped off his Super Hornet. In his mind, he'd simply done his job—it wasn't any different from what his grandfather and so many RAF pilots did during the Battle of Britain, forcing those V1 rockets off course. But his was captured by a half-dozen sailors aboard *Decatur* and uploaded on social media, where it had gone viral.

Demetrius would trade all of the praise in a New York minute for a chance to meet his daughter and be with Ghalia again.

Feeling damn lonely, he pulled out the picture and studied her, then Jasmine.

And the realization of what was truly important in his life made him question his future as a naval aviator. Perhaps the time had finally come to turn in his wings and leave the good fight to a new generation of pilots, hungry like he'd been two decades before, fearless, even immortal, with nothing to lose.

Jasmine's blue eyes looked back at him from the picture.

"Dammit, I know she's mine," he said.

"Talking to yourself now, man? The hell?"

Demetrius sighed and pocketed the photo. Gonzales joined him.

"That again, Jade?"

"Leave it alone, Speedy."

"I need to get you laid, man. It'll be easy now, you're a hero. Hell, they're talking about a Medal of Honor. If that doesn't get you some action, man, nothing will."

Demetrius sighed again.

"Seriously, Jade. We need to put this little war to bed, man."

"No argument there."

"So we can get our asses back to Japan, and I can get *your* ass in bed with someone that'll bring you back to your damned senses."

"Really?"

"You're being played, man, and—"

"Jade! Speedy!"

They turned around.

Commander Bassett glared at them.

"The fuck you doing out here? Mucker's got a fucking search party looking for your sorry asses!"

"Just holding his hand, Skipper," Gonzales said.

"*What?*"

"Our boy's heartbroken," Gonzales offered.

The big man blinked, then shook his head. "For the love of—" Bassett started.

"Fuck you, Speedy," Demetrius said.

"There! Our boy's back," Gonzales grinned.

"Goddammit, sailors! Stop *fucking* around! I want your butts down in the ready room in five!"

"What's happening, Skipper?" Demetrius asked.

"New orders, gentlemen."

"What kind of orders, sir?" Gonzales asked.

"Speedy, does this look like the goddamned ready room to you?"

Bassett spun around and disappeared through the yellow bulkhead muttering obscenities.

"What do you think's happening, Jade?"

"Not sure," Demetrius said, starting for the island. "But I'm getting this nasty little feeling that shit's once more about to roll downhill . . . straight for us."

CHAPTER 50
Code Breaker

"Codebreaking is like art, dude."
—Sally Kohl

40,000 FEET OVER THE SOUTH CHINA SEA

It took a little while, but the girl and the Fucking New Guy—John Savage—were getting it done.

Gorman and Harwich flanked Sally Kohl on the sofa aboard the Agency jet, a Bombardier Global 600 with international range.

The youngest and oddest member of Harwich's SOG team, an MIT prodigy with a passion for computers and tattoos, had caused them to storm out of Qatar and point the jet in this direction three hours ago, after breaking into one of the satellite phones. Its most called number in the past week had the country code 81: Japan.

Then an hour ago, Jason Savage, the thirty-something tech guy who had joined them in Qatar and currently sitting across from them, had extracted the next two digits of the number: 90. That meant it was a mobile phone in the Tokyo area.

Now the two techs worked on extracting the rest of that number from the encrypted device. It was plugged into their respective laptops, running CIA proprietary de-encryption software.

Gorman was fascinated by how they bounced code off of each other, attacking the firewall from both ends in a way that suggested professional familiarity even though they met just hours ago in Qatar. But, as Savage explained, the beauty of hacking was that you very seldom knew, or needed to know, your fellow hackers. It was all about the code.

"How much longer?" Gorman asked Sally.

"You can't rush these things," she said, pushing back the purple glasses perched at the end of her nose. "It's like art, dude."

She made a sweeping gesture for emphasis, never taking her eyes off the screen. The calavera bride and groom tattooed on her forearm flew past Gorman's face.

Savage grinned.

In complete contrast to the little tattooed nerd, Savage was clean cut, medium build, and very smooth, his fingers dancing on the keyboard, a maestro in a high-tech overture.

Gorman and Harwich exchanged a look. Both had been at the Agency long enough to remember when you couldn't even get a job interview at Langley if you had visible tattoos.

"Back to you," Savage said.

"Got it," Sally replied, clicking furiously for a few seconds and adding, "Back to you."

"Got it," Savage replied.

A high-tech game of ping-pong.

"Here you go," Sally announced, pointing at her screen. "Got the number for you . . . and a location."

The screen changed to a map of the greater Tokyo area, and a blue dot appeared. "There's your guy . . . or gal, hanging out near the bay."

CHAPTER 51
New Faces

"This isn't the time for your soft American approach."
—Naree Kyong-Lee

EAGLE PASS, TEXAS

Monica sat behind a laptop in the living room of her ranch house and tried very hard to ignore the fact that her brothers had been butchered the day before.

In her line of work, there was huge value in mastering the art of mental compartmentalizing. She learned long ago the power of being able to cubbyhole not only information but feelings, especially when emotions stood in the way of getting the job done.

It took everything she had to apply herself to the job at hand.

Stark was behind her, with Naree, Danny was with the helicopter, Ryan up on the roof in overwatch, and Juan kept an eye on their still unconscious female guest in Monica's old bedroom.

"Here we go," she said as a video materialized. "Our people got it from the Bear Creek Country Club. This is the camera facing Bear Creek Cemetery Road, which connects the highway to the southern fence around DFW."

The screen showed a two-lane road running along the edge of a parking lot. A white van emerged on the right side of the video.

Monica froze the image when the van drove through a patch of light spilling from the parking lot and onto the road, capturing a clear profile of the driver.

"And there's our mystery guest," Monica said. "Driving away from the airport ten minutes after the attack. And the manager confirmed the van ain't theirs, which can only mean . . ."

"And you said she looks like the same woman you saw leaving here with the two Japanese men in the van?" asked Stark.

Monica took a deep breath and managed a nod, forcing control over the anger blistering her gut like molten lava, because that woman in her room might have been involved in torturing and slaughtering her brothers.

"She *was* involved," Naree said. "And she'll tell us *everything* we need to know."

Stark turned to the petite Korean woman. "And she will, but *I* am leading the questioning."

Naree crossed her arms. "If she is who we think she is, then we need to be *ruthless*. This isn't the time for your soft American approach."

Stark shook his head. "The hell, Naree? Who said anything about a soft—"

"Look," Monica said. "If she was involved, and if the cartel wants her dead, then that suggests to me she could be the key to closing this."

"You're right, Cruz. If she was responsible, acting on orders from the cartel, why would they turn around and try to kill her?"

"Right," Monica agreed. "She has to be privy to information that the cartel doesn't want to get out, and that could be the proof we need to prevent World War Three."

Monica pulled up a YouTube video of USS *Decatur*. Crews were battling the flames.

"We need to get to the bottom of this mystery to keep it from escalating," Monica added. "And besides, there's a pretty good chance that the woman was involved in the murders of my brothers."

Naree made a face.

"Your *brothers*?"

Monica was breaking her own rule, but she needed to keep the woman under control. So, she took a moment to explain.

"I am very sorry," Naree said, and to her credit, she seemed sincere.

"Yeah, so am I," Monica said, "But this guy here . . . look, he's really the best there is when it comes to—"

"He might be the best when it comes to ops," Naree interrupted. "But I sure fooled him back in Seoul. Power of the pussy. Had you eating from my hand, didn't I, my sweet *Shiraki?*"

Monica gaped.

"Goddammit," Stark snapped. "That's enough. The mistakes I made back then are mine. They won't happen again. If you blink wrong while you are a guest of my country, *my sweet Naree*, there won't be enough of you left to put in an envelope and mail to that shithole you call home."

Naree leveled her eyes at him, assessing, then gave him a slight nod.

"She's awake!" Juan shouted from the bedroom.

Monica was first down the hall with Naree and Stark in tow, reaching the guestroom, which actually used to be *her* room—back when she had shocked her family by announcing her desire to save the world and enlisting in the Army after September 11, 2001.

The decision had broken her father's heart, he had planned for Monica and her two brothers to take over the ranch after his death.

Her eyes gravitated to the single bed against the wall, beneath an old pennant from her Eagle Pass High School next to a framed photo of the Eagle Pass Lady Eagle softball team, taken right before she left for boot camp at Fort Bliss, in El Paso, Texas.

The shelves opposite the bed held a handful of trophies, her varsity letter, a couple of dirty softballs, her old glove, and other memorabilia from a life she had long forgotten.

And now, as the reality of her brothers' murders sank in, it dawned on her that this ranch she had fought so hard to escape from now belonged to her—along with the responsibility of running it.

But she couldn't worry about that now.

She returned to the present, to Juan standing at the edge of the bed helping the stranger sit up, handing her a bottle of water.

"She doesn't get any fucking water until she tells us what we need to know!" Naree exploded, trying to take the bottle away but Juan blocked her.

"Back off," the big warrior warned sternly.

"Dammit, Naree," Stark said. "Final warning to dial it the fuck down."

"It wasn't your leader this whore killed, *Shiraki!*"

"That's true, Naree," Monica interceded. "But she may have been responsible for the death of many of our federal agents, police officers, military personnel, plus my brothers and—"

"I *will* help you," the woman said with a heavy accent, making them all turn in her direction. The expression on her face proclaimed her desire to repay the bastards who tried to kill her. Then, in sharp contrast with the fury in her dark eyes, she calmly took a sip from the bottle of water.

Naree started to say something, but Stark raised his hand. "Why should we believe anything you tell us?"

"Because," she said, "The asshole who tried to have me killed has my son."

CHAPTER 52
Lockdown

"If there's one thing I learned from Tío Chapo, it's to always assume the worst."
—Ricco Orellana

CULIACÁN CITY, NORTHWESTERN MEXICO

The cartel boss stood up behind his desk at the news his main bodyguards, Miguel and Roman, just delivered.

"How is it possible?" Ricco asked. "How is it *fucking* possible that over a hundred men could not take care of one goddamned woman?"

"According to the reports, *jefe*," said Roman, "a helicopter came out of nowhere and rescued her. It had no markings, but we're pretty sure it was the gringos because it was seen heading north, over the wall."

Ricco shook his head. Even before the helicopter had shown up, Mireya had managed to take out a couple of dozen men, some of them *sicarios*. And if indeed, she had fallen into the hands of the Americans, after Ricco had tried to have her killed . . .

Goddammit!

Pinching the bridge of his nose, he said, "I want her dead. Send the word. They can name their price. The gringos are going to put her in one of their jails. Get one of our people on the inside to take care of it. *Immediately.*"

"Yes, jefe. We'll send the order—"

"And then pull everybody in here. We're going into lockdown."

"Lockdown?" Roman said. "You don't think that—"

Ricco pointed to the portrait of Joaquin Guzman. "If there's one thing I learned from Tío Chapo, it's to always assume the worst, Roman. That's how we stay ahead in this business. And speaking of that, get Governor Chavez on the phone. It's time that fat bastard earned the millions I've been paying him."

"What about the boy?" Miguel asked.

Ricco frowned, considering that.

He had planned to explain to Antonio how his mother was killed by the Americans. Now, he might have to think of something else, of another way to explain the situation.

Or kill him.

But for now, he preferred the former.

"Keep him locked in his room—until this thing blows over. Then I'll have a talk with him."

Ricco dismissed them and stared out the panoramic windows overlooking the city and the Gulf of California beyond it. His defenses were in place. He had over five hundred men protecting the mountain retreat, including two hundred armed police officers from the State of Sinaloa.

If the Americans wanted to come after him, they would be in for one hell of a fight. Because another thing he had learned from his predecessors was that survival—success—belonged to the best prepared and the most determined.

And if all else failed, he had his vault, the panic room where he could survive for days if needed, certainly long enough for reinforcements to reach his estate from the military bases in the valley, where he clothed, sheltered, armed, trained and owned another two thousand soldiers, plus their families.

Let the gringos come and try, he thought. *Let them fucking come.*

CHAPTER 53
Covert Deal

"How many shadowy deals did Lincoln approve that never made it to the annals of history, but which contributed to the ultimate success of the Union?"
—President Laura Vaccaro

TREATY ROOM. THE WHITE HOUSE. WASHINGTON, D.C.

"I advise against that, Madam President. The consequences if it gets out . . . I can't even begin to imagine the repercussions."

Vaccaro remained standing, staring at the painting of Lincoln surrounded by his top generals.

She wondered just how many compromises the legendary president had to make to win that terrible but necessary war. How many unsavory characters he'd had to tolerate for the greater good, for the bigger picture?

Some of those alliances were well documented—Lincoln's clandestine intelligence gatherings, which he exploited to win the war. It included a long list of spies, some heroes, other unsavory characters—but all necessary to provide critical intelligence, including enemy strategies and deployments for crucial battles.

But Vaccaro wondered how many more secret alliances Lincoln had made?

How many more shadowy deals did Lincoln approve that never made it to the annals of history, but contributed to the ultimate success of the Union?

She finally turned to face John Wright, waiting, his entire posture radiating disapproval.

Colonel Stark had managed to secure a woman named Mireya Moreno Carreón, who was part of the team that shot down the Embraer in Dallas. The woman claimed responsibility for shooting down the two Black Hawk helicopters transporting the DHS contingent to Eagle Pass.

Under orders from Ricco Orellana.

Now, Stark maintained the woman could provide the information necessary to take Orellana from his retreat in the mountains of Sinaloa—if they acted quickly.

In exchange, the woman wanted total immunity plus witness protection for her and her son, currently a hostage of Ricco Orellana.

And all that was required to move forward was her approval.

Looking into the eyes of her most-trusted advisor and former comrade-in-arms, Vaccaro said, "Damn the consequences, John. Get it done, and give Stark anything else he needs."

Wright nodded.

"And what about the other . . . mission I approved?"

Wright checked his watch and said, "It's starting now."

CHAPTER 54
Stealth

"That's why you're going in F-35Cs, Jade, so you don't get your ass shot down."
—USN Captain Jared "Mucker" O'Donnell

USS RONALD REAGAN (CVN-76). THE SEA OF JAPAN

In spite of his current state of mind, Lt. Cmdr. Jacob Demetrius managed a smile under his oxygen mask as the yellow-shirted catapult officer secured the nose wheel of his F-35C Lightning to the Catapult One shuttle.

He pasted the picture of Ghalia holding Jasmine to the side of the full-panel-width glass cockpit touchscreen, which was integrated with his helmet-mounted display system.

His smile widened, and not just at his family but the simply beautiful and futuristic panel in front of him, making every jet he'd ever flown look like they belonged in a museum.

Gonzales taxied his F-35C up to the shuttle of Catapult Two, and its crew went to work. He would launch precisely two minutes behind Demetrius and follow the exact same GPS flight path at the exact same speed so they would have guaranteed separation in the clouds.

For most fighter jets, it was a dreadful night to fly, with ceilings at 800 feet and visibility less than a mile. But for the F-35C, it was perfect, especially given the nature of their top-secret mission.

"All set, Speedy?"

"Good to go."

"Radio silence on take-off," Demetrius said.

"Roger."

Demetrius placed his right index and thumb on the sidestick controller to tilt it in every direction. The joystick-like governor sent digital pulses to the Lightning's fly-by-wire system, which in turn moved the corresponding control surfaces in the desired direction.

He advanced the throttle to the military setting and flicked the external lights, letting the cat officer know his jet was ready. The cat officer in turn dropped to a deep crouch and extended his right arm in the direction of the bow.

Demetrius staged the blower of the single Pratt & Whitney F135 turbofan, engaging the afterburner when the sudden tug from the steam-driven catapult shoved him into his seat.

The flight deck blurred past as he volleyed off the bow, rocketing straight into the clouds, where he retracted the landing gear and reduced power to military setting after achieving a positive rate of climb.

He turned to a preassigned GPS track directly to the Weiyuan Dam, a large hydroelectric dam on the Yalu River, which divided China from North Korea.

Per the briefing, radio silence was critical to their mission, so Demetrius had his radio muted and the AN/APG-81 active electronically scanned array radar off, making him invisible not only to North Korea's coastal defenses, but to American forces and even Gonzales.

He checked the digital clock on the panel. If everything went according to the plan they were briefed on by Captain O'Donnell, seven pairs of F-35As, the Air Force variant of the Lightning, had already departed Kadena Airbase in Okinawa to hit the other hydroelectric dams on the Yalu River.

He leveled off at twenty thousand feet, remaining just below the speed of sound for the forty minutes it took him to reach the coast, where he jettisoned his external tank and switched to internal fuel, shutting off all external lights.

With a radar signature equivalent to a large bird, the naval jet entered North Korean airspace on a hostile sortie, the first since the signing of the Korean Armistice Agreement in July of 1953.

And here I am, Demetrius thought, still in the clouds, relying on his instruments to navigate this $109-million modern marvel into the world's most dangerous airspace.

And that reminded him of the short conversation he'd had with O'Donnell at the end of the briefing.

"*What happens if we get shot down, Skipper?*"

"*That's why you're going in F-35Cs, Jade, so you don't get your ass shot down.*"

Demetrius silently prayed not only that the stealth claims made by the engineers at Lockheed-Martin were correct, but that the Chinese, in their constant effort to try to outpace the Americans, had not come up with a counteroffensive weapon.

CHAPTER 55
Ghost Hunter

"Want to go hunting for ghosts?"
—General Mina Kyong-Lee

PANGHYON AIRFIELD. PYONGAN PROVINCE, NORTH KOREA

"Someone's up there, General, and it isn't us."

Mina Kyong-Lee and Major Byung Ko were observing the operator of a new-generation Chinese radar.

The system emitted high frequency electromagnetic waves with very long wavelengths and wide beams, which painted the skies with a type of radar energy designed to detect fifth-generation stealth fighters from hundreds of miles away.

"From where?" Mina asked.

"It may be from the direction of the American fleet," the operator replied. "But it's hard to tell for sure."

"How many?"

"Unknown."

Mina made a face.

"Can you pin its location?" Byung asked.

The operator shook his head. "That's the main drawback of this system, Major. It tells me there's something there, but I can't characterize it for you."

"So," Mina said. "This new Chinese system that Beijing claims will make fifth-generation fighters obsolete can tell me there's a stealth threat out there, but it can't tell me how many or get a precise enough fix to target it?"

"It's really a work in progress," the operator said, then pointing at the traditional radar systems across the room. "But at least it's better than those. They're completely blind."

Mina glanced at the operators staring at their blank radar screens. "Great. So, what are our options?"

"Well," the operator replied. "Sooner or later, they will have to turn on their weapons systems to target whatever it is they're trying to hit, especially in this weather. And when they do, they'll be visible for the duration of their attack, but it could be long enough for us to counterattack."

"Assuming we're already in the air and close enough?"

"Correct."

"Can you at least tell me the general area?"

"Based on what I'm getting, I would guess—and mind you it's only an *educated* guess—somewhere in the Jilin Province. But I don't know how many planes we're dealing with and—"

"Good enough," Mina said. She turned to Byung. "Want to go hunting for ghosts?"

Demetrius flew in from the east, cruising at 600 knots through a wet evening in monsoon season, still with zero visibility.

Although he knew Gonzales was some twenty miles behind him on the same course, Demetrius still felt a strange sense of loneliness from flying without a wingman.

He couldn't remember the last time he had flown without someone watching his back.

The navigation system started blinking, informing him he was within fifty miles of his target.

Throttling back, he lowered the nose, dropping from twenty thousand feet to begin his bombing run.

He went to turn on the AN/APG-81 scan array radar, per the flight plan, but something made him hold back.

Doing some quick math, Demetrius decided to wait until he was twenty miles from his target. The same fancy radar system that allowed him to place his munitions with insane accuracy had the undesirable side effect of broadcasting his position to anyone in the region, painting a big X on his back.

The trick was to minimize the time anyone on the ground or in the air could pick up his radar signal before he switched it off and returned to ghost status.

He frowned. In hindsight, he should have had a discussion with Gonzales about not turning on the radar until they were closer to the target.

And he still could—by breaking radio silence, but he decided to stay the course. With luck, Gonzales would be cautious anyway.

Forty miles. Ten thousand feet. Six hundred knots.

Demetrius kept his eyes on the GPS screen, maintaining his rate of descent.

"Haemosu Niner Six, I'm showing one target at your seven o'clock, one hundred sixty miles, descending through fifteen thousand feet at six hundred knots."

"Copy that," Mina replied, turning to that heading, adding, "Burners, Byung."

"Roger."

The twin Saturn turbofans rocketed the Sukhoi to Mach 2.2

Thirty miles. Seven thousand feet. Six hundred knots.

The flight plan called for a ninety-degree turn to the south to follow the Yalu River, which separated North Korea from China.

Demetrius competed the turn, remaining on the North Korean side of the river following the prescribed GPS approach to his target.

Twenty miles. Three thousand feet. Six hundred knots.

Alright. Here we go.

He powered up the AN/APG-81, which took less than thirty seconds to finish its boot up sequence and advertise his presence to all Chinese and North Korean radar operators in a five-hundred-mile radius.

But it gave him a view of traffic in the region. He picked Gonzales' F-35C twenty miles behind him, including his weapons systems radar already engaged even though Gonzales was forty miles out.

Shit, Speedy. You should have—

His radar also picked up two bandits a hundred and thirty miles behind Gonzales closing fast.

"Speedy," Demetrius said, breaking radio silence. "Behind you."

"I see them, Jade. Picked them up when I turned on my radar. But they're still too far away."

"Haemosu Niner Six, I'm showing a second target at your twelve o'clock, twenty miles ahead of the first, descending through twenty-five hundred feet at six hundred knots."

"Copy that," Mina replied still immersed in the clouds. "Byung, R-27s."

"Roger."

Mina enabled her two R-27EM radar-guided missiles, each with a maximum range of 106 miles, and quickly assigned one to each intruder and cut them loose.

The thirteen-foot-long missiles quickly accelerated to Mach 4, vanishing into the clouds.

She followed their courses on her radar screen, along with two missiles fired by her wingman.

Ten miles. Two thousand feet. Six hundred knots.

Demetrius broke from the clouds and transitioned to night vision. The darkness came alive in a palette of greens, revealing a wide river dotted with small pockets of lights.

He stayed on the east bank, out of Chinese airspace.

This remote region was far from major cities, and that suited Demetrius just fine.

His missile warning system went off. Gonzales came through the radio again.

Jade. Incoming vampires. Four. Eighty miles out.

"Too far away. We'll be long gone. Stay on target."

At a distance of three miles, and holding two thousand feet, Demetrius inched over to the western side of the complex to release two BLU-238/B submunitions and immediately pushed full power and entered a sharp climb and turn back east.

The weapons glided on a parabolic path for thirty seconds. An electric charge layering their composite skins disintegrated, releasing hundreds of bomblets, each a metal armature enclosed by a twine of copper wire—or stator winding—feeding a bank of capacitors plus a core of HEP—high-explosive plastic.

At an altitude of just fifty feet over the western side of the hydro-electric facility, the cloud-like weapon glided over three of the plant's six generators plus associated transformers and other high-voltage equipment. The capacitors in each bomblet distributed an electrical current through the stator wires, and this surge created a magnetic field that triggered a fuse mechanism that ignited their explosive cores.

The blast came through the armature of each bomblet like a wave, enveloping the stator winding and creating a short circuit that severed the coiled wire from its power source. And it was this moving short circuit that compressed the magnetic field, generating a localized and quite intense electromagnetic pulse that permeated through anything in its five-hundred-foot-radius kill zone, including the plant's delicate electronics.

Demetrius shut off his radar, once more becoming a ghost, At the same time, across the facility, hundreds of thousands of short circuits sparked like fireworks. The individual blasts of HEP disintegrated the bomblets, turning their highly-classified technology into sizzling ash that washed away in the slipstream.

A ghost jet dropping a ghost weapon, Demetrius mused. He banked east holding two thousand feet. The few lights across the region were going out.

Two minutes later, he heard three clicks of the mic. Gonzales had released his load over the eastern side of the hydroelectric facility.

And that's how it's done.

Demetrius climbed back up to twenty thousand feet and headed home.

"Haemosu Niner Six, I'm showing only one target now at—"

Mina frowned.

"Panghyon control, please say again."

Silence.

"Panghyon control, Haemosu Niner Six. Come in."

More silence.

"General?" Byung said. *"What is happening?"*

"Not sure," she replied, as both intruders vanished from her radar, and the four missiles they had fired started to wander.

She shook her head. Just like she was able to fire missiles the moment those stealth fighters turned on their acquisition radars, so could the Americans fire missiles at North Korean radar installations as they searched for enemy aircraft.

But then she thought of something: whatever it was that the Americans had hit, they had already turned off their radars, meaning they had completed their mission and were likely headed back for their carrier in the Sea of Japan.

Mina was pretty certain they would be conserving fuel, which meant they were headed in a straight line for home.

And that gave her an idea.

Looking at the map on the tablet strapped to her right thigh, she plotted a course from where the American radars had gone off to the last known location of the American aircraft carrier.

And the line linking the two ran just fifty miles south of her current location.

"Burners, Byung! On me!" she said, swinging the control column to the right.

She accelerated inside the clouds and turned, ignoring the accumulating G-forces pinning her into her seat.

Mina remained in the clouds, deciding to climb to fifteen thousand feet, hoping that the American jets would not be higher than ten thousand feet above her, the vertical limit of her two advanced R-74M all-aspect infrared missiles.

She enabled the missiles, letting their heat-seeking electronic brains, capable of detecting heat sources up to eight miles away, scan a sixty-degree cone of airspace directly in front of her.

She glanced at her map; twenty miles to the assumed departure point of the American stealth jets.

"Arm the R-73s," she ordered.

"Roger. Arming."

Mina throttled back when she reached the imaginary departure line and turned east, like she presumed the American jets had.

Both R-73 missiles emitted high-pitched beeps, confirming they had detected a heat source somewhere within the 60-degree-search cone centered on her new heading of 080.

"Got something," she announced.

"Got company, Jade."

Demetrius frowned. He had just crossed the coast and was over the Sea of Japan. "What are you talking about?"

"IR warning. Someone's trying to get an IR lock on me."

Demetrius eyed his warning lights but all was quiet. Then again, he was twenty miles ahead of Gonzales—his wingman was still over land but close to the coast.

He shook his head.

Demetrius had expected the North Koreans to be firing radar-controlled missiles at them the moment they enabled their target acquisition radars—and they had. But those missiles had lost them the instant he and Gonzales had shut off their radar.

He couldn't understand how someone had managed to sneak up behind them. The very best IR seeker heads had a detection range of around five to ten miles, so someone had been able to track them to get this close and—

"Missile lock!" Gonzales announced.

Got you, Mina thought and squeezed the trigger twice, releasing both missiles.

The twin R-73Ms rocketed to Mach 2.5 in seconds, their electronic brains locked on the single heat source three miles ahead.

"Goddammit! Vampires in the air! Two of them! Releasing flares!"

Demetrius turned his F-35C one-eighty degrees, back toward the coast. He enabled his target acquisition radar, picking up Gonzales' bird eighteen miles away—as well as two bandits on his tail. He detected the two missiles Gonzales was trying to evade.

The system tracked the enemy aircraft and provided firing solutions for two AIM-120 AMRAAM missiles, which he fired in sequence, watching their bright exhaust vanish into the clouds.

Returning to the radar, he tracked Gonzales' jet as it turned hard ninety degrees to the north to position itself at a right angle to the incoming missiles in a classic evasive maneuver.

"Enemy missiles in the air! Twenty seconds to impact!" announced Byung.

Mina frowned when the second American jet turned on its radar and fired missiles at her and Byung from a distance of twenty-five miles. And she couldn't counterattack because she had already shot her two mid-range radar-guided missiles, and now her two IR missiles. All she had left was the 150 rounds in the Sukhoi's internal 30mm Gryazev-Shipunov cannon reserved for close encounters.

"Evasive!" she shouted, turning her jet ninety-degrees to the missile locked on her, releasing chaff, going into full burner, and dropping the nose, accelerating to Mach 2.6.

As the G-forces hammered her into her seat, Mina saw the closest American jet on her radar performing a similar evasive maneuver to fool her two IR missiles. Fortunately, the "M" variant of her

R-73s included not only a greater range but much improved infrared counter-countermeasures. The missiles were much better at ignoring flares than prior generations.

The first missile went for the hot decoys, but the second remained on target.

"Fooled one! But the other vampire's on me, Jade!"

"Get the hell out of there, Speedy!" Demetrius shouted. On his radar the second missile was dangerously close to Gonzales' F-35C. "Eject! Eje—"

Gonzales pulled on the ejection handles just as the missile struck his exhaust, detonating its sixteen-pound fragmentation warhead. It wreaked havoc inside the turbofan, triggering a catastrophic explosion that propagated to the front of the fighter in a fraction of a second.

The blast briefly enveloped Gonzales while the Martin-Baker MK-16 ejection seat rocketed him away from the doomed jet in a parabolic trajectory.

A self-destruct switch built into the base of the ejection seat detected separation from the airframe, triggering complete destruction of the stealth fighter and its top-secret avionics beyond the initial explosion from the missile—a safety feature to prevent technology from the plane from falling into enemy hands.

The radar signature of the F-35C vanished.

"Goddammit!"

Keeping an eye on the two departing enemy jets, Demetrius dropped his nose, marked the last radar contact on his map, shut off his radar, and headed straight for it.

"Torch Bearer Twenty, Dambusters Three-Oh-Three, need a helo and a driver," Demetrius said, giving the coordinates.

"*Dambusters Three-Oh-Three, Torchbearer Twenty, we're calling it in now. Stand by.*"

Mina broke out under the clouds releasing more chaff and cutting hard left, making a second ninety degree turn.

The dark terrain below her momentarily brightened when the missile detonated almost a mile behind her, fooled by the last round of chaff. She pushed the Sukhoi beyond its design envelope, clutching the control column with both hands groaning from the G-forces.

But a moment later, a second flash followed by a fiery explosion marked the crash site of her wingman.

"Goddammit, Byung!"

She started circling the site, hoping to see a parachute.

Inside *Ronald Reagan*'s CATCC, Captain O'Donnell conferred with Commander Bassett.

"They're deaf, dumb, and blind, Mucker," Bassett said. "If there was an ideal time to send a rescue helo into North Korea, tonight would be it."

O'Donnell nodded. "Send the Alert Five to relieve Jade. Might as well send the works to get our boys back."

Demetrius transitioned back to night-vision. He circled the GPS coordinates where Gonzales had bailed.

"Speedy, Jade. Come in."

Silence.

"Speedy? Dammit. Come in, man."

Debris rained from the clouds, some of it on fire. Just east, a blue-and-white canopy sank toward a hilly meadow a couple of miles from the beach.

Good man.

"Torch Bearer Twenty, Dambusters Three-Oh-Three. Got eyes on my wingman," Demetrius reported, and he updated the coordinates.

"Dambusters Three-Oh-Three, Torchbearer Twenty, helo on the way. ETA forty-five minutes. Alert Five in fifteen."

"Torch Bearer Twenty, be aware there's no movement on the ground, and I have no radio contact with my wingman. Only visual. He landed in a clearing and is not moving.

"Dambusters Three-Oh-Three, Torchbearer Twenty. We copy. What's your fuel situation?"

"One hour left."

"Dambusters Three-Oh-Three, RTB. Repeat, RTB."

Demetrius frowned. The controller was ordering him to return to base, which would mean abandoning Gonzales before the Alert Five got here. His gaze went from the picture outside, where he could see the parachute on the ground, to the picture inside—the one of Ghalia and Jasmine.

Dammit, he thought. *I can't. I just can't. I'm sorry.*

"Negative," he said with determination. "I'm *not* leaving my wingman."

Burning debris in the distance, resembling rain, marked the destruction of one of the American jets.

Mina spotted a shadow circling the debris.

I see you, she thought, flipping a switch to arm the cannon and turning toward the enemy jet.

"Goddammit, Jade. Get your ass back here!"

Demetrius frowned when Bassett came on the line.

"I have the fuel, sir. I'd like to keep an eye on Speedy until—"

The side stick trembled in his hand as the unmistakable sound of a 30mm cannon blasted behind him, ripping across his port wing.

Shit!

"I'm under attack!" Demetrius shouted into the radio, pushing full power and cutting hard left as alarms blared inside his cockpit.

A glance outside and he cringed at the half dozen fist-size holes along his wing.

But he could still maneuver, getting himself out of the line of fire and enabling the target acquisition radar.

The system instantly picked up the bandit that had somehow snuck up behind him, and Demetrius fired an AMRAAM.

The missile went out, accelerating briefly then turning to come around behind the radar-painted enemy, who blasted a final volley of 30mm violence, then breaking off the attack.

More warning lights lit up his panel, including his turbofan, which stopped generating thrust.

Demetrius shouted, "Punching out, boys!" and reached for the ejection handles. His eyes landed on the picture of Ghalia and Jasmine still taped to the control panel. There was no time to reach it.

Goddammit.

And that was the last thing he saw. His vision tunneled when the Martin-Baker seat rocketed him away from the doomed jet seconds before it self-destructed, tossing him upside down and to the side before he blacked out from the G-forces.

Mina had just a couple of seconds to react as the missile came up behind her. Freshly out of chaff, she did the only thing she could: pull on the ejection handles.

Night turned to day as the Zvezda K-36D ejection seat kicked her away from the Sukhoi a second before the missile went up the turbines, detonating them along with her unused fuel.

She felt the intense heat as well as a terrible piercing pain in her left shoulder and in her abdomen as the rocket pushed her away from the inferno.

Her world spun in every conceivable direction and she trembled from the burning shockwave she had punched through.

She felt another tug, followed by a loud snap as her canopy blossomed overhead.

Just before she passed out, Mina saw another canopy a couple of thousand feet away from her.

CHAPTER 56
Lights Out

"One dam malfunctioning . . . yes, okay. But all of them? And at once?
—Joon Song-Ju, North Korean Minister of Infrastructure

RYONGSONG RESIDENCE. PYONGYANG, NORTH KOREA

Choe Ryong-Ju and General Pak Yong-Gil contemplated the darkness enveloping the capital city.

The door swung open, and Joon Song-Ju, the young official in charge of the nation's infrastructure, wearing only a robe and slippers, was pushed in at gunpoint by half a dozen soldiers. Two more soldiers remained in the anteroom flanking a beautiful woman with a bloody lip and a bruised cheek wearing a robe. She was hugging herself and sobbing quietly.

"The Supreme Leader, rest in peace, had your predecessor shot for incompetence," Pak said. "Tell me why we shouldn't do the same with you and that whore?"

The young official, his hair messy, his partially closed robe revealing a pale chest and equally pale legs, stuttered, "We . . . we were attacked!"

"Attacked? How, you idiot?" Pak challenged. "Our bases never reported any attacks! The plants malfunctioned, and you were in your office screwing one of your secretaries!"

"But this was nationwide," Joon said, mustering the courage to stand up to Pak's armor-piercing glare surrounded by the business ends of half a dozen Kalashnikovs. "The dams along the Yalu . . . they are *all* down."

"*All?*" Choe pressed.

He nodded. "Unbong, Weiyuan, Amnok, Sup'ung, and even Taechon," he said, referring to the hydroelectric dams that supplied over seventy percent of the power to the nation, including Pyongyang.

"And the coal plants?" Choe asked?

"Chonch'on'gang and Pukch'and are still operational, but they're small, and the sudden spike in demand has shut them down," Joon said.

Choe and Pak exchanged surprised looks.

"One dam malfunctioning . . . yes, okay," Joon said. "But *all of them*? At *once*? You can take me out back and shoot me, but this isn't my fault. The facts suggest that something else has occurred."

Choe motioned for the soldiers to leave the room saying, "Take the woman home. Let her be."

Choe patted Joon on the shoulder and said, "Come, sit. Let's talk this through."

The three men sat at the table.

Joon shook his head. "I'm not sure how this happened . . . you are right, General, no explosions were reported by the plants with shortwave radios. But they all reported that the transformers malfunctioned—short circuits is what the engineers claimed."

Choe turned to Pak. "An EMP, maybe? Like we did to their fleet?"

Pak removed his cap, set it on the table, and exhaled through his nostrils in visible frustration. "But . . . there have been no reported detonations in the atmosphere. If this was indeed an attack, then it was done with a new weapon—something we have not seen, until now."

"One moment the power stations were operating normally," said Joon, running a hand through his tousled hair, "and then our communications are cut off, leaving us dependent on shortwave radios. And I am sorry about the woman, comrades, but the stress of the past few days—"

"Is that how you're getting your reports, Pak?" Choe asked, not caring to hear that last part.

Pak nodded. "The few that are coming through, yes. But I can't contact the majority of our forces, especially in the DMZ or along the coast. And that means we can't launch the next phase of *Azure Dragon* as planned."

"It has to be the Americans," Choe said.

Joon said, "Perhaps, though the power outages affected the bordering Chinese provinces. Would the Americans be foolish enough to do that? To challenge Beijing?"

Choe considered his options. President Xi had warned him that something like this could happen.

"The Americans have used this tactic before," Pak said.

Choe studied the veteran general's weathered face.

"The Persian Gulf War in 1990," Pak added. "President Bush first blinded Iraq, cutting off communications across the country—turning off the lights. And then—" Pak ran the tip of his thumb across his neck. "It was swift and effective. And President Vaccaro did the exact same thing last year to Pakistan."

"So . . . what are you recommending?"

"Stay on plan. We resume the second phase as soon as we're able to send the word out."

"How long will that be?"

Pak turned to Joon, who took a deep breath, and said, "A day. Maybe two? We need to restore power in coordination with our Chinese counterparts since these are joint facilities. Then we can re-establish communications and—"

"Fine," Choe said. "Go and get the lights back on. And quickly. Your life and those of your whores depend on it."

As the young official left, Choe turned to Pak. "President Xi asked me to hold off launching the next phase until the Americans finish the investigation they claim to be conducting. Do you think it's possible that Xi turned off our lights? Perhaps to keep us from launching any more attacks?"

Pak shrugged. "At this moment, I'm guessing *anything* is possible. It would certainly explain why only the power plants along the Yalu River were affected since we share that power."

Choe considered that, then said, "Either way, whoever is behind this has temporarily succeeded in forcing us to hold back. Have we heard from Naree again?"

"Not since yesterday. She was supposed to be in some task force, trying to find this so-called proof."

"Get ready, then," Choe said, standing and turning back to the windows. "As soon as the lights come back on. Get ready, old friend. We will *not* suffer the same fate as Iraq and Pakistan. We will *not* go down without a fight."

CHAPTER 57
Risky Business

"If doing it costs me the presidency . . . so be it."
—President Laura Vaccaro

**TREATY ROOM. THE WHITE HOUSE.
WASHINGTON, D.C.**

"We have the location, Madam President. Are you sure you don't want to coordinate the takedown with Mexican authorities?"

Vaccaro asked, "Do you recall how that actually worked out with El Chapo?"

Wright and Jacobson exchanged glances.

"Well . . . I know he's in ADX?" Wright replied, referring to the Administrative Maximum U.S. Penitentiary in Florence, Colorado, the nation's highest security prison. There, the famous drug lord had joined some of America's worst offenders, including Unabomber Ted Kaczynski and Oklahoma City bombing conspirator Terry Nichols.

Vaccaro nodded. "Yes, John, but he was arrested *twice*, and *twice* he escaped from Mexican federal prisons. And he continued running his operation from prison. Hell, he had goddamned suites in those Mexican prisons with fine food and fine whores brought in daily. It wasn't until he was arrested a *third* time and finally extradited here that he was isolated from his operation. I can't afford to have the same thing happen with Orellana. I want his ass either dead or in *our* custody. And *yesterday*."

Wright traded another look with Jacobson.

Jacobson said, "So far, we have succeeded in keeping this special team under wraps, Madam President. The incident in Karachi never happened, and neither did the short excursion that Stark took in Mexico. But this—this is going to get out and—"

"Lisa, John, I just turned off the lights in North Korea to hopefully slow them down and buy us some time. Now, I need to take advantage of the time we bought. And I can't think of a better way than delivering to them the people responsible and preventing this thing from escalating any more than it already has.

"And if doing it costs me the presidency, so be it. My job is clear: protect the country. If I allow myself or any of you to factor in the possibility of political repercussions, then we *will* fail. It's precisely why you, John, and Colonel Stark rescued me back in country fifteen years ago. Remember?"

She looked John Wright straight in the eye, and for an instant, Vaccaro could see his young and handsome face as he carried her toward a waiting Chinook in the middle of a firefight.

The president took a deep breath, and so did Wright. "It was the mission, John, and I needed help," she added. "I see this situation the exact same way. Yes, it's what I did a year ago, and it's what I'm doing now."

CHAPTER 58
Storm Troopers

"If I was going to kill you, I would have done so by now."
—Mireya Moreno Carreón

GULF OF CALIFORNIA, NORTHWESTERN MEXICO

They came in low and fast from the southwest under a starry sky, rounding the pristine beaches of Cabo San Lucas after a short refueling stop aboard USS *Lake Champlain*, a Ticonderoga-class missile cruiser operating just outside of Mexican territorial waters.

In the copilot's seat of the Black Hawk, Stark contemplated the distant lights of resorts lining the southern tip of the Baja California peninsula, where tourists relaxed in a world that couldn't be any more distant from the violence he was preparing to unleash.

Danny slowed them to a hover five miles from the coastline near Culiacán.

"Any moment now," Stark said, watching a display.

"I can't believe we're back in this shit town again after all these years," Danny commented.

Green dots blinked to life on the screen, an equal number of bright plumes materialized in the western sky.

"Yeah. Seems like a lifetime ago," Stark said, changing the display to a night-vision feed from the RQ-4 Global Hawk UAV 40,000 feet over their target.

The drone's view was overlaid on a map marking the fortifications around a compound in the Sierra Madres. The defenses included half a dozen batteries of radar-guided surface-to-air missiles.

The SAM systems were actively searching for targets, which made them targets for the eight Tomahawk cruise missiles fired by *Lake Champlain*, each zeroing in on an individual radar signature.

But an additional six Tomahawks were fired toward the coordinates provided by the Global Hawk, marking the location of garrisons protecting the mountaintop retreat—according to intelligence from Mireya.

"Time to go," Stark said, and the Blackhawk accelerated to its maximum speed of 180 knots.

"Missile strikes in two mikes," Danny said, the coast blurring under them. "And we're up in three mikes."

Stark turned in the crew chief's seat to face the main cabin, where Monica handled the starboard Browning and Juan handled the port side. Ryan sat next to Monica with his Barrett. All three were wearing night-vision goggles.

Naree was on one of the starboard seats and Mireya occupied the seat across from her. Everyone was gunned up, wearing body armor, throat mics, earpieces, and night-vision goggles.

His eyes settled on Mireya. She had already proven as feisty as Monica and Naree.

Stark made the call to bring her along for three reasons.

One, she had demanded to come and get her son, assuming he was still alive.

Two, she had already proven to be a deadly operator.

And three, the most important: with no time to dry run this op somewhere with a mockup of the target for at least a few hours, the next best thing was to have a guide—plus an overwhelming show of violence in the form of the 1,000-pound warheads crowning each Tomahawk.

And those factors, combined with the electronics jamming that would shower the compound in another minute, courtesy of an EA-18G Growler, gave them a better than average chance of success.

The Growler, the electronic warfare version of the two-seater F/A-18F Super Hornet, was sourced out of Coronado NAS by Wright, but it was expedited to this location within the hour after Juan had contacted his former superior officer and explained the situation.

Of course, there was the thing with Mireya taking down the Embraer and two Black Hawks loaded with DHS personnel.

But President Vaccaro had already signed off immunity in exchange for her active cooperation.

It wasn't ideal, but it wasn't the first time the U.S. government made a deal with an unsavory character for the greater good.

Naree, of course, still wanted to put a bullet between Mireya's eyes, especially after she confessed to having delivered the knockout punch to the wounded jet trying to return to DFW.

Stark frowned, remembering how he had to restrain Naree, tossing her over his shoulder and carrying her outside kicking and screaming.

"She killed him, *Shiraki!*" she had shouted after Stark set her down. "The bitch just confessed!"

"Which makes it even more critical that we keep her alive. She can help us get to the man who gave the order."

"But—"

"Your nation is on the brink of getting erased from the map, Naree. They launched a direct attack against our fleet in the Sea of Japan. Do you remember what happened to Pakistan a year ago? To Iraq during the Gulf War? Hell, even to Germany during World War Two? Is that what you want for North Korea?"

Naree was visibly flustered.

"President Vaccaro is showing extreme restraint by not unleashing the full might of our military forces on your nation because she knows they're reacting to what they believe they know. That woman is the key to convincing Pyongyang. In fact, if we bag Orellana alive, you'll be taking him back to North Korea to face trial under your laws."

"You—you never told me that."

"I just found out, when I was on the phone with Washington."

And that had been enough to settle her down, giving Stark the time to plan this mission with Mireya's assistance, plus the crew of *Lake Champlain*.

"Three minutes!" Stark announced. "Ready?" he asked Naree.

She nodded. "You?"

Stark patted the MP7A1 strapped to his chest below a row of mixed grenades secured to his utility vest.

Naree lifted her chin toward Mireya. "I still don't trust her with that gun."

Mireya opened her eyes and glowered at Naree, completely unafraid. "If I was going to kill you," she said, "I would have done it by now . . . starting with you."

Naree shook her head. "She'd better not screw us, *Shiraki*."

"My son is all I care about. Once he is safe, you can do whatever you wish with me," Mireya said.

"Count on it," Naree replied.

Mireya ignored her and turned to Stark. "Make sure he puts us down by the helipad. That's where he will run when all hell breaks loose."

Stark nodded before looking over at Monica and Ryan, who seemed to be engaged in a conversation.

"So, did you like it?" Ryan asked, inspecting the dark terrain through the Barrett's night-vision scope.

"Like what?" Monica replied.

"The ranch gig."

She looked at him. "Seriously? *Now* you ask that? When we're about to—"

"Why not? Might not have time later. Look at what happened last time: you took off right after the mission."

"Pretty fucked up sense of timing," Monica grumbled.

She glanced at his perfect profile. Even with his face darkened the bastard was still one handsome devil, and Monica hated herself for being attracted to him.

"Well? Did you?"

She sighed. "Good days and bad days, like everything else."

"But overall?"

"Peaceful. Certainly none of this shit. Why you ask?"

"After Chief Larson and Mickey . . . dunno. Just been thinking."

Now, *that* was a surprise, and something stirred inside her.

"Thinking? About what?"

Multiple flashes, followed by distant booms echoing across the valley, marked the Tomahawks reaching their targets.

"One minute!" Stark shouted. "It's starting! We go in sixty seconds, and we need to be out in three minutes max!"

❖

The mountain shook from the explosions, rattling the compound, which fell into the twilight of emergency lights.

"It's starting," Ricco said to Roman. Alarms blared across the mountaintop. "Get me the garrison commander."

"Lines are dead," Roman said.

Ricco pointed at the emergency lighting. "But the emergency power is supposed to—"

"I know, which leads me to believe they're not picking up because . . ."

"Damn," Ricco said.

"And the cell phones are not working."

"The cell phones?" Ricco said, wondering how that was possible when he owned all the mobile towers in the state, giving him full control of communications.

"I can't reach *any* of the garrisons," Roman added, "or our men at the missile posts—assuming they're still there after those explosions."

Ricco considered his options.

"But our security system up here is on battery backup, still operational. And I just radioed the state police headquarters in Culiacán," Roman said, holding a two-way radio. "They're fifteen minutes out."

Ricco pointed at the blank TV screens. "Why are the cameras out?"

"They're tied to the computer system, which is rebooting. It takes several minutes to come back online."

"Who's out there now?"

"I don't know," Roman replied. I can't get the outpost above the helipad."

"Get the kid and my pilot to—" Ricco paused when he heard the whirring of an incoming helicopter.

"Scratch that! Go get the boy and come back here! I have another plan."

❖

"Time!" Stark shouted. He jumped out first, followed by Mireya, racing across the edge of the helipad.

Five seconds.

The clearing was flanked to the east by a hill—in flames from one of the Tomahawks. It had taken out a garrison post, where, according to Mireya, a dozen men and two machine guns had guarded the helipad.

A three-story Spanish-style mansion projected east of the helipad. And to the west was the access road connecting the estate to the city below.

Monica and Naree followed him, one behind the other, then Ryan, who ran toward the other side of the clearing to set up his sniper's perch covering the access road and their planned egress.

Ten seconds.

Danny kept the helo ready for a quick getaway, rotor whirling. Juan remained in the Black Hawk behind the Browning machine gun.

Stark led the stack with Mireya covering his right and Naree his left. Monica brought up the rear.

Fifteen seconds.

"This way," Mireya said, pointing to a pair of glass doors beyond a big Sikorski tied down to the ramp.

Stark considered tossing a couple of grenades toward it but decided against it. Right now, his only immediate exfil option was the Black Hawk. If something were to happen to it, they would be stranded here until another helo could be sent to get them out.

They reached the doors, which were locked, so Stark cut lose a volley of rounds, but all he did was graze the bullet-resistant glass.

Twenty seconds.

"Hold on," Mireya said, entering a code on the digital pad next to the doors, which was apparently on battery backup.

The locks disengaged, and she led the way to another door, this one made of metal.

Stark nodded at Mireya as he reached for a concussion grenade.

She entered a code, and inched the door open just enough for Stark to toss the flashbang.

"Fire in the hole!" he shouted and they all stepped back. The pressure wave from the blast slammed the door open.

He cruised through the haze, finding three men crawling on the floor next to their UZIs. Two had their hands on their ears. The other was struggling to get up.

"Is he here?" Stark asked.

Mireya inspected them quickly and shook her head. "Just guards," she said. "This is the receiving area. For Ricco's guests."

"See if they know anything," Stark said.

Mireya knelt by the least dazed guard and pressed the muzzle of her gun against his groin shouting in Spanish. Stark inspected the lobby-like room; a set of sofas, tables, and a bar along the back.

Thirty seconds.

"They say he's in his study. This way," Mireya said.

Monica and Naree flex-cuffed the guards. Mireya chose another door, tearing out into a corridor with Stark on her heels. Naree and Monica were behind him.

They covered the fifty or so feet of hallway to another security door, made of steel.

Forty seconds.

Again, Mireya did the honors, unlocking it and going through, reaching what appeared to be a large office with panoramic windows. Part of it resembled a living room, with sofas and tables, another bar, and three walls of portraits.

Stark's eyes narrowed at framed pictures of Osama bin Laden, Saddam Hussein, Pablo Escobar and even Manuel Noriega.

"The fuck is this?" Monica said. "The hall of dirtbags?"

"Ricco's office," Mireya said.

"Where the hell is everyone?"

Stark shared Monica's concern about too few guards and no Ricco Orellana. They had already burned through their first minute.

"Movement at the bottom of the hill," Ryan reported. *"Looks like a convoy of trucks coming up from the city. They'll be here in a few."*

"Roger," Stark replied pointing at the large desk. "Laptops and phones."

Mireya looked around suspiciously.

"What is it?" Stark asked.

"The soldiers from the city," she said, "They wouldn't be coming unless Ricco was here, and in trouble. It's his backup plan."

Monica and Naree went to work, stowing the hardware in their rucksacks. Mireya headed for another security door across the room.

But it opened before she could get to it.

Standing just behind and to the right of Mireya, Stark swung his weapon but held his fire. A large Hispanic man dressed in black with a kid roughly ten years old.

"*Mami!*" Antonio shouted. The man held him with one heavily tattooed arm, using him as shield and pointing a pistol at the boy's head with the other.

"Don't you fucking hurt him, Roman!" Mireya shouted.

"Stay back, all of you," Roman warned.

"Put the boy down," Stark ordered, lining up the man's head but unwilling to take the shot because the boy was moving too much.

"Let him go!" Mireya demanded.

"I swear, I'll kill him!" Roman shouted. He looked at Mireya. In doing so, he exposed the left side of his face. "Everyone just back off and—"

A round punched through his left eye, spattering the wall behind him.

"*Mami!*" the boy shouted again, running to Mireya. She hugged him and wiped his bloody face.

"Nice shot," Naree said to Monica, who stood there holding her pistol with both hands.

"Goddammit, Cruz!" Stark shouted

"I saw an opening and took it," Monica replied with a shrug.

"Where the hell's Orellana?" he asked Mireya, checking the mission timer. A minute and forty seconds.

Mireya tilted her head at the wall. "Panic room."

She went to it, and Stark made out the seams of a security door.

Pounding on it with her rifle, Mireya shouted, "I'm out here, *chingado!* Come out and face me like a man!"

But no one came out.

The unmistakable sound of a .50-caliber echoed outside.

"Romeo?" Stark said.

The headlights of the first truck rounded the final switchback. "Got movement up here," Ryan reported.

The troop carrier accelerated up the last stretch of road, right below his vantage point.

Taking out the slack on his Barrett, he centered the driver from a distance of almost a thousand feet and fired.

Blood sprayed the inside of the windshield and the truck swerved sideways, crashing into the mountain and blocking the road.

Soldiers began to jump out of the vehicles and race up the road.

"A little help over here, guys!"

"On our way," Danny replied, shifting the Black Hawk just to the right of Ryan and releasing a Hellfire.

"Nice, Danny," Ryan said matter-of-factly. The missile shot down the road blasting into the lead truck and the one behind it.

Danny turned the Black Hawk sideways to expose the road to the business end of the starboard Browning manned by Juan.

"Just bought us a little time," Danny reported. Staccato gunfire rattled from the helipad, followed by the powerful blasts from the Browning. *"But we really need to get the hell out of Dodge."*

"Blow it," Stark told Monica.

"It's a very thick vault," Mireya warned. "Explosives will not—"

"These ones will," he said.

Monica reached in her rucksack and went to work on the hidden door, taking forty seconds to rig it with PETN.

Pentaerythritol tetranitrate, or PETN, a close cousin to nitroglycerin with far more bite, was the most powerful and compact explosive made, its shaped charge designed to direct its steel-piercing chemical violence directly into its target, in this case, the perimeter of the door.

"Get your kid to the helo!" Stark told Mireya, turning to Naree. "And you, go with her!"

Stark remained with Monica as she inserted the detonator into the explosives and they stepped into the hallway.

Two minutes and twenty seconds.

"Fire in the hole!" she shouted, pressing a button on the remote control.

The powerful blast shook the room. Stark moved through the haze it created, followed by Monica, the smell of cordite assaulting his nostrils.

The thick door was blown off its hinges. To the right, a man was moaning on the floor.

Monica produced the last known photo of the cartel boss on her phone. She compared it to his face. Stark kept watch by the door to make sure no guards stormed the office.

"It's a match," she said. Monica took the man's weapon, a gold-plated Desert Eagle, and flex-cuffed him.

Stark frowned at the shiny weapon. Monica shoved it in her rucksack and he threw the semiconscious cartel boss over his shoulder.

"Get those too," Stark said, pointing at another laptop and satellite phone.

Three minutes.

Too long.

Monica put them in her rucksack and then took point. Stark followed, hauling Orellana, the pistol grip of his MP7A1 in his right hand and keeping his left under the barrel.

They joined the commotion outside, where Juan was blasting the access road with the Browning and Ryan picked up individual targets with the Barrett, causing quite the combined mess.

It was loud. It was blinding. And it was damn effective.

Their focused and overwhelming violence kept the troops at bay while Mireya, Naree, and Antonio raced toward the helicopter's port side door.

Three minutes and twenty seconds.

Stark pulled a couple of smoke grenades from his utility vest and tossed them behind him, fogging their six to prevent someone exiting the house from getting a clear shot and—

It happened almost in slow motion, and in a bizarre way. It even reminded him of that rooftop in Afghanistan.

Just as the grenades spewed their inky red contents across the clearing, a figure emerged through the glass doors holding a pistol, which he aimed toward Mireya, Naree, and Antonio.

"Get down!" he shouted, and swung his MP7SD in that direction, but because he was carrying Orellana, it took him a fraction of a second longer, allowing the man to fire twice.

Stark placed three rounds in his center mass, and someone dropped by the helicopter.

He turned and confirmed it.

Mireya was down.

Goddammit!

Juan jumped off the helo to pick up the wounded woman. Antonio screamed at her side.

Monica tossed three more smoke grenades toward the road Juan and Ryan were demolishing with their .50-caliber barrage.

They reached the Black Hawk, and Stark flung a stunned Orellana inside. Juan hauled the bleeding Mireya, and Monica and Ryan climbed aboard. Ryan strapped the flex-cuffed drug lord to a seat on the starboard side of the cabin.

"Any time now, Danny!" Stark shouted, sitting on the Black Hawk's port window.

The dual turbines spooled up and the helicopter leaped into the night sky. Naree went to work on Mireya and Stark tossed a combination of incendiary and fragmentation grenades into the road below. Monica got behind the port-side Browning and joined Juan, who was back at his starboard station blanketing the hill with overwhelming fire.

A moment later, the road and surrounding woods ignited with multiple overlapping blasts that lit up the night. And that, combined with the dual and deafening onslaught from the Brownings, plus the reddish haze from the smoke grenades, stripped the determination from anyone below long enough to allow them a clean getaway.

Stark remained on the port-side door next to Monica.

He stared at the devastation they had caused in just over four minutes—one minute longer than he had planned.

As the gunfire subsided, the wailing sounds from the rear of the helicopter filled the cabin.

It was Antonio, kneeling by Mireya's side as Naree applied Quikclot patches to her wounds, one in the middle of her chest and the other in her abdomen.

Naree worked feverishly on the Mexican woman.

"My . . . boy," Mireya whispered, reaching for one of Naree's hands.

The North Korean woman glared at the assassin, the person responsible for the death of her Supreme Leader, and she couldn't help but be taken aback at the irony of it all, trying to save the woman when just ten minutes ago she wanted to put a round in between her eyes.

"Your boy is fine," Monica said as she knelt by her and applied pressure on the bandages.

"Please . . . look after . . . him," Mireya mumbled, her pleading eyes narrowing, her pupils dilating.

"Please?" she added.

Mireya coughed, spraying Monica with blood. She leaned down to whisper something in the woman's ear that Naree could not make out. But whatever it was, Mireya managed a brief smile.

"Mami! Mami!" the boy screamed when Mireya went into convulsions.

Stark held little hope for the *sicario* woman. Wounds like hers were usually fatal, especially the one that had torn through her sternum.

The boy continued screaming, clinging to her. Naree and Monica tried to stop the dual hemorrhages.

Mireya went still.

Naree pressed two fingers against the woman's neck and shook her head.

And it was at that moment, that the boy looked up at Stark with those eyes that reminded him of . . .

The veteran colonel took a half step back.

Christ.

He turned away from a sight he could no longer stomach and went to the front, where Juan and Ryan guarded their prisoner.

The mountain burned from the Tomahawk strikes, the Hellfires, and the grenades, casting a reddish glow into the night sky.

"I never forget a face," Orellana said with a serenity Stark found unsettling. "And I remember yours."

Stark turned, for the first time taking a good look at the man responsible for this. And he blinked at Ricco Orellana's different colored eyes.

2004.

The desert south of Culiacán.

A gold-plated Desert Eagle.

Stark reached inside the rucksack and pulled out the weapon, examining the tiger stripes etched on the barrel, and at the initials on the pistol grip: M.O.

"You're . . . *the kid?*" More memories flooded his mind, not only that night but from the rooftop in Afghanistan—combining with the cries of another child mourning another loss.

"I am. And you and everyone you love is dead," Orellana said. "I will make sure of it. And—"

Monica slapped a strip of duct tape over his mouth and slipped a bag over his head. Stark just stood there dumbfounded by what had to be the most bizarre coincidence of his life.

"That's as much as I want to hear from you, asshole," Monica said, picking up the kid and hugging him, trying to console him. She took a seat next to Ryan, who slid his arm behind her shoulders and pulled them closer.

Stark found the sight bizarre, and took a seat in the middle of the cabin trying to gather his thoughts.

But the child continued to cry and his memories triggered a flashback of Chief Larson blowing up, of his friend spraying him with blood sacrificed on the altar of freedom, spilled so that his brothers might live.

He tried to reconcile the fact that this gangster was that very same boy who tried to kill him all those years ago.

Christ Almighty, he thought, feeling as if he had just crossed some sort of boundary from the real to the surreal.

The crying faded away, and Naree joined him. Ryan whispered something in Monica's ear that made her smile—something Stark realized she should do more often. Monica was one hell of a warrior, and she was as beautiful as she was tough.

Stark's eyes gravitated to the hooded man, and he couldn't help but wonder what dark forces had turned a boy into such a monster—and then he had to wonder if that was in store for Antonio, a kid who had already experienced more horror than most adults experienced in their lifetime.

"Monica sedated him," Naree said, patting Stark on the knee. "Are you okay, *Shiraki*? You look . . . I don't know, like you just saw a ghost?"

Stark drew a deep breath and lost himself in those coal-black eyes that took him back to those nights in Seoul.

He slapped down the part of him screaming it was wrong to enjoy being with her, because he found solace in her eyes that he'd never found anywhere else.

And in that moment, the hardened veteran was in dire need of comfort.

"I'm here for you," she said, reading his mind and moving the hand from his knee to his face.

"Do you get the feeling sometimes," he asked. "That that you may have done what you do for longer than you should have?"

Naree caressed his camouflaged face. "All the time, *Shiraki*. All the goddamned time."

CHAPTER 59
Lines Down

"If we can't communicate with Pyongyang by phone, we'll have to do the next best thing."
—President Laura Vaccaro

TREATY ROOM. THE WHITE HOUSE. WASHINGTON, D.C.

"What do you mean she can't contact her people?"

John Wright exchanged a look with Jacobson, who just sighed.

"Well, we took out their ability to communicate, Madam President," Wright said.

"Cut off their lights, at least for the time being," added Jacobson.

"But look on the bright side," Wright said. "They've been quiet since the stealth strike. No missiles or sorties. So, it's working . . . for now."

Vaccaro pursed her lips.

The very same strategy that put a damper on North Korea's aggression was now preventing the North Korean woman from contacting Pyongyang to let them know that Vaccaro was ready to turn over custody of Ricco Orellana, along with proof of his connection to the *Yakuza*—courtesy of Gorman and Harwich—to North Korean authorities.

And that, in addition to whatever economic package President Xi Jinping was negotiating with Pyongyang, should be enough to put this mess to bed.

Of course, there wouldn't be any negotiations until the lights came back on.

She needed a way to work around the blackout and get the information she needed delivered to North Korea.

"John, Lisa," Vaccaro, said, "if we can't communicate with Pyongyang by phone, we'll have to do the next best thing."

CHAPTER 60
Tension

"I can see when a man has had enough, when someone has been broken, ripped from the inside. And I see that in you."
—Naree Kyong-Lee

31,000 FEET OVER THE PACIFIC OCEAN

"You look like shit, *Shiraki*."

Stark was exhausted, he hadn't been able to sleep much since he lost Larson on that rooftop.

They had departed Coronado NAS six hours ago, heading to Kadena Airbase in Okinawa, where he would be given further instructions.

He'd spent the last hour up in the cockpit with the pilot, a young Air Force captain, until it became obvious he wanted a little P&Q.

The Air Force VIP jet, a modified Gulfstream G550, was quiet. The only illumination came from two rows of dimmed LEDs running along the floor.

Monica and Ryan were huddled on the long sofa at the rear of the cabin already sleeping, as was Juan, in a pair of bucket seats, next to a handcuffed, gagged, bagged, and strapped down Ricco Orellana. Danny occupied the entire row in front of them, sleeping.

For once, his pilot was getting a break.

They had left Antonio in the care of a Navy social worker at Coronado charged with helping him cope with Mireya's death.

But Stark knew better.

The kid, for lack of a better word, was . . . well, fucked.

He had seen his mother shot dead, plus God only knows what else, living under the umbrella of the Sinaloa Cartel.

The boy had that look in his eyes—that same look as a young Orellana in 2004 and the suicide kid on that rooftop.

The eyes of a—

"Come," Naree said.

She sat sideways at one end of the sofa in the front of the cabin, her back against the armrest, and she was tapping the space in front of her. Her boots were already off on the floor.

Stark considered the invitation, rubbing the spot on his chest marking the bullet he had taken for her in that tunnel. It still hurt like a mother.

"Let me take a look," she said.

"It's nothing."

"*Shiraki*," she said. "I can see when a man has had enough, when someone has been broken, ripped from the inside. And I see that in you."

Stark didn't know how to respond—this woman he had not seen in years was somehow spot on. The violence he had experienced, and not just in the past few days, was having a cumulative effect on his state of mind.

I'm so goddamned exhausted . . .

"Come, *Shiraki*," she ordered a second time. "Rest your head right here." She tapped her lap. "Now."

Stark knew it was wrong, but all of the other seats were taken, and according to the pilot they still had over eight hours ahead of them in this bird.

God knows I need to rest.

So, he complied, removing his boots and stretching out on the long sofa, resting the back of his head against her chest. Naree wrapped her legs around him, setting them on his thighs.

He inhaled deeply, eyes closed, hands on his lap.

"Good boy," she said, reaching for his T-shirt and pulling it up to his shoulders.

"Is that necessary?" he asked, lifting his head to glance down the dark cabin.

"Relax," she whispered. "Everyone's out."

Her fingers traced the edge of the fist-size injury.

"That's one nasty bruise."

"Just character building."

"And life-saving," she said, reaching down his right forearm. "What's this?"

Stark drew another deep breath as she fiddled with the carbon-fiber bracelet.

"Belonged to a dear friend . . . he was killed because of those damn missiles. In Afghanistan. Two days ago."

"Sorry," she said.

"Me too. Saved my life."

"Like you saved mine? I guess as you Americans say, you paid it forward?"

Before he could reply, she said, "*Lerne Leiden?* What does it mean?"

"German for learn to suffer."

"I see," she said. "And the rest?"

"Without complaining."

"What?"

"That's what the rest of the words mean: Learn to suffer without complaining. But they were destroyed . . . along with my friend."

Naree kissed his forehead, forcing his head back on her lap, softly rubbing the area around his sternum.

Damn, he thought.

"There," she said, working her way up to his shoulders and digging her fingers into his sore muscles, the backs of her feet rubbing his thighs. "Remember?"

Stark remembered. They'd spent hours like this, sometimes in bed, sometimes in a bathtub, but always with Naree behind him, legs wrapped around him, working the tension in ways he never thought possible.

Naree magically produced a mini bottle of Cava de Oro tequila.

"What the hell?" he said.

She twisted the top, took a sip and brought the bottle to his lips.

"Remember?"

"Hell yes," he said, letting the alcohol warm his core, enjoying it as much as her touch—against reason, logic, any argument he could imagine.

"My turn," she said, finishing it, setting it aside and doing one of the best things she ever did to him: massage his head.

She used her thumbs and fingers to rub the sides of his head, working her fingertips around his temples, up and down his neck, and across his forehead.

Oh, Christ.

Stark kept his eyes closed, letting her take away the strain of battle, the guilt of surviving, and the uncertainty of tomorrow—if only for a little while.

And somewhere along the way, just as he had done so often so long ago, Colonel Hunter Stark fell asleep in her arms.

CHAPTER 61
Wakey Wakey.

"Great. Just great. I'm in a damn potato field."
—USN Lt. Commander Jacob "Jade" Demetrius.

OUTSIDE WONSAN, NORTH KOREA

Demetrius opened his eyes and saw clouds parting, revealing stars and a yellowish first quarter moon.

But the pressure on his head, and on his chest and back, tunneled his vision.

He tried to fight it, tried to stay awake, but the darkness took him.

And in the darkness, a face resolved.

Her face.

Demetrius remembered every moment, every sound and smell from that unforgettable week—memories he'd clung to, moments he'd used to help get him through the madness of war.

Ghalia's lips twisting in that captivating smile that had robbed him of his senses, of his reason—that had given him the release he'd sought after weeks of facing death during long sorties over Pakistan.

"Wake up, love," she whispered. "Wake up."

He reached out to her but she was fading, floating away from him, from his life.

"Get up!"

Demetrius opened his eyes again, blinking the dream away.

This time he managed to sit up, though not without wincing. His body was sore, especially his back, following the painful spinal compression from getting shot out of his jet like a damn rocket.

He lifted his visor and glanced at his watch, realizing he had been unconscious for ten minutes.

He touched his chest and felt the Glock 19 pistol still secured to the front of his flight suit.

Verifying that his Emergency Locator Transmitter was broadcasting his location to the rescue helo, he reached for his radio, selected the Bluetooth interface with his helmet to avoid unnecessary noise, and whispered, "Torchbearer Five-Six, Dambusters Three-Oh-Three."

"Dambusters Three-Oh-Three, Torchbearer Twenty. Great to hear your voice. Hook Three-Seven is twenty mikes out. Hornets in five."

Demetrius nodded, swallowed, then said, "Roger. Gonna look for Speedy."

"Dambusters Three-Oh-Three, we're showing his ELT two thousand feet south from your current position."

"Roger."

Demetrius stood, stretched to try to work out the soreness, then shouldered the survivor's pack connected to the bottom of his rig and took a couple of minutes to hide the canopy.

He went through the pack, finding a flashlight that incorporated a compass and a bottle of water.

Twisting the top, he took a few sips, looking around him. He was in a meadow, and when he focused on it, he realized he was in the middle of an agricultural field.

Evenly-spaced rows of some ankle-high green plants as far as he could see in every direction.

Reaching down, he pulled one out exposing the roots, which were round.

Tossing it aside, he mumbled, "Great. Just great. I'm in a damn potato field."

A red and white canopy caught his eye. It broke up the scenery, but not to the south, in Gonzales' location, and it was much closer than a couple thousand feet.

This was west, the direction he had last seen the Sukhoi that snuck up behind him, and probably less than five hundred feet away.

Drawing the Glock, Demetrius made his way toward the rig, covering the distance in less than a minute.

But when he reached it, he quickly holstered the weapon and took a knee by the inert pilot, still helmeted and lying sideways on the ground.

There was a dark stain on the right shoulder, bleeding, and he used his SOG knife to tear off the fabric to expose the wound. When he did, he exposed a brassiere underneath.

"What the . . ."

He unstrapped the helmet, worked it off the head, and revealed the face of a woman. Short black hair framed a narrow and pale porcelain-smooth face with very fine, almost doll-like features and a pointed chin beneath full lips.

He returned his attention to the wound. Something had pierced the shoulder, probably shrapnel from her jet. He found the exit wound, still bleeding.

The woman began to shudder and mumble in Korean, lips quivering. She was going into shock.

Reaching in his survival pack, Demetrius grabbed two QuickClot patches, slapped one on each side of the wound. It made the woman cringe in obvious pain.

Catlike eyes opened wide for a couple of seconds, staring at him with feral intensity. She tried to sit up but collapsed, grimacing, a hand on her belly.

He turned her onto her back and gently moved her hand out of the way, revealing another patch of dark blood.

"Shit," he said, and started cutting into the flight suit around her waist. He exposed a piece of charred metal embedded between her navel and her groin.

It was already half dislodged, so he got another patch of QuickClot ready. Grabbing the piece of metal between his thumb and forefinger, he whispered, "Very sorry about this," and yanked it out.

The woman screamed and once again collapsed.

He pressed the patch on her wound and this time she didn't flinch at the chemical reaction.

Demetrius looked around him, realizing the likelihood of anyone coming to her rescue was low, especially since they'd shut down the power.

The QuickClot was doing its magic but he didn't think the pilot, already in shock, would survive long without medical care. For all he knew, she was bleeding internally.

"Dammit," he whispered. He made his decision, picking her up and heading south, where his wingman was supposed to be.

And as he did, he heard the beautiful sound of jet engines approaching from the east.

The face of the helmeted pilot came in and out of focus, accompanied by intense pain from her shoulder and her belly.

Mina tried to fight back, to sit up, to scream, but her body had been taxed beyond functioning, and she succumbed.

Where are you taking me?

Let me be!

Leave me here!

Bastard!

But the stranger continued walking, carrying her for what seemed like a few minutes, then setting her on the ground.

Mina opened her eyes briefly, catching the helmeted man leaning over another figure on the ground, then darkness returned, enveloping her.

"Dambusters Three-Oh-Three, Hook Three-Seven. One mike out. Pop smoke."

"Roger," Demetrius replied, tossing a smoke grenade and ignoring the blue haze billowing out, working the multiple lacerations on Gonzales' chest.

His wingman had not fared well during his ejection. The top of his chest was peppered with shrapnel and burns, as well as both arms. But he was still breathing, and unlike the North Korean pilot, his wounds appeared superficial though much more extensive—he had been caught in the fireball.

The helicopter was close, and Demetrius stood and waved his arms, The Hornets circled overhead.

"We've got you, Dambusters Three-Oh-Three. We've got you."

CHAPTER 62
Tochõ Grab

"That's who you are, Nakamura-san: a lowlife piece-of-shit banker."
—Bill Gorman

TOKYO, JAPAN

Minori Nakamura was running short on time.

The senior partner of Institech-Japan, one of the country's largest and best-connected hedge fund management institutions, had spent the day catching up on his regular work after spending two days traveling with one of his largest clients—at the cost of ignoring everything and everyone else, including his family.

But he was finally up to date and hopefully in time to catch the second half of his daughter's piano recital at the prestigious Tohogakuen School of Music.

He hurried down the steps from the *Tochõ*, the local name for the Tokyo Metropolitan Building that housed his offices on the fortieth floor. The high rise quite conveniently housed the headquarters of the Tokyo Metropolitan Government, where Nakamura spent half his time wheeling and dealing through the complicated and highly-discreet negotiations required by his complicated and highly-discreet clients.

He reached his stretch Mercedes Benz limousine, which waited for him at this precise location every evening, and climbed in, aching for the gin and tonic his driver always had waiting for him.

The moment he closed the door, he realized something was wrong—terribly wrong.

Nakamura gaped at two men sitting across from him in the club-style seating. One held his gin and tonic, the other held a gun fitted with a sound suppressor. And in between them sat a heavily tattooed girl who could not be older than twenty wearing thick purple glasses and clicking away on a laptop.

Next to him sat another man, but younger than the two across from him, holding another laptop.

Gorman handed the surprised hedge fund manager his drink, which he took with both hands. His eyes darted between him and Harwich, who had a Sig Sauer P220 pistol trained on him.

"Good evening, Nakamura-san," Gorman said, clasping his hands.

Nakamura took a sip of his drink, enough to wet his lips. In perfect English, he said, "Do you have any idea who I am?"

Gorman nodded, then looked at Sally. "Show him who he is."

Sally turned the laptop around so the screen faced Nakamura. It showed a bank transfer totaling $200 million from three numbered accounts at Improsa Bank in Costa Rica belonging to Ricco Orellana, to a numbered account at the National Bank of Bahrain, Saudi Arabia.

Then Jason Savage turned his laptop's screen, showing the funds were further transferred to a numbered account at Sumitomo-Noruma Holdings, right here in Tokyo, minus a ten percent transaction fee to Institech-Japan—all with Nakamura's approval signature.

"That's who you are, Nakamura-san," Gorman said, "a lowlife piece-of-shit banker facilitating the payment for three hundred missiles stolen by the *Yakuza* from a Toshiba warehouse three months ago."

Gorman produced a photo of Nakamura's wife and daughter entering the Tohogakuen School of Music.

He nearly spilled his drink.

"It would be a shame to miss the recital, Mister Nakamura. I'm sure your daughter is quite a player."

"Like his father," Harwich added.

"You are not here . . . to arrest me?"

Gorman grinned. "Of course not. We're here so we can help each other out."

"Help each other?"

Harwich leaned forward, the gun still trained on the bank executive. "You help us with what we need to know, and we help you make your recital . . . and maybe the rest of your miserable fucking life."

"What . . . what is it that you need to know?"

CHAPTER 63
Rollercoaster

KADENA AIRBASE. OKINAWA, JAPAN

"What's next, *Shiraki*?"

Colonel Stark hung up his satellite phone.

Even someone as battle-hardened as he was had to roll his eyes at the speed of events unfolding around him, resembling nothing short of a rollercoaster ride.

But at least he was refreshed, having spent a good portion of the flight sleeping in Naree's arms. His mind was clear and his body energized, ready for the challenge ahead.

And that challenge meant finishing this before the window that Vaccaro created closed.

Satellite imaging revealed a couple of the dams along the Yule River showing signs of life, and soon they would be back online.

Stark used the antenna of the satellite phone to point at one of the Chinooks on the tarmac. He said to Danny, "Our ride . . . to the *Reagan*. Go."

Danny nodded and headed for the helicopter.

"And?" asked Naree. Monica looked on.

He shook his head. "All I know is that we have four hours to get there. More instructions will follow. So, get our guest aboard. Wheels up as soon as Danny can get us airborne."

CHAPTER 64

Information

"You haven't lost your touch, Billy!"
—Glenn Harwich

TOKYO, JAPAN

If there was one thing Bill Gorman appreciated after two decades in the intelligence business was the value of information.

You could have the finest operators in the business, the most dedicated and skilled warriors on the planet. But without the right intel, none of that training and expertise mattered.

This was the fundamental reason why Gorman had chosen intelligence over the operative world. The right information at the right time and place—along with the right plan—could allow a few hands to pull off, quietly and efficiently, a job that would otherwise require a small army of highly trained soldiers, not to mention the accompanying shitload of shooting.

And tonight, Gorman was banking on that tried-and-true principle. He and Harwich sat in a black Toyota Land Cruiser across the street from Club Camelot, a popular and luxurious nightclub in Tokyo's bustling Shibuya Ward.

They had luck on their side tonight: Club Camelot was not only the place Akira Tanaka was partying tonight, it was a club popular with expats, meaning Gorman and Harwich wouldn't draw attention.

Unlike most other clubs in town, where westerners stuck out among a Japanese population where the average height was five-foot-five-inches, the clientele here included Canadians, Australians, Europeans, and Americans.

At precisely 11:45 p.m., Akari stepped outside the establishment in a tight black dress and high-heeled boots smoking a cigarette, her short black hair swirling in the evening breeze.

The Yakuza boss blew smoke toward the long line of people waiting to get in, and started toward her waiting silver Range Rover accompanied by two bodyguards, one of whom opened the door for her.

The Rover took off and Gorman went after it, following closely for several blocks down Inokashira-dori Avenue, until it turned north on Spain-zaka Street and pulled up to the Shibuya Coffee shop, just as Nakamura told them she would.

The woman was a creature of habit.

The same bodyguard who had opened the door for her stepped out, looked around, and let his principal out. Akira whisked past him and went inside. The bodyguard, along with the second one, followed her in. The driver remained behind the wheel.

Gorman pulled in front of the Rover, got out, and went inside the coffee shop, clutching a small can of pepper spray.

As he stepped up behind the trio at the counter, one of the bodyguards looked in his direction, and Gorman unceremoniously sprayed his face. The man dropped to the floor screaming, and he sprayed the second bodyguard, who landed next to his thrashing associate.

Before Akira could turn around, Gorman struck her just behind the right ear, shocking the web of nerves and triggering a vasovagal episode. Akira fainted from the sudden drop of blood pressure and literally fell into Gorman, who tossed her over his shoulder.

The driver had witnessed the attack through the window and was climbing out of the SUV, reaching inside his coat. Harwich tasered him, leaving him twitching on the sidewalk.

Gorman tossed Akira in the rear seat and climbed in behind her. Harwich drove off.

The entire incident had taken less than twenty seconds.

Gorman flex-cuffed her hands behind her back, slapped a strip of duct tape over her lips and slipped a bag over her head. Harwich shouted, "You haven't lost your touch, Billy!"

Ten minutes later, they turned on Sotobori-dori Avenue, which took them directly to the American Embassy, where they caught a helicopter to Tokyo-Narita International Airport.

CHAPTER 65
Double Vision

"You're all over the news, love. Looks like I've shagged a world hero."
—Ghalia Khan

USS RONALD REAGAN (CVN-76).
THE SEA OF JAPAN

Lt. Commander Demetrius figured he'd earned the right to monopolize the espresso machine in the Ready Room, where he was in the middle of enjoying his third cup.

He'd spent the majority of the night and morning at Gonzales' side after a Navy surgeon extracted a dozen pieces of shrapnel from his chest and treated his burns. His wingman was pretty banged up and currently quite sedated, but he was expected to make a full recovery.

Demetrius checked on the North Korean pilot, who turned out to be a general by the name of Mina Kyong-Lee.

Even with the two wounds, she was faring much better than Gonzales. As it turned out, they were both superficial, and thanks to his quick reaction, the blood loss had been stopped and replenished through a couple of transfusions.

He used a laptop to initiate a Skype call with Ghalia. After everything that he'd been through, he needed to see her face and hear her voice.

"Wotcher, love," she said, rubbing her eyes. She was wearing a white robe.

Demetrius frowned. It was two in the afternoon in Abu Dhabi, had he caught her sleeping?

"Sorry about that, baby," he said. "Didn't mean to wake you."

"It's alright," she said. "Little bugger was hungry. Fancies a feed every couple of hours. Finally put her down."

"I just wanted to hear your voice…"

"You're all over the internet, Love. Over ten million views, and now all over the news too," she interrupted. "Looks like I've shagged a world hero."

Demetrius grinned, then sighed. "It's been blown out of proportion," he said. "I was just doing my—"

"Bollocks. That was about the most heroic thing I've ever seen. So proud of you. Really."

"Thanks, baby."

"You alone, love?"

"Ah, yeah," he said.

"Then, this is for my hero," she said, parting the robe. "Fancy them?"

Oh, man, Demetrius thought, touching the screen, deciding that was the most beautiful sight he'd seen since Qatar, reminding him why he had fallen so damn hard and so damn fast for her.

"Thank you, baby. I really needed that."

"This and much more awaits you, love."

As he was about to reply, Commander Bassett burst into the Ready Room followed by a man he had never seen.

"Shit," Demetrius said, looking up and then back down at the screen. "I gotta go, baby."

Ghalia smiled, closed the robe, and blew him a kiss.

Demetrius terminated the call and looked at the stranger, a stocky, bald-headed man with an angry face and a tan that said he was definitely not from this region, where the weather for the past few months had been anything but tropical.

He wore black tactical gear and was followed by a Hispanic woman, tall and thin but muscular, also in tac gear.

"Jade, meet Colonel Hunter Stark. He's on a special assignment, along with FBI Special Agent Monica Cruz."

Too tired to talk and quite annoyed at the interruption, Demetrius lifted his cup of coffee in greeting, still seeing Ghalia in his mind.

Another woman stepped in, dressed for combat.

"What—what the . . . *fuck?*" Demetrius gaped at the Asian woman with short dark hair and a face that was a perfect match to the North Korean general he had rescued less than five hours ago. He even shook his head and blinked twice to make sure that he wasn't seeing things.

"Jade?" Bassett asked. "What's going—"

Demetrius pointed. "That one . . . she looks just like the North Korean pilot who shot me down."

The Asian woman stepped to the front of the line, standing across the table from Demetrius, staring at him like he had three heads.

"Goddamn," he added. "The resemblance . . . crazy."

"This pilot," the woman said. "When did she shoot you down?"

"A few hours ago," he replied. He spent a minute explaining what had taken place.

"So, you brought her here?" she asked.

Demetrius shrugged. "It was that, or leave her to bleed to death. So, yes."

"Where is she?" she asked.

"Uh . . . in sick bay. I just left—"

"Take me to her. Now."

CHAPTER 66
Controlled Crash

"Looking pretty pale there, Billy Boy."
—Glenn Harwich.

GRUMMAN C-2 GREYHOUND.
THE SEA OF JAPAN

"Not so bad today, sir!" shouted the female petty officer third class over the twin turboprops of the high-winged aircraft. Her patch read, FRENK. "Should have seen the weather the last couple of days. Now, *that* was bumpy!"

Holding an airsick bag in his hands, Gorman tried to hang on to the hastily eaten tuna roll he had consumed waiting for the Navy plane at a private terminal at Tokyo-Narita International Airport.

To Gorman's dismay, she was holding a half-eaten Snickers bar. She took a huge bite and chewed, saying, "Best not to fight it, sir!"

Goddammit, Gorman thought, tightening his jaw as his stomach convulsed again.

"Looking pretty pale there, Billy Boy!" Harwich shouted from across the aisle. He sat next to the *Yakuza* boss. She was still bound and hooded.

Gorman wanted to tell him to go to hell, but his stomach contracted again, and this time he just let it all out into the bag.

"Final approach!" Frenk shouted, took a seat next to Gorman, and strapped herself in.

The Greyhound dropped out of the sky like a broken elevator, then surged back up.

"The fuck?" Gorman shouted, feeling another spasm.

"Perfectly normal, sir!" Frenk assured him. "Quite bumpy near the water."

The fuselage slammed onto the flight deck with spine-compressing force and a deafening bang. The airframe shook to the point Gorman feared it would come apart.

Then he was slammed into his restraining harness as the Greyhound decelerated to a stop in less than three seconds.

"Jesus," he mumbled. "Are we . . .?"

"Welcome to *Reagan*, sir!" Frenk said.

Gorman tried to unbuckle the shoulder harness but couldn't get a grip on the release handles.

"Here, sir," she said, holding the Snickers bar in her mouth, leaning down and working the release of his six-point seatbelt.

Harwich stood, unbuckled Akari, and tossed her over his right shoulder.

"Take your time, Billy," he said.

Gorman gave him the finger. Frenk finally released him, and he was able to get up.

He followed her out the rear ramp and onto a flight deck that was heaving in the rough seas.

But as they walked across the deck toward the carrier's island, after he spotted a couple of naval officers with Colonel Hunter Stark waiting by a bulkhead, Gorman dropped to his knees and vomited again.

CHAPTER 67
We Are Family

"Got shot down by that one over there, but not before I took him out, and his wingman."
—General Mina Kyong-Lee

USS RONALD REAGAN (CVN-76).
THE SEA OF JAPAN

Naree found Mina sitting up in bed drinking a can of Coca Cola with a straw. She was wearing a pair of khaki slacks and a white T-shirt, but she had a bandage on her shoulder and another across her abdomen.

The sisters stared at each other dumbfounded. Naree went to the bed and hugged Mina.

They remained like that for a time, without words, just enjoying that familiar feeling neither had felt since that afternoon in Pyongyang when Naree left to start her journey as a spy in America. It had been a tearful farewell, but each understood their role in keeping their nation safe, and both had played that role to the best of their ability.

Slowly, Naree pulled away, holding her sister at arm's length, regarding her beautifully stubborn face, delicate, and almost colorless framed by coal-black hair, a reflection of herself.

Mina finally spoke. "What in the world are you doing here?"

"I could ask you the same thing," Naree replied.

Mina's eyes went to Demetrius, standing next to Stark. "Got shot down by that one over there . . . but not before I took him and his wingman out—and mind you, sister, they were in those fancy stealth jets that are supposed to be invisible. Shot his American ass right out of the sky."

"She sure did," Demetrius concurred. "But not before I put a missile right up her tailpipe."

Mina shrugged and said, "He did keep me from bleeding out and brought me here."

"Yeah," Demetrius said. "There's that."

"Now, Sister," Mina said, "what's *your* excuse for being caught in an American ship?"

Naree shook her head. "Long story, but I'm with the bald one."

Mina glanced at Stark. "He looks angry."

"Until you get him in bed, then he's a teddy bear."

Mina nearly spilled her drink. "*Sister?*"

"An assignment in Seoul, during the Olympics."

"I remember," Mina said. "I was training in Beijing. You tricked some American contractor into letting you inside the Olympic village?"

Naree nodded.

"*Him?*"

Naree nodded again. "Ancient history," she said, turning to look at Stark. "Isn't that right, *Shiraki?*"

"Can we get on with it? We don't have time for this shit."

Naree turned back to Mina, who said, "Yes . . . angry."

"Anyway," Naree continued, "we've been tracking down the people responsible for the assassination of our Supreme Leader and—"

"What are you talking about? The word I got from our *Samchon*—who got it from you—is that this was the work of the *Ibon-nom* assisted by . . . them." She pointed at Stark and Demetrius.

"Yeah, well, that's what it looked like in the beginning, but it wasn't the case, and I must contact Pyongyang. Unfortunately, your friend there, apparently managed to shut down power across North Korea. So, no calls."

Mina glowered at Demetrius, who crossed his arms defensively. "I follow orders just like you."

"And we not only have irrefutable proof," Naree added, "we have two of the masterminds responsible for the murder."

Mina blinked. "*Really?*"

Naree nodded. "A Mexican drug lord who purchased the missiles from a *Yakuza* boss, who stole them from a Toshiba warehouse. I'm taking them both home so they can be punished for what they did."

"And how are you planning to do that?" Mina asked, "with the whole country in a state of emergency and lacking communications?"

Stark said, "We were hoping you might be able to help us with that, General Kyong-Lee."

CHAPTER 68
Sitting Ducks

"It's starting, Pak. The attack has started. And we're fucking sitting ducks!"
—Choe Ryong-Ju

RYONGSONG RESIDENCE.
PYONGYANG, NORTH KOREA

"We have two bases back online: Pyongyang Airbase, and Wonsan, closer to the DMZ," General Yong-Gil said. "The rest should be operational between now and tomorrow morning. A few radar installations are coming back online."

"Any noise from the Americans?"

Pak slowly shook his head. "None so far, but we still have too many areas in blackout status, and radar installations require a lot of power. There could be an attack underway, and we would not know it until we heard the bombs."

Choe still refused to believe this was happening. Never in the modern history of North Korea, at least since the armistice, had the entire country been in a state of total helplessness.

"Any word from Beijing?" Pak asked.

Choe sighed. "Still cut off. But they tell me we will reestablish communications in a few hours."

"We can't launch the second phase of the *Azure Dragon* with only two bases," Pak said. "Hopefully we will be ready by tomorrow."

Choe shook his head, "That's assuming we still have the ability to do so."

"Yes," Pak said. "What are your orders?"

"Tell the bases we have contact with to be on high alert," Choe said, looking at the garden and fountains beyond the panoramic windows behind his desk. "So we can launch when ready and—"

The door swung open and Pak's assistant, a young captain, appeared.

"What is it?"

"A message, sir, from Panghyon Airfield."

Pak stood abruptly. "From Panghyon? What is it?"

"Their radar has picked up several contacts, eighty miles from shore."

Choe stared at his lifelong friend. "It's starting, Pak. The attack has started. And we're fucking sitting ducks!"

Pak shook his head and said, "Not quite, old friend. Not quite."

CHAPTER 69
The Kansas City Shuffle

"Colonel, I sure as hell hope this con of yours works out."
—Monica Cruz

CHINOOK TWO-OH-SIX.
SEA OF JAPAN

Danny pushed the helicopter to its operational limit of 180 knots, grazing the rough seas—so close that Stark could feel the sea mist.

He knelt between Danny and Mina, currently occupying the copilot seat. She was trying to reach anyone on the radio. Naree continued to try to get someone on her satellite phone, but so far neither had gotten anything in return but very annoying and frustrating static.

Like a mirage, the coastline materialized, its rocky cliffs stabbing a layer of low clouds. Mina had chosen the route, claiming that it would take them through the least defended part of the country, and more so if the electricity was still out.

"Here we go, sir," Danny said, working the control column and the collective lever, picking up some altitude to clear the approaching hills. "We're getting above surface clutter. If there's anyone looking, we're about to become quite visible."

"Then let's hope our diversion works," he replied, walking to the rear of the cabin, where Harwich and Gorman flanked Akari Tanaka, still wearing a bag over her head. Across from them sat Juan and Monica guarding their second prisoner, wearing a bag and flex-cuffed.

Ryan occupied the rear, the Barrett in between his legs, his head leaned back against the headrest, mouth open as he snored away.

Stark shook his head and took a seat next to Monica, strapped in, and said, "It's about to get interesting."

"Yeah," she replied. "You know, Colonel, I would have been totally oblivious to all of this had the bastards chosen to dig a tunnel anywhere else but my front yard. I mean, what are the damn odds?"

"It was fate, Cruz."

"Fate," she snorted. "Well, Colonel, I sure as hell hope this con of yours works out."

Stark smiled. The Kansas City Shuffle was an old con that relied on the mark, meaning the North Koreans, realizing they were being conned and then trying to foil the con they thought to have uncovered—and in the process falling for the real con.

In this case, the Chinook was the real con. The Super Hornets of Carrier Air Wing Five would be the fake con and he hoped any North Korean defenses or radar installations that were back in operation would fall for it.

It was a good plan, but few plans ever survived the first shot.

CHAPTER 70
Big X

"Well, if we have to be targets, this bird is the place to be."
—USN Commander Damian "Hound" Bassett

DAMBUSTER THREE-OH-THREE. SEA OF JAPAN

"Dambusters Three-Oh-Three, Torchbearer Twenty, we're showing clear airspace between you and the coast."

"Roger," Demetrius replied, switching to the intercom. They were flying BARCAP racetrack patterns thirty miles from the coast, close enough to attract attention, far enough to have some maneuvering room. "I hope we know what we're doing, sir," he said to his lead, Commander Bassett.

"So do I, Jade."

"Might as well hang a big fucking X on our backs flying this way," he said, not relishing the idea of having to engage North Korean jets. He carried only two AMRAAM missiles and two Sidewinders—plus the 578 rounds in his nose-mounted Vulcan gun. The rest of his load was devoted to dual external fuel tanks that were allowing him and the other Super Hornets the time out here to create this diversion.

"Well, if we have to be targets, this bird is the place to be."

"That's what I thought about the Lightning, sir, and look how that worked out."

The Super Hornets continued their BARCAP, and on his radar, Demetrius could see the four other two-plane sections of Super Hornets from the Dambusters, plus another four two-plane sections from the Diamondbacks doing the same thing all on a north-south line covering most of the coast of North Korea.

In all, *Reagan* had deployed eighteen Super Hornets, all actively painting the distant coast with radar energy. And on top of that, six EA-18G Growlers were flying racetrack patterns at thirty thousand feet up and down the coast, blinding any radar installations that may have come back on line and any airborne bandits with their ALQ-99 radar-jamming pods as well as with their next-generation focused jammers.

Demetrius hope was that whatever North Korean forces were scanning the Sea of Japan would be in for one hell of a day of confusing radar work.

And that, and whatever magic General Mina Kyong-Lee could conjure on the radio, might be enough to keep everyone healthy until Stark and his team could reach their destination.

CHAPTER 71

Insertion

"And there goes the plan."
—Colonel Hunter Stark

CHINOOK TWO-OH-SIX.
NORTH KOREA

"Goddamned North Korea," Monica muttered as the helicopter zoomed over the beach at sunset, continuing up the closest rocky hills, dropping back down over a lush valley leading to the interior.

Naree raised an eyebrow.

"No offense intended," Monica added.

"None taken."

Monica elbowed Ricco Orellana in the ribs. The drug lord, still bagged and flex-cuffed, let out a whimper. "And we're in this mess because of you, asshole."

Naree nodded and said, "Again."

And Monica did, ramming her elbow into his side and earning another high-pitched moan, followed with words muffled by the duct tape.

"Save it, dumbass," Monica added. "Where you're going nobody *habla*."

Stark was still trying to come to terms with the fact that this man was the boy back in 2004.

He stared out the window at a countryside that was quiet—deadly quiet—and dark. No lights. No missile warnings. No radars pinging them. No radio. Just a combination of valleys followed by forested mountains and more valleys under the dim grey light of a crescent moon.

"We really shut off the lights in this place," Harwich said.

"Sure did, Glenn," Stark replied. "And it doesn't look like they're coming back on any time soon."

They flew for an hour. When they reached the outskirts of Pyongyang, at least according to the GPS, Danny kept them flying at treetop and Mina was trying to raise someone on the radio, hammering away in machine-gun Korean.

The capital city was dark, except for an island of light near its center.

"Ryongsong," Mina said. "That's where we need to—"

"Missile warning," Danny said, throwing the helo into a sharp left turn and releasing flares, which lit up the sky around them like a Fourth of July fireworks display.

And there goes the plan, Stark thought He braced himself between the seats. Mina continued working the radio.

Danny turned the Chinook in the opposite direction and almost on its side, discharging a second batch of flares.

"It's gonna be close!" he warned. Two plumes shot up from a field to their left.

The first missile went for the flares, exploding in a fiery cloud.

But the second missile passed the decoys and stayed on them.

Danny cut left, positioning the helo at a ninety-degree angle to the incoming vampire, unloading a third volley of white-hot flares, lighting up the sky around them.

The missile went for the flares, but it exploded before Danny could put enough distance between them.

The blast shook the Chinook to its frame. Stark felt it in his bones, rattling his teeth. The control panel lit up with warning lights.

"I'm losing turbine pressure and we're fresh out of flares," Danny announced. "We won't survive another missile."

Stark turned to Mina. "Whatever you gotta do, General, you'd better do it fast!"

❖

"Dambusters Three-Oh-Three, Torchbearer Twenty, we're showing two bandits at your nine o'clock, one-eight-five miles climbing through two thousand at Mach one point seven."

"Oh, shit," Demetrius said. "Here we go again."

"Let's go combat spread, Jade," Bassett said, and the Super Hornets took up a parallel formation a quarter mile apart and turned toward the North Korean coast.

"Master arm on," Basset added.

"Roger," Demetrius replied, turning on his weapons systems, dreading the thought of another dogfight over North Korea. At their current closing speeds, they would meet the enemy jets roughly twenty miles inland.

The Raytheon APG-79 radar system picked up the incoming bandits and provided firing solutions for the two AAMRAM missiles under his wings. The naval aviator began to pray for a miracle.

The last thing anyone wanted to do was shoot down two North Korean jets when Stark and team were trying to reach Pyongyang in one piece.

"We just got a report of an unidentified helicopter over the city," reported Pak, holding a two-way radio as he rushed in the office.

"Over the city? I thought you said all of the activity was offshore, and we've deployed two interceptors," Choe said, referring to the two Sukhoi-35s they had scrambled from Pyongyang Airbase since they still could not reach any of the coastal bases.

Pak shrugged. "Just picked it up. One helicopter. Our perimeter defenses fired two missiles at it."

"Only one helicopter? And we fired . . . who gave the order?"

"That's the standing order to protect the capital."

"Sir," a male voice broke in through the radio.

Pak frowned. "Yes? Did you shoot it down?"

"Ah, negative, sir. They evaded the first missile and took some damage with the second. We're still tracking it."

"Then fire again! Do not let it get close to the palace!"

"But, sir, there's someone aboard who wishes to speak with you . It's General Kyong-Lee."

Pak was not a man easily surprised, but this shocked him to the bone.

Mina? Here? Is it a trick?

Pak exchanged a glance with Choe, who motioned for him to put her through.

"Connect her to me now! And hold your fire!"

"Yes, sir . . . just a moment, sir."

Static cracked on the radio before the connection came through, backdropped by the sound of a helicopter.

"Why are you in our airspace? Identify yourself!"

"This is General Kyong-Lee from the—"

"Mina?"

A pause, followed by, *"Yes, is this—"*

"This is General Yong-Gil."

"Samchon? SAMCHON! Stop shooting at us!

CHAPTER 72
Reception

"Of all the godforsaken places I thought I'd never set foot in."
—Monica Cruz

RYONGSONG RESIDENCE. PYONGYANG, NORTH KOREA

Smoke trailing from one of the turbines, Danny set down the crippled Chinook near a large fountain just east of the Ryongsong Residency, amidst a small army of soldiers gathered beneath the yellowish glow of floodlights.

Of all things in this world that Colonel Stark thought he'd do, landing an American helicopter at the North Korean equivalent of the White House in the middle of an American-triggered blackout and under DEFCON 4 rules had to be at the very bottom.

And yet . . .

The sisters stepped out first, screaming in Korean at the tight cordon of soldiers, who seemed hesitant at first, then slowly making a hole for them.

Stark and Monica followed them, escorting a bagged, gagged, and flex-cuffed Ricco Orellana. Harwich and Gorman walked behind them flanking their *Yakuza* prisoner. Juan remained in the Chinook with Danny, who was already looking into the damage.

In addition, the CIA men carried two laptops, one belonging to Ricco Orellana and the other secured by Harwich and Gorman during their raid in Karachi—both containing the financial transactions confirmed by Nakamura, Akari's accountant—that vindicated the governments of Japan and the United States in the tragic assassination of Kim Jong-un.

"Of all the godforsaken places I thought I'd never set foot in," Monica said, briefly drawing Stark's attention.

"And yet," Stark said out loud. They passed the guards and followed the twins up a set of steps to a courtyard.

Two men waited by a fountain illuminated in red, white, and blue, ironically, North Korea's colors. One wore a dark suit; the other a dark-green military uniform bearing the gold shoulder bars and large silver stars denominating him not only a general, but as Marshal of the KPA.

The general's tight features under his peaked cap softened. Naree and Mina went straight for him and hugged him as the man in the suit looked on.

Words Stark couldn't hear were exchanged for a minute or so. He looked about and realized he was surrounded by the wrong ends of dozens of AK-47s.

This better work, he thought. Naree and Mina pulled in the man in the dark suit into their discussion.

Then, after what seemed like an eternity, as Stark contemplated the fine Russian weaponry pointed at him and his team, Naree finally motioned him to approach.

"About damn time. Stay put, Cruz," he told Monica.

The women flanked the general, one on each arm. The skinny man in the dark suit stood with his hands behind his back.

"*Samchon*," Naree said. "This is Colonel Hunter Stark, the man appointed by President Vaccaro to lead the investigation. *Shiraki*, meet General Yong-Gil, Marshal of the KPA."

Stark saluted the general, almost a foot shorter than he was, and who saluted him back before extending a hand, which Stark pumped.

"A pleasure, General," Stark said. "Though I wish we could have met under different circumstances."

"Indeed, Colonel," Pak said. He indicated the man in the dark suit. "This is Choe Ryong-Ju, our new Supreme Leader."

Stark stepped over to and extended a hand, which Choe shook looking him in the eyes.

"If what I hear is true, Colonel," Choe said, still holding Stark's hand with impressive force for being so lanky, "then there is much to be discussed between our nations."

Stark tilted his head toward his people gathered by the bottom of the steps. "We have the proof, the real perpetrators, and . . ." Stark produced his satellite phone. "I have a direct line to the President of the United States."

CHAPTER 73
Final Volley

"Jade? What the hell's that at your three o'clock?"
—USN Commander Damian "Hound" Bassett

SEA OF JAPAN

"Dambusters Three-Oh-Three, Torchbearer Twenty, we're showing two bandits at your nine o'clock, forty miles climbing through six thousand at Mach one point six."

It was a clear night. Demetrius, however, would not see the threat on the western horizon for another minute, even though the Advanced Hawkeye controllers as well as his radar told him the two bandits were certainly there.

"Hold your fire," Bassett said, reminding everyone on frequency of the revised rules of engagement: no one fires unless fired upon.

Yeah, Skipper, Demetrius thought, keying the mic twice to acknowledge. They reached the coast, cruising at ten thousand feet. *You're not the one who got shot down by these bastards less than twenty-four hours ago.*

But the he stayed the course, ignoring his back sore from the recent ejection, approaching the jets, who had not fired at them.

What's on your minds assholes? he thought, his eyes went to the spot where he always taped the picture of Ghalia and Jasmine, now long gone.

He eyed the fuel gauges instead, which told him they had less than an hour of fuel left before they would have to hit the tanker circling over—

Demetrius spotted four columns of fire down the coastline, roughly three miles from his position.

"Jade, what the hell's that at your three o'clock?"

Demetrius frowned. Usually, flashes from the ground meant surface-to-air missiles, but none of his warning systems indicated that anyone had a lock on him.

"Dunno, Skipper. Taking a closer look."

He moved the stick to the right and banked the Super Hornet to get a better view.

"Shit," Demetrius said when he got within a mile. "They're ballistic missiles—big ones!"

"Dambusters Three-Oh-Three, Torchbearer Twenty, we're showing two bandits at your twelve o'clock. Ten thousand feet. Twenty miles."

"Roger," Bassett replied.

"Well, Skipper," Demetrius said over the squadron frequency. The two Sukhois were getting awfully close. "The hell we do now?"

"Go after the missiles, Jade," Bassett ordered. "I'll handle the bandits."

"Roger," Demetrius said, pushing the F/A-18 toward the ballistic missiles slowly lifting off into the night sky.

In sixty seconds they would be out of reach. Instinctively, he pushed into afterburners and entered a shallow dive, activating the nose-mounted Vulcan 20mm cannon.

He came in from the south at 700 knots, placing the gun's sight on the closest missile, just barely clearing the silo. He fired two short bursts, consuming nearly one hundred rounds of his 578 load.

Nothing. The missile continued to climb.

Demetrius adjusted his fire and tried again. Two more bursts and the missile disintegrated less than a hundred feet above its silo, going off in a bright cloud.

One down. Three more to—

"Jade. Tally. Single. Seven o'clock low," Bassett warned. "I'm behind the other one."

Demetrius frowned. One of the two Sukhois was just four miles behind him. On his radar, he could see the other bandit twisting and turning away from Bassett ten miles away.

An alarm told him the Sukhoi had achieved a missile lock on him.

Screw him, he thought, continuing on his trajectory for the ballistic missiles even though it gave the Sukhoi a great position in a dogfight. But he didn't have a choice; he had to stop those ballistic missiles.

Instead of trying to shake the bandit, Demetrius did a one-eighty turn and came back around for a second pass at the missiles.

This time, he selected one of his two AIM-9 Sidewinders. Its infrared seeker head immediately locked on to the ballistic missile and began buzzing.

Demetrius released it, and the 180-pound missile shot out from under him, reaching its target a few seconds later.

The resulting explosion created a larger ball of flames.

Two more to go.

The missile warning went off, telling him the Sukhoi had fired a at him.

Demetrius pumped flares and threw the Super Hornet into a wickedly tight turn to place himself at a ninety-degree angle from it, leveling off and releasing more decoys. Rolling the jet onto its back he dove toward the coast.

The missile went for the flares, exploding a safe distance to his left, but the Sukhoi closed in behind him as he leveled off, fifty feet above the ground.

He silently cursed the North Korean jet. The last two ballistic missiles, roughly a thousand feet above him, gathered speed.

When the Sukhoi got closer, Demetrius got a radar lock on it and fired off one of his AMRAAMs, just as he had to shoot down Mina yesterday.

The missile rocketed away and did a tight turn to go after the Sukhoi, who broke off in an evasive maneuver.

Demetrius once more pushed full throttle, entering a vertical climb in full afterburners.

Off to his left, the Sukhoi dispensed chaff, twisting and turning.

Good luck with that, he thought. The Super Hornet rocketed toward the heavens at the bright plumes of the two missiles Demetrius was determined not to let escape. But the vampires had already gone supersonic.

He glanced at his multifunction display, which told him his indicated airspeed was only 500 knots and dropping as he thundered past ten thousand feet. He would not be able to use the cannon.

Dammit. They're getting away!

He selected his second Sidewinder and when the buzzer went off, he released it.

The heat-seeking missile streaked upward as its electronic brain tracked the closest of the missiles.

The Sidewinder closed in on the large missile, its 25-pound warhead going off with a bright flash.

His airspeed dropping below 375 knots, Demetrius waited for something to happen, but the North Korean missile continued on its upward drive. Then he understood. The hottest part of the ballistic missile—where the Sidewinder had locked on—was over a dozen feet below the missile's nozzle. The Sidewinder's warhead had done nothing to the rocketing ballistic missile.

He selected his second and final AMRAAM and let its radar system lock onto the ascending missile, and he released it. His airspeed dropped below 200 knots.

The radar-guided missile hurtled skyward. Since the North Korean missile was only one mile away, the AMRAAM automatically switched to its own internal target-acquisition program.

His amber stall light came on: airspeed 120 knots.

Shit.

Topping out at twenty thousand feet, Demetrius inverted and dove to avoid entering a spin. The third ballistic missile burst in midair as the AMRAAM struck the nose.

When he managed to regain enough airspeed to level off, Demetrius glanced back at the heavens. The last vampire was now a distant light in the night sky.

I'll never catch it.

"Jade! Single at your six!" warned Bassett. "Took care of mine. Coming to you now."

Demetrius glanced at the radar and spotted the Sukhoi rapidly closing on him. It had apparently shaken off the AMRAAM. Problem was, he was fresh out of missiles and had less than 200 rounds in his cannon.

He executed a series of tight turns, dives, and a climb, trying to get behind the Sukhoi to no avail.

"Can't shake him, Skipper."

"Hang in there, Jade. I'm thirty seconds away."

The Sukhoi opened fire.

Demetrius cut left, a river of bullets ripped across the starboard wing, creating small clouds of white debris that washed away in the slipstream, invoking images from yesterday.

Dammit!

He broke left and checked for cautions.

None.

"The bandit is closing in again, Jade!"

"Bastard's trying to get another angle!" Demetrius replied. He dove below ten thousand feet at Mach one.

Another stream of rounds blasted across his port wing.

Demetrius threw the stick to the left and placed the jet in a tight turn, pulling maximum G. He watched the vapor pouring off the wingtips as he sank into his seat. His vision tunneled and his limbs tingled. His G-suit inflated, keeping his blood from accumulating in his legs.

Fighting the hammering gravitational forces, Demetrius followed the evasive move by pushing the stick forward. Now the G's turned negative, shoving him up against his restraint harness. Blood rushed to his face and the world changed to palettes of red as the capillaries in his eyeballs inflated.

The pressure eased, allowing him a glance back.

The Sukhoi couldn't match him through the maneuver, but soon was on his tail again.

Demetrius eyed his fuel gauges: eight hundred pounds. He had consumed a great deal by using the burners to catch those missiles, and he was close to flying on fumes, probably not enough to keep him airborne ten minutes. And with the Sukhoi on his back, he couldn't head for the tanker flying fifty miles out. Bassett was still over five miles away.

Too far.

So, the naval aviator did the only thing he could do: he pulled back on the throttles.

"Jade? The fuck are you doing?"

"Give us some space, Skipper."

"No, wait! I'm almost there."

Demetrius checked the airspeed indicator: 500 knots.

"I'm out of time, Skipper!" he said and cut back throttles even more, watching the Sukhoi catch up to him.

Demetrius reached for the air brakes lever, the flap lever, and the landing gear handle.

The first few rounds pierced the port wing. Several more ripped across the titanium layers of the starboard wing.

Demetrius slapped the landing gear down and pulled up all air brakes and lowered flaps. Then for the second time in twenty-four hours, he pulled on the ejection handle.

The canopy was blown clear, and the windblast crashed against his chest.

His body was thrown up, to the side, and flipped upside down. The G's pushed down on him with titanic force. The sky and the moonlit ground changed places in a blur, but his senses were quickly clouded by the extreme pressure on his already abused body.

His vision narrowed and his limbs tingled. His mind hung at the edge of unconsciousness but he refused to fall into it, holding on until his ears registered the sound he so desperately hoped he would hear.

His body was further propelled through the air when the shockwave from the midair collision reached him.

Got ya!

In spite of the harrowing pain, Lieutenant Commander Jade Demetrius managed a thin smile.

His last conscious moment came from the jerk of the parachute deploying, it temporarily shielded him from the brilliant fire of the explosion.

Then there was peace.

CHAPTER 74
Confusion

"Now we wait . . . and pray."
—Colonel Hunter Stark

RYONGSONG RESIDENCE. PYONGYANG, NORTH KOREA

"Who the hell fired them?" Choe demanded, pounding his desk with a fist.

Stark had his satellite phone, which he was using to communicate real-time with Admiral Kostas and Captain O'Donnell on the bridge of USS *Ronald Reagan*. They had just relayed to him that North Korea had fired four ballistic missiles at the fleet. Three had been shot down by a Navy pilot flying BARCAP, but one got away and was currently in a ballistic trajectory toward the fleet.

He regarded the two seemingly confused leaders flanked by Naree and Mina. Harwich, Gorman, and Monica had gone off with a contingent of North Korean agents to transfer the prisoners to their custody. Juan and Danny were still with the Chinook, looking at the damage done by the missile, and apparently assisted by a contingent of North Korean mechanics.

"I'm trying to get the details," Pak said, getting off his radio, but there is a lot of static interference. The only operational base in the vicinity is Panghyon, by the coast."

"I should have been there," Mina said. "That's my base."

"What kind of missiles?" Choe asked.

"Hwasong-15s," Mina replied, referring to ballistic missiles capable of hitting targets anywhere in Japan. "That's all we had left after the first wave."

"Dammit," Pak said. "And what warheads?"

Mina shook her head. "Nuclear."

"My people want to know if the last one can be remotely destroyed," Stark said, holding up his satellite phone.

Mina frowned. "Of course, but to do that, we need to communicate with the base operator."

Choe pressed a hand to his forehead. General Yong-Gil somberly shook his head and whispered something.

Stark held the phone to the side of his head and said, "That's a negative on the self-destruct, gentlemen, and I have confirmation it is nuclear-tipped. So, do what you have to do, but stop jamming North Korea so Pyongyang can communicate with its bases and make them stand down."

"*Will do, Colonel,*" Kostas replied. "*Thanks for delivering the package.*"

The line went dead.

"Now what?" Choe asked.

"Now," Stark said, "Now we wait . . . and pray."

CHAPTER 75
Defensive Measures

"Don't fail me, babies."
—USN Commander Joanna Watson.

USS ANTIETAM (CG-54). SEA OF JAPAN

Commander Joanna Watson, watched the Aegis weapons system track the incoming ballistic missile from behind the operator, Petty Officer Third Class Carla Martinez.

"What's the range?" Joanna asked

"Thirty miles high, ma'am," Carla replied. "It's entering its terminal phase. Vampire in range in fifteen seconds."

"Fire when ready," Joanna said.

Taylor joined her.

"Vampire now in range," Carla reported as the incoming missile dropped below the 20-mile ceiling of Antietam's ERAM missiles. "And they're off," Carla added.

The Vertical Launching Tubes forward of the bridge came alive, firing a dozen ERAMS, which rocketed into the night sky at a sixty-degree angle under the power of their solid-propellant boosters.

Don't fail me, babies, she thought.

Everyone on the bridge stared at the large display, watching the rising ERAMS converging on the single missile arcing down over the fleet, five miles up.

"Eight seconds to impact," Carla announced. "Six . . . four . . . three . . ."

Four of the ERAMs detonated close enough to the Hwasong-15 to knock it off course.

But they did not destroy it.

The digital gyros inside the ballistic missile tried to readjust but failed, and the massive missile went spinning toward the ocean.

At an altitude of two thousand feet, an altimeter trigger fired a circular charge of high-explosive plastic, which in turn compressed the one-kilogram sphere-shaped plutonium 239 payload.

As the HEP increased the density of the plutonium, a neutron initiator collided against a single plutonium atom with a force great enough to split it in half, releasing a small amount of energy in the form of light and heat. That released a few more neutrons, which in turn collided with other plutonium atoms, causing further fission, which released even more neutrons.

The multiplication, which took close to eighty generations to absorb the plutonium mass, was over in one millionth of a second, producing the energy equivalent to 20,000 tons of TNT.

"Mother of God!" Joanna shouted as a flash lit up the horizon, replaced by a rapidly-developing fireball rising up to the sky roughly ten miles away.

The ball reached about five thousand feet in height before cooling off, forming the familiar mushroom-shaped cloud with a column of smoke and steam.

"Good job, people," Captain Taylor said, pointing at the radar screen, which showed the original parabolic trajectory of the ballistic missile, as well as its projected trajectory, which would have placed it right over the fleet. The ERAMs had forced it to fall short. "You knocked it off course. And with ground zero at least ten miles away, we're good here."

And he was right.

Even though the sound that reached Antietam was intimidating, the wind and heat that soon engulfed them was a mere fraction of the inferno that had been the few square miles surrounding ground zero, where the blast wave, heating the air to incandescence, had moved outward in all directions at an initial velocity greater than the speed of sound.

Soon a second blast reached the cruiser from the opposite direction as cool air rushed back to fill the partial vacuum created by the explosion.

Joanna took a few pictures of the fiery cloud with her phone, and she was glad she pulled it out when she did, because in another minute it vanished in the dark skies.

"Well," Taylor said. "That's something you don't see every day."

"Nope," she replied. "Definitely not."

EPILOGUE

"I hold on to the lives we're saving because that allows me to live with the lives I've lost."
—Colonel Hunter Stark

THE WHITE HOUSE. WASHINGTON, D.C.

For the first time in his life, Colonel Hunter Stark walked into the Oval Office.

A smiling President Laura Vaccaro, dressed in a dark-blue skirt suit stood up from behind her desk, came around it, and met Stark in the middle of the room, right over the presidential seal.

They shook hands.

Stark remembered the first time he had met the president back in 2006, then a hotshot Air Force A-10 pilot who had just saved his bacon in southern Afghanistan providing air cover to his team. He had seen her holding a tray at the DFACs facility at KAF adjacent to the Canadian coffee shop.

Her auburn hair wasn't as fiery now as it had been, swinging behind her as she made her way down the food line. But the determination in those steely blue eyes was still there, regarding him today just as they had in country, as the colonel awkwardly introduced himself under the amused faces of his crew sitting nearby.

"It's been a long time, ma'am. Thanks for the invite," he said. "It's an honor."

"No, Colonel," she replied, still holding his hand firmly. "The honor is all mine."

Vaccaro had plenty of reason to smile. In an unprecedented press conference, the new North Korean leader, Choe Ryong-Ju, had issued a statement to the world, praising President Vaccaro for her leadership during this crisis, not only preventing what could have easily become World War Three, but concluding an investigation that captured the assassin of Supreme Leader Kim Jong-un.

It had gone a long way to forestalling any movement in Congress to go after her for the covert operation conducted the year before.

It had certainly quieted Congressman McDonald. At least for now.

If there was one thing Stark had learned after a lifetime of fighting America's wars, was the short shelf life of any sort of political status, especially a good one. He was certain that sooner or later, another effort to impeach her would flare up.

And, ironically, by those whose lives were made safer by her decisions, Stark thought. But that was the reality of the dog-eat-dog world of Washington politics.

But for now, the president certainly had a reason to smile, and Stark decided that, like Monica Cruz, Vaccaro should do it more often. Her face truly lit up.

"You've done your country—and the world—a great service, Colonel," she said. "Your work saved the lives of millions, and for that I salute you."

Stark felt overwhelmed and uncomfortable. Flattery always made him uneasy.

After an awkward pause, Vaccaro added, "Now, shall we?"

Stark gave her a nod.

They stepped out of the Oval Office through a different door into a small anteroom where John Wright waited for them holding a small box, roughly the size of a paperback.

There was no one else present, precisely what Stark had requested.

He didn't want it. In fact, he had politely declined it because he knew Chief Evan Larson would have turned it down. His best friend had done what he did for the love of the brotherhood, not for some piece of metal and ribbon.

But the president insisted.

And if there was anything Stark had learned about Laura Vaccaro, it was that she always got her way. She did compromise on not inviting the press.

Stark faced the president. Wright approached them and opened the box, revealing a Medal of Honor.

"The President of the United States," Wright began, "authorized by Act of Congress, March 3rd, 1863, is awarding in the name of Congress the Medal of Honor to Master Chief Evan T. Larson for conspicuous gallantry and intrepidity at the risk of his life above and beyond the call of duty."

Stark felt the depth of those words as once again, he relived the events on that rooftop, the ultimate sacrifice that the big chief had made so others might live.

There is no greater love, indeed.

Chief Larson had certainly gone above and beyond, and Stark could not think of anyone better in the team to receive such coveted decoration.

Stark took the award on behalf of Chief Larson since he didn't have any living relatives, as was the case with the rest of his team. But he also took the award on behalf of the many fallen brothers and sisters that he had lost through the years.

"Thank you, Mister Wright," Stark said. "And thank you Madam President."

Vaccaro said, "No, Colonel. Thank *you*."

EAGLE PASS, TEXAS

Monica Cruz had dropped everything and headed to her ranch as quickly as she could.

Cattle ranches didn't run themselves, and with her brothers and every ranch hand killed by the Sinaloa Cartel—or by her own hand—she was pretty much alone.

But not for long.

It took her just a week of interviewing to secure the help of enough ranch hands, most of them Mexican. Although she knew it was against the law to hire illegal immigrants, Monica was desperate for help. And besides, given what she and her family had gone through, she figured that the United States government owed her this favor.

After three long days of organizing her new crew and setting them off to perform their tasks, Monica sat in her back porch armed with her Winchester .308 and a cold Lone Star. She was dressed in a pair of tight Wranglers, a black button-down cotton shirt with the sleeves rolled up to her elbows, her old pair of Luccheses, and her late Brother Michael's Stetson, which actually fit her perfectly.

She took a sip and closed her eyes in silent pleasure as the cold drink cut through the desert dust.

Slowly, she opened them and let her gaze sweep the clearing beyond the porch, starting with the entrance to the tunnel, which she had once more collapsed.

And this time for good, she thought, having spent a full day setting off charges along its entire length to keep any more unwanted visitors out.

But she had gone a step beyond that and converted the first few feet of the tunnel into a memorial wall, where she had deposited her brothers' ashes and had two marble plaques etched with their names.

One could argue that the burial was a bit unorthodox, but it filled Monica with a sense of closure and of peace, especially since she now knew that their deaths had not been on her. The Mexican Cartel dug tunnels constantly, and it was just bad luck that this particular one ended where it did.

Bad luck indeed.

Monica took another sip. She could argue that what had brought the world to the brink of a third world war had been sheer bad luck.

Bad luck that Kim Jong-un's plane had malfunctioned.

Bad luck that Vaccaro asked President Bush to yield his jet.

And damn bad luck that Ricco Orellana had decided to exact revenge at that particular moment for an event that took place nearly two decades earlier.

And there was the promise she had made to the dying *sicario* woman on that helicopter, a promise she wasn't sure she would be able to keep.

Antonio Moreno Carreón was currently in the care of a Navy social worker at Coronado Naval Air Station. Monica had already filled out the necessary paperwork to try to become his foster mother, but the death that seemed to follow her made her wonder if she was indeed what the damaged child needed to help him find his way out of the shadows.

But she had to at least try.

The Navy was processing her request, which included letters of recommendation from Stark and even the White House, and she should hear something back within the week. Monica had even started interviewing potential nannies to help her with what would be a very long and difficult journey. But at least she had this ranch, where she hoped that the same demanding work that had helped her vanquish some of her demons this past year might lessen the pain in Antonio's mind, allowing him to step closer to the light.

She could only hope.

And perhaps pray.

And there was Ryan . . .

Monica shook her head. Just as had been the case a year ago, Monica had departed quickly, without saying goodbye, figuring that goodbyes never did anyone any good. They just prolonged the inevitable.

So, she had packed up and hopped on the first flight out of Kadena upon their return from North Korea and come straight here.

Monica heard a car engine in the distance, coming up the access road to the highway.

She set down the Lone Star, grabbed the Winchester resting next to her, and stepped off the porch, holding the weapon across her chest, barrel down, right hand on the finger lever, left one under the barrel.

A black SUV came into view, making its way down the last quarter mile stretch of road, past the tunnel, and came to a stop in front of her.

Monica lowered the rifle as the driver got out, and shook her head. Dressed in a pair of faded jeans, a green T-shirt, and a baseball cap worn backwards, Ryan Hunt closed the door and gave her a half wave.

"Ryan? What the fuck?"

He didn't reply. Instead, the former Delta sniper went to Monica, smiled that great smile of his, moved the rifle out of the way, and embraced her.

She wanted to resist. In fact, she wanted to punch him in the face or kick him in the balls.

Or both.

But she didn't.

Instead, she let him hold her for a moment, slowly pulling away and asking again. "What are you doing here?"

He grabbed her by the hand and took her to the SUV, opening the rear door behind the driver. The window was half open and smoke swirled from it.

"I'm harboring a fugitive," he said.

"What are you talking about?"

"Just escaped from Brooke Army Medical in San Antonio," Ryan finally said. "And I had to assist."

Monica tried to move around Ryan to get a look into the passenger seat, but she didn't need to.

Michael Hagen stepped out with the help of a cane.

The former Navy SEAL, who had saved Monica's life a year ago in Monterrey, wore a pair of gym shorts, a black T-shirt, and a titanium prosthetic below his right knee.

"Mickey!" Monica said, and hugged him. He managed a thin smile on a face sporting a couple of new scars, including the one traversing his chin.

"We figured this would be a better place for his recovery," Ryan added. "Plus, they wouldn't let him smoke."

Hagen took a drag and exhaled bullishly through his nose tilting his head back.

"Plus, I was afraid he was going to start stabbing people," Ryan added. "So, what do you say?"

This time it was Monica's turn not to reply. Instead, she wrapped an arm around each of her brothers-in-arms and guided them toward the house.

KADENA AIR FORCE BASE. OKINAWA, JAPAN.

Lieutenant Commander Jacob Demetrius stared out the window from his hospital bed.

A cold front had moved through the region, bringing freezing rain and clouds the color of gunmetal that only added to the gloom in his state of mind.

He glanced at the open box containing the Medal of Honor that had been awarded to him yesterday morning by the President of the United States via a video call and physically placed around his neck by Admiral John Kostas, commander of the *Reagan* carrier strike force still deployed in the Sea of Japan, who had flown out here to do the honors.

While he was certainly glad, and even flattered, that a grateful nation had graced him with its highest military award, Demetrius wanted nothing more than to see Ghalia and his newborn daughter.

And he had stated it that way to his commander in chief upon receiving the award—to the dismay of Kostas.

"Is there anything our country can do for you, Commander?" President Vaccaro had asked.

"As a matter of fact, there is, Madam President."

The video chat had ended shortly after, and Kostas had returned to *Reagan*, leaving him in his current state of pain and misery.

The double spinal compression from his back-to-back ejections had pinched the nerves between L1 and L4, leaving him temporarily dependent on the meds that the good doctors here didn't give him often enough.

He winced in pain at another jab, and instinctively reached for the call button, pressing it twice.

"Goddammit," he mumbled, closing his eyes and taking a deep breath, shifting his body, trying to get more comfortable. But he could never do it. Any way he lay down, or sat, or even walked, was painful.

And what was worse was that soon he would be hooked on the damn opioids.

But Kostas had promised him that he would be going under the knife shortly, as soon as they could get a top surgeon flown in from Tokyo—apparently among the world's best at this type of surgery. Last he'd heard, the man was due to be here tomorrow.

And not a moment too soon, he thought, pressing the button again.

"Where the fuck is she?" he mumbled, closing his eyes again.

"Where the fuck is *who*, love?"

Demetrius opened his eyes at the voice he had not heard since—

"Bollocks, love. You look like shit."

In spite of his current level of pain, the naval aviator managed a smile when she stepped up to the bed holding a baby—his baby.

"How . . . how did you . . ." he started to ask, but he already knew the answer.

Ghalia pressed a finger against his lips and smiled that amazing smile, depositing Jasmine on his lap.

"Meet your daughter, love."

As Demetrius held her in his arms, Ghalia leaned down and kissed him softly on the lips, pressing her forehead against his.

And just like that, as Commander Demetrius embraced his family, all was right with the world.

ARLINGTON NATIONAL CEMETERY. ARLINGTON, VIRGINIA

Under an overcast sky, Stark regarded the seemingly endless graves marking the mortal remains of honored dead.

There were rows and rows of them. Most were known, a few unknown, but the men and women buried here shared one thing: All had lived and died for the preservation of liberty, of peace.

Of our freedom.

Different generations lay next to one another, from those who served in the Revolutionary War, to the Mexican War, the Civil War, the Spanish-American War, both World Wars, Korea, Vietnam, Grenada, the Baltics, and the seemingly endless War on Terror.

All had come when their country had called them. All had served without complaint, without regret.

All had died with honor.

Stark took a knee by a freshly dug grave, by a new white headstone at the end of a row up on a hill beneath a stately oak. At the top of the stone, etched in black, was a cross since Chief Larson had once claimed to be a Christian.

Beneath the cross, it read:

EVAN T. LARSON
MCPO
US NAVY
AFGHANISTAN

Stark held three small American flags, and he pressed the staff of one of them into the soft turf next to the headstone.

Then he did something else.

The colonel produced a small gardening shovel and used it to cut a two-inch wide track into the grass at an angle, lifting it just enough to insert the Medal of Honor, lowering the turf back onto it. With luck, no one would notice it, letting his best friend and warrior rest in peace next to his well-deserved honor.

For all time.

It gave Stark some semblance of solace to be the only one who knew of this award besides Vaccaro and Wright, and of its final resting place.

"Till we meet again, Chief," he said, standing, snapping to attention and giving him a final salute.

The colonel went in search of two more graves, laid side by side. They belonged to Robert and Joseph Stark.

Bobby and Joey.

And he planted small flags by their headstones.

It had been years since he had buried them here, but the pain was always there, though he had somehow learned to live with it.

Finally, Stark headed for the rented Honda and drove to his hotel for a little R&R. In three days, he was scheduled to hook up with Danny Martin in the CIA jet at Reagan International and fly to San Antonio, Texas, to look into Hagen, who was supposed to be finishing his rehab there. Juan Vasquez was back in Coronado tying up a few lose ends before joining Stark in San Antonio, along with Ryan who was supposed to catch up with them there. Harwich claimed to have another assignment ready for his team in Colombia, something about babysitting the family of a drug-lord-turned-confidential-informant.

Ten minutes later, Stark pulled up to the valet at the Four Seasons, where Wright had put him up in one of the top-floor suites, and where

Stark planned to spend the following three days catching up on his sleep.

He tipped the valet kid and strolled through the double glass doors, making a beeline for the elevators.

But he didn't get past the sofas and chairs surrounding a bar across the hallway from the front desk.

A woman sitting at the bar stood slowly and turned around.

Naree smiled beneath her very soft black hair at his obvious surprise—a smile that stirred a longing for recklessness he knew he would regret in the morning.

It was wrong for her to be here, luring him back into those shadows he had so desperately tried to put behind him.

And it would be stupid for Stark to allow her do so again.

There was no future with Naree Kyong-Lee. Their ideologies were as far apart as the ocean separating their worlds. And at this juncture in his life, Stark felt the need for something more than just another night of carnal pleasure in the arms of the enemy.

But whatever semblance—whatever vestige of will power he had left, vanished the instant she held up a bottle of Cava de Oro.

ACKNOWLEDGMENTS

Dianne Brandi, for her unflagging support of this book series. All authors should be so lucky.

Ellen Campbell, for her first-rate editorial job.

Alice Frenk, for her proofreading assistance.

Kevin Summers, for his formatting and cover work.

And last but not least, the authors would like to thank their wives, Angela Hunt and Lory Pineiro for their encouragement and support during the writing and rewriting of this story.

Colonel David Hunt is a military TV analyst with 30 years of military experience including extensive operational experience in Special Ops, counterterrorism and Intelligence Ops. Most recently, Colonel Hunt served as tactical adviser in Bosnia where he facilitated all national intelligence matters for the Commander in Chief.

Prior to this, he served as counterterrorism coordinator to the Summer Olympic Games in Seoul, Korea. In this capacity, Colonel Hunt planned, choreographed and implemented the first United States national response for an Olympic event in Korea in conjunction with Korean National Intelligence and the Korean Crisis Response Agency.

He has served as a security adviser for the Federal Bureau of Investigation as well as state and local police officials. A graduate of Harvard University's John F. Kennedy School of Government, Colonel Hunt holds a Master's degree in English from Norwich University.

He is the author of the New York *Times* Bestseller *They Just Don't Get It*, as well as *On the Hunt, Terror Red,* and the *Without Mercy* series of books.

R.J. Pineiro is a 35-year computer industry veteran and military researcher who spent the first three decades of his career at Advanced Micro Devices, Inc. in the engineering and manufacturing of microprocessors, the soul of today's computers, tablets, and phones. During his term at AMD, he rotated through Microprocessor Design and Test Engineering, Information Technology, Program Management, led test factories in Singapore and Suzhou, China, and retired in 2012 as Vice President to focus on his books.

R.J. Pineiro holds a degree in computing engineering from Louisiana State University. He is also an instrument-rated pilot, has a black belt in martial arts, is a firearms enthusiast, and enjoys the privileges of his open water SCUBA diver certification.

He is the author of many internationally acclaimed novels, including *Avenue of Regrets, Chilling Effect, Highest Law,* and the *Without Mercy* series of books.

For more information
on the authors
please visit
www.rjpineiro.com

For more information
on the Hunter Stark
Series of novels,
please visit
www.withoutmercy.org

Made in the USA
Columbia, SC
22 September 2020